PRAISE FOR DANI'

The Pretty D

'Everything a summer read should be … Warm and …

'*The Pretty Delicious Café* is brimming with romance and eccentricity. A refreshing take on romantic comedy, it reminds us about the importance of family, friends and the opportunity of fresh beginnings. Danielle Hawkins' fans will not be disappointed with her latest and people new to her will not be able to put it down' Better Reading

'… hits the mark with its quaint and cosy setting, smattering of eccentric small-town characters and budding romance' *Weekly Times*, Melbourne

'*The Pretty Delicious Café* is another delightful read from Danielle Hawkins. It's light-hearted, self-deprecating and charming, with quirky and engaging characters who draw out the themes of friendship, family and living life to the full' *The Blurb* magazine

'*Pretty Delicious* is a story of determination, of love, of allowing oneself the freedom to follow their dreams rather than allow themselves to be restrained by self-doubt or burdened by that which they cannot control. It is a story of friendship – Lia and Anna – and the power of reconciliation and forgiveness. The characters, with their flaws and neuroses are heartbreakingly real, and thus easy to identify with' The Bookseller New Zealand blog

'I loved this book, I love the characters and I love the sense of family' Beauty & Lace Book Club pick

'Author Danielle Hawkins … has a talent for witty and convincing dialogue and this, in particular, gives *The Pretty Delicious Café* verve and humour. She's also a skilled sculptor of characters and I enjoyed the cast she assembled for this, her third foray into fiction' *Otago Daily Times*

'Danielle Hawkins' quirky humour and easy style make this a great summer read' *Dominion Post*

'A girlfriend lent me this book during the holidays – saying 'it's just delightful, you need to read and review this' … Delightful is a perfect description … it really is a wonderful story, with quirky and relatable characters, fast, witty dialogue and lots of humour' NicShef♥Reading #1 reviewer Amazon

Dinner at Rose's

'It's so good that it's hard to believe it's a first novel. It had better not be her last. Please, Danielle' – Lee Matthews, *Manawatu Standard*

'What really carries it is the quality of the writing. The dialogue is absolutely spot on. You would almost believe the author wrote for TV or writes sitcoms. It's very, very funny' – Paper Plus, Winter Reads

'A cross between *All Creatures Great and Small*, *Bridget Jones's Diary* and something the Topp Twins would write if there was only one of them and she was straight, this is a very funny book' – *Next* Book Club

'It was page 4 when I saw this and knew it was going to be a good book: "You really should consider becoming an eccentric yourself. It makes life so much more interesting"' – Jessica, GoodReads

'I LOVED this book and devoured it quickly' – Georgia, GoodReads

'This book … has to be the most satisfying in this genre that I've ever read' – Kathleen Dixon, GoodReads

Chocolate Cake for Breakfast

'Another sweet, gently funny depiction of life in the back blocks of New Zealand' – *Next* Book Club

'This is a delightful, contemporary romance' – *Herald Sun*

'Helen is frankly delightful – intelligent but oh-so-human … a plausible, relatable storyline and hugely appealing characters. A charming summer read, and a giggling good time' – *Australian Women's Weekly*

'Helen reminds me of a modern day James Herriot and her often hilarious adventures in this dairy country will have you laughing (although if you're squeamish this may not be the book for you!)' – Bec, GoodReads

'This is pure escapism and I thoroughly enjoyed this read' – Carol, Reading Writing and Riesling

'This book is like chocolate cake for breakfast: addictive' – Bree T, GoodReads

Danielle Hawkins lives on a sheep and beef farm near Otorohanga in New Zealand with her husband and two children. She works part-time as a large-animal vet, and writes when the kids are at school and she's not required for farming purposes. She is a keen gardener, an intermittently keen cook and an avid reader. Her other talents include memorising poetry, making bread and zapping flies with an electric fly swat. She tends to exaggerate to improve the story, with the result that her husband believes almost nothing she says. Danielle has written four novels: *Dinner at Rose's*, *Chocolate Cake for Breakfast*, *The Pretty Delicious Café* and *When It All Went to Custard*.

when it all went to custard

Danielle Hawkins

HarperCollinsPublishers

HarperCollins*Publishers*

First published in Australia in 2019
by HarperCollinsPublishers Australia Pty Limited
ABN 36 009 913 517
harpercollins.com.au

Copyright © Danielle Hawkins 2019

The right of Danielle Hawkins to be identified as the author of this work has been asserted by her in accordance with the Copyright Amendment (Moral Rights) Act 2000.

This work is copyright. Apart from any use as permitted under the Copyright Act 1968, no part may be reproduced, copied, scanned, stored in a retrieval system, recorded, or transmitted, in any form or by any means, without the prior written permission of the publisher.

HarperCollins*Publishers*
Level 13, 201 Elizabeth Street, Sydney NSW 2000, Australia
Unit D1, 63 Apollo Drive, Rosedale, Auckland 0632, New Zealand
A 53, Sector 57, Noida, UP, India
1 London Bridge Street, London, SE1 9GF, United Kingdom
Bay Adelaide Centre, East Tower, 22 Adelaide Street West, 41st floor, Toronto,
    Ontario M5H 4E3, Canada
195 Broadway, New York NY 10007, USA

ISBN 978 1 7755 4141 7 (paperback)
ISBN 978 1 7754 9172 9 (ebook)

Cover design by Michelle Zaiter, HarperCollins Design Studio
Cover images: Clothesline by Andrey Pavlov/stocksy.com/725113; Sheep by David Marano Photography/Getty Images; all other images by istockphoto.com
Internal images: Emojis by shutterstock.com
Author photograph by Marama Shearer, Thrive Photography
Typeset in Baskerville Regular by Kirby Jones
Printed and bound in Australia by McPherson's Printing Group
The papers used by HarperCollins in the manufacture of this book are a natural, recyclable product made from wood grown in sustainable plantation forests. The fibre source and manufacturing processes meet recognised international environmental standards, and carry certification.

Chapter 1

I wasn't enjoying the afternoon of 23 February even before I learnt that my husband was having an affair. It was very hot and I was on the phone with a deeply unpleasant woman who'd just fenced off her neighbour's driveway. I had a lot of pressing work to do, and the knowledge that her complaints were nothing to do with Building Control and I wasn't the person who should have spent the last nineteen minutes listening to them was not improving my outlook.

Pushing a swag of hot hair off my forehead, I changed the phone from one ear to the other and said, 'Yes, but I'm afraid –'

'He *cut* the wires! *Wilful* destruction of my property! And he had the *gall* to tell me it was none of my business what he planted! I suppose it'll be none of my business when his horrible flax bushes block off the creek and there's a foot of muddy water in my house, either!'

'Mrs Cotter, I don't really see why –'

'You people seem to be very concerned about *his* rights, but what about *my* rights as a ratepayer?'

'You don't *have* the right to cut off his access,' I said.

'That driveway is on *my land*!'

'Yes, but you signed a right-of-way agreement. We've got it here on file.'

At which point she hung up.

I put the phone down and returned to the plans on my desk. It rang again immediately; it was Lyn at the front counter.

'Please, not Mrs Cotter again,' I said.

'It's not,' said Lyn. 'Someone here to see you.'

I did a little chair-dance of annoyance, but venting frustration on Lyn had long-lasting and unpleasant repercussions, so I merely said, 'Okay. Coming.'

Having traversed the three corridors and two flights of steps between my office and reception – the Tipoi District Council building was designed in the sixties by an architect who, in his determination to create something truly unique, had overlooked such trifling concerns as lighting, ventilation and internal flow – I found our next-door neighbour Andrew Faulkner at the front counter. He looked hot and dusty and he smelt like wool grease, and I wondered what emergency had brought him straight into town out of the yards.

'Hi, Andrew, how's it going?' I said.

'Jenny. Could I have a word in private?'

'Yes, of course,' I said, slightly unnerved. 'Um ... outside?'

I led the way out to the small paved area between the street and the police station fence, which contained two painted wooden bench seats and a raised garden bed filled with stunted orange marigolds. The sun beat down fiercely and rebounded off the concrete paving stones, and the air shimmered with heat. 'This is revolting,' I said. 'Come back in and we'll talk in the staffroom.'

'No, it's okay. You'd better have a seat.'

Beginning to be nervous, I sat down on the edge of a bench and squinted up at him.

He crossed his arms, uncrossed them again and dug his hands into his shorts pockets. 'Christ,' he said. 'Right. So, um, I just found your husband in bed with my wife.'

'Oh,' I said inadequately.

'Sorry,' he added.

'You – you mean …?' Which was stupid, because there was only one thing he could possibly have meant.

'Yes.'

'Did they see you?'

'Yes,' he said again.

'What did you do?' I croaked.

'Turned around and went away again. What was I supposed to do?' His thin brown face crumpled suddenly, like a hurt child's. Andrew Faulkner had always seemed, from what little I knew of him, to be a grave, stoic sort of man, and it's extra horrible watching unemotional people suffer.

'Andrew, I'm so sorry,' I said softly.

His head shot up. 'You *knew?*'

'*No!*'

'I've got to go,' he said. 'I've got sheep in the yards.' And, turning, he hurried across the street to where his ute was parked.

I sat in that sweltering little concrete courtyard, waiting for the onslaught of anguish and rage. It seemed slow in arriving, and eventually, probing my mental state as you probe a sore tooth with the tip of your tongue, I decided with some surprise that what I felt seemed largely to be relief.

* * *

Returning to my desk I looked at the building plans, decided that they may as well have been in Swahili for all the sense I could make of them, shut down my computer and left. I collected one small, indignant child from day care ('It's not *time* to go home! I haven't had afternoon tea!') and one from school ('I want to go swimming! You never let me do *anything* I want!'), then headed homewards up the valley between smooth, steep, grassy hills burnt a delicate fawn by the summer sun.

'Are we going to Nana's?' Nathan asked as I swung up my parents' driveway, eight hundred metres before our own.

'I'm just going to see if you can stay here for a little while this afternoon,' I said.

'Why?' asked Lily.

'Oh, I just need to – to go down the farm with Dad, and it's so hot and sticky I thought you might rather not come.' This was a fairly safe bet; the kids quite liked farming once they were out there, but they were invariably unwilling to go.

Pulling up beneath the big oak tree beside the implement shed, I opened my door and said, 'I'll just run down and check whether Nana and Granddad are home.'

They weren't. Returning to the car, I found the children wrestling in the front passenger footwell.

'It's mine! *Na*-than! Mum, Nathan's got my daily diary and he won't give it back!'

'She's not sharing!' Nathan wailed, bursting into noisy tears.

'Back in your seats NOW!' I shouted.

Two pairs of big brown eyes lifted to mine, widened, filled and overflowed.

'Oh, guys, come off it,' I said tiredly. 'Jump in your seats and I'll buckle you back up.'

'Aren't we s-staying with Nana?' Nathan sobbed.

'She's not home.'

'But I don't w-want to go down the farm! It's too hot! I'm as-*sorsted*!'

'Cheer up, sausage,' I said. 'Let's see what we find when we get home.'

What we found at home was a very twitchy Dave, pretending to read the paper at the kitchen table.

'Daddy!' Lily cried, abandoning her schoolbag in the middle of the floor and throwing herself at him. 'Do we have to go down the farm?'

'No,' he said, pulling her onto his knee.

Human shield, I thought sourly.

'How was school, Lily-billy?'

'Shineya and Paige went on a plane in the holidays, and they had a TV on the front of their seats! And Shineya said there was a whole channel just for Barbie movies! And –'

'Nathan, don't lick the Marmite lid!' I said sharply.

Dropping it, he scurried across the kitchen to climb onto Dave's other knee.

'Oof,' Dave said. 'Steady on there, Nath.' Putting an arm around each of his offspring he eyed me smugly over the top of Lily's head.

At that point, the rage I'd been expecting arrived. It filled me from top to toe, scorching and electric. I could have wrestled a rabid gorilla and won; lifted a freight train; leapt tall buildings in a single bound. How *dare* the snivelling weasel sit there hiding behind his children?

'Would you guys like an ice block?' I asked.

Lily and Nathan bounded to their feet. 'Yes!'

'I'll get them!'

'I want orange!'

Dashing past me, they wrenched open the freezer door.

'You have to eat them outside,' I said, smiling shark-like at my now unprotected husband.

Within seconds they'd vanished outside, ice blocks in hands, and were sitting cross-legged under the persimmon tree on the far side of the lawn.

'So,' I said, leaning my elbows on the kitchen counter. 'Is she the love of your life, or was it some sort of brain explosion and you don't know what came over you?'

Dave gave a miserable, half-defiant shrug.

'Any comment? Anything at all? No?'

'For God's sake, Jenny!'

I straightened with a jerk. 'Dave, it is *not* unreasonable for me to be pissed off about this!'

He picked at the side of his right thumbnail and said nothing, and the silence grew and spread between us.

'What are we going to tell the kids?' I said half to myself, looking out over the lawn to where Nathan was now hanging from a low branch by one hand and one knee, waving his ice block like a baton.

'What do you mean?'

'Well, you're going to be moving out. They'll want to know why!'

Dave sighed heavily. 'Yes, alright, I've stuffed up. But there's no need to take it out on Nathan and Lil.'

'How dare you?' I said, whirling back to face him. 'How *dare* you imply I'd upset the kids just to get back at you? Of *course* I'm not going to tell them you've been fucking Toni Faulkner!' I don't swear much, and I winced at the ugliness of the word as well as at the image it conjured up.

'Sorry,' he said helplessly.

I pressed my hands to my eyes. 'I guess we'll have to sit them down and give them the standard speech about how we both love them very much but we don't want to be married to each other anymore.'

There was a long pause before he said, 'Can't we – shouldn't we try? Get some counselling or something?'

After another, longer pause I dropped my hands and looked at him. 'Do you honestly think we've got a marriage that's worth saving?'

* * *

'So where is he?' asked my sister Rebecca the next evening, when, having heard the news from Mum, she rang for further details.

'He's staying in town with one of his friends.'

'Not with *her*?'

I tucked the phone between ear and shoulder so I could take the washing off the line while I talked. It was just after eight, and the sun was setting in dusty golden splendour behind the Faulkners' woolshed on the skyline. 'Well, not at her house, anyway. She's moved out too.' Which meant that their affair, if it was ongoing, was presumably being conducted either in Travis Lynch's spare bedroom or at the Palm Court Motor Lodge, a charmless hostelry set back about two metres from the edge of Tipoi's heavy traffic bypass. Neither location seemed particularly romantic, a thought which consoled me slightly in the watches of the night. Not much, but slightly.

'What's she like?' Rebecca asked.

'Pale and thin and completely devoid of personality, as far as I can tell. But she obviously has hidden depths.'

'God, what a tosser he is. What did he have to say for himself?'

'Oh, he didn't mean for it to happen, he was lonely, I'm too wrapped up in the kids, I need to accept some responsibility, we should go to counselling ...' I pulled a sheet off the line and started to fold it. Tessa the elderly fox terrier, inherited the year before when Dave's grandmother went into a rest home, came around the corner of the house and flopped down on her side beside the washing basket. She would much have preferred to stay in her comfortable bed in the living room, but if I insisted on wandering around outside I needed to be supervised, and no-one could accuse Tessa of failing in her self-appointed duty. If Tessa had been human, she would have been the sort of woman who vacuums pointedly around you when you sit down to have a cup of tea.

'He'd really try counselling?' asked Rebecca.

'Apparently,' I said.

'That's good, isn't it?'

'I don't want to fix it,' I said slowly.

'Well, you're angry, of course,' she said.

I dropped my sheet into the washing basket and reached for the next one. 'Yes, but – you should be friends with your husband, shouldn't you? And we're not.'

There was a blank pause before she said, 'But what about the farm? Who'd run it? You couldn't expect Dave to stay around if you split up; you'd have to buy him out. And then how would you afford to pay someone to manage the place? You can't ask Mum and Dad.'

No-one pours cold water down your neck like my little sister. 'I don't *know*!' I said. 'I don't know how any of it would work. It's been one day!'

'Look, I'm just *asking*,' she said sniffily. 'No need to jump down my throat. Maybe I should kick Sean out, too. He's such a bastard. He never helps me at all. And Caleb's teething at the moment – I've had no sleep for weeks ...'

Finishing the washing, I picked up the basket, pulled Tessa's ears and crossed the back lawn to the veggie garden. The litany of Rebecca's troubles continued while I picked four lemons, cut a head of broccoli, went back inside and filled the kitchen sink with water.

'I haven't had a break since God knows when,' she said.

I held the broccoli under water to flush the earwigs from their homes between the stems. 'Haven't you just been out on the boat?'

'Well, that's hardly a relaxing holiday! Watching Caleb twenty-four seven – Sean's hopeless. I doubt he'd notice if Caleb fell overboard!'

Sean, to my knowledge, was a reasonably hands-on father, but I just said, 'Mm,' as I skimmed half-a-dozen panicking earwigs off the water's surface with a sieve and tipped them out the kitchen window. 'How was the fishing?'

'Not bad, actually. I got a twelve-kilogram kingfish the day we came home. Hey, Jen, why don't you come down for a girls' weekend? Get a bit of distance; put things into perspective. We could go out dancing –'

'Dear God, no,' I said, scooping out another earwig.

'Why not?'

'I can't think of anything I'd like less than staying up till eleven o'clock to go out with a lot of sneery seventeen-year-olds.'

'Why sneery, may I ask?'

'Don't you remember being seventeen? I thought people in their thirties who went to nightclubs were sad, pathetic old losers.'

'Well, they're not,' she snapped.

'I'm sure they're not. But I still don't want to be one of them. I like sleep.'

'You want to be careful, Jen. You're getting alarmingly middle-aged and boring.'

'Quite possibly,' I said, taking the broccoli out of the sink and inspecting it for further signs of insect life. There were many; I'd removed most of the earwigs but none of the resident caterpillars. Growing vegetables in summer is very discouraging. Too many other things want to eat them.

'Nice new men don't just miraculously appear on your doorstep and sweep you off your feet,' said Rebecca. 'You have to go out and find them.'

What a truly horrific thought. 'Didn't you want me to stick with the old one?'

* * *

Nine caterpillars and another two earwigs later, she rang off. Leaving the broccoli on the draining board I made myself a cup of tea and sat down with it at the kitchen table. What *would* happen to the farm if I divorced Dave? He and I didn't own it; we owned the stock and machinery, and leased the land from my parents. The farm earned enough – barely – to pay the lease, a large amount of interest to the bank and Marcus the worker's wages; we drew only a tiny allowance in the hope of eventually beating the mortgage into submission, and lived almost entirely on what I earned working Wednesday to Friday for the council.

Pulling a copy of the *Farmer's Weekly* towards me, I started writing numbers in the margin with Lily's purple glitter pen.

Assets
2000 ewes at – I shrugged and took a stab *– $120 per head*
1400 lambs at $80
220 cows with calves at foot at $1500(?)
100 weaner bulls at?
70 heifers?
Tractor, 2 motorbikes, post rammer, shearing plant, hydraulic cattle crush???

I put down the sparkly purple pen. This was hopeless. If I wanted to make an even slightly accurate guess, I needed the depreciation schedule from the latest set of accounts and some current stock prices.

Anyway, we owed the bank five hundred and fifty thousand dollars. Our total assets and total debt probably balanced out, more or less, so if we sold up we'd come out with half of nothing each. I rested my head in my hands. Surely that wasn't right. Dave had run the farm for eight years – would he be owed eight years' worth of undrawn salary? And even if not, there was no extra money in the system to pay a manager. Maybe *I* could manage the farm, I thought doubtfully, and was immediately beset by panic. Living on a farm does not a farmer make, even if you do the accounts and help out occasionally in the yards. I didn't know when a paddock should be shut up for silage or how to fix a water leak; I couldn't hang a gate or calve a cow.

So if I left my cheating husband, we'd have to terminate the farm lease and my father, who was thoroughly enjoying his retirement, would get back all the worry and responsibility of running the place. But Dad wouldn't want to do that indefinitely, so then what? Either I would have to step up, or the farm – heaven forbid – would have to be sold. The farm my great-grandfather and his brother broke in, fresh off the boat from England, having lost both parents and a sister to consumption on the voyage. I remembered Great-Granddad – a frail wisp of a man with a sweet, shy smile. He smelt of aniseed and tobacco smoke, and he used to let me help fill his pipe.

And apart from all of that, Dave and I splitting up would bring Lily and Nathan's nice stable home tumbling down around their ears.

Dave wanted to try to fix our marriage – well, I'd just have to try too. Be more patient and less preoccupied; readier to laugh at his jokes and slower to snap.

I can't, I thought in sudden panic. *I can't bear it.* And although I knew I was being silly and melodramatic, I pushed my forgotten tea out of the way, rested my head on the table and cried.

* * *

I was still crying when I heard a car come down the driveway and pull up on the other side of the house. Dave, I thought drearily. The picture of repentance, no doubt, and wearing his best lopsided smile. Dave's best smile was mischievous and rueful and intimate, with a hint of dimple. *Yes, I'm trouble*, it said, *but we both know I'm gorgeous, and though women everywhere adore me* you're *the only one who really understands me.*

I *did* understand him, sadly; the smile would have worked a lot better if I hadn't.

I pulled a square of kitchen towel off the roll at the end of the bench, blew my nose, squared my shoulders and went to meet him at the door.

'Jenny, darling,' said my mother as I opened it, hastening up the steps and throwing her arms around me. Dad, behind her, grasped my shoulder and gave it a little squeeze.

'Hi,' I whispered, overcome with relief and gratitude. My parents, although always delighted to see me in their house, normally visited mine about once every other year.

'That *stupid* man. I could kill him,' said Mum fiercely.

'Shh. The kids are asleep,' I said, standing aside to let them in.

'Of course. Sorry, darling. Brian, could you make a cup of tea?' Leading me across the kitchen to the table, she pressed me into a chair and sat down beside me, holding my hand. 'Don't cry, love. He's not worth it.'

I nodded and blew my nose again, pushing the paper with my margin notes casually away.

'Where's he staying?' Mum asked.

'In town, with Travis.'

'Sonia says *she* didn't come in to school today.'

I wondered for a moment what Sonia not going to school had to do with anything before realising that the *she* was Toni Faulkner, who had taken a part-time job in the office at Lily's school when she and Andrew moved into the district two years ago. No wonder she hadn't been at work; she'd been busy leaving her husband for mine.

'She's a strange woman,' said Mum. 'Quite unfriendly.'

'Apparently not always,' I said dryly.

Dad rounded the kitchen counter bearing one Dora the Explorer and two Bunnykins mugs of tea, a packet of chocolate biscuits under his arm.

'Brian,' said Mum with weary disapproval.

'Only cups I could find,' he said, carefully putting everything down and pulling out a chair.

'They're fine. Thanks, Dad.'

Silence fell while we sipped our tea. It was eventually broken by Mum, who sighed and said, 'Never mind, love, you're better off without him.'

'He wants to try to patch things up,' I said to the tabletop.

'*Does* he?' she asked, brightening.

'Mm.'

'You're not going to, are you?' said Dad.

I looked up in surprise. 'Well, I – for the kids' sakes ...'

He grimaced.

'*Brian*,' said Mum, taking my hand again.

I barely noticed. 'But you like him, Dad!'

Dad snorted.

'*Don't* you?'

'Not much.'

'But – but what about the farm? We – I – wouldn't be able to afford to keep leasing it. I'd have to pay Dave out *and* pay a manager.'

'Don't worry about the farm. We'll figure something out.'

'What?' Mum and I said together.

'I don't know. Something.'

'Dad,' I protested, half laughing.

He sent me a long, level look over the rim of his Dora mug. 'Don't you *Dad* me, young Jennifer. Now, if your life will be blighted without that waste of space, you stay with him by all means. But if you're thinking of letting him come crawling back just so you can pay the damn farm lease, then you need to get a grip.'

I reached out blindly with my spare hand and took his, and he smiled. 'Good grip,' he said.

Chapter 2

The next few months were reasonably awful. Dave and I had a series of long and unhappy conversations, during which he ranged from remorse to frustration to blame to regret and back, and I maintained a dogged, miserable resolve. It was sad and exhausting, and telling Lily and Nathan that Dad wasn't ever coming back home will rank forever as one of the least fun experiences of my life, but finally things were settled, and we picked ourselves up out of the wreckage and started rebuilding some new version of normality.

Dave moved out of Travis's spare room and got a job managing a bull-beef unit on the other side of town – a thoroughly unsatisfactory job in every respect, he said, which he accepted only for the sake of his children. He had the kids on Wednesday nights and every second weekend. He disliked this arrangement because he didn't see them enough; I disliked it because both kids, but Lily in particular, were shattered and distraught every Thursday; and the kids disliked it because it was so obviously inferior to the old routine.

After much discussion, the cows were sold to pay for Dave's share of our joint assets. The plan was to graze dairy calves in their place, which would require no capital outlay and provide a nice reliable monthly income. Marcus the worker agreed to stay on, with a pay rise to reflect an increase in responsibility and with Dad in a supervisory role. It was all a bit precarious and understaffed, but it seemed to work, at least in the short term.

* * *

One grey and gusty Friday afternoon in May, as I drove up the hill home, I rounded the corner before the woolshed and saw Dad climbing stiffly off his four-wheeled motorbike to shut the road gate. Pulling over, I opened my window to talk to him.

'Afternoon,' Dad said. A handful of golden poplar leaves whirled across the road between us and plastered themselves against the windscreen of my car. 'What's up?'

'I went in to Wrightson's about that pipe, but they don't have one in stock,' I said. 'They're ordering it in; it might be here tomorrow.'

'No rush.' He bent to look in at Lily's window. 'How was school?'

'Okay,' said Lily.

Nathan struggled briefly with his seatbelt, got it open and crawled out of his booster seat to perch beside me on the centre console. 'Watch me, Granddad, I'm a sloff.' He linked his hands behind the headrest of my seat and hung off it, head flung back.

'A what?'

'A sloff. Hanging upside down in the branches.'

'Oh,' I said. 'A sloth. Excellent choice.' It might be nice, I thought dreamily, to be a sloth. I believe they sleep for twenty-three hours a day.

'Good man,' said Dad. 'Now, Jenny, I had a call from John a day or two ago.'

'John?'

'John ... what's his name? Oh, you know, used to work for Royce.'

'Mercer,' I said, after a moment's thought. 'John Mercer.' A small, weather-beaten man with terrible teeth, he'd been a shepherd on what was now Andrew Faulkner's place, and he used to give Rebecca and me Curiously Strong peppermints from a little flat tin that lived in the breast pocket of his shirt. We didn't much like the peppermints, but we appreciated the thought.

'That's the one. John Mercer. Saw him at the sale yesterday. He's retired now, and he's at a bit of a loose end; he was wondering if he could rent Grandma's cottage.'

'It's not fit to be lived in, is it?' I said doubtfully. The cottage had no insulation, and it had been empty for about twenty years.

'Oh well, we could give it a bit of a spruce-up, couldn't we?'

'Mu-um,' said Lily from behind me. 'I'm *tired*. I want to go *home*.'

'It'd have to be a pretty major spruce-up,' I said, ignoring her.

'Well, maybe he could come and look at it, and if he thinks he can make it habitable he can have it for nothing.'

That sounded good to me. If he wasn't going to pay any rent, surely I wouldn't be obliged to de-spider the place. Although I *had* better go and look at the roof. 'I'd better check that it's sound, first,' I said. 'Can't you just imagine the headline in the *Tipoi Times*? MAN KILLED WHEN BUILDING CONTROL OFFICER'S HOUSE FALLS ON HIS HEAD.'

'True,' said Dad. 'It would be a poor look.'

No small ginger-and-white dog met us at the back door when we reached home, the significance of which escaped me until I went inside to find the contents of the kitchen rubbish bin evenly distributed over a four-metre radius. Said dog was in her basket, industriously chewing a plastic bag that had contained mince. Her stumpy tail wagged once and then stilled as our eyes met, and her ears went flat back against her head.

'The rubbish is all on the floor!' announced Nathan, master of the obvious statement.

'Yep,' I said. Tessa passed me in the kitchen doorway like a plump, hairy torpedo and shot to safety under the car.

'You forgot to put her outside this morning,' Nathan said.

'Yep.'

'That was silly, wasn't it, Mummy?'

'Nathan, could you just *not* talk to me for a minute?'

'Okay,' said Nathan cheerfully, and pounded down the hall to his bedroom. Nathan was completely incapable of doing anything quietly, even if he wanted to, which he didn't.

'Lily!' I called. 'Come inside now.'

Lily, listening to the radio in the car, glanced at me without interest and leant forward to turn up the volume. I ran back down the steps, opened the car door and jabbed the radio's 'off' button.

'It's my favourite song!' she cried.

'Do *not* ignore me when I talk to you!'

'I didn't *hear* you!'

'Yes you did! Now go and have a shower, and use the soap!'

With shoulders drooping, she descended from the car.

'Take your bag!'

'I hate you,' Lily shouted, grabbing her bag by one strap and bolting indoors.

I sighed as I followed her into the rubbish-strewn kitchen. Just last night I'd read an article on Facebook, that bottomless well of trite parenting advice, about helping your children work through the trauma of their parents' separation. You must never snap; never shout; always respond to testing behaviour with boundless, unrelenting love and acceptance. Bugger.

I cleaned up the rubbish, retrieved the kids' lunch boxes and found a note in Lily's schoolbag bidding me to a school fundraising meeting on 20 May at nine a.m. in the staffroom. This morning, in fact. *Never mind*, I thought. *I can ring in the morning and apologise for missing it. Again.* And then, *Oh, shit, it's the twentieth and I haven't paid the bills.*

We had macaroni cheese for dinner, with peas in so I'd feel like the sort of mother that provides her children with at least an occasional vegetable. Nathan sorted his peas out and arranged them in rows at the side of the plate, and Lily said she wasn't hungry and she'd like to go to bed.

We did baths and teeth and stories, followed by a panic when Lily remembered that she hadn't done her homework and the hurried composition of a poem about autumn. Then I cleaned the kitchen and sat down at the table with the laptop and this month's bills. There was a GST return due too, and I'd need to code two months' worth of accounts before I could file it.

I loathed doing accounts, but because they were exponentially more loathsome if left to accumulate, I usually kept them up to date. Lately, however, I'd done nothing but pay the bills and the wages on the grounds that it was All Too Hard At The Moment. I should have known better. I was just as tired now as I'd been three months ago; just as upset about the decline and fall of my marriage; and I had twice as much accounting to do as normal.

At seven fifty-four, surrounded by piles of paper and halfway through the month's KiwiSaver contributions, I heard a car come down the driveway, turn and stop on the gravel in front of the carport. Approaching visitors were invisible from the kitchen and living room windows, which all faced down the valley towards town. Your first sighting was of their feet through the glass panel at the bottom of the kitchen door, and if you really didn't like the look of the feet you had a split second in which to hide behind the living-room sofa. (A childish response to unwanted callers and one which, after vaulting lightly over the back of the sofa to escape a neighbour selling natural skincare products the previous month and landing on a plastic stegosaurus, I had decided it was time to give up.)

This evening's feet were male, clad in grubby white sneakers, and I didn't recognise them. I opened the door to find Dave's friend Travis, holding a supermarket bunch of murky purple alstroemerias and looking nervous.

'Hi, Travis,' I said.

He thrust the flowers at me. 'Hey, Jenny. Can I come in?'

'Of course. Wow, thank you so much; they're lovely …' They weren't all that lovely, and I was overdoing it. 'I'll just put them in water.'

'So,' he said, following me across the kitchen. 'How's it all going?'

Tessa heaved herself out of her basket with a deep sigh and pattered across the floor to greet him.

'Oh – it's going.' I smiled bravely and immediately felt annoyed with myself.

'It must be hard,' he said, stooping to pat Tessa. She cowered ostentatiously, just for effect.

'I *don't* beat her,' I said. 'Even when she deserves it. It's just a bid for sympathy. Cup of tea?'

'You wouldn't have any herbal stuff, would you?'

My sole box of herbal teabags was labelled Be Happy, and I saw Travis look at it with a sympathetic little smile.

'That looks like a paper blizzard,' I said, indicating the table, 'but actually it's a highly organised system, so we'd better not disturb it. Come and sit in the lounge. How's work?' Travis owned a small but fast-growing plumbing business in Tipoi.

'Fine. Busy.'

'Gingerbread man?' I offered brightly, putting the tin down on the coffee table. 'I'd go for the ones without icing, if I were you – Nathan was chief icer, and he tends to lick the knife between biscuits.'

'Dave's a wreck,' said Travis.

I sat down heavily in an armchair.

'He's *gutted* that he hurt you. Jen, couldn't you give him another chance? It wasn't even an affair, just a – a stupid impulse.'

I balanced my tea carefully on the chair arm and looked at my sock-clad feet. *Oh, please, not now*, I thought. It's so exhausting, defending your position when you're not sure it's the right one.

'You guys were so good together,' he continued. 'I really thought you two would go the distance.'

'Did you?' I asked, sufficiently surprised to look up. 'Why?'

'Well, I guess because you're such a pin-up couple. You know – popular, good-looking, nice kids …'

Crikey. 'Well, there you go,' I said. 'Proof that you can never tell from the outside what anyone's marriage is really like.'

'He stuffed up, Jenny,' said Travis earnestly, his pleasant, open face creased with distress. 'People do. It doesn't necessarily mean they're wankers.'

'I *know*. I do, honestly. I'm not just – just sticking to my guns because he's embarrassed me and I want to punish him.'

'No, of course not, I didn't mean –'

'We were a *lousy* couple. He thought I was boring, and I thought he needed to grow up. We should never have got married in the first place.'

Travis opened his mouth and shut it again, and I felt like the sort of person who tells children there's no Santa Claus for the fun of seeing their little faces fall.

'Sorry,' I said. 'Have another gingerbread man.'

He left soon afterwards, crushed, and I returned to my accounts. KiwiSaver contributions at three percent of gross income, and employer contributions tax at ten point five percent of that, so net employer contributions were …

'Mummy,' said Lily, appearing like a small pyjama-clad ghost at my elbow.

'What are you doing awake, love?'

'Should you and Daddy never have got married?'

'Lil! No!'

'That's what you said. I heard you.' She started to cry.

I pulled her onto my lap and hugged her tight. 'No. Lily. Stop it, my darling. I did say that, but –'

'Then you wouldn't have had me and N-Nathan.'

'You and Nathan are my favourite people in the whole world. Hands down. Even when you're revolting. Hey, listen.' I gave her a little shake, and she raised her face from my shoulder and looked up at me with wet, tragic brown eyes. I smoothed her hair back. 'The thing with me and Dad is …'

'Is what?'

'We just weren't … getting on very well. We weren't nice to each other, and we were making each other grumpy. And if being with someone makes you unhappy, I think it's best *not* to be with them. Otherwise you get in the habit of snarling at each other, and you turn into a horrible person.'

'Why can't you just say *sorry*?' Lily asked, resting her hot little forehead against my neck. 'Just promise to be nice to each other.'

'We've tried,' I said. 'But … you know how you and Mandy just don't get on? You're both lovely people, but you can't play together without arguing.'

'She's not lovely. She's really annoying.'

'I bet *she* thinks she's lovely.'

'Well, she's not.'

'See?' I said. 'If you feel like that about someone, it's best not to hang out with them. It just makes both of you bad-tempered.'

Lily sighed. 'I wish everything was like it used to be.'

'Oh, sweetie, I know,' I said. 'People always feel like that when things change. But then you get used to it, and it's not so bad after all. It might even be better.'

She sighed again.

'Better go and hop into bed, love, or you'll be tired and cranky in the morning.'

'I want to sleep with you,' she whispered.

'Okay. You go and jump in my bed, and I'll come when I've paid the bills.'

'I want you to be there now.'

'I have to do this first.'

Lily started to cry again, noiselessly, the tears welling up and trickling down her cheeks to fall off her small pointed chin. It was quite unbearable to watch, and I wondered desperately, for perhaps the thousandth time, whether it's brave or horribly selfish to end an unsatisfactory marriage. Does it set a worse example to stay with someone you've got nothing in common with because leaving would cause such an almighty upheaval, or to cut and run? Is it nobler to lie on the bed you've made or to admit you made it wrong and start again?

'Oh, Lil,' I said. 'Go and get your pillow, and I'll move all this stuff into Dad's and my – into my room.'

She went straight to sleep beside me, her lashes still wet and her fierce little face smooth and peaceful. *We'll be alright*, I promised silently. *I won't spoil them because I feel guilty, I won't run Dave down no matter how much he annoys me, and I won't ever make them choose between us.* On which noble resolve I sighed, opened the laptop and began coding accounts.

Chapter 3

'Nathan!' my father cried the next afternoon, clapping his hands over his ears. 'For the love of Mike!'

Nathan, who was standing on Mum and Dad's sofa with his head flung back, wrapped in a hairy brown rug and baying at the ceiling, looked at him reproachfully. 'I'm a wolf, Granddad, howling at the moon.'

'How about being a stalking wolf, creeping up silently on your prey?' I said.

'Alright,' said Nathan, jumping off the sofa.

'You'll have to move incredibly slowly and patiently, so you don't scare the deer.'

'Who's the deer?'

'Caleb?' I suggested.

'No, he's a baby wolf.'

'Okay then, Granddad's armchair. But remember you need to stalk *quietly*.'

'I know, I know,' said Nathan impatiently, waving me to silence and dropping into a crouch.

'That boy,' said Mum, smiling. 'Just look at Caleb copying him.' Rebecca's little boy Caleb was squatting at Nathan's heels, clutching his cuddly blanket around his shoulders with one hand and sucking the thumb of the other.

'No, baby wolf,' said Nathan sternly. 'You must wait for me at the cave. There.' He pointed, and Caleb crawled obediently under the coffee table.

'How's work, Bex?' I asked. Rebecca ran a Pilates studio in Wellington; a very upmarket one, all gilt-edged mirrors and shiny blond wood, where she conducted intensive one-on-one lessons for an exorbitant hourly rate.

'Insane. Booked solid,' she said, shaking her sleek black hair back off her face. Rebecca, Mum and I all take after Mum's mother, who came from the Ukraine. We have dark hair, slanted hazel eyes and wide cheekbones, and with enough makeup we look striking and vaguely exotic. (Though, on the less glamorous side, if not for rigorous hair-removal regimes we would all three grow moustaches.)

'Have a piece of cake, love,' Mum said. She pushed a plate of fruit cake towards her younger daughter, who eyed it with amused scorn.

'No, thanks.'

'You've no need to worry, with *your* figure.'

'Mum, I *have* this figure because I don't eat cake.'

'Jenny?' Mum asked.

'Thanks,' I said, taking a piece and consoling myself with the thought that if it is indeed true that once you pass forty you have to choose between a nice bum and nice skin, in not too many more years Rebecca would have a face like a raisin.

There is, however, no need to give up *entirely* on one's bum. 'Can I have a private Pilates lesson later on, so I can feel like one of the rich and famous?' I asked.

'Sure. That piece of cake's worth forty extra squats.'

'Totally worth it,' I said, taking a defiant bite.

'What's young Sean up to this weekend?' Dad asked, looking up from the glossy magazine Bex had brought with her.

'He had a presentation to finish for work, and he wanted to go mountain biking. And he was hoping to catch up with a friend for coffee.'

Dad assumed the exact same expression that Bex had used to decline cake.

'Men sometimes go out for coffee these days, Dad,' I said. 'Even straight ones.'

He gave me a long, flat look over the tops of his glasses, and I grinned.

'Aaarghh! Hi-ya!' Nathan cried, leaping out from behind the corner of the sofa and attaching himself to Dad's leg. Caleb trotted after him and cast himself upon Dad's other foot.

'Good Lord!' said Dad. 'Kung-fu wolves!'

Lily, who was colouring in across the table, looked up, rolled her eyes and bent back over her page. She had, now she was seven, put aside childish things – I was hoping she'd pick them up again shortly.

Marcus the worker appeared at the patio door suddenly out of the rainy dark, setting off the security light; the sound of his approach had been drowned out by the noise of the wolf attack.

'Hello, Marcus! Come on in,' Mum called as he opened the door. 'Boys! Settle down, please! Too noisy!'

Marcus, looking like a model in an outdoor clothing catalogue, pushed back the hood of his raincoat and smiled. 'No, thanks, Lorraine. I won't come in – I was just wondering if I could have a hand on Monday morning to drench those calves.'

'Have we got anything to drench them with?' Dad asked, putting Caleb down.

'I called the vets' this morning and asked them to leave some stuff in the after-hours box,' said Marcus. 'I'm going through town tonight, so I'll pick it up.'

'You're wonderful,' Mum said.

He glinted at her, shut the patio door and vanished into the night.

'Gosh, we're lucky to have him,' said Mum. 'How many young men do you know who are out in the rain working at quarter to six on a Saturday night?'

'Well, *he* certainly thinks he's pretty awesome,' Bex said.

'He can think he's as awesome as he likes,' I said. 'We'd be lost without him.'

* * *

Later that evening, once our respective children were in bed, Rebecca came up to my place wearing space-age microfibre leggings, a ravishing apricot-coloured hooded top and Dad's gumboots.

'Gorgeous top,' I said, meeting her at the door.

She stepped out of the gumboots and came in. 'I'll send you one. I sell them in the studio. Since when do you have a dog?'

Tessa had bustled across the kitchen and was nosing at her socks. 'I'm sure we had Tessa last time you were up,' I said. 'She belonged to Dave's grandmother.'

'Why have *you* still got her, then?'

'She's a nice old sausage. I'd miss her. And Dave's never said anything about taking her to live with him.'

'That'd be right,' she said. 'How is the lovely Dave, anyway? Dad says he's giving you grief about the kids.'

I sighed. 'He wants to have them half the time, week and week about. And – and I guess that's fair, really, but it just doesn't *work*. He can't get away from his job five nights a week to pick up Lil from school, and he can't take Nathan with him on the farm all day, so I'd have to have them until five thirty, and then he'd collect them or I'd drop them off, and it's a half-hour drive from here to his place. The thought of putting two tired kids into the car every night and driving them across the district so they can have tea and go to bed just seems completely brain-dead to me. But apparently,' I finished, 'I'm using the children to punish him.'

'I'm sure you're not,' said my sister vaguely, having lost interest somewhere in the middle of this little tirade. 'Come on; let's do this. Got any mats?'

I led her into the living room, where I'd pushed the coffee table aside and laid down a yoga mat and a beach towel. Rebecca appropriated the mat and stood, slim and straight, at one end.

'Okay,' she said. 'Feet shoulder width apart, weight spread evenly, tummy pulled in … Shoulder blades down, Jen. *Down*. That's better. Now, deep breath in, then breathe out as you roll down.' She folded gracefully towards the floor. 'Breathe in, then roll slowly up again. Suck in your tummy. Navel to spine.'

'I am,' I said.

'Maybe you should cut down on carbs.'

'Do you give your paying clients these helpful tips?' I asked.

'Of course not,' she said. 'You look pretty good, actually. You're tall enough to pull off a few extra kilos.'

'Thanks,' I said, only a little bit sourly.

After some preliminary stretches she set me about five hundred crunches, and to rub salt into the wound she did them too, with additional extra-for-experts leg raises and while maintaining a stream of nonchalant conversation: '– with balsamic vinegar and a handful of pine nuts. Sean wants another baby.'

'Ugh,' I said, crunching doggedly. 'Do you?'

'Eventually. Although it'll be a nightmare, with running the studio.'

'Unghhffno pair?' I said. ('Even with an au' had coincided with the up stroke of my four-hundred-and-ninetieth crunch.)

'Doesn't help with the sleep deprivation. You really struggled when Nathan was little, didn't you?'

'Don't think ... it was ... too bad.'

'What about that weekend when we came up, just after he was born?'

I collapsed onto my back. 'That weekend when he was ten days old, when I had mastitis and Lily had an ear infection, and we were shearing?'

Tessa, who had been watching me with her chin on her forepaws, got up and came to stick her nose in my left ear. I swatted her weakly. 'Tessa, stop it!'

'Hey!' said Rebecca. 'Do you want this session or not?'

'I don't *do* this for three hours a day like you do. I think all my abdominal muscles have torn themselves off their attachments.'

'I doubt it. Alright then, roll onto your stomach. Arms out at right angles from your body, palms facing forward ... Shoulder blades down. *Down!*' She got up and came to crouch beside me, laying a hand between my shoulders. 'God, you're tense, Jen.'

'Yeah, you get that when your marriage disintegrates.'

'You're the one who wanted out.'

I closed my eyes and felt hot tears leak out at the corners. 'I know. Still hurts.' It may not have been the love the poets dream of, but you share a lot of experiences over ten years. 'And I'm worried about the farm.'

'What about it? You've got Supermarcus, haven't you?'

'Yes, but we're just coping with the day-to-day stuff. There's no longer-term plan.' Well, except that I'd started listening to Beef + Lamb New Zealand farmer education podcasts in the car.

She rubbed my back gently. 'You'll figure it out. You're the strongest person I know.'

'No I'm not,' I muttered.

'Yes you are,' she said firmly, evidently feeling that I'd had enough sympathy as was good for me. 'Okay, squeeze your shoulder blades together – tighter – tummy button to spine … Now lift your chest up off your mat.'

Chapter 4

We pregnancy-tested the ewes on a clear, bitterly cold day in early June. I was late, having been detained at the school gate by Amy Wallace, head of the Pukewai School fundraising committee, who was looking for a sucker to run a jumble sale.

I rounded the side of the woolshed at a run, pulling my woollen beanie down over my ears. The man who did our sheep ultrasound scanning was a grim and humourless fellow, and without me there either Dad or Marcus would have to mark the ewes, which would mean only one person pushing sheep up the race, which would mean delays …

But no. John Mercer, new tenant of Grandma's cottage, was stationed at the side of the scanning crate with a can of spray paint in each hand. He wore an ancient nylon tracksuit and a limp roll-your-own stuck out of the corner of his mouth. 'Jenny,' he said, graciously inclining his head.

'Hi, John. Thanks so much; I'm really sorry I'm late.'

'Single!' called the scanner, and John sprayed a blue dot on the ewe's back.

'Maybe you could help push them up,' he suggested kindly.

'You must have things to do …' I said.

'Nothing that can't wait.'

'Dry!' the scanner said.

Glowing with competence and satisfaction, John marked the next ewe red and drafted her out into a side pen. Dad, at the far end of the race, winked at me. I smiled back and climbed over the rails to stand at the side of the race.

'Do you want to separate off some of these skinny ewes?' John called back to Dad as I pushed a bony old matron into the crate.

'Single!'

'Marcus?' Dad asked.

'Not now,' Marcus shouted, chivvying another twenty ewes into the pen at the back of the race.

'It'll be easy enough to draft 'em out,' John persisted. 'I can just put them with the dries for now. I remember I used to say to Royce, "Royce," I'd say, "if you want them to put on weight you're going to have to feed them. If you keep doing what you keep doing, you just keep getting what you keep ge—"'

'Next!' barked the scanner.

'Yes, good idea, John,' I said hastily, and Marcus's lips tightened.

We stopped work just once, for half an hour's lunch break, and it was after four o'clock when the last ewe ran through. The scanner got slowly and stiffly to his feet, stretched his back and stripped the long plastic glove from his right arm.

'Well, that's a good job done,' said John, extracting his tobacco from inside his tracksuit jacket with shaking hands. After a long and inadequately dressed day, he had turned an alarming shade of purplish grey.

'Back a bit from last year,' said the scanner as Dad and Marcus came up the race towards us. He squinted down at the screen of his machine. 'A hundred and forty-one percent in the mixed-age ewes and a hundred and twenty in the two-tooths.'

'How many dries?' I asked, linking my arms behind my back to try to relieve the tightness in my shoulders.

'A hundred and twenty-four.'

Almost twice as many not pregnant as the year before. Shit. What had we done wrong? 'Have any of them aborted, do you think?'

'No more than one or two,' the scanner said. 'Nothing significant.' He bent down to pick up his machine and carried it away around the corner, adding over his shoulder, 'More likely to be condition. Fairly light, some of them.'

They were indeed, I thought worriedly, looking out over the mob John had drafted off. They'd been in the yards all day, of course, so they were bound to look a bit hollow – and the very thinnest and mangiest sheep is always the one standing front and centre – but even so ...

'Sorry, chaps, but you get that in a drought,' said Marcus tightly.

Dad clapped him on the shoulder. 'No-one's blaming you, son,' he said. 'There's always a tail end. We'll separate them off and sprinkle them through the cattle block for a month, and they'll be new animals.'

'Wouldn't hurt to give them a drench, either,' said John, cupping his hands around his cigarette to light it.

Marcus looked at him with flat dislike. 'Well, I haven't got time today, I'm afraid.'

'No, no,' said Dad. 'Of course not. Where do you want these girls? They can just stay here below the shed for now, can't they? We'll sort them out in the morning.'

'I'm on it,' said Marcus wearily, going to untie his dogs from the back of the yards.

* * *

At eight sixteen two mornings later, I was hunting frantically through a mountain of clean washing for my black merino work jersey when there was a tap at the glass sliding door just behind me. I spun around, startled, and saw John standing on the deck, swathed in an enormous plastic raincoat.

'Oh, hi, John,' I said, unlocking the door and pushing it open. 'Is everything alright?'

Nathan, with a Marmite sandwich in one hand and my red tights tied around his head to make a Ninja Turtle bandana, dashed into the living room. 'Mum! There's a rat under Lily's bed!'

'Dead or alive?' I asked.

'Dead. Its guts are all coming out.'

'Then it can wait. Sorry, John, it's a bit of a crazy time of day around here.'

'Hello there, young fella,' said John, leaning against the doorframe in a leisurely way that made my heart sink. 'Are you a Red Indian?'

Nathan sighed as if the stupidity of adults was a cross almost too heavy to bear. 'No, I'm Rapha*el*.'

'Who?'

'Can you please get your bag and jump in the car, love?' I said. 'And tell Lily to, as well.'

'Lily!' Nathan roared. 'Get in the car!'

'Don't stand there and yell; go and *find* her. Go, go.' I flapped a tea towel at him, and he whirled and ran off. 'Sorry, John, we're running late, I'm going to have to dash …'

'Those light ewes,' John said. 'Did you decide to put them back in with the others?'

'What?' I said stupidly.

'And he never drenched them.'

'Oh, I'm sure –'

'He didn't. I may be old, but I'm not stupid. He ran them around again on Monday night after you'd gone and drafted off the dries, and then he chased the skinny ones straight out the back of the yards with the rest.'

'I – I'm sure there's a good explanation …' Oh, dear Lord, please no. I needed to know that *someone* in my life could be trusted to do what he was supposed to without direct supervision. Poor old John – he was lonely, no doubt, and he'd been giving Marcus the doubtful benefit of his outdated wisdom, and Marcus was too immature to be tolerant.

'Of course there's a good explanation,' said John, standing up straight again. 'He's a lazy little bastard and he's taking advantage of you.'

I took a deep breath. 'Well, I can't do anything about it just now; I'm late for work. Thanks for telling me, John. I'll look into it.'

'You do that, m' dear.' And he clomped down the porch steps and off across the sodden lawn.

* * *

On our way down the hill that morning, I worried about Marcus's possible insubordination while Lily patronised her brother.

'What's two plus two?' she asked.

'Four,' said Nathan promptly.

'Yes, well, that's *easy*. What's four plus four?'

'Five.'

'*No*, Nathan. Four plus four is *eight*. What's two plus three?'

'I don't know,' said Nathan crossly.

Lily sighed. '*Five*.'

'Lily, for goodness' sake,' I said. 'How on earth is he supposed to know when he hasn't started school yet?'

'I'm *helping* him. He needs to learn.'

'He will, when he gets to school. Oh no.'

'What is it?' Lily asked.

'Mrs Wallace,' I said, pulling onto the gravelled verge in front of the school. She was talking to Christine Denny at the gate, but her real quarry, I feared, was me. 'Right, have you got your bag, love?'

'Should I take my bag for Dad's too?' It being Wednesday, they were spending the night with Dave.

'No, I'll leave it at day care with Nathan's, and then you don't have to remember it.' I got out of the car to kiss her, and she flung her arms around my waist. 'Have a good day, chicken. I'll see you tomorrow.'

'I'll miss you, Mummy.'

'You too. But you'll have a great time at Dad's.'

'Will you ring and say goodnight?'

'Of course,' I said.

'Good morning!' cried Amy Wallace, approaching. 'How are you today, Lily?'

'Good, thank you,' Lily said to her shoes.

'I haven't seen you at netball. Aren't you playing this year? It's not too late, you know. I'm sure we could find you a spot.'

Lily gave something between a shrug and a squirm.

'Arwen's just *loving* her netball.' (I'd been told, although I wished I hadn't, that Arwen's name was a happy reminder of the night of her conception, on which her parents had had a *Lord of the Rings* movie marathon.) 'She's doing so well with her shooting, now. You must take Lily to netball camp next year, Jen; you'll be amazed at how her confidence will improve.'

'Mm,' I said.

'Now, I've got the list of phone numbers for the jumble sale ...' She paused to fish a piece of paper from her handbag. 'Here it is. It's so sweet of you to volunteer. I can't *believe* it's the same Saturday as Aaron's family reunion; we *never* go away ...' She lowered her voice sympathetically. 'How *are* you, anyway?'

'Great,' I said brightly.

'And the kids?'

'They're doing really well.'

'Little angels,' she said, turning to the car to wave at Nathan – who was, unfortunately, probing his nose thoughtfully with his index finger.

* * *

'Good afternoon, Mrs Reynolds!' said Ray de Vries playfully as I came in through the council building's automatic doors fifteen minutes later. I'd been starting work at eight forty-five since Lily had gone to school two years before, but Councillor de Vries, bless him, was not noted for his rapid assimilation of change.

'Hi, Ray,' I said. 'How's it going?'

'Not bad, not bad. Family all well?'

'Fine, thanks.'

'I saw Dave at the squash club last night. Let him off the leash for a night, eh?'

I smiled vaguely.

'I bet *he* was a bit slow to get going this morning. Ah well, mustn't keep you.' He trundled off towards the lunch room, and I headed upstairs.

I didn't ever plan to grow up and be a building control officer – it just sort of happened. I got a degree in mechanical engineering, largely because my high school careers adviser said engineering was no field for a girl, and before Dave and I moved home to the farm I worked for a company in Auckland that designed and made biomedical equipment. I had no background whatsoever in building or construction, but there were no other engineering-type jobs going in Tipoi and, luckily for me, no other applicants. I liked my job, although the building department was chronically understaffed and I spent the occasional hour in the middle of the night wondering if, on my deathbed, I'd really feel that all these hours trying to reconcile the Building Code and the Resource Management Act (which overlap but contradict each other) had been worthwhile.

Worthwhile or not, I spent the morning doing paperwork and the afternoon at a commercial building site on the edge of town, where I found that the foundations were marked out three metres to the left of where the plans said they should be. This led to a long and wearying debate, during which the owner said (many times and with steadily increasing wrath) that only an officious little bureaucrat would worry about such a minor detail, and I replied (almost as many times and with steadily decreasing sincerity) that I was very sorry, but that as well as being illegal the change would compromise the on-site sewage system, which wasn't quite as minor a detail as he seemed to think.

After this uplifting encounter, I spent two solid hours answering emails, and left work feeling tired and flat. I called in to see Mum and Dad on the way home, and found them eating poached eggs in front of the TV with their plates on their knees.

Mum looked up as I opened the patio door. 'Egg, love?' she offered.

'Yes, please. I'll get it. Anyone want a cup of tea while I'm at it?'

'Why not?' said Dad.

'How was your day?' Mum called as I broke two eggs into a perspex jug of cold water.

'Reasonably dire. How was yours?'

'Fine. Kathleen and Geoffrey were here for lunch, so that was nice.'

'Really?' I asked, and Dad snorted with laughter.

'Yes, really,' said Mum firmly. 'They've just got home from visiting Joshua in Argentina. They had a wonderful trip.'

'Cool.' The microwave beeped, and I took the jug out and peered at its contents. The egg whites were still raw, so I put it back in.

'They asked after you,' Mum said. 'Kathleen was very sympathetic.'

'Mm.' Aunty Kath was very good at commiserating with other people's misfortunes – it was rejoicing in their triumphs that she struggled with.

'She's planning to ring you,' said Mum, and just then there was a medium-sized explosion. She hurried in to find me scraping egg off the inside of the microwave. 'Oh, *really*, Jenny.'

'Sorry, Mum.'

'It's so much better just to do them on the stove,' she said, taking the jug and tipping my unexploded egg down the sink.

'Hey, I could have eaten that one!'

'It's as hard as a rock,' she said, hurrying it down the plughole with the dish brush. 'You can't eat it.'

'Well, I can't now.'

Lips folded into a thin line, she filled a pan with water and thumped it down on the stovetop. 'Go and talk to your father.'

Startled by what was surely an extreme reaction to a very minor culinary disaster, I said, 'No, Mum, your tea will get cold. Go on. I promise not to blow up anything else.'

'I'd rather just do it myself, please,' she said shortly.

Dad grimaced sympathetically as I went back into the living room.

'What on earth's bugging her?' I mouthed.

He shrugged.

'Hey, Dad,' I said, perching on the arm of the sofa, 'John called in this morning and said Marcus didn't drench those thin ewes; he just put them back in with the main mob on Monday night.'

'Really? Why would he do that?'

'Laziness, I suppose,' I said. 'If he did.'

'Funny thing for John to say if he didn't.'

'Well, he obviously doesn't like Marcus, for some reason or other. He might just be trying to get him in trouble.'

'Look, I don't know,' said Dad. 'I haven't seen the ewes since we scanned.'

I fiddled absent-mindedly with an earring. 'Would you mind wandering out and having a look at them?'

He sighed.

'I don't want to have a go at Marcus unless he's done something wrong,' I said.

'I don't know that you want to have a go at him anyway.'

'Not have a go at him,' I corrected. 'But if he *is* slacking off, surely it's best to pull him up on it.'

Dad sighed again.

'Dad?'

'Just – don't go in with guns blazing, eh?'

'No, of course not,' I said, taken aback.

'You do sometimes, you know,' said Mum, putting her head around the corner.

'When?' I tried not to sound defensive but failed miserably.

'Well, leaving David, for a start.'

'What?'

'Lorraine,' said Dad weakly.

'Yes, he made a mistake. And by *God* he's paying for it. *Everyone's* paying for it.'

'Lorraine!' Dad said again.

Bursting suddenly into tears, Mum turned and fled.

I sat and stared after her with my mouth open.

'She doesn't mean it,' said Dad, rubbing his face with his hands. 'Kath's been winding her up about the dire consequences of divorce.'

I stood up. 'How helpful of her. Right, I'll see you later.'

'Jenny ...'

'It's okay,' I said, although it wasn't. I opened the patio door. 'It's fine. Night, Dad.'

Chapter 5

I was cooking dinner the next evening when a clamour arose from down the hall. 'Gross! *Na*-than!'

'Mu-um!'

'What is it?' I called, sprinkling sugar into my pasta sauce directly from the canister to save the two extra seconds it would take to use a teaspoon and, of course, adding three times as much as I wanted. 'Damn!'

'You never moved the rat!' Nathan shouted. 'It's still under Lily's bed!'

'It's *rotting*!' Lily added. 'I'm going to spew.'

I reached her bedroom to find both children making elaborate gagging sounds, hands clapped over their mouths. 'For goodness' sake, guys,' I said, kneeling beside the bed and dragging one small, stiff rat out by the tail.

'You left its guts behind!' Nathan shrieked.

'Where?'

'There!'

'That's a pipe cleaner!' I said, dropping it at his feet. 'Now, shower time, please – tea's nearly ready.'

I bore the rat outside and hurled it far out over the orchard fence, washed my hands and returned to the stove. I added more salt to the sauce to cancel out the sugar, tasted it, grimaced and decided we'd worry it down if I was heavy-handed with the cheese. There was a noise behind me; assuming it was Nathan, fan of the stand-under-the-water-for-ten-seconds-and-then-get-out method of showering, I said without turning around, 'You cannot *possibly* have had time to wash your willy.'

'Um,' someone said, and I turned to see the tall, lean figure of Andrew Faulkner in the kitchen doorway.

'Oh,' I said. 'Hi.'

'Hi.'

'Mum!' Lily shouted up the hall. 'Nathan hasn't washed his willy!'

I looked at Andrew, who was evidently wondering whether the child had some sort of willy health issue or if he had merely entered a household with an unnatural penis fixation, and dissolved into helpless laughter.

'Mu-um! Lily hit me!'

'He hit me first!'

From outside came a series of hysterical, high-pitched barks from Tessa, answered by a rising snarl. Andrew turned and ran down the back steps, with me at his heels.

Tessa was bouncing up and down at the entrance of the carport, rigid with affront and bristling like a hedgehog. Facing her in the twilight, lips drawn back and hackles up, stood an old, grey-muzzled huntaway. It launched forward, grabbed Tessa by the scruff of the neck and shook her like a terrier shakes a rat.

'Meg!' Andrew roared. 'Drop it!'

His dog looked at him to see if he really meant it, decided he did and grudgingly opened her mouth. Tessa flew past me up the steps and inside.

Andrew grabbed his dog by the collar. 'You miserable old tart,' he snapped, and she lay down flat and whined.

'What happened?' Lily cried, appearing in the kitchen naked and dripping wet.

Rounding the corner behind her at a gallop, Nathan slipped on the wet lino, skidded and fell over. He squeezed his eyes shut, opened his mouth and roared.

Lily began to cry as well, presumably in sympathy.

I picked Nathan up and stood him on his feet. 'Hey, come on, you're alright. Go and get dressed now, okay?'

'There's blood,' Lily whispered, pointing with a shaking finger at a red drop on the kitchen floor.

Nathan looked at it in horror and burst into fresh sobs.

'It's not yours, sweetie,' I said, pulling his plump, wet little body up against me. 'Tessa just had a scrap with Mr Faulkner's dog.'

'T-te-ess-sa,' Nathan wept, instantly changing tack.

'She's okay. I'm going to look at her right now while you go and get dressed.'

Tessa was under the blanket in her basket, and she whimpered when I pulled it back. 'Come here, small idiot dog,' I said, kneeling down beside her.

She cast me a piteous look. One ear was bleeding, torn very slightly at the tip.

'Well, you did kind of ask for it, didn't you?'

In a gesture so laden with pathos that I almost heard violins, Tessa extended one trembling paw and laid it on my knee.

'Diva,' I said, running a hand gently along her back. She flinched, but I couldn't find any obvious wounds.

'Is she alright?' Andrew asked from the doorway.

'I think so. Just a bit bruised. I don't think your dog actually broke the skin, apart from that tiny little nick on her ear.'

'No, well, she doesn't have many teeth. Look, I'm really sorry.'

'It's fine,' I said, getting up. 'I'll perform a diagnostic test.' Opening the fridge door I found a leftover sausage and broke it in half. 'Tessa! Sausage?'

Tessa clambered smartly out of her basket and pattered across the floor. Then, remembering that she was supposed to be badly injured, she lifted a front paw and whined.

'Poor Tessa,' I said, giving her half the sausage. 'So misunderstood. So brave. So uncomplaining.' I offered the other half to Andrew, who looked underwhelmed.

'Is that for me or my dog?' he asked.

'Either. You can share it, if you like.'

This admittedly feeble witticism received not even the hint of a smile. 'I just called in to let you know I've run half-a-dozen calves that were on the road in through the gate beside your parents' place,' he said.

'Thank you.'

'Not a problem.' He frowned at the sausage, turning it over between his fingers. 'I, er, guess Marcus will be moving the rest of them on pretty shortly. Feed's looking a bit short where they are.'

Now, that's just not the sort of comment farmers make to one another. It crosses very much the same line you'd cross by advising an acquaintance that she should consider making an appointment to do something about that unsightly facial hair. So either the man was an unmitigated busybody, or he felt things were so dire that he couldn't, in all conscience, say nothing. And of all the things Andrew Faulkner might have been, a busybody was not one of them. 'I'll look into it,' I said slowly.

'All good. Catch you later.' And, looking greatly relieved to have discharged his duty, he went quickly away.

* * *

My thoughts, as I served up three bowls of tomato spaghetti with extra cheese, ran in worried circles. How short of feed *were* those calves? I should damn well know; they were by the road, and I passed them at least twice a day. Why hadn't I looked at them properly? I should have. But I'd have noticed if they didn't have anything to eat, wouldn't I? And so would Dad. Wouldn't he? And then there were those thin ewes ... I was going to have to talk to Marcus, but without offending him, because we needed him way more than he needed us. How short of feed *were* those calves ...?

'Mum. Mum. Mum. Mum. Mum,' Lily was repeating across the table.

'Hmm? Yes? What's up, love?'

'You're not listening.'

I shook my head to clear it. 'You're right. Sorry, kidlet, tell me again.'

'We really, really want to go and see Granny and Poppa and Uncle Marty. *Please* can we?'

'Yes, of course,' I said, surprised. 'I'm not quite sure when, but I guess Dad will take you some time. Have you asked him?'

'He said you won't let us go.'

'Why on earth wouldn't I?' I said indignantly, before remembering that I must not, under any circumstances, allow Lily and Nathan to be drawn into some stupid he said/she said argument between Dave and me.

'Because you're punishing him,' said Lily.

I took a deep breath.

'She's really mad,' Nathan observed, eyeing me over the rim of his glass.

I stuck my tongue out at him, and he giggled. 'Never. Tell you what, guys, I'll talk to Dad and we'll decide when he's going to take you. I think going to see Granny and Poppa is a great idea.'

'Will you come too?' Lily asked.

I shook my head.

'Why *not?*'

'Well, it's – it's just a little bit awkward, now that Dad and I aren't together.'

'Don't you like them anymore?'

'Of course I like them. I love them,' I said, although to be honest I could have taken Dave's father or left him. 'Hey, guys, don't worry too much when Dad and I are a bit snarky with each other. We'll get over it eventually.'

'Shineya's dad broke her mum's hand,' said Lily. 'That's *true.*'

'*Really?*' I said, horrified.

'She went to hit him and she hit the edge of the cupboard instead. She had to have her arm in a cast and everything.'

I smiled. 'I don't really think that's Shineya's dad's fault.'

'No, it *was,*' said Lily. 'Shineya's mum said it would never have happened if he wasn't so annoying.'

'Actually, she may have a point,' I said. 'Who wants ice cream?'

* * *

Having done the bedtime thing, I returned to the kitchen and looked reluctantly at the phone. Who to start with? Hostile husband? Potentially incompetent worker? Apathetic jumble sale helpers? Or perhaps I should really go for gold and ring my mother, in case she had any more supportive comments to make. I sighed, metaphorically stiffened my upper lip, and dialled Marcus's number.

'Yo,' he said, answering on the fifth ring.

'Hi, Marcus, it's Jen here.'

'Oh, hi, Jen. How's it going?' I could hear background music, something with a throbbing beat and breathy vocals, and a girl laughing softly. The overall impression was one of romance and seduction, and I felt both intrusive and middle-aged.

'Good, thanks,' I said. 'I won't hold you up – Andrew Faulkner just called in to say he's chased a few calves that were on the road into the paddock by Mum and Dad's.'

'Good man,' said Marcus. 'I'll get right on to them in the morning.'

'They're looking a bit short of grass where they are,' I said hesitantly.

'Yeah, that paddock looks terrible from the road, doesn't it? There's still quite a bit of feed on the sides, but I'll move them tomorrow anyway. And I'll have a look for a hole in the fence they might have got through, and fix it up.'

'You're a legend,' I said, feeling quite limp with relief.

'Hey, you have a good night, okay?' he said warmly.

'Will do. Um, just one more thing I wanted to catch up with you about …'

'Mm?'

'Those light ewes.'

'Yep, what about them?'

I took a steadying breath. 'Did you separate them from the others, in the end?'

There was a pause on the other end of the line, and then he said a little stiffly, 'Yes, of course. I drenched them first thing Tuesday morning and put them in the waterfall paddock. Wasn't that what you wanted?'

Oh, hell, I'd offended him. 'Yes, absolutely,' I said hastily. 'Thanks heaps, Marcus, that's great.'

'Was that all?'

'Yes. Hey, I'm sorry; I didn't mean to interrogate you.'

'No worries. Goodnight.'

'Goodnight,' I said, but he'd already put the phone down. I considered calling Dave, followed by a few potential jumble sale helpers, then decided it was all just too hard and retired to the sofa to watch ancient reruns of *Porridge* instead.

Chapter 6

The next day was Friday, and it was Dave's weekend to have the kids. I left work at two forty-five, collected Nathan from day care and Lily from school, made them pikelets with golden syrup for afternoon tea, emptied their lunchboxes, read Lily's school newsletter and put it in my pocket to hand on to Dave, packed their clothes for the weekend and their schoolbags for Monday morning and thrust them both into the shower.

'*Nathan!*' Lily shrieked. 'Mum, tell him not to piddle on my foot!'

'Nath, it's poor form to piddle on people's feet,' I said absently, looking at my reflection in the bathroom mirror and wincing. This wouldn't do at all. I wished to confront my cheating husband looking the epitome of poised and effortless chic, not the epitome of harassed fatigue.

'What if a jellyfish stinged them?' asked Nathan. 'Then you *have* to piddle on them.'

'Really?' I asked, pulling the hair tie out of my ponytail and dragging a brush through my hair.

'It was on TV.'

'Well, there you go.'

'Yes, but a jellyfish didn't sting me,' said Lily snippily.

'Glad to hear it,' I said. My hair was alright – I'd straightened it the day before and it fell in a dark, moderately shiny sheet to my shoulders – but there were purple smudges under my eyes and a spot on my chin. I rummaged through the bathroom drawer for a tube of liquid foundation.

'Why are you putting on makeup?' Lily asked.

'Oh, because I'm looking a bit old and tired.'

'I think you look beautiful, Mummy,' said Nathan.

'Me too,' Lily said.

'You guys are awesome,' I said. 'Right, jump out; it's time to go to Dad's.'

* * *

'I like Daddy's house,' Nathan said as we turned up the long gravel driveway leading to Dave's farm cottage.

'*Nathan,*' Lily hissed, scowling at him.

'That's great,' I said heartily.

'I can play on the iPad as much as I want.'

Dave opened the door and came out to stand on the little strip of porch, backlit from inside. He was wearing jeans and a long-sleeved T-shirt I didn't recognise, and he'd had his hair cut. He looked boyishly, startlingly attractive. 'Well, if it isn't my very favourite children,' he said, smiling.

'We're your *only* children!' Lily cried.

'That's not the point. Come here, you.' He picked her up and spun her around, and she squealed with delight. 'You get more beautiful every time I see you.'

'Thank you,' she said demurely.

Dave let her slide to her feet. 'Nathan, my main man! How's it hanging?'

'Can I play on the iPad?'

'Not until I've had a hug, you can't,' said Dave, turning him over and suspending him by the ankles while he shrieked with laughter.

It was *wonderful*, I told myself firmly – as I ferried car seats, bags, Nathan's cuddly blanket, Lily's Flower Fairy sticker book and two pairs of gumboots from the car to the porch – that Dave was such a good father.

'Well, guys, have a great weekend,' I said, putting down the last load.

'I'll miss you, Mummy,' said Lily, turning to hug me. 'Will you be okay by yourself?'

'Of course. I'll be able to party all night without you scuzzle-butts holding me back.'

'You will not,' said Nathan. 'You'll put on your pyjamas and do work on the computer.'

I laughed and then sighed. 'Sad but true. Have you got anything special planned, Dave?'

'Maybe we could go fishing tomorrow. What d'you reckon, kids?'

'Yes!' Lily cried. *'Awesome!'*

'Dad! Mr Faulkner's dog bit Tessa!' said Nathan.

'Mr Faulkner's dog?' said Dave, frowning.

'But *luckily*,' said Lily, 'she doesn't have any teeth so Tessa just got a big fright.'

'I was telling it!' Nathan wailed.

'You did tell it, buddy,' said Dave. 'Right, bags inside. Chop chop!'

As the children scurried inside I fished Lily's school newsletter out of my jeans pocket and passed it over. 'Just to keep you in the loop.'

'Thank you.' He smiled at me crookedly. 'New shoes?'

I looked down at my red canvas sneakers. 'Mm. New shirt?'

'It feels wrong.'

'The shirt?' I asked, raising my eyebrows.

He shook his head. 'Moving on. Buying something without you approving it.'

Dave had never asked for my approval before buying things, but I knew what he meant. 'You did well. It's a nice shirt.'

'Thanks. I like your shoes. Want to come in for a coffee?'

'Oh,' I said, surprised and pleased. But it wouldn't do to get Lily's hopes up. 'Um, no, I'd better keep going.'

He gave me a wistful little smile. 'Okay. Have a good weekend.'

'You too. Hey, Dave – please don't tell the kids I won't let you take them to see your parents.'

He said nothing.

'You know I'd never do that.'

'How the hell would I know that? You've done a lot of things I never thought you'd do,' said Dave, following the children into the house and shutting the door behind him with a bang.

* * *

I spent the first half of the drive home castigating myself for ruining that fragile attempt at a truce. Why couldn't I keep my mouth shut? Why couldn't I just leave well enough alone? I kept *doing* this; kept antagonising people instead of working with them. What was *wrong* with me? Dave, Marcus, the charming fellow from yesterday's site visit, who had rung my manager that morning to complain ... If one person's pissed off with you, the problem could well be with them. But when you've alienated half the people you associate with, it's time to start looking good and hard at the common denominator.

Although, on the other hand, why *shouldn't* I take exception to Dave telling the children I wouldn't let them see their grandparents because I was trying to punish him? And he hadn't even tried to justify himself; he'd just attacked. Much easier than trying to defend the indefensible, of course – ignore the charges, and go straight to making Jenny feel guilty. He was very good at it, which was only to be expected after years of practice. And I, guppy that I was, fell for it every bloody time.

Never mind, I thought drearily, changing down a gear as I passed Mum and Dad's mailbox and started up the last hill home. Just because you've been a guppy for thirty-five years doesn't mean you have to stay a guppy for the rest of your life. And now I would stop this foolish downward spiral of self-loathing, make myself a nice risotto, read my book, take a bath *all by myself* and finish looking at that consent for the Millers' ensuite bathroom.

The moon was rising above the hills and the big horse chestnut by the bottom road gate, grown from a conker by my father as a small boy, cast a delicate fretwork of shadows across the road. It was a lovely, clear winter's night – there would be a serious frost by morning. I'd better go out and cover my baby jacaranda when I got home. Winter temperatures in New Zealand's King Country aren't really conducive to growing semi-tropical trees, but the thought of a cloud of lavender blossom on the bottom lawn was so seductive that I was determined to give it a try.

As I rounded the corner before the woolshed I remembered I'd left my woolly hat in the yards on Monday when we were scanning, and turned in through the gate to collect it. I parked the car in front of the woolshed, climbed the rickety wooden steps to the door, went in and groped for the bank of light switches on the wall. Breathing in the familiar scents of dust and lanolin, I made my way through the catching pens behind the wool board, shoved open the heavy wooden sliding door that led out into the covered yards and ran down the ramp.

I'd left my hat on a shelf beside the drafting gates at the head of the race. I picked it up, cast a careless eye around the yards and stopped, frowning. The drenching race was slap up against the drafting race, and I'd spent about seven hours on Monday looking into it while I pushed ewes into the scanning crate. It hadn't been in use that day, and various odds and ends had been dropped into it to keep them out of the way: a couple of old shearing combs, an orange extension cord, an empty plastic water bottle. They were all still there, unmoved. One loop of the extension cord made the same neat letter *e* as it had on Monday, and the combs still lay almost, but not quite, at right angles to one another. No sheep had been through there.

'Marcus, you scummy little scumbag,' I said aloud.

There were no lights on in Marcus's little weatherboard house just up the road from the woolshed, and I was relieved not to have to decide whether to confront him now. I drove the five hundred metres home, let a reproachful Tessa off her chain in the carport and ran up the kitchen steps, anger starting to displace my initial shock. After tipping a little heap of dog biscuits into Tessa's bowl, I snatched up the phone.

'Hello?' Mum said.

'Is Dad there?'

I heard her breathe in. 'Jenny, I'm sorry if I hurt your feelings the other night.'

'What? It's fine, Mum. I just need to talk to Dad.'

'Here he is,' she said sadly.

'What's up?' Dad asked, taking the phone.

'Marcus didn't drench those thin ewes.'

'What?' he said, sounding entirely bewildered.

'I asked him last night if he'd put them back in with the rest of the mob after all –'

'Oh, Jenny,' he said, sighing.

'– and he said no, of course not, he'd drenched them all on Tuesday morning and run them out to the waterfall paddock.'

'So?' Dad prompted.

'So, I just called in at the woolshed to pick up my hat, and the drenching race is full of rubbish. There is no way any sheep have been through it since Monday. So he lied.'

'Jenny ...' Dad said again.

'He told me straight out that he'd drenched them. He was all stiff and offended about it. *Did* you go and have a look at them?'

'No, I haven't got there yet.'

'And Andrew Faulkner called in last night to say that perhaps we'd better move the calves across the road from your place. He was obviously really uncomfortable about saying anything – I'm sure he wouldn't have unless things were looking pretty bloody dire.'

'Calm down, love,' said Dad.

'Did *you* notice those calves had nothing to eat?'

'Jenny, stop it,' he said firmly. 'There's no point in working yourself up into a state. No, I haven't looked closely at the calves, but I will in the morning. And I'll have a talk to Marcus. I really don't think it's a good idea for you to go charging in and reading him the riot act.'

'Well, no, but if he's lying to us ...'

'We'll sort it all out tomorrow. Now, you go and have a drink. Have you got the kids this weekend?'

'No, they're with Dave,' I said tiredly.

'Well, that's good, you can really put your feet up and have a bit of a rest. Okay?'

'Okay. Thanks, Dad.'

'Not a problem. Goodnight, love.'

* * *

I had two glasses of wine and a long hot bath, but neither relaxed me. This was bad. This was smooth, expert lying to cover up deliberate disobedience, and that wasn't something a little talk with someone could fix.

I should have kept a closer eye on Marcus, and so should Dad. But I didn't know enough to be in charge, and he didn't really care. He'd never wanted to assume responsibility for running the place again; he wanted to enjoy his retirement in peace.

The difficulties ahead – removing Marcus, with the appalling amount of red tape that firing bad employees entailed; finding somebody else; fattening up two thousand pregnant sheep in the middle of winter; trying, somehow, to make enough money out of the whole operation to keep paying the mortgage – loomed like something out of a nightmare. And I was so tired, and there was nobody to help me, and I couldn't say it was all too hard and it wasn't fair when I was the one who'd precipitated the whole situation ...

I lay in the cooling water, weeping with self-pity, until Tessa, who was sitting on the bathmat beside me, lifted her greying nose to the ceiling and howled.

I sighed, sat up and splashed my face with water. 'Oh, it's alright, I'm just being a drip. Let's go find something to eat.'

Chapter 7

There was a spectacular frost in the morning, carpeting the lawn in silver and furring the boards of the deck. The Tipoi flats at the foot of the valley were blanketed entirely in fog when I went out to uncover my jacaranda tree, and the bush-clad ranges behind them rose through the mist like islands in a white sea. The air was clean and fresh and lovely, and although none of last night's problems had gone away, they seemed a lot less dire in the sunshine.

I had two Cameo Creams for breakfast, which is acceptable when your children aren't there to be corrupted by your unhealthy lifestyle choices, tied up Tessa, who was no asset on a long walk, climbed the orchard fence and set off downhill towards the creek. Tessa, smug and collarless, joined me at the third gate.

The main creek through the farm – named either the Mangapotu or the Mangapika Stream, depending on which map you happened to consult – was a particularly charming one with a stony bottom. Over the last few hundred thousand years it had, with admirable perseverance, cut itself a broad, curving valley, which divided the farm more or less in two. I followed the valley down, enjoying the low-pitched chuckle and clatter of the water, and Tessa took point duty, grunting importantly as she investigated random smells in the grass. The sunlight crept down the hillside towards us, turning the grass from grey to green, our breaths steamed and mist rose in lazy curls from a narrow, bush-filled gully on my left. It was all quite ridiculously lovely, with every grass head and fern frond outlined in tiny, glittering ice crystals. I dug my cold hands into my pockets, crossed the creek via the new concrete bridge (put in the year before, after Dave and the tractor fell through the old wooden one) and struck up a grassy ridge towards the sunshine.

I headed in a wide curve back towards the woolshed and home, not keeping to the tracks but bearing diagonally up across the faces of the hills, and carrying an increasingly heavy Tessa for increasingly long stretches. 'You're a horrible little animal, you know that?' I told her, and she reached up to lick my ear.

We went through a mob of lambs, recently shorn and sparkling white. Tessa whined and wriggled in my arms, desperate to chase them, and I clamped her more firmly beneath my elbow. They looked good, I thought – clean and plump; in plenty of grass. Perhaps things weren't as bad as I'd thought last night. Perhaps Marcus *would* lift his game, once Dad had spoken to him. Perhaps. I hadn't – we hadn't – kept a close enough eye on things, but we'd do better. Maybe we could institute a fortnightly meeting and drive around ...

I skirted the shoulder of the last hill, put Tessa down with relief, rounded the end of the bamboo hedge below the yards – home, I'd once believed implicitly, to a family of pandas – and found the ewes.

'Oh, dear God,' I said.

I wasn't far below the woolshed, at the top of a little holding paddock that opened into a fenced laneway. The laneway ran along the crest of a narrow ridge, with a gate at each end and one on either side, allowing stock to be sent in several different directions from the yards.

But all the gates were shut. Two thousand ewes were packed into that laneway like sardines, fetlock deep in mud. We'd scanned on Monday, and it was Saturday now. Five days.

Tessa barked shrilly, and every head went up. Two thousand ewes pressed forward towards us, yelling at the tops of their voices, and in the face of this unprecedented reaction Tessa the Apex Predator retreated, whimpering, and hid behind my legs.

I ran down the holding paddock, vaulted the fence at the bottom and sped on beside the laneway. The sheep on the other side of the fence followed me, pressing so fast and hard that I was afraid there would be a smother. I stopped at the first gate I came to, opened it and dragged it back against the fence.

Ewes surged through, a dozen abreast. I stepped forward to try to slow the rush, but they were beyond caring about me. I retreated back along the fence line and watched helplessly as they shoved and jostled, pouring through the gate like an avalanche.

And then it was over. The last few unfortunates, who'd been jammed against the gate posts in the crush, limped past me and dropped their heads to start grazing. The air was filled with the soft, juicy sound of tearing grass.

One ewe, so covered in mud that I could only see the whites of her eyes, lay in the gateway. She must have lost her footing and gone down beneath the stampede. She threw her head sideways and struggled feebly, and then subsided, panting.

'Shh, baby,' I said foolishly, picking my way across the slick, ankle-deep mud to lift her.

I rolled her up to sit, and she flailed wildly, throwing herself back down into the mud. I seized two handfuls of filthy wool and lifted her again, and this time as she thrashed a back leg collapsed beneath her. She slumped between my hands, eyes rolling and her leg bent at a nauseating, impossible angle.

I pushed her over to lie with her broken leg uppermost, so it was at least reasonably straight, and shuddered as I saw a white gleam of bone showing through the mud.

'Oh, sweetie,' I whispered. 'I'm so sorry. I'll run straight home for a knife. I won't be long ...' I pushed myself to my feet, slipping in the mud, and hastened back towards the gate.

As I reached the road fence behind the woolshed, a battered green ute came up the road past me, slowed and pulled off onto the grass verge. 'Is everything al–' Andrew Faulkner said through the open window, before his voice was drowned by a frantic volley of barking from both Tessa and his dog, who was on the back of the ute.

'Meg!' he said sharply, turning in his seat to glare at her. The old huntaway, who had been showing every sign of launching herself off the deck of the ute to gum Tessa to death, subsided reluctantly.

Tessa chose to take this as a sign of surrender, and went up an octave or so.

'*Stop it!*' I shouted, shaking her.

There was a moment of quiet, broken almost immediately by a renewed outbreak of hostilities between the two dogs.

'THAT WILL DO!' Andrew roared. He got out of his ute, tied his dog to the front of the deck with a short length of chain, and came up to the fence. 'What's wrong?'

'A ewe, just down the hill – she's broken her leg, and I can see the bone sticking through. It's ...' My voice was rising, and I pulled myself together with an effort. 'I'm on my way home for a knife.'

'I've got one,' he said. 'Hop in.'

'I'm filthy,' I said, looking down at my mud-slicked jeans. 'I'll get on the back.' I climbed the fence, Tessa under my arm, and approached the deck of his ute, to be met by a low, menacing growl.

'Better hop in,' said Andrew dryly.

In I hopped, putting Tessa down in the footwell, and Andrew did a U-turn in Marcus's driveway just up the road. The four-wheeler was parked in front of his house but there was no car in the garage – he must have gone out, the rotten little swine.

'It's awful,' I said abruptly. 'You'll be appalled; the ewes haven't had anything to eat for nearly a week. The gate at the bottom of the laneway was shut, and nobody noticed ...' As he turned in at the woolshed I added, 'Keep going to the far end; it's just down the hill.'

He parked at the top end of the bamboo hedge and turned off his engine. It stopped with a shuddering cough.

'Down here,' I said, getting out. Tessa jumped down behind me. 'It's just awful.'

We rounded the hedge and surveyed the scene below in all its Somme-like horror. Several more grim little heaps, I now saw, lay half submerged in the mud. Dead of starvation? Suffocation? I felt sick with horror and guilt, and filled with shame that Andrew Faulkner, acknowledged district-wide as a seriously sharp operator, should be witnessing this cruel, unforgivable stuff-up.

'The one with the broken leg's down at the bottom,' I said shakily. 'It was my fault – they stampeded through the gate when I opened it, and she must've got trampled.'

'It's okay,' he said, opening the gate into the yards.

'It is *not*.'

He didn't reply, but started down through the holding paddock towards the nearest of those pitiful mud-caked shapes. There were five, besides the ewe with the broken leg, one of which was still breathing. Andrew took out his sheath knife and cut her throat without a word before carrying on down the hill.

'Thank you,' I said, as he straightened up from the last ewe, still kicking spasmodically as the blood pooled scarlet in the mud beneath her.

'You're welcome.'

'God, what a hideous cock-up.'

'Not your cock-up, though, is it?'

'Yes,' I said. 'It is, ultimately. It's my – Dad's and my – responsibility. And I knew Marcus was cutting corners; you told me, and so did John Mercer ...'

Andrew grimaced, not unsympathetically, and started back towards the ute.

We climbed the hill in silence, but as we reached the yards again I said, 'There's a tap on the corner of the woolshed if you want to wash your boots.'

'Thanks.'

I led the way, and he gestured for me to go first. 'No, after you,' I said. 'I'll walk home; Tessa's far too dirty to go back in your ute.'

He glanced at Tessa, who had accompanied us on our grim little pilgrimage and now looked as if she'd been taken by the ears and dunked like a teabag in liquid mud, and smiled. It was the first time I'd ever seen him smile, and it worked a startling transformation. He was really quite good-looking – not unlike Bruce Springsteen, circa *Born to Run*.

'It's tricky when your legs are five inches long and the mud's six inches deep,' he said. 'If you can hold her, I'll rinse her off with the hose.'

I held Tessa around the chest while he hosed her legs and sides, and then lifted her to stand on her back legs so he could do her stomach. She was most unimpressed, whining and shivering and generally giving her very best impression of a dog bravely attempting to endure the unendurable.

'I'm so sorry about your clothes,' I said, releasing the cowering victim and looking at the mud caking the bottoms of Andrew's jeans.

He looked up briefly from hosing his boots. 'They'll wash. I even have a machine for it.'

'Wow.'

'I know. Pretty impressive.' He handed me the hose. 'I'll go and fetch the ute.'

This time, as he pulled up beside me, it took a mere 'Stop it!' from me and a 'Sit!' from him, in tones of extreme menace, to quiet the dogs. 'They're improving,' I remarked, getting in.

'Practically best friends,' he said.

I smiled, and then said blankly, as we turned onto the road, 'Marcus's dog kennels are gone!' There had been two shiny, new kennels with brightly galvanised runs under the ancient grapefruit tree between house and garage. 'Unless he's just moved them …'

Andrew braked abruptly and turned up his driveway. He must have noticed me stiffen beside him, because he said, 'His car's gone; he's not here now, anyway.'

'With any luck he's gone for good.'

'Then you won't get to yell at him.'

'I don't ever want to see him again,' I said. 'It'll be much easier if he's just packed up and left than if we need to start issuing written warnings.'

He parked the ute. 'I think you can fire someone on the spot for that sort of carry-on,' he said, jerking his head in the direction of the woolshed.

'Well, you'd think so, but employment law is pretty heavily biased in favour of the employee ...' I got out, the ubiquitous Tessa at my heels, and crossed the lawn to the little house's back door.

This was surrounded by black plastic rubbish sacks, some intact but several of them split and oozing bottles, bits of plastic and assorted decaying food scraps.

'*And* he doesn't recycle,' Andrew said behind me. 'Clearly an arsehole.'

'Clearly.' I tried the door, found it unlocked and led the way into the kitchen. The sink was full of dirty dishes, and the rubbish bin had either fallen or been pushed over, scattering used tissues and plastic wrap and partly gnawed mutton bones across the floor.

'Bugger,' Andrew said. 'He hasn't left for good.'

'He might have – we furnished the house. Tessa, you horrible dog, drop it.' I crouched down to relieve her of the chop bone she'd just picked up, but she bolted past me up the hall. I followed, running her to ground in the master bedroom.

'Come *here*,' I said.

She came.

'Drop it.'

The chop hit the floor and rolled under the edge of the bed, and I crouched down to retrieve it. 'Oh, good God.'

'What?' Andrew asked, appearing in the doorway.

'A whole lot of used condoms – *Tessa! OUTSIDE!*'

Tessa, who was investigating the nearest condom with interest, shot out of the room and back down the hall as though she'd been fired from a gun.

Andrew eyed me warily.

'It's alright,' I said crossly as I straightened, chop bone in hand. 'I'm not going to start screaming and throwing things.'

'Wouldn't blame you at all,' he said. 'Lousy little shit. But on the bright side, I think he *has* packed up and gone.'

'Why?'

'No clothes, no toiletries, no books or pictures, and you can see a place in the lounge where someone's taken away a couch or something ...'

'I suppose he must have gone yesterday, while I was at work.'

'Leaving his rubbish as a happy memento of your time together.'

'What a guy,' I said. 'Andrew, how bad a job *was* he doing? I mean, not this week, but in general.'

'Well, I don't know ...'

'Yes you do,' I said flatly.

He sighed and ran a hand through his greying dark hair. 'Pretty bloody mediocre,' he admitted.

My eyes prickled, and I blinked fiercely. And I hadn't noticed ...

Andrew looked highly alarmed. 'Look, come on, it's starting to feel like lunchtime,' he said. 'I'll give you a lift home.'

Chapter 8

'Oh no,' said Mum, dropping her hands into her lap. 'Oh *no*.'

Dropped off by Andrew at my own house, I'd paused only to reinstate Tessa's collar, tightening it by one hole, and tie her up before driving back down the road to Mum and Dad's. I paused at their mailbox to see if the calves over the road had been moved, saw with some surprise that Marcus had actually found time in his busy schedule to open a gate for them, and carried on up to the house. There I found my parents lunching on soup and homemade bread, and promptly spoilt their appetites by pouring out my tale of horror and woe.

'We'll have to take the four-wheeler and tow them up to the offal hole,' I said. 'And then we'd better go right around and check the whole farm, in case there's some other disaster I haven't found yet.'

'Christ, what a horrible thing to happen,' said Dad, rumpling his hair up at the back as he did in times of strain.

'I guess it was dark on Monday night when he pushed them out of the yards, and he never went back to check them.'

'Mm.'

'And neither did we,' I said.

'Don't think about it anymore, love,' Mum said. 'What's done is done. We can't change it now.'

'And then his *house*. It's just disgusting. There's rubbish everywhere, dishes in the sink – he didn't even strip his bed or pick his used condoms up off the floor.'

Dad winced. 'Charming,' he said.

'Do you think your talk on the phone with him on Thursday might have had anything to do with his going?' Mum asked gently, laying her hand over mine.

I snatched my hand away. 'Mum, I *had* to ring him to let him know about the calves Andrew Faulkner found on the road! And then, while I had him on the phone, I just asked – very tentatively – about the ewes, and he told me he'd drenched them all and put them in the waterfall paddock on Tuesday. He sounded pissed off about being questioned, and I *apologised*!'

'Don't be like that, Jenny, I just thought that perhaps …'

'I expect he was planning to go on Friday anyway,' Dad said, pouring oil on troubled waters. 'That's the day his pay goes through, isn't it?'

'Yes. In advance.'

'Have you tried calling him today?'

I shook my head.

'Well, we probably should.'

'Can you do it, please?' I asked, and he sighed and got up.

'No good,' he said, putting the phone down again thirty seconds later. 'It just went straight to the answer phone thingy.'

'Shouldn't you leave a message?'

'Yes, I suppose so,' he said unenthusiastically.

'Sorry, Dad.'

'Where are we going to find another worker like him?' said Mum, following her own special line of thought.

'With any luck, my sweet, we won't,' Dad said, and I laughed despite myself.

'Oh, well, I *know* that, it's just –'

But what it just was we were destined never to find out, because at that moment my pocket began to play the theme song from *Get Smart* (I love the theme song from *Get Smart*). I pulled out my phone and looked at the screen. It was a local number, but not one I knew. 'Hello?' I said, answering it.

'Jenny? Andrew Faulkner here.'

'Oh. Hi.'

'I've got my younger brother staying here, and he's quite keen on the idea of doing some casual farm work for a few months.' His voice was deep and quiet and unhurried, as soothing as cold cream on sunburn. 'Just thought I'd mention it, in case you wanted someone in a hurry.'

'Well, *yes*!' I said. 'I mean, probably – we haven't even … Look, thank you so much! Can we meet him?'

'I'll bring him over, if you like.'

'That'd be brilliant. When? I'm down at Mum and Dad's, but I'll –'

'Why don't we just come down there?'

'Yes,' I said. 'Wonderful. Thank you so much.'

'Be there in ten minutes,' he said, and hung up.

'Who was that?' Mum asked as I put my phone down on the kitchen bench.

'Andrew Faulkner,' I said, smiling.

'I didn't realise you knew him so well.'

'I don't. It's just that he's got a brother staying who might be able to help out on the farm for a few months. Isn't *that* the luckiest coincidence of all time?'

'Depends on the brother,' Dad said.

'Well, we'll soon find out. They're coming down to talk about it.'

'Down *here*?' Mum said.

'Yes. In ten minutes.'

She leapt to her feet. 'For heaven's sake, Brian, finish putting those groceries away! The place looks like a bomb's hit it! Jenny, put some wood on the fire, please.'

I went obediently towards the burner in the corner. 'Mum, he's just seen that hideous crime scene up at the woolshed; I don't think he's going to be all that distressed by a few groceries on the bench.'

She was flying around the kitchen and didn't answer, so I picked up the empty wood basket and went outside to fill it.

'This sounds like them,' said Dad as I came back in. He put a pile of newspapers down on the end of the kitchen bench.

'*Brian!*' Mum said. 'Don't put those there!' She snatched them up again as if they'd been copies of *Penthouse*, looked around wildly, and thrust them under the table onto the seat of a chair. Then she hastened to the door as two men came down the path. 'Hello! Come in!'

Andrew Faulkner's brother wasn't at all like him on first impression – or, as I was to discover, on any subsequent impression either. He was fair where Andrew was dark, and he looked both considerably younger and considerably more approachable. He had a wide, engaging smile, broad shoulders, cropped sandy hair and a sprinkling of freckles across his nose. I thought, as I watched him greet Mum, that he seemed oddly familiar. He bent to unlace his boots, and it was as he stood back up and our eyes met that I placed him.

'Oh!' I said. 'Hi! It's Harry, isn't it?'

'Hi!' he replied in the bright voice people use when they have no idea who you are but are hoping to remember before you realise it. And then he *did* remember. His smile vanished and his eyes widened in horror.

This was disconcerting, to say the least, and I took a step backwards.

'You've met already?' Mum asked.

'Um, yes,' I said, pulling myself together. 'At a really dire party in Wellington, about a year ago. I never realised you two were brothers.'

'It's a small world, isn't it?' said Mum.

'It is indeed,' said Harry hoarsely.

'In that case, you'd know our younger daughter Rebecca, too.'

'Er, no, I'm afraid not.'

'Really?' Mum said. 'She owns a Pilates studio in Wellington. She meets all *sorts* of glamorous people. Amanda Marshall – you know, the news presenter – comes for sessions, and she's recommended Rebecca to *several* of her friends.'

Harry smiled mechanically.

'Afternoon,' said Dad, coming forward and holding out a hand to each man in turn. 'Brian Smith.'

'Harry Faulkner,' Harry said.

Andrew merely nodded.

'Nice to meet you,' said Dad.

Meanwhile I was busy replaying that party in my head, looking for horrendous and hitherto unnoticed social lapses on my part. It had been held in an art gallery; the cutting-edge sort where the exhibits aren't actually recognisable, to provincials such as myself, as Art. Bex had been invited by a client and had taken me for moral support. Finding on arrival that she knew more people than she'd expected to, she left me in a corner while she networked, and I fell into conversation with a nice but unhappy young man. Harry was a hunting guide, of all the unlikely people to meet at such an event, and he'd been brought along by his architect boyfriend. They'd had a fight on the way there about Harry's reluctance to come out of the closet, and the boyfriend, who was somewhere on the far side of the crowd, was now pointedly ignoring him ...

Oh. Understanding arrived in a flood of relief. He must still be in the closet. And he was afraid, poor man, that I'd out him. I smiled at him reassuringly.

'I understand thanks are in order for your help with that horrible situation with the ewes,' Dad was saying to Andrew.

Andrew gave a small nod.

'Terrible thing to have happen. We knew young Marcus was a bit cocky and inexperienced, but ...'

'Mm.'

'Er ...' Dad said. And then, giving up on this laborious and one-sided conversation with palpable relief, 'So, Harry, what brings you to this neck of the woods?'

'The thought of home-cooked meals and high-speed broadband, mostly,' said Harry. 'I've been down in the Kawekas for the last few months, working as a hunting guide, but the boss was a bit of a prat.'

'What sort of hunting? Deer?'

Harry nodded. 'Red deer, mostly, around there. A few fallow.'

'Ah. And you've got a farming background?'

'Yes. The parents had a sheep and beef farm near Feilding – they sold up a few years ago and moved to town. I've worked as a fencing contractor and a musterer, but for the last few years I've been culling goats on conservation land, and working as a hunting guide.'

'Any management experience?' Dad asked.

'Not a huge amount,' Harry said. 'I've run Mum and Dad's place for a couple of three-month stints, while they were travelling.'

Damn, I thought. Another stop-gap. But beggars, after all, cannot be choosers.

'What we're going to be needing,' Dad was saying, 'is someone who can manage the day-to-day stock work, fix up a hole in a fence, feed out a bale of silage here and there …'

'I think I could handle that.'

'Well, shall we go for a drive around the place and see what you think?'

They went in Dad's ute, which had only two seats. I'd have had to ride on the back if I'd gone with them, and it seemed that my input wasn't required, so I accompanied Andrew up the path from the house to where our respective vehicles were parked beside the implement shed.

'Thank you for everything today,' I said.

'Hmm? Oh, no worries.' And without further ado he got into his ute and drove away. I smiled to myself as I opened my car door. He must have used up today's – or perhaps even this week's – quota of social chit-chat.

Chapter 9

I spent the afternoon making a start on cleaning up after Marcus, in rubber gloves and an old pair of Dave's overalls. This was an underwhelming experience, but we could hardly expect Harry, assuming he wanted the job, to start it by taking out someone else's festering rubbish.

The next morning, heading down the road to pick up where I'd left off, I had a sudden thought and carried on past to turn into John Mercer's driveway two hundred metres further down the hill. I rounded a straggly conifer hedge, parked in front of the garage and stared. The tired weatherboard cottage that, only six weeks previously, had lurked in the middle of a camellia thicket now rose stark and gleaming above a forest of stumps. It had been painted a clear, bright lilac, and it looked exposed and embarrassed, like an elderly lady who's just been interrupted in the bath.

As I got out of the car, John appeared around the side of the house, carrying a coil of high tensile wire and with the inevitable drooping cigarette in the corner of his mouth. 'Morning,' he said.

I gestured towards a glossy lilac-coloured wall. 'Wow.'

'We're getting there,' he said. 'Come and tell me what you think of my new path.'

I followed him around the back of the cottage, where a new and meticulously pieced mosaic path led from the washroom door to a tiny woodshed. It was a floral pattern; the petals were made of broken-up orange pebblecrete pavers and the centres of the flowers were alternating green and brown beer bottles, hammered bottom-up into the ground. It had obviously taken a vast amount of time and effort, and it was one of the nastiest things I'd ever seen.

'Wow,' I said again. 'What a – a labour of love, John.'

John smiled and scuffed the bottom of a bottle coyly with his foot.

'And the lawns, and the gardens – and the house ...'

'A lick of paint soon brightens a place up.'

'It does indeed,' I said.

'It's a nice, cheerful colour,' he said. 'And it was marked down *eighty* percent, if you can believe it.'

I could believe it quite easily. 'That was good luck,' I said. 'John, I just wanted to let you know—'

'And I've fixed up the compost bins over here,' he said, ushering me across the lawn. 'See? When you want to empty them out, you just lift the boards out of their slots.'

'Now *that*,' I said sincerely, 'is cool. I wish mine did that.'

'Well, we can organise it. No trouble at all. You get the timber and I'll come over and put them up for you. Now, come and have a look at this.' He led me around to the cottage's back porch, where, in a little square of earth beside the steps, a delicate green shoot was unfurling beneath a pane of glass propped up with sticks.

'What is it?' I asked, crouching down to look more closely.

'It's a choko vine,' said John proudly. 'Haven't you heard of chokos?'

'Yes, I –'

'Marvellous things. Roast 'em, boil 'em, make 'em into pies if you want to … Wait here a minute.' He climbed the porch steps, took off his gumboots and vanished inside.

'Here you are,' he said, reappearing at the door. He held out a pale green fruit, roughly the size of a quince. It was hard and smooth, more pointed at one end than the other, and folded in on itself like an old, toothless mouth at the blunt end.

'Never get any bug damage,' said John. 'And they keep forever. Try it. Cut it up and add it to your Sunday roast.'

'Thank you,' I said, taking it. 'I'd better carry on, but I just wanted to thank you for letting me know about Marcus. He's gone.'

'Has he now? Good riddance.'

'Yes,' I said with feeling. Should I tell him the grisly details, I wondered, or just leave it at that?

'I could see that he was taking the Michael,' said John, nodding wisely. 'John, me lad, I said to meself, that little bastard's taking advantage of the Smiths. They've never run the most progressive of operations, it's true, but this is bloody ridiculous.'

Leave it at that, I decided. 'Well, um, thank you,' I said, trying with indifferent success not to feel offended.

'So you'll be looking for someone else, I suppose?'

'Actually, Andrew Faulkner's brother's going to help out for a few months.'

'Andrew Faulkner? Bloke who bought Royce's place a couple of years ago?' said John.

'That's the one.'

'Well, I suppose this brother of his can't be any worse than the last lot, can he?'

'That's right,' I said, smiling. 'Things can only improve. Right, I'd better keep going. Thank you for the choko.'

'Children not with you today?' he asked, accompanying me back around the cottage to the car.

'No, they're with their father this weekend.'

John sighed. 'It's tough on little ones, isn't it? Call me old-fashioned, but I still think it's hard to beat the good old nuclear family. Mum, Dad and the kids.'

'Well,' I said lightly, 'I suppose that depends on the family.' I reached out to open the car door.

Leaning a hand on the roof, John cut me off neatly. 'Me old mum used to say that people think marriage is a case of finding your true love and living happily ever after, when in actual fact it's a case of finding someone near enough and then compromising for the rest of your life.'

'True,' I said. 'Anyway, I'd better …'

'Marriage is too easy to get out of, these days. People don't commit for better or for worse; they ditch the whole thing as soon as the going gets tough.'

'Sometimes,' I said. 'But then again, sometimes they try really hard, and adjust their expectations, and try again, until finally they hit a wall. See you later, John.'

* * *

It was funny, I thought, donning my rubber gloves in preparation for an assault on Marcus's shower, how so many people felt that their opinions on how you were running your life would be of interest and assistance. One tended first to meet the phenomenon during pregnancy. Then it increased exponentially once the baby was born – breastfeeding, naps, dream feeds, starting solids, toilet training, day care ... if not managed correctly, every one of these vital aspects of child raising could, apparently, lead to ill health, psychological damage and near-certain delinquency in your offspring. And if, by some miracle, you managed to navigate these many shoals, you could still ruin your children's lives by divorcing their father ...

Looking up at this point in my bitter little soliloquy, I noticed that the shower cubicle was sparkling, which was such a pleasing side effect of my tantrum that it ended it.

By one thirty, I'd finished cleaning the kitchen and bathroom and had vacuumed the floors. The windows were still to be done, and the closer I looked at the ceilings the more cobwebs and fly spots I saw, but I had at least removed most of the overt grime. I sighed, stretched and went home for lunch.

I was sitting at the table with a curry powder and tinned peach toasted sandwich (my own invention, which had yet, inexplicably, to catch on among my friends and relations), a cup of tea and a wildflower seed catalogue when I heard a vehicle come down the driveway. With a grunt of effort, Tessa clambered out of her basket and pattered across the kitchen floor to meet the visitor at the door.

'Come in!' I called, circling *Linaria vulgaris* for further consideration and turning in my chair.

'Hi,' said Harry Faulkner, cautiously pushing the kitchen door open.

Tessa rolled over onto her back and waved a beseeching forepaw.

'Foolish beast,' said Harry, crouching down to tickle her tummy.

I stood up and carried my cup into the kitchen. 'Hi. Cup of tea?'

'Sounds good.'

'How did the farm tour go?' I asked, refilling the kettle and switching it on.

'Great,' he said. 'It's a beautiful spot.'

'It is, isn't it? Apart from the hideous sheep concentration camp below the woolshed.'

Harry made a polite, noncommittal sort of sound as he straightened up again.

'So, after seeing the worst, do you still want the job?'

'Yeah, I think so,' he said.

'Awesome. I've been thinking that it's time we started being a bit more systematic about things. You wouldn't happen to know any good farm advisers, would you?'

'No, sorry,' he said. 'Andrew probably does, though.'

'Would you mind asking him?'

'Yeah, of course.'

'Thank you,' I said.

'I, um, got the impression your dad would be quite keen to help out, too,' he said.

I reached a cup down from the cupboard above the counter and turned to face him, slightly puzzled. 'With the farm work, you mean? He does. Not quite so much with the day-to-day stuff, but whenever there's a big job.'

'Cool. And I think he'd quite like to help with the, er, decision-making, as well.'

'He does,' I said again. 'Well, in theory, anyway. I'm afraid neither of us has been doing much decision-making ... You know that my husband – ex-husband – was running the farm up until a few months ago?'

He nodded.

'So, what with marriages turning to custard and farm leases being wound up, a few things may have slipped through the cracks. Like making sure the worker was actually working.'

'Understandable,' he said, smiling.

But what was it he'd just said? *I got the impression your dad would be quite keen to help out ...* 'What did Dad say to you, exactly?' I asked.

'About what?' said Harry, looking suddenly nervous.

'About wanting to help.'

'Just – just that he might be able to give a few tips, but he didn't want to cramp your style ...'

Really? Had my father *really* absolved himself of responsibility for the current disaster by implying that he'd been powerless to fix things because I wouldn't listen and wouldn't take his advice? I put the mug down very carefully on the edge of the bench, noticed that poor Harry was now looking quite alarmed, and tried to smile.

'I have no style,' I said lightly, opening the fridge to get out the milk. 'Any tips gratefully received. Now, did you and Dad talk about money?'

'No. Apparently that's your department.'

'Marcus was on fifty thousand a year. Does that sound reasonable?'

'Oh, um ... yeah, sure. Fine.'

'It's not amazing, I'm afraid. But finances are a bit stretched at the moment.'

'Fifty thousand is fine,' he said.

'And every second weekend off?'

'Great.'

'D'you want to be paid weekly or fortnightly?'

'Couldn't care less.'

'Okay ... Fortnightly, then. I'll download one of those new employee tax forms before you go. Oh, and the job comes with a house. Did Dad show it to you?'

'No.'

'It's the little white one opposite the woolshed. I haven't quite finished cleaning it yet, but we could go down and have a look now, if you like.'

'Actually,' he said, 'I might stay with Andrew for the meantime. He's not a bad cook.'

'Cool,' I said. 'Were you after tea or coffee?'

'Tea. White with one, thanks. Chances are I *will* want the house in a week or two, when Andrew gets sick of me and chucks me out.'

I laughed. 'Surely not.'

'Hard to believe, I know.'

'Come out onto the deck,' I said, pouring boiling water into two mugs and sugaring one. 'The view down the valley's a lot nicer than the view of my washing pile.' Passing him his mug and a packet of biscuits I led the way outside, retrieving my toasted sandwich en route.

'Stunning view,' said Harry, sinking into a canvas chair. 'The genius who built Andrew's house plonked it right at the bottom of a gully.'

'Royce Murphy,' I said. 'I remember when that house was built; it was architecturally designed, and the Murphys were incredibly proud of it.'

'Have you been inside? It's horrible.'

'Not for about twenty-five years. I remember there was a

brown shag pile carpet in the living room, and my sister and I thought it was the height of elegance and luxury.'

Tessa wandered outside and flopped down on her side at my feet.

'The whole *place* is brown,' said Harry. 'Brown-tinted windows, brown wallpaper, brown aluminium joinery ... it's like living inside a turd. No wonder Toni left.'

I paused with my sandwich halfway to my mouth and looked at him in surprise.

'What, didn't you know Andrew's wife had buggered off?' he said. 'It was a few months ago now.'

'Yes, I knew,' I said. 'She buggered off with my husband.'

'Oh, shit,' said Harry. 'Sorry.'

I smiled at him, shrugged, and took a bite of my now cold and soggy toasted sandwich.

'Your husband left *you* for *Toni?*'

'You don't like her much, do you?' I asked, considerably uplifted by the naked disbelief in his voice.

'Sour, miserable bitch. Never understood what Andrew saw in her. So are she and your husband still around here?'

'No,' I said. 'Well, he is; I think she went back to Feilding.' I looked at him thoughtfully over the rim of my mug. 'You and your brother don't really stay up to date with each other's personal lives, do you?'

'Nope.' He reached for a chocolate biscuit. 'You'll have realised he, uh, doesn't know I'm gay?'

I nodded.

'I'd like to keep it that way,' he said, picking at a flake of lichen on the arm of his chair and not meeting my eyes.

'I won't tell. But would he care?'

Harry laughed shortly. 'Yes.'

Well, no doubt he knew his brother better than I did. 'Excellent,' I said, breaking a short but uncomfortable silence. 'That gives me a wonderful opportunity for blackmail, if I'm ever in the mood.'

He looked startled, and then smiled.

'Are you still with your partner?' I asked tentatively. 'Chris, wasn't it?'

'Yes. Yes, it was Chris. No, we're not still together.'

'I'm sorry.'

He shrugged. 'Ah well; you win some, you lose some.' He took another two chocolate biscuits and ate them together, like a sandwich, in two bites.

Chapter 10

I arrived at Dave's place at eight o'clock the next morning to find the living room door locked and the curtains drawn. Following a narrow concrete path that led around the side of the house, I saw the children sitting up at the kitchen counter eating toast in their pyjamas, eyes fixed unwaveringly on the TV across the room. Dave wasn't there.

I smiled and waved through the window. Nathan ignored me completely – his father once made him a peanut butter and gravy sandwich while he was watching TV, just as an experiment, and it went down a treat – but Lily's face lit up with gratifying delight.

'Mummy!' she cried, running to the door to let me in.

I picked her up and hugged her hard. 'Hey, little chicken. How was the fishing?'

'We didn't go. We went to the Warehouse instead, and I got a skirt and two pairs of tights and a T-shirt with sparkles and some new boots!'

'Wow!' I said, letting her slide to her feet. 'You're going to be looking pretty sharp at school today.'

'I *know*! Shineya and Lexie are going to be jealous *as*! I'll go and get dressed right now.' She dashed through the nearest doorway and into Dave.

'Hey!' he said, laughing as she rebounded off his bare chest. 'Careful there, Lil, or you'll cause a major wardrobe malfunction.' He adjusted the towel – the small and skimpy towel – around his slim hips, propped his shoulder against the doorframe and crossed his arms. His skin, still damp from the shower, gleamed as his muscles shifted. 'Morning, Jen.'

'Morning,' I said, hovering somewhere between amusement and annoyance. You really couldn't accuse Dave of being complex and hard to read – his subtext couldn't have been clearer if it had been written in large capitals across his forehead. *Hey, look at this! Not bad, eh? And have you noticed this pec definition? I'll just give a little flex ... See? Do you miss all this? Do you? Huh?*

'Did you have a good weekend?' I asked, lifting my eyes from his sculpted torso. Had he waxed his chest?

'Yeah, it was great. We got up to all sorts of mischief. How about you?'

I made a face. 'Pretty action-packed, actually. Marcus is gone.'

'Shit. Why?' asked Dave, standing up straight in surprise.

'Left in the middle of the night without telling anyone, and isn't taking our calls,' I said.

'Huh. Must've got a better offer, I suppose.'

'I guess so. Then I discovered on Saturday that he'd left all the ewes shut in that little bit of race below the woolshed since Monday. It was appalling.'

'Oh, hell.' Dave settled back against the doorframe, letting his towel slip just a fraction. 'Maybe running the farm's not quite as easy as you thought, eh?'

I'd never thought, or said, that running the farm was easy. 'No,' I said shortly.

'So what now?'

'Someone else has just started. Andrew Faulkner's brother.'

His eyebrows lifted. 'Well, well.'

I refrained, with a certain amount of effort, from replying with: *'Yes, Andrew Faulkner's brother. I expect you recall Andrew's wife?'* and said instead, 'I'd like to get a farm consultant out to have a look at the place, too. Do you know of anyone?'

'You want *me* to find *you* a farm consultant?' he asked.

'Dave, admit it, you'd be offended if I *didn't* ask your opinion.'

He grinned disarmingly. 'True.'

At this point Lily emerged from her bedroom into the hall behind Dave with a cry of 'Tada!' She was wearing black leggings with a fishnet pattern in hot pink, a black T-shirt with a sparkly rainbow-coloured unicorn on the front, and pink vinyl boots with a little spike heel. 'Do you like my new clothes, Mummy?'

'Um ...' I said weakly.

'I don't *care* what you think! Daddy bought them for me, and *he* thinks I look pretty!'

'So do I,' I said. 'I'm just not sure –'

'I'm not going to listen to you!' Lily cried, hurtling back through her bedroom door and slamming it behind her with a bang that shook the house.

Dave shook his head slowly. '*Epic* fail, Jen,' he said.

'What were you *thinking*?' I hissed. 'She looks like a prostitute!'

'It was what she wanted! Don't be such a snob.'

'I'm *not*.'

'You are too!'

'Okay. Whatever. Nathan! It's time to go.'

Nathan looked away from the TV briefly. 'Hi, Mum.'

'Hi, love. Can you go and get your bag? It's time to go.'

'Soon,' he said, his eyes back on the screen.

Dave crossed the kitchen, picked up the remote on the end of the bench and turned the TV off. 'Better go, dude,' he said. 'Mum's on the warpath.' Then, 'Hey, come on, Jen – smile. You wouldn't want the wind to change with a look like that on your face.'

I smiled – or, to be perfectly honest, I bared my teeth – and he laughed.

'Too easy,' he said, pulling the towel from around his waist, slinging it around his neck, and sauntering naked down the hall.

* * *

As if that wasn't a sufficiently irritating start to the day, Amy Wallace pulled up beside me as I parked the car in front of Pukewai School twenty minutes later. 'Good morning, everybody!' she carolled, opening her door. 'How are we all?'

'Very good, thanks,' I said, lifting Nathan out of his car seat and swinging him onto my hip. He was heavy, and he was perfectly capable of climbing out by himself, but on the other hand I hadn't seen him for nearly three days. He wrapped his arms around my neck and rubbed his cheek against mine, and I kissed the top of his curly head. 'Lil, is there a jersey in your bag, love?'

'I don't want one,' said Lily.

'You don't have to wear it; just have it there in case.'

'I don't *want* a jersey.'

'Lily,' I said, 'get a jersey.'

'One of those mornings, is it?' Amy asked, handing Arwen her schoolbag. Arwen was short and squat with sandy hair and eyelashes and a perpetually open mouth, and every time I saw her the nasty, sarcastic bit of my brain labelled her privately as Child Least Like An Elvish Princess.

I smiled vaguely and put Nathan down so I could rummage in Lily's weekend bag. 'Here you go.'

'I'm not going to wear it,' Lily snapped.

'Good for you.' I unzipped her schoolbag and poked the sweatshirt in.

Crumpling suddenly, she threw her arms around my waist and burst into tears. 'I'm sorry, Mummy,' she sobbed.

'That's okay, love,' I said.

'I don't want to go to school today. I just want to be with you.'

'Well, it seems a bit of a shame not to show everyone your new clothes, now we're here,' I said, stroking her hair. 'Want me to come up to your classroom with you?'

Lily nodded against my shirt.

Amy fell into step beside me as we crossed the road. 'I was talking to Louise Russell last night,' she said. 'She was saying she hadn't heard from you about the jumble sale yet.'

'No,' I said. 'I made a start on the list last night, but I haven't got to her yet.'

'Mm. The Barkers hadn't heard, either, but Mary Ann promised a cake, if you could just confirm that with her.'

'Will do,' I said. 'Thanks.'

'Mrs Reynolds, when can I come to your house?' a small girl shouted from the top of the monkey bars.

'Get your mum to ring me, and we can make a time,' I called back.

'I don't *want* her to come,' Lily muttered. 'She smells like pineapple.' An odd criticism, surely.

'Then there's Cathy Muller,' Amy continued. 'She said she might be able to give us some old curtains and things.'

'Great,' I said.

'They might need a wash, of course. I know Jim smoked for years.'

'Come *on*, Mum,' said Lily, tugging at my hand.

'Mustn't interrupt when grown-ups are talking, Lily,' Amy told her, wagging a playful finger.

Lily started to cry.

'Oh dear,' said Amy, giving me a meaningful look. 'Everything's all a bit much at the moment, isn't it, Lily honey? Don't worry, I wasn't really growling.'

'Right, Lil, we'd better get up to your classroom before the bell rings,' I said with false cheer. 'See you later, Amy!'

Nathan peeled off and headed for the sandpit as we hastened up the path towards the front door, and Lily and I went inside.

'Hi, Lily!' chorused a pair of little girls. 'Hi, Lily's mum!' They vanished, giggling, through the doorway of Room Two as Lily's current best friend Shineya came hurtling out.

'Look!' she cried, brandishing a skinny arm bearing a dozen neon plastic bangles. 'Gran bought them for me at the market! *And* I got some candy floss, *and* a doll!'

'I got new boots,' Lily said.

'Tonelle's got some like that,' said Shineya dismissively. 'But the heel came off. You can have a bracelet if you want.'

'Can I have that one?' Lily asked, pointing to a pink one.

'No. You can have this one.' Shineya pulled off a lime green bangle and handed it over.

Lily put it on, examined it from several angles, and smiled. 'Cool. Thank you.'

'Actually, maybe not that one,' Shineya said. 'You can have the white one.'

'But I like this one!'

'They're my bracelets.'

'You *gave* it to me!'

They went into the classroom still arguing, and I was about to follow when Lily's teacher came down the hallway from the staffroom. Mrs van der Wetering was a pleasant-looking woman in her fifties with the brisk, competent, somewhat overbearing manner that teachers so often develop after thirty-odd years of benign classroom dictatorship.

'Good morning, Jenny!' she said.

'Hi! How's Peter's hip?'

'Wonderful,' she said. 'He's still using a stick, but the pain's almost gone. His temper's *miles* better than it was; he should have had it done years ago.'

'That's great,' I said. 'Sonia, I've been meaning to ask you – how's Lily doing?'

She raised her eyebrows slightly. 'Just fine.'

'No problems with her behaviour?'

'Not at all. How's she been at home?'

'We've had a few tantrums here and there,' I said.

'I don't accept tantrums in my class,' said Sonia firmly. 'Look, Lily's doing very well, considering. She gets on nicely with the other children, her reading's excellent. Her maths isn't quite so good, but we'll get there. Just carry on as usual at home. She'll be testing the boundaries – that's perfectly normal, when there's been an upheaval like you've had – so make sure you're consistent. Don't start feeling guilty and letting her get away with bad behaviour, whatever you do. Doesn't do them any favours at all.'

'You're right. Thank you,' I said, repressing a smile. Sonia's son, locally famous for never receiving any parental discipline or guidance at all, had been in Rebecca's class at school.

'And how are *you* doing?' Sonia asked, looking me up and down.

'Very well,' I said.

'Hmm. You look tired.'

This was discouraging, since, as everyone knows, looking tired is the same as looking unusually plain. 'No, I'm fine,' I said lightly.

'Hmm,' said Sonia again. 'Well, I'd better get on. See you, Jenny.'

* * *

Monday and Tuesday were industrious and domestic. I refereed the children's arguments, baked with Nathan, tested Lily on her spelling words, drove around the farm with Harry, made an appointment with the farm consultant recommended by Andrew for the following week, rang about fifty people to solicit contributions for Saturday's jumble sale, planted my garlic, bathed Tessa (who had vanished for an afternoon and returned smelling of something very dead) and cleaned up a puddle of sick which suggested that she had partaken of as well as rolled in the carcass.

Rebecca called at half past nine on Tuesday evening to tell me how insanely stressed she was and to extract further details of our recent farming crisis.

'Do you spend your entire *life* on the phone?' she asked when I picked up the receiver.

'Yes, currently,' I said. 'I've rung pretty much everyone in the district to beg for donations for the school jumble sale.'

'How on earth did you let yourself get roped into *that*?'

'Pure stupidity. How are things?'

She sighed. 'Hideous. I'm so busy I don't know which end of me's up, and Sean's away at a conference all next week.'

'Bummer,' I said. 'How's my favourite nephew?'

'He's alright. He's got a cold, of course, but that's standard.'

'Just think: after another year or two of day care he'll have encountered every virus known to man, and he'll be immune to everything.'

'Man, I hope so,' she said. 'I hear you've been having all sorts of drama on the farm.'

'We sure have. Did Mum tell you I got a text from Marcus yesterday?'

'No! What did it say?'

'*Won't be back. Keeping final week's pay in lieu* – which he spelt L-O-O – *of holiday pay*.'

'What a guy,' she said. 'I suppose it's not worth trying to get him to pay it back?'

'No, I don't think so.'

'And you thought he was the best thing since sliced bread.'

'There's no need to rub it in,' I said.

'Ah well, live and learn. What's the new worker like?'

'Very nice.'

'But does he know what he's doing?'

'He seems to,' I said. 'He and Dad ran the ewes through the middle yards today and drafted off a skinny mob, and he's feeding out silage to the calves, and fixing fences.'

'Well, that sounds promising. But then, as we both know, you have a history of being fooled by people who look capable.'

'*Must* you imply that I'm a gullible moron?' I asked plaintively.

She laughed. 'How old is he?'

'Late twenties? Early thirties?'

'Mum says he's quite good-looking.'

'Yeah, I suppose so.'

'Oh, come on, Jenny, don't pretend you haven't noticed.'

'I'm not. Hey, did Mum tell you we've got a farm consultant coming out next week? I thought that just hoping the grass would grow wasn't the most proactive approach.'

'Don't change the subject,' said my sister.

I sighed audibly. 'Yes, Harry's cute. No, I'm not considering having a wild affair with him. Okay?'

'Fine,' she said. 'We'll talk about farm consultants, if that's what you want. Dad reckons they're mostly just failed farmers.'

'Does he,' I said flatly.

'*Man*, you're in a lousy mood.'

'I know. I'm tired. Sorry. How are the new classes going?'

'Booked solid,' said Bex. 'Massive waiting list.'

'Hey, that's wonderful! Good on you!'

'I know, but Sean's so unsupportive. He's skiving off to Queenstown all next week for work, and *now* he reckons he's going to stay on and go skiing for the weekend. Never mind me and Caleb …'

The recital of Sean's inadequacies could, and almost certainly would, take some time. I collected a nail file and a bottle of Cherry Shimmer nail polish, and settled myself on the kitchen floor with my back against the pantry door to transform my toenails into ten little works of art. At least I could achieve something positive while we were at it.

Chapter 11

The next day was Wednesday, which meant work for me, school for Lily, day care for Nathan, and Dave's night to have the children. A missing-sneaker crisis delayed us in leaving home, and having dropped Lily off at the school gate, I sped on into town and hustled Nathan up the path to the front door of Kiddies' Corner.

Waylaid inside by the manager, who was having an argument over a culvert pipe with Todd Granger from the council's roading department, I was fifteen minutes late to work. This earned me a dirty look from the mayor's PA, self-appointed auditor of the work ethics and moral hygiene of all council employees. There were four new consents on my desk, fifty-seven unread emails in my inbox and we had a departmental meeting at ten. In loo of a lunch break, I checked a list of legal specifications for culvert pipes, which confirmed that Todd Granger was talking through a hole in his head, and took a little walk to see the roading manager at the other end of the corridor.

The roading manager was a tall, stooped man in his fifties with a perpetually harassed expression and thinning hair. He looked up from his desk as I tapped on his open door and said, 'Oh. Jenny. What can I do for you?'

'I've had a complaint –' He flinched, and I corrected myself to, 'I mean, a query from Sue Downey at Kiddies' Corner. They've just resealed their driveway, and Todd's told them they need to dig it up again and put in a bigger culvert pipe.'

'And …?'

'And they don't,' I said. 'The existing one's fully compliant. So I just wanted to let you know I'm going to override Todd and confirm with Sue in writing that it's all good as it is.'

'Todd won't be happy,' he said weakly.

'I'm not all that happy either,' I said. 'I'm sorry, Charlie, I know it'll cause a bit of unpleasantness, but this kind of drivel is a waste of my time, and it makes council look like a pack of incompetent dickheads.'

He flinched again. 'Send me the letter first, please,' he said.

'Will do,' I said. 'Thanks, Charlie.' I smiled at him and left. It would have been nice to think that he would now summon Todd to his office and tell him off for being an officious, self-important twerp, but I knew he wouldn't. Feeling slightly aggrieved, I went to make myself a cup of coffee.

It was half past one, and the staffroom was nearly empty. Lyn from the front desk and my fellow building control officer Greta were perusing an EziBuy catalogue at the table, and taking my coffee I went to sit with them.

'You need to call Phillip McClintock,' Lyn told me, looking up. 'He rang about an hour ago – he said he's left several messages on your answer phone and you haven't got back to him.'

'I haven't quite made it to my phone messages yet,' I said.

'I'd get on to it, if I were you. He didn't sound happy.'

'I'll ring him shortly,' I said. 'Anything nice in this month's catalogue?'

'I quite like this wraparound dress,' said Greta, flicking over a couple of pages and pushing the catalogue across the table.

'Pretty,' I said.

'It's not bad,' said Lyn. 'Not the red, though. Not your colour. Jenny, you look exhausted.'

'So I'm told,' I said glumly.

'Maybe you should have a chemical peel,' suggested Greta. 'I had one last year – it was awesome. My skin was so soft and smooth afterwards.' Greta was twenty-six, blonde, petite and very pretty, and she needed a skin peel like Cameron Diaz needs liposuction.

'Perhaps I'll try it,' said Lyn, who, after a lifetime of heavy smoking, looked like a nice Shar Pei. 'Is there an industrial-strength version? Battery acid and a wire brush?'

I laughed, choked, inhaled a sinus full of coffee and folded over in pain.

'Are you alright?' Greta asked.

'Doh!' I said, digging frantically in my pocket for a handkerchief and clapping it to my nose.

Lyn grinned, stood up and carried her empty plate over to the sink.

'Hey, Jenny, I'll give you a discount voucher for the skin place by the National Bank,' Greta told me. 'It's twenty dollars off, and to be honest I'll probably never get around to using it before it expires.'

I sat up and inhaled cautiously. 'Thanks, but I don't think …'

'Why not? You work really hard; it's time you did something nice for yourself.'

'Well,' I said, 'I *was* thinking I'd give it another five or ten years and then have a major revamp. I'm sure you get some sort of package discount if you get yourself peeled and waxed and botoxed and collagened and lasered all at the same time.'

Lyn paused on her way out of the room and looked back over her shoulder. 'Jen, honey,' she said, 'I'm sorry to break this to you, but if you wait ten years no-one's going to care.'

* * *

On this happy note I returned to my desk and rang Phillip McClintock, who was quite convinced that only petty small-mindedness had prevented me from returning his call earlier. We had a lengthy and unenjoyable conversation, following which I emailed Sue at Kiddies' Corner, cleared the rest of my messages and started on the plans for Malcolm Short's new woolshed.

At ten past five, Greta, heavily made up and wearing tight, shiny black jeans and a long, black woollen coat, put her head around my office door and said, 'You haven't got the kids tonight, have you? Come and have a drink.'

'That,' I said, pushing my chair back, 'is a bloody marvellous idea.'

'Awesome!' she said. 'I'm meeting my friend Miriam. You'll love her.'

We went out into the chilly dusk and across the road to the Tipoi Hotel, which had an open fire, rustic wooden tables, two whole walls covered in hunting trophies and several very nice local craft beers on tap. It was busy and loud, with the buzz and surge of conversation competing with both the rugby league game on the TV above the bar and this week's Top 40 music videos on a second screen near the door.

We got ourselves a drink each and found a free table, slightly closer to the fire than we wanted. 'How's the running going?' I asked, leaning back in my chair and unwinding my scarf.

'I've been having a few issues with my ankle,' said Greta. 'But it's coming right now. I've got a race this weekend. Hey, Miriam! Over here!'

Miriam, it turned out, was in week two of a relationship with a man she suspected could turn out to be The One. She and Greta plunged into a thorough dissection of last night's hot date, while I drank my cider and idly watched Justin Bieber's latest music video. Poor little mixed-up sausage, I thought – living proof, if more proof was needed, that fame really isn't good for you.

Dave's friend Travis wandered across the room with a beer in his hand, and I waved.

'Hi, Jen!' he said, veering in my direction. 'How's it going?'

'Good. How are you?'

'Great, thanks. Hey, have you got a minute?'

'Sure,' I said.

He pulled up a chair and sat down, saying, 'I know it's not your department, but I wondered if you knew who I should talk to about the car park beside the shop. You know, the one between me and the back of the medical centre.'

'Todd Granger, probably, if it needs an upgrade,' I said.

Travis grimaced. 'You wouldn't be able to have a quick word with him, would you? He's such a grumpy bugger.'

'I'm really sorry, Travis, but I don't think a quick word from me is going to help your cause. Todd and I had a bit of a run-in today.'

'Damn,' he said.

'But tell you what, if you just sort of casually mention in passing that you ran it by me and I didn't think it was part of council's jurisdiction …'

'Nice,' he said, grinning.

'Jenny Reynolds?' said someone just behind my left shoulder.

Turning in my chair, I saw a woman I recognised vaguely – a rather hard-looking woman about my age, with dead straight, peroxide blonde hair, heavy eyeliner and very high heels, who worked at Grubb's Accountants at the other end of the main street. She had a glass of wine in one hand and a patent leather clutch in the other.

'Hi,' I said, smiling at her.

She didn't smile back. Skewering me with a pale blue, deadpan stare, she said abruptly, 'You left your husband, didn't you?'

'Yes,' I said, surprised.

'Good on you.'

'Um, thanks.'

'I fucked him.'

I opened my mouth, realised I had nothing to offer in response to this and closed it again.

'It was a couple of years ago. I didn't know he was married – I'm not into that shit. Made me feel sick when I found out. I've seen you around town with your little girl and boy … I wasn't the only one, either. Anyway, good on you. You're way better off without him.' And turning on her heel she hurried off through the crowd, leaving Travis and me staring after her in shock.

'Are you alright?' he asked after a while.

'Did you know?' I croaked.

'No. Shit, no!'

I got blindly to my feet. Greta said something to me that I didn't catch, but I thought I had about ten seconds before losing the plot entirely, and that the public bar of the Tipoi Hotel really wasn't the place to do it. Snatching up my handbag, I bolted for the exit.

It was cold outside, and as the door closed behind me the noise from the bar stopped as suddenly as if someone had flicked a switch. Then it started again as the door opened and Travis came out.

'Hey,' he said gently.

'Hey.' Breathe in. And out. And in, and – 'I'm going to kill him.'

'Maybe – maybe she was making it up,' he said.

'Why would she?'

'I don't know. Maybe she knows he wants you back, and she's hoping to get you out of the picture ...'

'You reckon?' I said, in a tight, brittle voice.

He sighed. 'No.'

'Neither do I.'

A short silence fell. 'Jenny, I swear to you that I had no idea,' he said, breaking it.

'That's – good. Makes me feel – a bit less – stupid.' The muscles in my chest seemed to have seized, and it was quite hard to breathe.

'You're *anything* but stupid.'

'I'd better go.'

'No,' he said. 'Let's find somewhere quiet and get something to eat. You're white as a sheet.'

'I just want to go home,' I said, tears prickling.

'You shouldn't be by yourself.' He gave me a tentative hug. 'Come on. Come back to my place. I'll heat you up a baked bean or something.'

* * *

We went to Travis's house, a chilly, un-homelike, concrete block place overlooking the railway line. He made baked beans on toast, which I don't much like but couldn't taste anyway, and maintained a flow of inconsequential and soothing small talk while we ate them.

'These curtains are pretty horrible, aren't they?' he said. 'I suppose I should do the place up a bit, but it doesn't really seem worth it when I'm hardly ever home.'

'Hmm?' I said. 'Yes. True.'

He looked at me worriedly. 'Jen, don't feel bad. Dave's a dribbling idiot, that's all. It's no reflection on you.'

'All this – this *crap* he's been feeding me, making me feel guilty for not giving him another chance when he made one tiny little mistake ... Did you hear her say she wasn't the only one? How long d'you think he's been cheating on me? *Years*, probably!'

'Well, if he has been, he's the dumbest man on the planet. You're smart, and kind, and – and beautiful ... Any man who needs to screw around when he's got someone like you at home isn't worth another thought.' He reached across the table and squeezed my hand gently. 'Okay?'

Oh shit, I thought suddenly. Travis was the rescuing type – his girlfriends were always poor things, ill-treated by life. I straightened, smiled at him brightly and pulled my hand free. 'Actually, I'm glad that woman told me,' I said. 'Now I don't have to waste any more time wondering if I made the right decision when I kicked him out.' I got to my feet. 'Thanks so much for dinner, Travis. You're a legend.'

'You're welcome. If there's *anything* I can do, at *any* time ...'

'That's really kind of you,' I said. 'Right, I'd better go – poor old Tessa will be most unimpressed about being home alone for so long.'

He stood up too. 'I'll drive you back down to the council to get your car.'

'No, it's only a two-minute walk,' I said, hastening across his kitchen to the door. 'Honestly, don't bother. Good luck with the car park. Don't forget to tell Todd how unhelpful I was when you asked me about it.'

* * *

Tessa was touchingly delighted to see me when I got home. I fed her, had a shower and climbed into my warmest, snuggliest pyjamas. I felt cold and sick and stupid. *I wasn't the only one, either,* she'd said, and I had no reason to believe she was lying. How many others? And since when? How *could* he?

I'd better make myself a doctor's appointment, I decided, hugging my knees. Heaven only knew what venereal diseases the rotten sod had brought home. I shivered, swiped a hand angrily across my wet eyes and went to bed, if not to sleep.

* * *

I was already regretting the involvement of Dave's chivalrous friend Travis in my marital woes, but I regretted it increasingly over the course of the next day. The first concerned text message arrived at breakfast time:

How are you doing?

All good, thanks, I replied.

Can't believe he could do this to you, he sent back.

Then eleven fifteen's message read, Are you free for lunch?

Thanks, but work crazy today, I replied. Also, I had a doctor's appointment at one.

Checking my phone on the way back to work, I found, Have told Dave he's a massive loser. Fresh from getting up close and personal with a steel speculum, I couldn't have agreed more, but I didn't reply because I couldn't think of any remark that wouldn't encourage further communications.

After school that afternoon the kids and I spent a pleasant and productive hour outside in the wintry sunshine. While I weeded the bed underneath the lemon tree, Lily practised her cartwheels on the lawn and Nathan collected snails from the depths of a clump of Siberian iris, loaded them onto the back of a toy dump truck and trundled them across the lawn to tip them through the fence.

My cell phone beeped as we came back in, and Nathan ran to fetch it from the end of the kitchen bench.

'I can read it!' said Lily.

'*I* will,' Nathan said, holding the phone an inch away from his nose and breathing on it heavily.

'You cannot! Mummy, he can't read!'

'I can too!'

'Can I have it, please?' I asked. 'Seeing as it's my phone.'

Nathan bore the phone across the room and handed it over, smiling smugly at his sister.

'*Mum!*' Lily cried.

Just scored 5 kg of smoked marlin. Would you like some? read the message.

I sighed.

'Can I read it?' asked Lily plaintively.

'What? Oh, sure, love.'

'Just – sc–' Lily started, and stuck. 'What does it say, Mummy?'

'It's Travis wondering if we'd like some smoked fish.'

Both children made noises of disgust.

I like smoked marlin, but reclaiming the phone I wrote, Thanks so much, but no.

You don't know what you're missing. How was work? came the reply.

I bit my lip, frowning. If I replied, I'd lay myself wide open to a long, cosy text conversation. If I didn't, it would be mean.

'Mummy?' said Lily softly.

'Yes, love?'

'Daddy said he would come home again if you let him.'

It took a few moments for that to sink in. '*What?*'

'Would you, Mummy? If he said he was really, *really* sorry?'

I took a deep breath. 'No, sweetie.' She burst into tears and ran out of the room.

'Can I have a sandwich?' Nathan asked.

'Hmm?' I said, returning my phone to its spot on the bookshelf. Maybe it was mean, but it would be meaner to encourage him. 'Yes, okay. Marmite or honey?'

Chapter 12

The farm consultant, as recommended by Andrew Faulkner, came the next Tuesday morning. Arnold Keller of Morgan and Keller Consulting Ltd was a large, jovial man of about forty, with receding hair, a modest paunch and very tight moleskin trousers.

After shaking hands with Dad and Harry, he greeted me briskly with, 'Nice to meet you, Jessie. Black with two sugars, if you're boiling the billy.'

'Right,' I said, slightly taken aback. 'Hi.'

He ate three scones with his mouth open, addressed himself almost exclusively to the men and seemed surprised when I accompanied them outside to drive around the farm. But he did sound like he knew what he was talking about, and Andrew thought he was alright, so I smoothed down my feminist hackles and told myself firmly that a boorish expert was better than a charming incompetent.

We'd returned to the house and were listening meekly to Mr Keller's assessment of our current situation (poor) and future prospects (not *completely* hopeless, providing his recommendations were adopted forthwith), when the phone rang. I turned in my chair to pick up the receiver attached to the fax machine.

'Hello, Jenny speaking.'

'Mrs Reynolds?' said a rather nasal female voice.

'Yes?'

'It's Deirdre here from the medical centre. I'm just calling with your test results from last week's smear.'

'Oh,' I said, disconcerted. 'Um ...'

'Now, I've got good news and bad news, I'm afraid.'

'Look, can I call you ba–' I began, conscious that conversation around the table had died down and that her voice really was quite penetrating.

But it seemed Deirdre had no time, or at least no inclination, for shilly-shallying. 'The *bad* news is that you have chlamydia,' she brayed. 'But the *good* news is that it's extremely easy to treat. I've spoken to Dr McKenzie, and she's written you a prescription. So if you'd like to just pop in and pick it up from the front counter, we'll have you sorted out in no time.'

'Great,' I murmured, crushing the phone to my ear in the hope of muffling that awful voice. The horror I might otherwise have felt at having some nasty venereal disease was entirely overshadowed by the horror of other people hearing about it. 'Thank –'

She raised her voice and swept on. 'It's just a single treatment of antibiotics. It couldn't be easier. But there are just a *few* other considerations. Your partner will need to be treated as well, otherwise you'll just pass the infection back and forth. So if you're having sexual intercourse in the meantime, it's *very* important to ALWAYS USE A CONDOM, alright?'

'Yes, thank you,' I said hastily.

'Anybody you've had UNPROTECTED SEX with is at risk of infection,' she roared. 'So you should contact ALL your recent sexual partners and let them know they need to come in and be checked out. Now, I'll put aside a brochure for you with your prescription explaining HOW CHLAMYDIA IS SPREAD, symptoms and possible complications ... And I'll pop in one on KEEPING YOURSELF SAFE DURING SEX, alright? Okay, you have a good day.'

Quivering with embarrassment, I hung up the phone. They must have heard. You could have heard that voice from the other end of the house, with your fingers in your ears. Why, oh *why* hadn't I just hung up on her? Being brought up to be polite is a dreadful handicap.

Dad broke the silence that had fallen around the table. 'Everything alright, Jen?' he asked.

He *hadn't* heard. Glory be! Perhaps no-one had ... But this hope died at birth as I glanced from Harry, examining his fingernails with his bottom lip caught firmly in his teeth, to Arnold Keller, who was looking me up and down in a distressingly speculative sort of way.

'Jen?' said Dad again.

'Sorry,' I said. 'Yep, all good. Where were we?'

'Those – ah – those four hundred lambs,' said Arnold, giving himself a little shake. 'They need to go as soon as possible. This week. And you need to apply nitrogen to the whole farm – thirty-five units per hectare ...'

* * *

'Well, he certainly didn't sugar-coat things, did he?' said Dad an hour later, as Arnold Keller backed his Range Rover around and headed up the driveway.

Harry smiled and shook his head.

'Jenny? What did you think?'

'I, um …'

'Are you alright, love?'

'I thought he was really good,' I said, pulling myself together. 'Just what we need. I'll call the stock agent tonight, shall I?'

'I suppose so,' Dad said. He sighed and stretched. 'We'd better run those lambs in and dag them tomorrow.'

'I can do them if you'll just give me a hand with drafting them,' said Harry.

'No, no,' Dad said. 'Can't let you do that. Give me a ring when you've got them up to the shed.' He crossed the gravel and got into his ute. 'Right, chaps. See you in the morning.'

'Good meeting, I thought,' said Harry, watching Dad's ute vanish around the corner of the driveway.

'Yep.'

'Where's young Nathan?'

'He's spending the day with Mum. Serious management meetings aren't really his forte.'

'Fair enough.' He hesitated for a moment and then clapped me on the shoulder. 'Cheer up. Nobody ever actually dies of embarrassment. Take it from me.'

I laughed, because it was that or cry. 'Oh, *God*.'

'At least your dad didn't hear.'

'Arnold Keller did!'

He grinned. 'Yeah, but I think he was quite impressed.'

'Thanks,' I said bitterly. Then, 'I really *am* going to kill him, now.'

'Who? Keller? That seems a bit harsh.'

'No! *Dave*. My slimeball husband.'

'Oh-h,' said Harry on a long note of enlightenment.

I looked at him, appalled. 'What, did you think I ...?'

'I didn't think anything,' he said hastily.

'Well, *don't*!'

He laughed, patted my shoulder again and went to start the four-wheeler.

Left alone, I looked at my watch. It was one fifty-three, which gave me nearly an hour before the school run. Mum had taken Nathan to Taupo to have lunch and go shopping with Aunty Kathleen, and wouldn't be back until at least four o'clock. I ran through a list of potential jobs – pay the bills, iron a selection of bed and table linen that had been donated for Saturday's jumble sale, read that unappealing wodge of legal documents on my bedside table – and decided that, in my current frame of mind, they were all completely unbearable. I went to turn the compost heap instead.

After half an hour's hard digging I was tired, dirty and reasonably calm. I straightened up, wiped my hot face on my sleeve and went slowly back to the house, leaving Tessa chewing a disintegrating child's sandal, lost several years ago and sorely missed, that I'd just exhumed from the depths of a compost bin.

I washed my hands and had a drink of water, and then, yielding foolishly to impulse, rang Dave's cell phone.

'Hi,' he said, answering on the third ring.

'I just had a call from the doctor's,' I said. 'I've got chlamydia.'

Silence greeted this announcement.

'Thanks,' I added coldly.

'It's not hard to treat,' he offered.

'How do you know?'

Silence again, not unexpectedly.

'So you knew *you* had it, and you didn't tell me.'

Dave sighed. 'Oh, fuck, here we go,' he said.

I hung up the phone and kicked the wall, which in socks nearly broke my toes and produced only a dull, unsatisfactory thud. *'Bastard!'*

Beside the phone sat a little spiral-bound diary – a birthday present from Mum, with a new page and a new inspirational message for each week. *Blame keeps wounds open. Only forgiveness makes them heal*, it informed me, beneath a picture of two teddy bears holding hands.

'Oh, piss off,' I said savagely, opening the rubbish bin and hurling it in.

* * *

It was four thirty when Mum brought Nathan home. Lily and I were outside picking lemons when we heard the car, and we rounded the corner of the house in time to see the last three-quarters of Mum's signature nineteen-point turn. My mother drives like a bat out of hell forward, but she's never come to grips with reversing. I'm not actually sure she realises that the direction in which you turn the steering wheel is reliably correlated with the direction in which the car goes.

Eventually she came to rest and got out of the car, leaving the engine running.

'Nana!' Lily cried, throwing her arms around Mum's waist.

'Hello, my darling! How was your day?'

'Just boring school. I wish I could have come with you,' said Lily sadly.

'It was boring at Aunty Kaffleen's too,' Nathan said, wrestling with the buckle on his booster seat. I opened his door to help him.

'Now that's not true, Nathan, love,' said Mum. 'We had a lovely time, remember? We threw stones in the lake, and we had some lollies ...'

'Did you save any for me?' Lily asked.

'Darling, no, I never thought of it. Never mind – I'm going shopping tomorrow, and I can bring you some then.'

'Okay,' Lily whispered bravely, blinking away tears, and I wondered, not for the first time, if she was going to be a confidence trickster when she grew up.

'Mum, thanks so much for having him. You're wonderful,' I said, lifting Nathan's booster seat out of her car and dropping it beside the back steps.

'You're welcome, love. How was your meeting?'

'Good, I think. We'll have to make some pretty major changes, but at least we've got a plan, now. Come in and have a coffee.'

'I'd better not,' said Mum. 'We've got people coming for tea. Oh, Rebecca and Sean are coming up this weekend; did you know?'

'No,' I said. 'Cool. Lucky them – they'll be able to come to the jumble sale.'

'Goodness, is that this Saturday?'

'Yes. You're making a cake, remember?'

'Yes, yes,' said Mum. 'That's fine.'

I smiled. 'Do you think Bex would like to man a raffle?'

'Somehow,' Mum said, 'I doubt it.'

'I could!' said Lily eagerly.

'You're going to Dad's this weekend,' I said.

'But I want to come to the jumble sale! *And* see Aunty Bex and baby Caleb,' said Lily.

'Sorry, love,' I said, tweaking the end of her ponytail. 'Next time.'

'It's not *fair*!'

'Well, life *isn't*, Lil.'

She whirled and ran inside, and Mum looked at me reproachfully. 'Jenny ...'

'*What*, Mum?' I asked. 'What am I supposed to do about it?'

'Love, I know that David made a mistake, but he really does regret it.'

'Does he?' I said grimly.

'Yes, he does. He rings, sometimes, and talks to me. And as Kathleen says, sometimes you just have to —'

I'd have filled her in on some of the details that Dave, I suspected, had left out of these chats — and added a few pithy comments on the value of Aunty Kath's opinion of my marriage — had not Nathan, who had vanished inside, reappeared just then at the back door. 'Mum, can you help me make a sandwich?' he called. 'I tried to put the butter on but it's gone all scrunched.'

'Nathan, it's nearly tea-time!' I said.

'I'm just *so* hungry,' he said pathetically.

'He's got butter all over the bench,' said Lily, popping up behind him. 'And he's used up *heaps* of bread.'

'I have not!'

'He has too! Ow! *N*athan!'

'We'll talk later,' Mum told me, squeezing my hand and getting back into the driver's seat. 'This isn't the time. Love you, sweetie.'

I sighed. 'You too.' And closing her door, I turned and went inside to mediate the sandwich crisis.

* * *

It was later that evening, when the kids were in bed and I was halfway through paying the bills, that it occurred to me that if Dave had given me chlamydia he might well have given it to Toni Faulkner too. Or vice versa, for that matter. I'm afraid I didn't care all that much about Toni's sexual health, but her husband was a decent bloke, and he deserved to know.

I finished the bills, ironed the jumble sale tea towels and polished the stovetop until I could see my face in it. My housekeeping standards are always at their highest when I'm using cleaning as a displacement activity.

I did eventually manage to force myself to look up Andrew's number and dial it.

''Lo?' said a deep male voice.

'Andrew?'

'No, it's Harry.'

'Oh,' I said. 'Right. Hi. It's Jen, here.'

'Hi,' said Harry. 'Did you get hold of the stock agent?'

'No, not yet! Thanks for the reminder. Is, um, Andrew there?'

'I'll just get him,' he said, sounding mildly intrigued.

'Thanks.'

After a medium-sized pause, an identical voice to Harry's said, ''Lo?'

'Andrew?' I said doubtfully.

'Speaking.'

'Oh, hi. It's Jenny Reynolds here.'

'Hi,' he said.

I took a deep breath and said in a rush, 'I just found out Dave gave me chlamydia. So – so maybe you should go to the doctor and get checked out too. Dave might have given it to Toni, and she might have given it to you. So, um, maybe you should ...' I trailed off, realising I was repeating myself.

There was a pause on the other end of the phone, and then he said very slowly, 'Okay.'

'And you might want to let Toni know. If you're going to be speaking to her ...'

'Yeah,' said Andrew, sighing. 'Thank you.'

'My pleasure,' I said stupidly.

He gave a sudden crack of laughter. 'Really?' he said. 'Thanks, Jenny.' And he put the phone down.

Chapter 13

'Okay, chickens! Into the shower, chop chop!' I said brightly on Thursday evening, feeling like Mother of the Year as I laid two sets of clean flannelette pyjamas across the heated towel rail to warm.

Nathan sat down in the middle of the hall and started to cry.

'Hey, sausage, what's the problem?' I said. 'Let me give you a hand with your buttons.'

'I don't *want* a shower!' Nathan wailed.

'But – you're green, dude. You look like Kermit the frog.' The nice student teacher at day care had transformed him into a ninja turtle (I found later that the paint she'd used stained fabric permanently, but such is life).

'But my doderent will wash off!'

'Your what?'

'*Doderent*,' said Lily in patronising tones, coming down the hall. 'Dad put it on him.'

'It makes me smell handsome,' Nathan wept.

'Oh,' I said, light dawning. 'Deodorant. Well, we can put some more on after your shower, if you like.'

This was deemed acceptable, although my Mitchum Powder Fresh roll-on was not. Eventually I tucked two small pyjama-clad figures smelling strongly of *Poeme* into bed, kissed them goodnight and went back up the hall to start on the dinner dishes.

I was on my hands and knees wiping tomato sauce off the floor beneath Lily's chair when I heard a vehicle come down the driveway. Tessa got up and clattered across the floor to meet the visitor.

It was John Mercer. 'Hello, little doggie,' he said, rubbing his hands together and shivering in the frosty night air.

'Hi, John. Come on in,' I said.

'Thank you very much, m' dear. It's cold enough out there to freeze the balls off a brass monkey, if you'll pardon my French.' He bent to unlace his shoes, a slow and tortuous process.

'Are you warm enough in the cottage?' I asked, pulling the door that led down the hall shut so our voices wouldn't wake the children.

'Ah. Now that's the, er, nub of the matter, as you might say.' He stepped out of his shoes, arranged them carefully side by side on the doorstep and came in, closing the door beside him. 'Kiddies not here tonight?'

'They're in bed,' I said.

'Of course they are. Nice place you've got here.'

'Thank you.'

'Bit of a leak in the roof, though,' he said, looking at the corner above the stove where the wallpaper had lifted and was curling at the edges.

'There was. It's been fixed, but I haven't got to that bit of wallpaper yet.'

'It'll only get worse, once it starts lifting like that. You want to get right on to it. Your little dog's left a puddle on the floor here.'

I looked. 'No, that's just the fridge leaking. It does that if the door's not shut properly.' I dropped my tea towel on the little pool of water and leant my shoulder against the fridge door to shut it.

'Looks like you could use a handyman around here, eh?' said John. 'Bring the place up to scratch. But anyway, what I'm *really* here for is to talk to you about heating the cottage.'

I bent to retrieve the tea towel, looking at him enquiringly.

'I've got a couple of oil heaters, but the cost of running them is absolutely ruinous. It's not easy to scrape by on a pension, you know. What I'd really like to do is put in a wood burner with a wet-back system. Might as well heat the water while we're at it, don't you think?'

'Well ...' I started.

'I can chop my own wood, then. Yes, I know' – he held up a hand to forestall the comment I hadn't been about to make – 'it's heavy work for a man my age, but I've got to keep meself out of mischief somehow, eh? And I'd rather drop in harness than sit in a chair with a rug over me knees waiting to die.'

Feeling that some encouraging comment was expected, but failing to think of one, I nodded.

'The thing *is*,' he said, 'it's a big expense when you're on a pension. And it'll really up the value of the place – not to mention all the other little improvements I've been making ...' He broke off at the sound of another approaching car. My lucky night, evidently. 'And who might this be? Popular young lady, aren't you?'

Tessa and I reached the door together, and she bustled down the steps as Harry opened his car door.

'Hi, Jen,' he said, bending to pull her ears. 'Major crisis.'

'What?' I asked, seized by fear. Broken tractor? Foot and mouth outbreak? Better job offer?

'I'm trying to make massaman prawn curry, and there's no star anise in the house.'

'Is that all? Thank heavens. I think I've got some. Goodness knows how old it is, though.' I didn't have much call for recipes including star anise these days; my family greeted any flavouring more exotic than chicken stock with deep suspicion. I hunted through the pantry and emerged triumphant with a little paper box.

'You're wonderful,' Harry said from the doorway.

'I know. Harry, this is John Mercer, who lives in the cottage by the woolshed. John, this is Harry Faulkner, who's taken over from Marcus.'

'Hi, John,' said Harry.

John nodded regally. 'So you're the new man, are you?'

'That's right.'

'I hope you'll be an improvement on the last model.'

'So do I,' said Harry.

'This is a good lady here,' John continued, nodding towards me. 'She's got a lot on her plate, so make sure you help her out.'

'Absolutely,' said Harry gravely.

'So it's your brother who bought Royce's place, is it?'

'Yes, that's right.'

'I see he's put kale in there alongside the airstrip. Too steep, that paddock; he'll make a hell of a mess feeding it off.'

Harry lifted his eyebrows just a fraction. Headlights swept the entrance to the carport behind him as yet another car came down the driveway.

'More visitors!' John cried. 'It's a giddy social whirl around here, eh?'

Tessa, who had been mooching around the kitchen, put her head on one side, stiffened and shot outside between Harry's legs.

'Steady on, old girl!' I heard Dave say, laughing, as he got out of his new ute. 'Okay, Tessa, that'll do.'

I looked past Harry's shoulder out the back door and saw Tessa fawning at his feet in a servile and unattractive way. Dave stirred the fur on her tummy with one foot, stepped over her and continued towards the door, a cellophane-wrapped pot plant under one arm. 'Daft dog,' he said. 'Hi, I'm Dave.' He held out a hand to Harry.

'Harry,' said Harry, shaking it briefly.

'Hey, Jen,' Dave said, smiling and offering me the yellow chrysanthemum he was holding. 'All go around here tonight. Kids asleep?'

I took the chrysanthemum – it's very hard *not* to take something you're handed – and turned to put it down on the bench behind me. This, I realised too late, was a strategic error as Dave nipped in behind me.

'Hi,' he said, seeing John.

John looked at me expectantly, but I was too cross for social niceties and he was forced to introduce himself. 'John Mercer,' he said, holding out a hand.

'Dave Reynolds. So you're living in Grandma's little cottage below the woolshed?'

'That's right,' said John.

'Nice to have someone in there, for a change,' said Dave. 'Doesn't do a house any good, standing empty.'

'It does not,' John said with emphasis. 'My goodness, the place was in pretty bad shape when I moved in. It's taken a lot of time and effort to fix it up, I can tell you.'

Dave nodded sympathetically, and I felt like the sort of slum landlord who refuses to fix the drains when the tenants are dying of cholera.

'I've just been chatting to Jenny about putting in a wood burner. These old bones get a bit creaky in the frost.'

'I bet they do. That place must be a bloody fridge at this time of year.'

'It's not the warmest,' John agreed, sucking air through a gap in his teeth and looking longer suffering and harder done by with every passing second.

Thinking it was time I took some control of this conversation, I said, 'I'll have a talk to Dad, John, and we'll see what we can do.'

'Much appreciated, m' dear. And now it's time I got out of your hair.' Going back across the kitchen he began, slowly and painfully, to put his shoes back on. 'I'm afraid I'll need to trouble you young chaps to move your vehicles.'

'You'll get past mine no trouble,' Dave said. 'Just back around into the gap by the water tank.'

I sent him a hard stare, which he pretended not to see. 'Actually, I think you'd better go,' I told him.

He pretended not to hear, either.

'Need a hand, Jenny?' asked Harry quietly from the doorway.

I fleetingly considered enlisting him as a bouncer, decided that the ensuing drama really wouldn't be worth it, and shook my head.

'Sure?'

'Yeah.'

'Okay. Night.' He ran down the back steps and strode across the gravel to his car, watched by a stiff and offended Dave.

'Oof,' said John, finally finishing his second shoe and pushing himself upright, hands on his knees. 'Feet are a bit further away than they used to be. Right, I'll be off.'

'Goodnight, John,' I said.

'Goodnight, m' dear.' He made it to the door, stopped and turned. 'Oh, how did you like that choko?'

'It was very nice,' I said, with more politeness than truth. I'd cut it up and roasted it, and although it hadn't been actually unpleasant it was barely worth the effort of chewing up and swallowing.

'Wonderful things, aren't they? So versatile.'

I just nodded, hoping that the less I said the quicker he would go away.

'I put one into a casserole last week. Cooked up really nice. I'll bring you some more sometime, if you can use them.'

'That's very kind,' I said, without much enthusiasm. 'But only if you can spare them.'

'For you, yes. Now, I can see you've got things to discuss, so I'll bugger off and leave you to it. Good to meet you, Dave … Say hello to those young rapscallions of yours from me. Bring them down sometime for a cuppa, if it's not too boring to come and see an old codger …' And gradually, in a cloud of half-finished and vaguely plaintive sentences, he shuffled away.

'Nice old bloke,' Dave observed, waving and shutting the kitchen door as John got into his car.

'What are you doing here?' I said, folding my arms.

He bent to stroke Tessa's greying nose with the back of a finger. 'Grovelling.'

'No point.'

'I know you're angry,' he said, straightening up. 'You've got every right. I've cocked up monumentally. But …'

Ah, I thought. The inevitable *but*.

'Don't look at me like that, Jen.'

'I do *not* want to hear about how you screwing around, and giving me chlamydia – *chlamydia!* – is actually *my fault!*' I said in a furious half-whisper.

'It's not your fault,' he said quietly.

'And how *dare* you tell the kids you'd love to come home but I won't let you?'

He sighed. 'I'm sorry. You're great, and I'm a loser. You've made that very, very clear over the years.'

Pulled up short by the actual pain in his voice, I stared at him.

'I know I should never have cheated on you. But *God*, Jen, do you have any idea how cold you can be?'

My heart gave a savage, painful little twist, and I gripped the edge of the bench behind me with both hands.

'I'd say something, and you'd shut your eyes, take a deep breath, and answer in that patient, what-did-I-do-to-deserve-this voice ... I'm not stupid. I'm not as stupid as you think I am, anyway.'

'I don't think ...' I faltered.

'Yes, you do. That's why –' He broke off and wiped the back of a hand across his wet eyes. 'Everyone needs a little bit of admiration and respect somewhere along the line.'

I looked fixedly at the floor, and for quite a long time neither of us moved or spoke. Then I lifted my head and looked at him. 'I'm sorry.'

'Me too,' he said. He reached out hesitantly with a hand, but I walked into his arms and hugged him. His arms came around me in return, and I rested my head in the hollow between his neck and shoulder. He was warm and comforting and familiar, and my anger dissolved in a wave of exhaustion. Tessa wormed her way in between us and sat on our feet.

'You know what?' I said, letting him go.

'What?'

'We really were the worst couple ever. People should bring out the best in one another, not the worst.'

'Trying to convince yourself you've made the right decision?' he said wryly.

I sighed and then smiled. 'You got it.'

'We could try again, Jen. The kids'd be so stoked ...'

'But –' I started, and his hands clenched in frustration.

'Don't,' I said, putting my hands over his. 'Hey, come on, Dave. We've already turned their lives upside down – we can't do it again unless we're absolutely a hundred percent –' I stopped talking again, this time because he was kissing me.

I recoiled, but he didn't let me go. He had taken my face in both hands, and he slid them up through my hair to cradle the back of my head. And thoroughly shaken by a flood of loneliness and guilt and doubt and desire, all jumbled up together, I kissed him back.

If he'd started taking my clothes off – if he hadn't asked, but just done it – I think I'd have had sex with him. It would have been a really stupid move, but I have a nasty suspicion that I wouldn't have let that stop me, and that I would have succumbed to the temptation of feeling loved and wanted again, if only temporarily. But my dubious self-control wasn't tested, because he didn't try. He just said, when at length he let me go, 'At least promise me you'll think about it.'

I nodded dumbly, and he turned to open the door. 'Night, love,' he said, and ran down the steps.

Chapter 14

Dave picked up Lily from school and Nathan from day care the next afternoon, and I was profoundly grateful not to have to face him. I stayed at work until six, finishing four of the five consents that had landed on my desk that week, and then drove slowly home, dined off two slices of buttered toast and three big glasses of red wine, wrapped several dozen lucky-dip prizes for the following day's jumble sale, went to bed and fell into a semi-anaesthetised and wholly exhausted sleep.

The result of this foolish course of action was that I woke up again at two with a splitting headache and stared at the ceiling for an hour and a half, thinking about Dave, the evils of drink, Dave, the advantages of two-parent households, Dave, the likelihood that he'd actually still want me if he thought he could get me and the odds he'd stay faithful once the novelty had worn off. My conclusions, as you might expect from conclusions reached at two in the morning, were not particularly optimistic.

Saturday was wet and cold, and I spent most of it at the Pukewai Hall. It was an unexpectedly fun day – Louise Russell from further up the valley, stately, grey-haired and scarily competent, came early and stayed all day to help. Louise looks like the chairman of a Privy Council but has the driest, wickedest sense of humour imaginable, and I want to be like her when I grow up.

It was after four by the time we'd finished cleaning up, and I drove home up the hill with half-a-dozen boxes of unsold bric-a-brac in the boot of the car, a bowl of cold sausages on the passenger seat beside me and stomach muscles that hurt from laughing.

Calling in at Mum and Dad's place, I found my brother-in-law sitting at the kitchen table, frowning intently at his iPad. He looked up as I opened the door, said, 'Hi, Jenny, how are you?' and immediately looked back down.

'Good, thanks,' I said. 'How was the flight?'

'Hmm? Yeah, fine,' he said, so absently that I went past him into the living room without subjecting him to further conversation.

I eventually ran Bex and Mum to ground in the master bedroom, where Mum was trying on clothes while Bex passed judgment from the bed. 'That's a nice blouse,' she was saying when I put my head around the door. 'Try it with those jeans.'

'Those jeans do nothing for me,' said Mum.

'Rubbish. Anyway, the shirt's long enough to cover your wobbly bits – hey, Jen!' She rolled to her feet in one lithe, graceful movement and came to kiss me.

I hugged her tightly, inordinately pleased to see her. 'Where's Caleb?'

'*Helping*' – her tone was very dry – 'Dad stack wood. How was your jumble sale?'

'Surprisingly good fun,' I said.

'How much did you make?' Mum asked.

'Four hundred and fifty-eight twenty,' I said. 'Minus bread and sauce and all that stuff.'

'Bloody hell,' said Rebecca. 'And how many hours have you spent?'

I let myself fall backwards across Mum and Dad's bed. 'Oh, about forty, I suppose. I know; it's painful.' But nobody else seemed to think so. The previous year I had put my foot in it *spectacularly* at a school fundraising meeting when I suggested that, for a change, we could send home a note to each family asking for an anonymous donation of whatever sum that family felt it would be worth paying for a whole year free from jumble sales, sausage sizzles, trail rides, raffles and fundraising chocolate bars. An icy silence had followed this proposal, eventually broken by Amy Wallace saying brightly, 'I'd like to see more certificates being given out at assembly, wouldn't you, ladies?'

'No kids this weekend?' Bex asked.

I shook my head.

'Excellent. Let's get pissed. Sean can be the responsible parent for a change. Mum! Jeans. Now.'

'You're a horrible bully,' said Mum, smiling. 'Oh, alright.' She wriggled out of her black trousers and into the jeans. 'Well?'

'Huh,' said Bex. 'You're right. Not good.'

I lifted my head. 'It's not *you*, Mum, it's the jeans,' I said.

'I did *say* –' she started.

'Yes, yes, never mind,' said Bex. 'Concentrate, please, Mother. We're supposed to be finding outfits for Rarotonga.'

'Rarotonga?' I asked, sitting up in surprise.

'Kathleen suggested it,' Mum said apologetically. 'She and Geoffrey have been before, and they've asked your father and I to join them this time. They rent a house big enough for three or four couples – apparently it's much nicer and cheaper than staying in a resort.'

And just think of all the time Aunty Kath would have to expand on her concerns about my marriage break-up. 'How long are you going for?' I asked.

'Ten days. But it's not decided yet. Your father's not sure he should be leaving the farm at the moment.'

'I'm sure we can stagger along without you for ten days.'

'Of course you should go,' said Bex firmly. 'If this new worker's as amazing as you all seem to think, he'll never even skip a beat. Hey, the rain's stopped – how about a walk, Jenny?'

We heard Dad's voice, with Caleb's little piping treble as a counterpoint, from the direction of the woodpile as we went up the path from the house to the implement shed. I veered in that direction, but Rebecca caught my arm.

'He'll want to come if he sees us,' she said. 'I just want a decent walk, for a change.'

'Okay,' I said, veering back again. A large, icy drip from the big oak tree by the shed hit the back of my neck and trickled down between my shoulder blades, and I shivered.

'Ugh, what a miserable time of year,' said Bex distastefully, looking at the dark, sodden undergrowth lining the driveway. 'Maybe I should go to Rarotonga with Mum and Dad.'

'And Aunty Kathleen,' I reminded her.

'Oh. Yeah. Anyway, I can't take the time off work.' She sighed. 'God, I'm tired. Sean's been away in Queenstown all week, lucky bastard.'

'Wasn't he going to stay and go skiing this weekend?' I asked, remembering.

'I told him he could damn well spend some time with his family for a change,' she said grimly as we started up the road.

I looked at her sideways. 'Bex, are you guys okay? You and Sean, I mean.'

'Why wouldn't we be?'

'You're pretty hard on him,' I said tentatively.

'That's rich, coming from you.'

'*Was* I horrible to Dave?'

'No more so than he deserved,' she said, which really wasn't all that reassuring.

'He says I treated him like an annoying little kid,' I said.

'Well, he *acted* like an annoying little kid.'

'But if you're treated like an annoying little kid it's probably very tempting to act like one. It's one of those chicken-and-egg things.'

She snorted. 'It sounds to me like one of those Dave-trying-yet-again-to-make-everything-your-fault things.'

This was quite possibly the case. And it was certainly a much nicer, more comfortable theory than the one where I had to accept a bit of responsibility too. I opened my mouth to cement my position as victim with tales of chlamydia and serial adultery – and then changed my mind. Yes, Bex would say that Dave was a lousy, rotten scumbag, but so what? It wouldn't actually make me feel any better. And – and if we *did* happen to get back together, the less my family knew about his goings-on, the better.

'Do you want to go up the road or down?' I asked.

'Up,' she said.

We had a nice brisk walk up the road to the bush reserve past Andrew Faulkner's place. The setting sun crept in beneath the clouds to tip every leaf and grass blade with gold, inciting a pair of bellbirds in a straggly tree lucerne at the edge of the reserve to effortless, liquid song.

'Gorgeous things,' Bex said.

'Mm,' I said, and sighed.

'What?'

'It's so lovely,' I said. 'And I don't even notice anymore.' When I was at boarding school and chronically homesick, I loved this place fiercely. I used to watch for a dozen private landmarks as the car wound up the last hill home – a small round hill, the crooked Dr Seuss-ish silhouette of an old pukatea tree, the horse chestnut at the bottom road gate … And now I whizzed up and down the road, looking neither right nor left, thinking of overdrafts and resource consents and what on earth I could cook with mince that wasn't spaghetti bolognese and that my children would still eat.

'Well, don't go into a decline about it, old bean,' said Bex, slinging an arm around my shoulders. 'You've had a few other things to think about. Come on, let's go home and have a drink.'

* * *

'Weren't they going to put in a new cell phone tower somewhere around here?' asked Sean just before dinner, taking his phone off the living room windowsill (where the coverage was best), looking at it, frowning and putting it down again. He was wearing a tight, charcoal-coloured merino top with a V-neck and a tighter pair of designer jeans, and he looked fashionable, expensive and just a little bit effeminate.

'My cell phone works all over the house,' Mum said. 'And it's just a cheap little one. What model have you got?'

'It's not the model,' I said. 'The Vodafone coverage is awful around here.'

'What *did* happen to that new tower?' Dad asked.

'It's still happening,' I said. 'But there was a big slip on the access road, and they'll have to wait for the ground to dry out a bit before they can get a digger there to fix it.'

'Never mind,' said Sean, crouching down beside his son, who was trundling an ancient wheeled cow across the floor. 'How are you going there, mate?'

'Rrr-*oom*,' Caleb said, crashing the cow into a chair leg.

'Hey, that's a bit rough! Poor cow!'

Caleb giggled and drove full-tilt into the nearest skirting board.

'Settle down, you thug!' said Sean, picking him up and tickling him.

'Don't get him all worked up!' Bex said sharply over Caleb's squeals of laughter. She came around the end of the kitchen counter carrying a bowl of scrambled egg. 'How about doing something useful for a change and giving him his dinner?'

Sean, with what I felt was admirable restraint, sat silently down at the table with Caleb on his knee, checked the temperature of the egg and offered Caleb a spoonful.

'Could you set the table, Jenny, love?' Mum asked, taking a stack of warmed plates out of the oven and putting them down on the end of the bench.

Getting up obediently from my chair, I said, 'Hey, Dad, John came to see me the other night. He's cold, and he says oil heaters are too expensive to run. He was wondering if he could have a wood burner in the cottage.'

'Well, I suppose he can, if that's what he wants,' said Dad.

'He wants us to pay for it.'

'Ah.'

'That's fair enough, isn't it?' Bex said. 'It's not like he'd take it away with him when he left.'

'Ye-s, but on the other hand he doesn't pay any rent,' I said.

'Why not?' asked Sean, shovelling scrambled egg into his son's open mouth.

'It's a very small cottage,' Dad said. 'And it was in a pretty poor state when he moved in.'

Sean smiled wonderingly and shook his head.

'It's not a *massive* loss of potential income,' I said, slightly ruffled by the smile. 'The going rate for one-bedroom cottages with no insulation in downtown Pukewai isn't very high.'

Dad bent down to retrieve a bit of egg that had escaped under the table. 'I suppose he'd better have his burner,' he said, sitting back up. 'Can't have him freezing; it's not a good look. And he's done a lot of repair work around the place, after all.' He offered the egg to Caleb, who took it and stuffed it into his mouth.

'Dad! That's been on the floor!' Bex protested.

He smiled at her. 'Do him good.'

'Brian,' Mum said warningly, tasting her gravy. 'Don't tease. Could you get out the cork mats, please, Jenny?'

'You're going to buy a wood burner for a tenant who doesn't actually pay rent,' said Bex.

'So it would seem,' Dad said.

'Generous,' said Sean dryly.

Bex pulled out the chair next to Dad's and sat down, clasping her hands around her knees. 'While you're feeling generous,' she said, 'might you consider helping your very deserving daughter and son-in-law buy a house?'

Dad's eyebrows went up. 'Don't you have a house already?' he asked.

'Yes, but not a very nice one.'

'Isn't it?'

'It's little and poky. It's got no off-street parking ...'

'Nobody has off-street parking in Wellington, do they?'

Bex ignored this. 'The thing is, we've found an *amazing* property in Seatoun. Sean, show Mum and Dad the house.'

'How?' he said. 'No wi-fi.'

'Can't you use your phone as a hotspot?'

'No doubt I could, if there was any cell phone coverage.'

'You could use my phone,' Mum offered. 'I get three bars, over there by the window.'

'No,' said Sean. 'I couldn't.'

'Of course you can. My pleasure.' She dried her hands on a tea towel and rummaged in her handbag beside the fruit bowl. 'I put some money on it just the other day.'

'No, Mum, your phone doesn't connect to the internet,' I said, counting out cutlery. 'Do you want mine, Sean?'

'Look, it doesn't matter,' said Bex. 'The point is, this house has *everything* we want — four bedrooms, room downstairs for a studio, sea views ... It's the house of our dreams.'

'What's it worth?' Dad asked.

She shrugged. 'One point six.'

'*Million?*' said Mum, looking up sharply from her gravy.

'Uh-huh.'

'Rebecca, my petal,' Dad said. 'How much spare cash do you think we have?'

'Oh, about four million dollars,' she said softly, resting her chin on her bent knees.

'What?' I said.

Dad frowned at me, got slowly to his feet and went across the kitchen to get a beer out of the fridge. 'Sean?' he asked. 'Girls?'

'No, thanks,' Sean said, and I shook my head.

'The thing is,' Bex continued doggedly, 'just how long *are* you going to hang on to the farm? It'll have to be sold eventually – why not do it now, and free up some cash so you can have a nice retirement?'

'Rebecca, love ...' Mum started.

'Things obviously aren't working, the way they are now. Look at the debacle you've just had with Marcus. I know Jenny's doing her best, but she's in over her head. What's the point of struggling on, not making any money, while the place keeps going backwards?'

I glared at her in mingled hurt and anger, and she said, 'I'm sorry, Jen. I know you don't want to hear this, but you're not coping. You're exhausted and miserable.'

'I am *not*!' I cried. Well, only a little bit. And only temporarily.

She gave me a long, sceptical look.

'Yes, alright, the last few months haven't been much fun, but that's what you *get* when your marriage falls apart!' I said.

'I think the point that Bex is trying to make,' said Sean, rescuing Caleb's plate just in time to stop him hurling it to the floor, 'is that to all intents and purposes sheep farming's a subsistence lifestyle. And that's fine, if you're doing it because you love it ...'

'But you *don't* love it,' Bex finished. 'Do you, Dad?'

'It's not quite as simple as that, Rebecca,' he said.

'Isn't it?'

'I've lived here all my life,' he said.

Bex smiled pityingly and shook her head.

'*I* love it,' I said abruptly.

'You love the scenery,' Bex corrected.

'And the lifestyle, and the community, and – and my garden.' And every tree and stone and blade of grass on the place. The farm wasn't just a business; it was our home and our way of life. It looked after us, and it was our duty – no, our *privilege* – to look after it.

She rolled her eyes, and I hadn't even said the mushy bit out loud.

'Stop it!' I snapped. 'It's *good* to love your home! It doesn't mean you're soft in the head!'

'You don't love it *that* much! You'd never have moved back here if you hadn't married Dave.'

'I know,' I said. 'But I've always been really grateful that I got to.'

'And now that you've given him the bum's rush, Mum and Dad have to stay here so you can keep living the dream?'

I dropped a stack of plates on the table with a thud. '*Jesus*, Bex!'

'*Girls!*' Mum wailed.

'Stuff this; I'm going home,' I said. And snatching up my shoes I went out through the glass patio door, closing it behind me with exaggerated care.

That was really dumb, I told myself as I paused on the deck, just out of line of sight, to cram my feet into my shoes. Not only because I'd stepped squarely onto the sopping doormat in my socks, but because dramatic exits, although momentarily satisfying, leave your opponents in possession of the floor.

Clutching my self-pity around me like a blanket, I groped my way up the dark path between the house and the implement shed.

The security light on the corner of the shed came on as I neared the car, just too late to stop me walking into a puddle. '*Fuck*,' I said viciously.

'Jenny,' Dad said behind me.

I turned around and watched him approach.

'You don't want to take your sister too seriously, you know,' he said.

'You do know that she has absolutely *zero* concern about whether I'm coping, or your retirement?'

'I know,' said Dad.

'So why don't you ever tell her to sit down and shut up?'

'Because years of experience have taught me that the storm passes more quickly if you say nothing.' He reached out and dropped a hand on my shoulder. 'Funny how you don't ever seem to have grasped that.'

'It just does my *head* in that she can say what she likes, and we all have to understand that she doesn't mean it; it's just her little way. And – and I try to be nice, and consider everyone else's point of view, and *everything* I do is wrong. I shouldn't have kicked Dave out just because he was sleeping with the next-door neighbour, I shouldn't have rocked the boat with Marcus just because he was doing a terrible job, I shouldn't be angry about Dave telling the kids he wants to come home but I won't let him ...'

'Who says you shouldn't?' said Dad.

'*You* do!' I cried.

'Pardon *me*?'

'Oh, not about Dave – that's just Mum – but you weren't exactly supportive over Marcus! First of all I was overreacting and antagonising him, and then you turned around and told Harry that you'd known he was a disaster for months, but I'm so stroppy and difficult you couldn't do anything about it!'

Dad winced and scratched his chin.

'You'd better go in,' I said. 'Your tea'll be getting cold.'

'Bugger my tea. Jenny, I'm sorry. I should have backed you up.'

'Thank you,' I said, wiping my wet eyes on the sleeve of my jumper. 'I – I'm sorry about all the whirling drama.'

'Come back down home and have something to eat,' he said.

I shook my head and smiled. 'She'll forgive me nobly because of all the stress I've been under, and I'll be forced to stab her with a fork.'

'We should probably avoid that. For Caleb's sake, if nothing else.'

'Exactly. Dad?'

'Mm?'

'Do you think she's right about the farm?'

He sighed. 'Well, she does have a point, of a sort.'

'I've been trying not to think about it, but I'm probably never going to be able to buy her out.' The theory had always been that Dave and I would, over twenty or thirty years, save enough to buy half the farm, and that I would inherit the other half. It was an ambitious plan with Dave farming full-time and me earning a salary, and without him it went from optimistic to hopelessly unrealistic.

'Don't worry about it,' Dad said. 'It's very early days, and no-one's going to do anything in a rush. Let's just hang fire for a while.'

'Mm.'

He put an arm around my shoulders. 'Who knows? You might meet a handsome young billionaire.'

'What a distressingly unfeminist solution,' I said, smiling.

'Well, then, we'll just have to diversify into luxury homestays and horse trekking.'

I reached up and kissed his cheek. 'Clichéd, but better,' I said. 'Night, Dad.'

'Goodnight, love.'

Chapter 15

'Knock knock!' said Nathan, bouncing up and down excitedly in his chair.

'No,' I said weakly. 'No more, please.'

'Knock *knock*!'

'Oh, al*right*. Who's there?'

'One-two-oh,' said Nathan.

'That doesn't make any sense!' Lily protested.

'Be strong, my darling,' I said. 'One-two-oh who?'

'One-two-oh … Bum!' He threw his head back and roared with laughter. 'Knock knock!'

'*No!*' said Lily and I in unison.

'Knock *knock*!'

'No, it's my turn!' said Lily. 'What do cows do on the weekend?'

'What?' asked Nathan.

'They go to the moo-vies. *Mooo*-vies. Get it?'

I groaned, but both children fell into gales of laughter.

'Moo-vies! Get it, Mum? Because cows go *moo*!'

'Yep,' I said. 'Brilliant stuff.'

'You tell one now, Mum.'

'Right. Um … what's yellow and very dangerous?'

This was met by twin blank stares.

'Shark-infested custard,' I said.

Nothing. Not a flicker.

'Really, guys? You don't think custard with sharks in it is even a little bit funny?'

'No,' said Lily.

'It doesn't strike you as a good metaphor for life in general? Even when it looks all smooth and sweet on the surface, unexpected dangers lurk beneath?'

'Never mind, Mummy,' said Nathan pityingly. 'My turn! Knock knock!'

It was Saturday, 8 July, the first day of the school holidays. The children were spending this week with me and the next with Dave, who was planning to take them to visit his parents in Napier. A howling easterly wind had been blowing since the previous night, and as we got up from the lunch table a particularly savage gust hit the side of the house, flinging a barrage of rain and wet leaves against the dining room windows. There was a crack like a gun going off from outside, followed by a long drawn-out groan and then a crash. The lights flickered, Lily screamed, Tessa barked and Nathan burst into tears.

Getting up, I went to look out the window. Seeing only rain, sodden lawn and battered shrubbery, I opened the kitchen door.

'Mummy! Don't go out there!' Lily cried.

'Don't panic, chicken. It's only wind. But I'd better just make sure the roof's still there.'

'What if it's *not*?'

'Then we'll fix it.' And with a bright, fake smile I put on my raincoat and gumboots and sallied out into the storm.

We still appeared to have a roof, which was nice, but a forty-year-old totara tree, part of the shelter belt between house and road, had fallen right across the top of the driveway. With my head bent against the weather I pushed past a head-high wall of wet, prickly foliage, climbed the bank and found that the half-metre diameter trunk had snapped clean off at ground level.

It was a chainsaw job, and chainsaws were beyond me. I chewed my right thumbnail, thinking. Dad, my primary go-to in time of need, was in Rarotonga. It was Harry's weekend off, and he'd gone hunting. John Mercer? No, he was far too frail. Dave, then. I sighed. I didn't want to ask Dave for help. It was a fortnight, now, since he'd kissed me, and I'd considered and agonised and reduced myself to a state of near-terminal bewilderment before applying this simple test:

How do I feel about getting divorced?
Sad. We promised to spend the rest of our lives together, and we stuffed it up. Bummer.
And how do I feel about not getting divorced?
Panic-stricken. Trapped. Like I'm drowning ...

Which seemed fairly conclusive. Telling Dave, however, was such an unpleasant thought that I'd spent the last ten days refusing to think it. Still, the conversation would have to be had at some point. And the kids and I were meant to be lunching with friends the next day, which is tricky if you can't leave home ... I turned and went slowly back to the house.

Dave's phone was turned off, and diverted straight to the answer phone. *'Dave here. Leave a message. You never know; I might even ring you back.'*

'Hey, it's me,' I said awkwardly. 'One of the trees at the top of the driveway's come down; I was just wondering if you could give me a hand cutting it up, so we can get out. Um, no worries if you can't, I'll sort something out.' I hung up the phone and turned to smile at the children. 'Would you like to watch *Despicable Me*?'

'What about the tree?' Lily asked.

'I can't get hold of Dad right now, but he'll probably call back in a while. It doesn't matter; we don't need to go anywhere today.'

'What if we *do*? What if someone gets sick? Or we run out of food?'

'Then ... we'll take the four-wheeler down through the paddock, and get Granddad's ute.'

'Or we could call the rescue helicopter,' Nathan suggested.

'Well, true,' I said. 'We could ask them to bring us some more milk. Go and turn on the TV, you turnip; I'll make you a Milo.'

* * *

Half an hour later I was washing the bowl of the electric mixer when Lily drifted into the kitchen, carrying my cell phone. 'Can I listen to music on your phone, Mum?' she asked.

'Okay. Don't you want to watch the movie?'

She shook her head, put the phone down on the bench and climbed up beside it. 'What's in the oven?'

'Caramel biscuits.'

'Awesome.'

She selected some breathy, insipid pop tune or other, and sang along word-perfect. I refrained from comment, but as her next choice started I asked, 'What's that, Lil?'

'Shawn Mendes,' she said, showing me the phone screen.

'And you actually *like* it?'

She giggled. 'Yes!'

'Deary, deary me,' I said, shaking my head.

'Do you want to pick a song?'

'Yes please,' I said, and she handed me the phone. What was a good song for a wet, stormy afternoon? Something uplifting … something you could sing along to … something good for headbanging, preferably … I scrolled down my playlist. 'Run to Paradise'. Perfect. I selected it, turned up the volume and pulled the hair tie out of my ponytail.

Lily watched me from the bench with a slightly patronising smile. I handed her a wooden spoon, and she took it gingerly.

'Microphone,' I explained, shaking my hair forward over my face. '"*Baby!* …"'

She slid to the floor, laughing, and we danced enthusiastically around the kitchen.

'Mum,' she said a little later. '*Mum!*'

I was on my knees playing air guitar, eyes scrunched shut and fingers dancing furiously across imaginary strings. An inspired performance, though I say it myself. I looked up at her enquiringly.

'Mr Faulkner's here.'

Suddenly cold with horror, I scrambled to my feet and turned to face the door. Andrew Faulkner stood in the doorway, wearing a raincoat and waterproof leggings. I fumbled for my phone and turned the music off.

'I knocked,' he said awkwardly into the resulting silence, 'but you were, um …'

Making a complete tit of myself. 'What's up?' I asked, my face burning.

'I see you've got a tree down across your driveway,' he said. 'I've got the chainsaw on the back of the ute.'

'Oh! Look, thank you so much, but don't —'

'It's not a problem.' He retreated, pulling the door shut behind him.

I dropped my head into my hands. Andrew Faulkner. Why him, of all people? He was so stern and efficient; so — so *grown up*.

'Don't worry, Mum, he thought you were funny,' said Lily. 'He was smiling.'

'Oh, good,' I said hollowly. The oven timer went off, and I took the biscuits out. 'Hey, Lil, I'd better go out and help him. You stay in here in the warm, okay?'

'Okay,' she said. 'Can I have a biscuit?'

'Yes, but wait five minutes for them to cool down.'

Still hot with embarrassment, I put on my raincoat and boots and walked up the driveway to where Andrew was working. The tree's trunk divided about a metre up into a mass of branches, so that cutting it up was like dismembering a prickly giant cauliflower. I began to drag cut branches up onto the side of the road and pile them on the wide grass verge beside the mailbox, watched indifferently by the old dog on the back of Andrew's ute. I was manhandling a particularly awkward branch onto the top of the heap when she suddenly sat upright, leapt down and shot past me like a black-and-grey streak.

I turned to watch her and saw, just below the fallen tree, the beginning of yet another geriatric dog fight. Tessa was making little rushes at her opponent's hocks while the other dog lunged at her, snarling. I ran between them and snatched Tessa up, and the old huntaway, furious at this untimely interference, reared up and bit my raincoat-clad elbow. She may have been short on teeth but there was nothing wrong with her jaw tone. '*Ow!*' I yelled. Tessa barked, squirming like an eel in my hands.

The chainsaw cut off and Andrew flew past, knocking his dog aside and pinning her to the ground. Tessa made another vigorous attempt to use me as a launching pad, pushing me off balance so that I went over backwards, still clutching her, into a heap of wet, spiky foliage.

'Mummy!' wailed Lily.

'*Stop* it, Tessa! Lily, why on *earth* did you let her out?' I asked, pushing myself up to sit.

'I – I'm s-sorry,' she sobbed.

'It's alright, love; it's not your fault.' I struggled to my feet, Tessa under my good arm. For some reason Andrew, clutching his dog's collar, was still on hands and knees. 'Thank you,' I said.

He hissed, which seemed uncalled for.

'Are you alright?' I asked.

'No,' he said between his teeth. 'Back.' His dog growled, and Tessa fairly gibbered with rage and frustration.

'*Mummy!*'

'It's *okay*, Lily! We'll go and shut her in the laundry.' I turned back to Andrew. 'Um – hang on. Back in a minute.' And with Lily at my heels I ran down the driveway.

I opened the back door, slung Tessa into the laundry and pulled the sliding door shut behind her. 'Nathan! Are you still watching the movie?'

'No, I'm drawing,' he called from the living room.

Ominous. 'On what?' I asked.

'My little pad.'

'Good man. Okay, Lil, you stay here and I'll go and help Mr Faulkner.'

'I'm scared,' she wept.

'You don't need to be scared. They're just a pair of silly old dogs. They'll be alright now that they can't see each other. But for goodness' sake don't let Tessa out till I get back, will you?' I kissed the top of her head, turned and ran back up the driveway.

Andrew was standing now, with his knees bent and hands on his thighs. His dog sat beside him, anxiously nosing his hand.

'What can I do?' I asked.

'Nothing.' He levered himself up straight, lower lip caught firmly between his teeth.

'Painkillers? Should I ring the doctor?'

'No. Just need – to get moving.' He took a tentative step and grunted in pain.

I hurried forward and put an arm around his waist, and the dog growled again.

'Meg,' he said in a voice like ice, and she dropped to her stomach with a little whine.

'Maybe if you just slide your feet it mightn't jar so badly,' I said.

He grunted again, put up a hand to grip my shoulder and shuffled around to face up the driveway.

'Where are you going?' I asked.

'Home.'

'You can't drive.'

He shuffled onwards, not replying.

'Hey,' I said, stopping dead. 'You can*not* drive yourself home like this.'

'It'll free up in a minute.'

A big, fat raindrop hit my face, and then another. 'It's going to pour any second. Please come down to the house for a bit.'

'No, thanks,' he said. 'You go in before you get wet.' He released my shoulder and shuffled on. The raindrops fell faster.

I watched him worriedly for a moment, sighed and went to fetch his chainsaw.

He made it all the way to the top of the driveway before his right boot slipped on a bit of exposed clay. He staggered sideways, and I dropped the chainsaw and threw both arms around his chest from behind, half shoving and half dragging him back upright.

'*Fuck*,' he said, his hand closing like a vice around my bruised elbow.

A big, black, shiny ute swept around the corner and stopped just in front of us, across the top of the driveway. 'Having fun?' said Dave sardonically, opening his window.

I dropped my arms from around Andrew's waist and took a hasty step backwards. And at that moment the heavens opened.

The rain fell in sheets rather than drops, and little clay-coloured streams danced between the stones at our feet. Water poured off the hem of my raincoat, soaking my jean-clad legs to the skin. Dave shut his window again smartly.

Andrew, moving as jerkily as a puppet, reached his ute, which was parked at the side of the road just in front of Dave's. 'Thank you,' he said as I lifted the chainsaw onto the back.

'Are you sure you're alright to drive?' I asked.

'Yes,' he said.

I looked doubtfully at the old dog beside him, her curly coat slick and dark with water. 'She can't jump up by herself, can she?'

'No.'

'Will she let me pick her up?'

'Better wait till I've got a good grip on her collar.' He bent, wincing, and grabbed it.

I couldn't hear her growling over the drumming of the rain, but I felt it. Her whole body vibrated as I lifted her. I put her down on the deck of the ute, from where she eyed me with unmistakable loathing, lips drawn back in a snarl.

'Does she hate everyone, or is it just me?' I asked.

'You more than most, I think,' Andrew said. Then he smiled. 'No, I'm kidding, she hates everyone.'

'That's alright, then. Hey, could you ring when you get home, so I know you've made it?'

'What on earth do you think is going to happen between here and there?'

'No idea. Just humour me?'

'Alright,' he said.

'Thank you.'

The rain was easing now, and Dave got out of his ute, wearing a cap and an oilskin vest. 'If you'd let me know you'd called in the cavalry, love, it would've saved me a trip,' he said.

For all sorts of reasons, only some of which I understood, I wanted to hit him.

Without another word or a glance for either of us, Andrew opened the door of his ute, got in with grim, painful determination, closed the door again, started the engine and drove away.

'Oh, for God's sake,' said Dave.

'Dave, you slept with his *wife*!' I snapped. 'Do you honestly think he should stand around and make polite conversation?'

He didn't pursue the subject. 'Why the hell were you standing in a thunderstorm cuddling Andrew Faulkner?' he asked.

'I wasn't,' I said crossly. 'He hurt his back.'

'And you were kissing it better?'

'Oh, stop it. He slipped. I was helping him up. And you're in no position to –'

'Yeah, yeah.' He strode down the driveway and picked up a branch too big for me to drag.

'I'll just check the kids are okay, and then I'll come and help you,' I said.

'Uh-huh.'

Lily and Nathan were in the kitchen when I opened the door, eating caramel biscuits. 'Lily's had five,' Nathan said quickly.

'So have you!'

'That's okay,' I said. 'But stop now, or you'll be sick. Could you both have a drink of water to wash the sugar off your teeth?'

'When are you coming inside?' Lily asked.

'When the driveway's clear. Another ten minutes, maybe?'

'Tessa's been barking.'

'You can let her out now. Mr Faulkner and his dog have gone.'

'Can I come outside?' said Nathan.

And see Dave. And get all excited. And want him to come in to see the cubbyhouse we'd made that morning, and … But there was no point in trying to avoid it; Dave, if I knew Dave at all, would only be prevented from coming in by me throwing a major wobbly. And I *had* asked him for help. 'Yes, if you want to,' I said. 'Dad's here helping with the tree. But put on your coat and boots first.'

There were two shrieks of excitement, and both children tore down the hallway, shedding biscuit crumbs, to get their coats.

'See you out there!' I called after them, reaching around the doorjamb to open the laundry door and release Tessa.

'Do I get to see the kids?' Dave asked, not quite belligerently, as I rounded the corner of the driveway once more. Tessa rushed up to paw excitedly at his shins.

'They're on their way,' I said, not quite smugly.

He grunted, bent and rolled a ring of totara trunk off the bank into the undergrowth.

I took a deep breath. 'Dave, I've been thinking about us getting back together ...'

'And?' he said, straightening up and turning to face me.

'It's not going to be a starter.'

There was a pause. 'And that's it, is it?' he said at last.

I nodded.

'Right, then.'

'I can't ...' I started, and then stopped.

'Bear the thought?'

'I was going to say "help it".'

'And that's better because ...?'

'It isn't,' I said miserably. *I will not apologise. I will not agree that this is my fault* ... The silence stretched between us. 'Dave, I'm s—'

'Daddy!' Lily shrieked, running up the driveway and hurling herself into his arms.

* * *

The four of us working together to finish clearing the driveway made a delightful picture of wholesome family life. Dave carried Lily and Nathan in turn on his back as he dragged branches, and the damp air echoed with childish laughter. I looked on and smiled, un-gritting my teeth at intervals.

'Can you come and see our cubbyhouse?' Lily asked as the last branch was thrown up onto the pile by the mailbox.

'If it's okay with Mum,' said Dad.

'Please, Mum, please, Mum, *please*?' said Lily.

'Yes, of course,' I said, unclenching my jaw again and wondering how much magnanimity it takes to cause a stomach ulcer.

We all shed our raincoats at the back door, and the kids ran inside. I caught Tessa and dried her on an old towel before letting her in after them, and then hesitated, looking at my sodden and muddy jeans. Six months ago I'd have stripped in front of Dave without a thought.

'You ain't got nothing I ain't seen,' he said, taking off his oilskin vest and dropping it over the back of the car.

'True,' I said. It did, after all, seem a bit precious to worry about a man who had watched me give birth – twice – seeing my knickers.

I peeled off my jeans and socks, and Dave remarked, 'Standards have slipped, I see.'

I turned sharply, and saw him looking with half-amused distaste at my unshaven legs. The distaste was understandable, I admit. When those of us with very dark hair neglect our depilatory routines the result is a bit alarming. *But.*

'Why *do* you want to get back together?' I asked suddenly. 'It isn't because you love me.'

'What?'

'You never let an opportunity to put me down go by. *Ever.*'

'Ah, the sweeping generalisation,' he said. 'Yet another Jenny specialty.'

'You'd better come and see the kids' cubbyhouse,' I said, stalking up the back steps and inside.

Chapter 16

At eight o'clock on Monday morning I was cleaning the toilet (and the cistern, and the floor, and the walls, Nathan's aim being somewhat erratic) when a four-wheeler came down the driveway and stopped outside. I came up the hallway to the kitchen, where I found Nathan holding forth to a bemused Harry Faulkner.

'*You* know, the thing with a bone in it, shaped like this …' Nathan was saying, drawing circles in the air with a chubby finger.

'With a *bone* in it?'

'Yes.'

'What do you do with it?'

'What?' said Nathan blankly.

'Do you play with this thing, or eat it, or what?'

'You *eat* it! It's *meat*.'

'You mean like a chop?' said Harry.

'No! It's made of *chicken*.'

'A drumstick? A chicken leg?'

'Yes!' said Nathan, smiling radiantly. 'Chicken's my favourite.'

'I like sausages,' Harry offered.

'Me too. And mashed potato, and ice cream, and ginger crunch, and chippies, and schnitzel, and icing, and –'

'Nathan,' I said. 'Shh.'

'But not punkin,' Nathan continued. 'Or bisketti out of a tin.'

'Well, I'm glad we've got that cleared up,' Harry said. 'Good morning, Jen.'

'Good morning. How was your weekend?'

'I've had better,' he said.

'It wasn't really ideal hunting weather, was it?'

'No. We walked back out on Saturday afternoon when the wind got up.'

'What a good idea,' I said. 'Much better than lurking in a wet tent in the scrub.'

Harry smiled a bitter, twisted little smile.

'Or not?' I asked.

'Or not.' He sighed and then gave himself a little shake. 'Windy here too, huh?'

'A tree went crash on our driveway,' said Nathan importantly.

'Yeah, I saw.'

'How's Andrew's back?' I asked. I'd found a two-word answer phone message saying, 'Made it,' on Saturday evening after Dave left, and hadn't felt, on the whole, that further communications from my end would be welcome.

'Oh, he's staggering around the place,' said Harry. 'He'll come right in a day or two.'

'Is he going to go and see the doctor, or a physio or something?'

'Pass,' Harry said. 'I haven't asked. He's in a filthy mood.'

'Well, I suppose that's not surprising,' I said.

'No, not at all. He's usually in a filthy mood.'

He was not, it seemed, the only one.

'We moved those calves yesterday, like you said, and let the two-tooths up into the cabbage tree paddock,' I said brightly.

'Mummy felled over and got sheep poo on her,' Nathan put in.

'These things happen,' said Harry.

'Lily and me laughed and *laughed*.'

'Good on you. Many trees down?'

'Nothing that needs dealing with straight away,' I said. 'One walnut out by the cattle yards, and a couple of big branches off the poplars in the waterfall paddock. The tracks are all clear, though.'

He nodded. 'Well, I'd better go and feed out,' he said heavily. 'I'll bring the tractor and trailer back later this afternoon and clean up that stuff at the top of your driveway.'

'No, I can pick it up,' I said. 'But it would be great if you could bring the trailer home. Thank you.'

'It's fine.'

'Come for lunch,' I said impulsively.

'I'm not the best company today.'

I smiled at him. 'Doesn't matter. Come anyway. Cheese scones or cinnamon?'

'Whatever. Cheese.' And he went sadly away.

* * *

It was quarter to one when he came back. The children and I had finished lunch, and they had retired, protesting slightly, for an afternoon nap. I got up from the table, where I was reading an article in the local paper headed TIPOI PRIMARY WINS NEW SPORTING EQUIPMENT! (two hundred dollars' worth – it was evidently a slow news week) and went to meet him at the door.

'Soup?' I askèd.

'Yes, please.' He kicked off his boots and bent to pull Tessa's ears. 'Where are the kidlets?'

'Asleep,' I said. 'Do you want a hot drink now or later?'

'Hmm? Oh, now. A cup of coffee would be good, thanks.' Accepting the soup bowl I held out to him, he drifted over to the table, sat down in my chair, took a scone off the plate at his elbow and began to shred it despondently.

'What's up?' I asked, filling the kettle.

'Nothing,' he said.

I preserved a tactful silence.

'Everything,' he amended quickly, just in case I was dim enough to believe him and leave it at that.

I managed not to smile, but it was hard. 'Work? Family? Relationship issues?' I asked.

'No, not work. The job's fine.' He picked up his soup spoon, looked at it vaguely and put it down again. 'I saw Chris yesterday.'

'Chris your ex-partner?'

'Mm.' Then, 'Made a total dick of myself.'

'Well, we all do that from time to time,' I said consolingly.

He dropped the remains of the scone and looked up at me. 'I drove to Wellington in the middle of the night and banged on his door, and …'

'He's found someone else?' I said gently, after a longish pause.

He nodded, and I saw a tear fall into his soup.

'Oh, Harry,' I said, going around the end of the counter and hugging his head against me.

'I know the guy,' he said into my shirt. 'I fucking *introduced* them.'

I stroked his hair, feeling absurdly maternal.

'Sorry,' he muttered, pulling away.

'It sucks,' I said gently.

'Yeah.'

'Eat your soup.'

He smiled a tortured little smile. 'Yes, Mum.'

'Good man. Then you can have a caramel biscuit.'

'Before you put me down for my nap?'

'That's the one. Harry, how did you meet Chris in the first place?'

'At a bar.' He stirred his soup pensively. 'My mate Mark – he was the only person who knew I was gay – took me to this nightclub in Wellington when I went down to see him for the weekend. I was so scared that someone I knew might see me there I nearly wet myself.'

A car came down the driveway and stopped, and I looked out the kitchen door to see who it was. John Mercer, wearing his favourite maroon nylon jacket and an orange woollen hat with a bobble, opened his car door and lifted a hand in greeting. I waved back.

'Who is it?' Harry asked, swiping a hand hurriedly across his eyes.

'John Mercer.'

'Oh, Christ, no.'

'Be strong,' I said. 'Hi, John!'

'Jenny, m' dear – I've brought you some more chokos,' he called.

'Oh. Thanks.'

Levering himself upright, John went around the front of his car, opened the passenger-side door and lifted an apple box with a grunt. I hastened out to take it from him.

'Thank you kindly,' he said, looking at the four-wheeler. 'That man of yours here, is he?'

'Harry? Yes. How's the new burner going?'

'Oh, can't complain,' said John. 'Any chance of scrounging a cup of tea?'

'Of course,' I said, although my heart sank. 'Come on in.'

I led him inside and put the box of chokos – there must have been two dozen of the damn things – on the kitchen bench. Harry grimaced at me from the table and went on with his soup.

'Don't worry about your shoes,' I said, as John bent stiffly to take them off.

He straightened up again. 'Thank you kindly,' he said again. 'Feet are a long way away, these days. Afternoon, young fella.'

'Hi,' said Harry shortly.

'That smells good.'

'Would you like some?' I asked.

'Don't mind if I do, actually.' Rubbing his hands together, he crossed the kitchen and sat down at the dining room table. 'That's a fair-sized tree you lost up by the road.'

'Yes,' I said, ladling soup into a bowl.

'It's a mistake to have too many trees on a section. They do grow, you know.'

As I delivered John his soup, I heard Harry mutter something under his breath that sounded suspiciously like: 'No shit, Sherlock.'

'Like that one,' he said, nodding out the dining room window towards the big *Magnolia denudata* at the edge of the top lawn. 'If that came down it'd hit your roof.'

'I love that tree,' I said. 'It'll be a – a visual symphony, in another month. Don't you dare even *suggest* cutting it down.'

John smiled tolerantly and shook his head. 'I see there's a dead ewe in the swamp below my place,' he said, turning to Harry.

'Is there?'

'Well, I suppose it doesn't seem very important when they're not your animals.'

Harry spooned up a mouthful of soup and didn't reply.

'When *I* was managing the place your brother's on now, I always treated the farm as if it were my own.'

'Really,' said Harry flatly.

'Do you take sugar, John?' I asked hastily.

'No, thank you, I'm sweet enough.' He took a scone and began to butter it thickly. 'Never used to take all me holidays. Not even a fraction. There's always *something* needing doing on a farm.'

'John, what do you suggest I do with these chokos?' I said with something approaching desperation.

Harry smiled. 'Well,' he said, '*I'd* recommend he takes the biggest one he can find and –'

I glared at him, and his smile widened.

'Oh well, work to do,' he said, pushing back his chair. 'Better crack on. Always something needing doing, as John says. Thanks for lunch, Jenny, it was delicious.' He kissed my cheek as he came past, and then opened the kitchen door. 'John.'

'You want to watch that fellow,' John said darkly as the four-wheeler started.

'What?' I said, letting my annoyance show more plainly than I'd meant to.

John shook his head. 'Give them an inch …'

'Oh, for goodness' sake, John. He's doing a really good job.'

'Hmph. Now, don't take this the wrong way, my dear –'

'John,' I broke in. 'I have never, *ever* heard *any* comment that came after someone saying "now don't take this the wrong way" that wasn't deeply offensive. So maybe just don't.'

'I'm only concerned that –'

'John!' I said sternly.

'You're vulnerable at the moment, m' dear. And sometimes when people are vulnerable they get themselves into situations that ...' Something in my expression must have penetrated even his armour-plated self-assurance; he didn't finish the sentence. 'I just wouldn't want to see you doing anything you might regret later on.' He smiled at me in a fatherly sort of way. 'But right you are; I won't say another word.'

* * *

The kids spent the second week of the school holidays with Dave, and I spent it at work. It made quite a pleasant change to be there full-time; I got so much stuff *done*.

On Tuesday I met my friend Ange Miller for lunch. Ange was small and blonde and energetic, with a most endearing habit of being incapacitated by laughter at inappropriate moments. She used her hands to express every mood and underline every statement, to the point where I suspected that if you held them still she'd be struck dumb. We'd been friends since meeting at antenatal class eight years before, but since she worked on Mondays and Tuesdays – she was branch manager of the Tipoi ANZ – and I worked Wednesday to Friday, managing to coincide for lunch was a rare achievement.

She was waiting at a corner table, touching up her lipstick, when I reached the cafe.

'Hi!' I said. 'I'm so sorry I'm late – I got held up on site.'

'It's fine,' she said, standing up to kiss me. 'Shall we go up and order?'

I looked at her surreptitiously as I followed her to the glass-fronted display case by the counter. She seemed rather thick through the middle; was she pregnant? She'd regained her figure after little Perry was born with sickening ease and rapidity, so she probably was – but there's nothing more depressing, if you've put on a few unwelcome kilos, than to have well-meaning friends start offering their congratulations.

'The spinach and filo thing that looks like someone already ate it is actually quite good,' she told me, rummaging in her handbag and emerging with a tube of antacid tablets.

'Is that a standard pre-lunch precaution, or are you pregnant?' I asked, throwing caution to the wind.

'Five and a half months. Didn't you know?'

'No – that's *wonderful*! Congratulations!'

'Thanks. I only stopped throwing up every time I looked at food a few weeks ago, and now I've got heartburn. And my hip's giving me all sorts of grief – I'm too old for this carry-on.'

'You gonna order?' the girl on the other side of the counter asked, wiping her nose on the back of her hand.

'We're getting there,' said Ange. 'Oh – soup of the day, and a pot of Earl Grey. With toast, please, not garlic bread.'

'It comes with garlic bread.'

'Well, just think of the saving you'll make by giving me naked toast instead.'

'It'll cost the same,' the girl said, eyeing her balefully across the cash register.

'That's *fine*,' Ange told her warmly, and then stuck her tongue out as the girl turned to pass the order through the kitchen window.

I grinned. 'BLT, please, and a flat white.'

Having paid, we retreated to our corner to start catching up on each other's news. 'Do you know what you're having?' I asked.

'Of course. Why endure unnecessary suspense? It's a boy.'

'Lovely. Are the kids looking forward to it?'

'Very much. Although Perry's quite convinced the baby will be able to play with him within a week of being born, no matter how much we try to explain, so he's in for a disappointment, poor little man ... How are you, anyway? I've been meaning to call you for *months*, but you know how it goes; you get busy and another week goes past. I'm sorry, Jen. Worst friend ever.'

'Of course you're not,' I said. 'Anyway, I haven't been feeling strong enough for socialising, these last few months. Pathetic, I know, but there it is.'

'I'd be the same,' said Ange. 'I'd just want to crawl into a hole somewhere and lick my wounds.'

'And then so many of the people we socialised with were *our* friends, not *my* friends. It's awkward; you don't like to ask people to choose ...'

'Yeah,' she said, screwing her face up in sympathy. 'Although from what I hear, nobody was very impressed by Dave's behaviour.'

'Thanks,' I said. 'Ange, had you ever heard of him having other affairs?'

'Oh,' she said, and sighed. 'Yeah, a rumour here and there. Did he?'

'Mm.'

'Moron.'

'Apparently it's partly my fault, for being so cold and hard.'

'You don't believe that crap, do you?'

'N-no,' I said uncertainly.

'Oh, come on,' she said. 'I've never heard such drivel in all my life. You're about as cold and hard as a toasted marshmallow. Pull yourself together, woman.'

I smiled. 'Yes, Ange.'

'You want pepper?' asked the waitress, appearing suddenly and sliding our meals in front of us.

'No, thank you,' I said.

'Cutlery would be nice, though,' said Ange.

'Over there.' She jerked her head towards a table in the corner and sauntered off.

'Service with a smile,' I remarked, getting up.

'How are the kids?' Ange asked as I returned, bearing cutlery and a glass of water apiece.

'Pretty good,' I said. 'Nathan's always happy – well, he seems to be; hopefully he's not hiding all sorts of deep psychological issues.'

'Nathan? I doubt it.'

'Me too,' I said, smiling. 'But it's all been a bit tougher on Lily.'

'Well, she's older.'

'Yeah. And she's always been a worrier ... How are yours?'

'Fine,' she said. 'Scarlett needs braces, and Perry's decided that vegetables are poisonous – you know, just normal stuff. Hey, I hear you've got a hot date tomorrow night.'

I choked on a mouthful of BLT. 'Where did you hear that?' I demanded when I had stopped spluttering and recovered enough to speak.

'Scarlett decided to flush a pair of trousers down the loo on Friday, and I had to call a plumber.'

Ah. Travis. Who had asked me around for dinner when I encountered him on a building site the week before, startling me so much I'd said yes before I knew what I was doing. 'Why did she do that?'

'They weren't pink,' said Ange glumly.

I laughed. Ange, when her daughter was born, was vehemently opposed to gender stereotyping. Frills, sequins, Lego Friends – all forbidden. She had ceremonially burnt a little pink stretch-n-grow with *Do my thighs look big in this?* on the front, and posted the video on Facebook.

'I know, I know,' she said. 'But back to your date.'

I groaned. 'I don't know what possessed me to say yes.'

'You might enjoy it. He's sweet.'

'But I'm not even *faintly* attracted to him. And he looks at me with these great big puppy-dog eyes, and I feel like a callous bitch.'

'Jen, grow up; it's only dinner. You don't have to sleep with the guy.'

'True,' I said. 'It's just … all a bit alarming …' The thought of ever embarking on a new relationship was only marginally less terrifying than the thought of spending the rest of my life alone.

'Yeah,' said Ange, wrinkling her nose sympathetically. 'I bet.'

Chapter 17

It *was* only dinner. And Travis was a very nice guy, I assured myself, and it would no doubt be a very pleasant evening.

It wasn't. We dined by candlelight, and although I tried hard to be brisk and matter-of-fact, either I failed or he was particularly obtuse, because as we rose from the table he suggested that we retire to the bedroom.

'No!' I said, horrified.

'Oh, God, I'm sorry!' Travis said.

Then we had a long and exhausting discussion about what a lovely and eminently desirable person he was, but that I was far too emotionally fragile to even *consider* another relationship. The whole thing was appalling. Just appalling.

Mum and Dad came home from Rarotonga tanned and filled with enthusiasm for foreign travel, although not for the welcome-home bag of chokos I'd thoughtfully left on their doorstep.

The days began to lengthen, the early plum trees were starred with pink and we vaccinated and set-stocked the ewes for lambing. Harry acquired a heading dog – a cheerful, ugly, moderately efficient beast with pink-rimmed eyes – and drifted into the habit of coming for dinner on Tuesdays when his brother was out playing squash. He was a good guest, eating everything I offered with flattering promptness, and we all enjoyed having him around. I hadn't realised, until I had another adult to talk to in the evenings, how lonely I was.

One gusty Monday afternoon in mid-August, I was sitting on the kitchen floor with a particularly dopey orphan lamb between my knees, trying to teach it how to suck, when the phone rang.

'Lil, could you get that?' I called.

Lily tore across the living room and picked up the phone. 'Hello, Lily Reynolds speaking,' she said. Then, 'Hi, Aunty Bex.'

'Tell her I'll call back in a minute,' I said, poking a red rubber teat into the lamb's mouth. It spat it straight back out.

Lily relayed the message, paused, covered the phone's speaker in a most professional manner and hissed at me, 'She says it's really urgent!'

'Okay,' I said, putting down my bottle of milk and holding out a hand for the phone.

'I'll just get her. Bye-bye, Aunty Bex. Here she is,' Lily said primly, passing it over.

'Hi, Bex.' Normal communications had resumed following last month's argument, after our standard week-long interval of frosty silence.

'I'm pregnant,' she said.

'Congratulations!' I cried.

'Thanks,' she said, and burst into tears.

'Aren't you feeling well?' I asked in concern.

'Oh, not too bad; it's not th-that …'

'Rebecca! What's wrong?'

'I don't know if this was the right decision!' she wailed. 'We've been h-having some problems …'

Lily picked up the lamb, which was lurching across the slippery lino like a first-time ice skater, sat down with it on her lap and gestured imperiously for the bottle. I passed it to her and got to my feet. 'It's okay,' I said soothingly. 'Remember how you cried for a month when you were pregnant with Caleb? It's just your hormones giving you the run-around.'

Bex sniffled.

'Anyway, honey bunch, too late now.'

'Thanks,' she said sourly.

'When are you due?'

'Tenth of April.'

'Awesome,' I said. 'So you get to be heavily pregnant over summer. Well timed.'

Lily pushed the teat back into the lamb's mouth. It sneezed, shook itself and started sucking. I pantomimed astonishment, and she beamed.

'You're a horrible, horrible person,' Bex said.

'I know. No, seriously, Bex, it's wonderful news. Have you told Mum?'

'Not yet. She's next.'

'She'll be thrilled.'

'Yeah,' said Bex. She sighed. 'I'm already a whale.'

'I'm doing a really good job, aren't I, Mum?' Lily said proudly.

'You are indeed. Not you, Bex!'

'No, I am. And I'm exhausted. And my skin's revolting.'

'I doubt it. What does Sean say?'

'He says I look fine. He wouldn't notice if I grew another head.'

'Mummy! It finished all the milk!'

'That's awesome!'

'It is?' said Bex.

'It is what?' I asked.

'Look, if this isn't a good time ...' she said coldly.

'No, no, it is,' I said. 'Lil, how about putting the lamb back in the box, now, before she wees on you?'

Lily, who had the lamb on her knee and was murmuring sweet nothings into one furry ear, did not respond.

'Speaking of weeing, I need to,' said Bex. 'Yet again.'

'I'll give you a call back in five minutes?'

'Nah, it's only you,' she said. 'I can pee and talk.'

'This one's called Buttercup,' said Lily. 'Do you like your name, Buttercup? She does, Mum! She nodded!'

'I must say I'm dreading having another baby in this house,' said Bex, her voice accompanied by tinkling sounds. 'All these bloody stairs, with prams and car seats and everything else.'

Ah. This sounded like the beginning of the next farm sale argument. 'Mmm,' I said, aiming to sound vaguely supportive without saying anything that could possibly be used against me.

Lily scrambled to her feet, sending little Buttercup sprawling. 'Mu-um! She weed on me!'

'Well, never mind. It's not the end of the world.'

'Especially when you're not the one ending up with scoliosis.'

'Pardon?' I said, completely confused.

'Are you actually listening?' Bex asked.

'I'm trying! Hang on. Lily, put the lamb back in the box and put your trousers in the washing machine. Right, Bex, you have my undivided attention.'

'I doubt it,' she said bitterly.

'Have you told Caleb yet?' I asked.

'No, not yet.'

'He'll be so excited.'

'I hope so,' she said. 'My friend's just had a baby, and she can't leave it alone with her three-year-old, or he beats it up.'

'I can't imagine Caleb doing that. He's lovely.'

'You wouldn't have said that if you'd seen him yesterday,' Bex said. 'He threw a massive tantrum in the supermarket when I wouldn't buy him some horrible mutant stuffed toy.'

'Perfectly normal,' I said, smiling.

'Hey, why don't you come down the next weekend Dave has the kids? Sean's got a friend who's just come back from working in Dubai and wants to meet someone nice.'

Lily emerged from the laundry, wearing her T-shirt and knickers and carrying a resigned looking lamb wrapped in Nathan's freshly washed bedspread. 'That's a *terrible* idea,' I told her.

'Why?' said my sister. 'Let's face it, you could use the practice.'

'I wasn't talking to you. Although your idea's terrible too.'

* * *

'Thank you!' I said, coming up the hallway after bedtime stories the next evening to find Harry, who had dined with us as usual, scrubbing the heavy ceramic slow-cooker bowl.

'You're welcome.'

Picking up the big plastic measuring jug I used for lamb milk, I half filled it with warm water, set it down on the electronic scales and turned them on. 'Can you feed the lambs for me at lunchtime tomorrow, while I'm at work?' I asked. 'Mum and Dad can't; they're going to Hamilton.'

'Yeah, sure,' he said, rinsing the bowl and upending it on the edge of the sink. 'How many are you feeding now?'

'Five.' Currently known as (although their names changed almost daily) Amelia, Snowflake, Fuzzy Wuzzy, Bob and Buttercup. 'The biggest four have two hundred and fifty mil each and the smallest one about two hundred – I'll write it all down for you.'

'Thanks,' Harry said. 'Did John bring you another couple last night? I met him halfway up the main track with a lamb under each arm.'

'No,' I said, sighing. 'He's going to rear them himself. But he came around for bottles and milk powder.'

'And no doubt to tell you there was a dead ewe by the creek.'

'He did mention it.'

'I bet he did,' he said.

'He doesn't have enough to do,' I said, scooping milk powder out of the bag at my feet. 'And he's lonely. And then of course he's terribly concerned that you and I are on the brink of a wild affair.'

'Little does he know.' He stared glumly into the washing-up water and said for at least the tenth time, 'What do you think Andrew would say if I told him?'

'That you and I were on the brink of a wild affair?'

He gave me a pained look.

'I don't know what he'd say,' I said patiently. 'Why don't you tell him and find out?'

'It's not that simple …'

'You know what?' I said, whisking lamb milk. 'It really *is* that simple.'

'He'll be disgusted.'

'I doubt it.'

'What if he is?'

'Well – then he is, I suppose. But I honestly can't see why he would be. And why would you care if he was?'

'It's all so easy when it's someone else's life you're talking about,' he said sourly.

I ran more water into my plastic jug. Eleven hundred mil ... twelve hundred. 'True. Don't tell him, then. It's completely up to you.'

Harry bit his lip. 'Chris said to call him, if – when – I've told my family.'

'When did he say that?' I asked.

'That night I went to see him.'

I put the jug down on the bench and turned to face him squarely. 'As in, "You tell them and then we'll get back together"?'

He gave something between a nod and a shrug.

'He said that even though he's with someone else?'

Another shoulder twitch.

'That seems a bit tough on the new boyfriend.'

'Nah, he's a fuckwit,' said Harry.

'Why did you introduce them in the first place, then?' I asked, briefly diverted from the issue at hand.

'You don't introduce your boyfriend to *nice* people,' he explained. 'They might make you look bad in comparison.'

'Of course. Good plan. Okay, then, no sympathy for him. And you really care about Chris?'

'Yes!'

'So what are you *waiting* for, you turkey?'

He sighed and shook his head.

I divided the lamb's milk between five bottles, screwed on the teats and put on my head torch.

'Would you be there?' he said, looking up suddenly. 'For moral support?'

'Sure, if you want.'

'Thank you,' he said, picking up two of the bottles and preceding me out the kitchen door.

* * *

At work the next day I was going through a set of architect's plans for a house and thinking resentful thoughts about people who focus solely on the look of the building they're designing without considering how the walls will join to the roof, when my cell phone rang. It was Harry.

'Hey,' I said, answering it. 'What's up?'

'Tonight,' he said. 'Can you come tonight?'

'Um ...' I started, puzzled.

'I'm going to tell Andrew. I've got to do it before I lose my nerve. Can you come for tea? You don't have the kids tonight, do you?'

'No,' I said, suppressing a small pang at the thought of missing *My Kitchen Rules*, the current highlight of my week. 'Of course I'll come. What time?'

'Seven.'

'Okay, see you then.'

Hanging up, I leant back in my chair and looked across at Greta, who was staring at her own cell phone with a dreamy little smile. 'New man?' I asked.

'Mm,' she said. 'Well, it's early days, but ... Here, look. Isn't he gorgeous?' She pushed herself off the edge of her desk and scooted around the corner to mine on her wheeled chair, holding out the phone. There on the screen, cheek to cheek, radiant with youth and beauty, were Greta and –

'Marcus!' I cried.

'You know him?' she said excitedly. 'How?'

'Oh, Greta ...'

'What?' she asked, stiffening.

'Remember I was telling you about the guy who was working for us, who did a runner?'

'Yes.'

'That's him.'

'Is it?' she said coldly.

Oh, hell. Should I labour the point? Should I tell her that he was an unreliable, self-centred little shithead? I looked at Greta's face and realised that it wouldn't make any difference to her relationship with Marcus if I did, but it would make an enormous difference to her relationship with me. 'Be careful, won't you?' I said, feeling it was a feeble remark as I made it.

'I will,' she said, more coldly still. 'Thank you.' And standing up, she pushed her chair back around the corner to her own desk.

The office atmosphere was tinged with frost for the rest of that afternoon, and it was a relief to go home. Supervised by Tessa I fed the lambs, took the washing off the line and drifted across the lawn to admire a little clump of *Iris reticulata* that was just coming into flower in the bed outside the living room windows. It was the time of year when the garden, mostly still bare and drab, begins to hint at loveliness to come – I counted four snowdrops and startled a pair of tuis that were bickering in my Nicky Crisp camellia. They took off with a noise like rustling taffeta to chase each other through the darkening orchard, and I smiled as I turned back towards the house.

At precisely two minutes past seven I turned off the road at the Faulkners' mailbox, all regret for cooking shows forgotten in anticipation of the evening's potential drama. The driveway plunged downhill and swept around a corner to end at an angular concrete patio edged with concrete benches, lit by a pair of bulbs in round plastic shades. I could see Andrew through a bank of floor-to-ceiling windows, stirring something on the stove, but there was no sign of Harry.

I parked the car and got out. There was a kennel on one side of the patio, from which a low, sullen growl issued as I passed it. 'Evening, Meg,' I said, and the growl deepened in response.

Andrew came across the room and opened the door. 'That will *do*,' he snapped in the direction of the kennel. 'Hi. Come in.'

'Hi,' I said, passing him a bottle of wine and starting to kick off my red sneakers.

'Better bring them in; the hellhound there might chew them.'

I picked up my shoes and stepped inside, toes sinking into the brown shag-pile carpet that had impressed me so much at age eleven. It was somewhat ragged now, and faded at the tips, like the coat of an elderly brown bear. There were long uncurtained windows with brown aluminium frames around three sides of the big open-plan living area, and a kitchen against the far wall. A television, a fat beige sofa and two brown leather armchairs were grouped in one corner and a spiral staircase with concrete treads led upwards from another. It had dated badly, as ultra-fashionable interiors mostly do, and the overall effect should have been one of dreary and excessive brownness – except that it wasn't, because the stair corner was as lush and green as a rainforest. There were plants everywhere, growing in pots massed on the windowsills, on the floor, on shelves and the ends of the concrete steps.

I've never been very keen on indoor plants, partly because I kill them with such depressing regularity and partly because they remind me of waiting rooms. These, however, were no ordinary indoor plants. Among many unfamiliar exotics were orchids, palms, a whole grove of the most delectable ferns, furry-leafed begonias with flowers of every colour from white to pale green to lemon to pink to scarlet ...

'Wow,' I said.

Andrew smiled slightly and turned back towards the stove, while I went to look more closely at the miniature rainforest.

'What's this gorgeous thing that looks like a cross between a primrose and an orchid?' I asked, examining a spray of pale lemon blossom.

'It's a pansy orchid,' he said. '*Miltoniopsis*, if you want to get technical.'

'Very classy.'

'It's very easy to grow.'

'I bet it's not, under my tender care,' I said. 'Someone gave me an African violet a few months ago, and I managed to kill it stone dead in two days.'

He looked at me over his shoulder, one eyebrow raised. 'Did you sit on it?'

'No! It just turned into brown sludge before my very eyes. All I did was water it and put it down on a bookcase.'

'Botrytis, probably,' he said, prodding something in a pot with a fork. 'Fungal infection.'

'What should I have done differently?'

'I expect you overwatered it.'

'Ah.' I smiled to myself as I adjusted my mental picture of the man to include Indoor Plant Specialist.

'I also make a mean pavlova,' he said, seeing and correctly interpreting the smile.

'Mine are only average,' I said. 'But you should see me with a nit comb.'

'It's always nice to have a skill,' he said gravely.

'Hey, Jenny,' said Harry, appearing through a doorway amid the greenery with his short hair standing up in damp spikes. 'Sorry – I didn't hear you arrive. Can I get you a drink?' He hurried across the room to the fridge. 'What've we got? Beer, orange juice, milk, water ... Crap. Haven't we got any wine?'

'Only the bottle Jenny brought with her,' Andrew said, taking a pot off the stovetop and carrying it to the sink to drain.

'Right. Glass of wine, Jen?'

'Yes, please,' I said.

'Andrew? What d'you want?'

'I'm alright at the moment,' he said.

'Did the lambs behave themselves at lunchtime?' I asked as I accepted my glass, aiming to put Harry at ease with idle small talk.

It didn't work. He stared at me, horrified. 'Shit,' he said. 'I forgot all about them. I'm so sorry.'

'It's okay. They're fine.'

'Shit,' he said again.

'Honestly, don't worry about it.'

'I can't believe I forgot. Poor little buggers. Jenny, I'm really sorry.'

I smiled at him. 'It really is okay.'

'God, you must think I'm the most unreliable bastard in the world.'

'Actually,' I said, 'I was just thinking that it's really refreshing to have someone say "Sorry, I stuffed up" without any excuses or self-justification.'

Andrew gave a slightly bitter snort of laughter.

* * *

Dinner, which was cooked and served by the senior Faulkner brother, was very good. We had sausages with onion gravy, mashed potatoes and green vegetables – simple, but nicely cooked and perfectly seasoned. The quality of the conversation, however, came a poor second to the quality of the food. Harry barely spoke and Andrew, although he replied civilly to my increasingly laboured remarks, didn't seem to feel obliged to make any of his own.

'That was lovely. Thank you,' I said at last, lining up my knife and fork with meticulous care.

'You're welcome,' said Andrew.

Harry stood up and began to clear the table, and I got up to help. 'No, I'll do it,' he said. 'Sit down.'

I sat down again.

'So,' said Andrew, leaning back in his chair and stretching his long denim-clad legs out in front of him. 'Harry said you were wondering about perhaps selling some of your lambs store this season?'

I looked at him blankly.

'Selling them to someone else to finish, rather than trying to grow them all big enough to go to the works,' he explained, downgrading his estimation of my farming knowledge.

'I know, but …'

'Was it the timing you were wondering about, or the numbers, or …?'

Harry shot me an anguished look over the gravy jug he'd just picked up.

'Oh,' I said. 'Actually, I *would* really like to pick your brains about that, if you could bear it.'

Andrew nodded patiently.

'Well, according to Arnold Keller, we really need to have all the lambs gone by March. But is it better to fatten as many as possible and then sell everything that's left, or sell some early?'

'She doesn't give a rat's arse about store lambs,' Harry cut in, his voice high and strained. 'I asked her to come tonight for moral support. There's something I have to tell you.'

Andrew raised his eyebrows questioningly.

'Okay,' said Harry, taking a deep breath. He looked down at the gravy jug he was still clutching to his chest, frowned and put it down on the table. 'Okay. So.' He stopped again, closed his eyes, opened them again and said, 'I understand that this won't be easy for you to hear. If you want me to leave, that's okay. I'll understand.'

'For Christ's sake, Harry,' said his brother. 'What is it?'

'I'm gay,' said Harry.

'Oh,' said Andrew, after a short silence. 'Right.'

'I'm homosexual. I like men.'

'Yes, thank you, that's very clear.'

'Do you want me to go?'

'Er, no,' said Andrew.

There was another, longer silence.

'So – did you want to know about store lambs, or not?' Andrew asked me at last.

'Is that it?' Harry said shakily.

'What did you want me to say?' Andrew asked.

'I don't know,' muttered Harry, either not noticing or not amused by the smile lurking at the corners of his brother's mouth. It is, after all, very disconcerting to meet cheerful indifference when you were all geared up for shocked disgust. 'But – this is a big deal for me!'

'So I see,' said Andrew.

I kicked him under the table, slightly harder than I meant to, and he looked at me quizzically. I frowned at him.

'Oh, alright,' he said. 'So, er, what brought this on?'

'Being gay's not a fucking *virus*, Andrew!' Harry said.

'Would you please stop trying to cast me as a raging homophobe?' Andrew snapped. 'I meant why the big disclosure? Why now?'

Harry shrugged. 'Tired of living a lie,' he said, sinking back into his chair.

'Fair enough.'

'Did – did you never wonder?'

'No,' said Andrew, sighing. 'Can't say I did. But then apparently I have no emotional intelligence whatsoever.'

'Mm,' said Harry, displaying a fairly severe shortage of emotional intelligence himself.

'Rubbish,' I said abruptly. 'Someone with no emotional intelligence has no idea how what they say and do might affect someone else. *You*, on the other hand' – I looked sternly at Andrew – 'know perfectly well that you're being an unsympathetic bastard. You're just doing it for fun.'

Andrew raised his eyebrows a fraction.

'And that's better?' said Harry.

'Um ...' I hesitated. 'Yes.'

'How?'

'Well,' I said, groping for a workable hypothesis, 'someone who's being a bastard on purpose might always decide to be nice for a change, but the bastard who doesn't even realise it is pretty much a hopeless case.'

'So I'm a deliberate bastard rather than an unwitting one,' said Andrew. 'Thank you.'

'You're welcome.'

'Once you two have finished flirting ...' said Harry sulkily, evidently feeling that his big news was failing to receive the undivided attention it deserved.

'What?' snapped Andrew, and I jumped as if I'd been stung. Surely you should be able to try to cheer a man up a trifle without being accused of flirting. But it occurred to me uncomfortably that the brother I should be focusing on was the one who'd just taken the momentous step of coming out, and I felt my face grow warm.

'Are you going to tell Mum and Dad?' Andrew was saying.

'Yeah, I suppose so,' Harry said.

'Won't that be fun?'

'How d'you think they'll take it?'

'Pass,' Andrew said. 'I'd imagine there'll be a certain amount of wailing and hand-wringing.'

'They might surprise you,' I suggested.

'Will,' said Harry. 'Not might, but will. They're mad.'

'Mad?' I asked.

'*He* works himself up into rages about the way the world's heading and writes letters to editors, and *she* – well, she's just on another planet.'

'You'd have to be, living with him,' Andrew said. 'Purely out of self-defence.'

'True,' said Harry.

'So are you going to go down this weekend?' Andrew asked. 'Might as well, now that you're on a roll.'

'Shit, no! I'll tell them over the phone.'

Andrew stiffened in his chair. 'What?' he said. 'What if they decide to come up here?'

'And talk me out of it? Nah,' said Harry. 'They won't leave the cat.' He smiled at me.

I smiled back at him. 'Told you it'd all be okay.'

'Yeah, rub it in; go on.'

'Why didn't you tell us years ago, you twerp?' Andrew said.

'Well, you weren't around,' said Harry, rearranging the salt shaker and the gravy jug. 'I knew for sure by the time I was seventeen, I suppose, but I couldn't have told any of the guys I hung out with; I'd have been a social outcast. And then I was bloody terrified about what the neighbours would say, let alone Dad …'

'And the longer you kept it to yourself the bigger deal it all seemed,' I said.

'Mm,' said Harry.

'Chump,' Andrew told him kindly.

'We don't all have your cast-iron, unshakable self-confidence,' Harry said, and a bleak expression I thought I understood flickered across Andrew's face. Having the person who's supposed to love you best of all decide you're not worth being faithful to would shake a self-confidence of solid rock.

I wrinkled my nose at him sympathetically, and he gave me a grave little nod of acknowledgment.

'Right,' he said, getting to his feet. 'Cup of tea, anyone?'

Chapter 18

Spring arrived, spreading delicately from snowdrop to daffodil to plum blossom before exploding in the wild, exuberant flood of green that still catches me by surprise every year. A flock of twenty tuis, very beautiful but with no manners whatsoever, descended on my Pink Cloud cherry tree, and two starlings built a nest in an old motorbike helmet of Dave's that was hanging on a nail beside the back door. The pet lambs (called, by this time, Snowy, Milly, Kevin, Bob and Piglet) grew from knock-kneed babies to strapping thugs, broke into the garden and mowed a patch of sunset-coloured tulips, and my baby jacaranda tree defied all the odds and actually produced a couple of buds.

At quarter to eight one Monday morning in mid-September, I hung the last pair of knickers on the washing line and picked up the washing basket. The air smelt fresh and spicy, and beneath an old, leggy rhododendron dappled sunlight fell on a carpet of bluebells and lime-green baby ferns.

I'm happy, I thought wonderingly, and my eyes filled with tears. I'd forgotten how nice it felt. I gave myself a little shake and headed for the house, pausing only – almost only – to grub up an enormous buttercup from the middle of a clump of dwarf agapanthus.

It was eight thirty when I got to Dave's place to pick up the kids, and Lily came out onto the porch as I got out of the car. 'You're late,' she said.

I ran up the steps and kissed the top of her head. 'I know. Sorry. I was weeding.'

Lily smiled with tolerant scorn. 'She was weeding,' she called back towards the house. '*As* usual.' She slipped a hand into mine. 'Guess what?'

'What?' I asked as we reached the door.

'Daddy's got a new girlfriend.'

'Oh,' I said stupidly.

'She's beautiful,' Lily added, looking at me sideways. 'And she smells nice.'

I was somewhat taken aback, less at the thought of the beautiful girlfriend than by the realisation that my seven-year-old daughter was trying quite deliberately to upset me, just to see how I'd react. 'Lucky Dad,' I said dryly.

'Don't be like that,' said Dave, crossing the living room towards us.

'I'm not being like anything,' I said, which, although true, was a stupid way of putting it. Some phrases come out defensive no matter how they're intended. I took a deep breath, and Lily looked at me expectantly.

'Lily, go and get your bag,' I told her. 'Morning, Nathan!'

'Hi, Mum,' said Nathan, who was sitting up at the breakfast bar, drawing something with a ballpoint pen.

'Get your bag, love, we're running late.'

'*You're* running late,' Dave corrected.

'True. And getting later by the second.'

'Easy, now, Jen. Settle down, eh?'

'Oh, stop trying to wind me up,' I said crossly.

He grinned. 'But it's so much fun.'

'Did you have a nice weekend?' I asked, making a face at him.

'Wonderful,' he said. 'As always.'

'It's such a beautiful time of year.'

'You say that about every time of year,' he pointed out.

'Isn't it lucky I have such a sunny, optimistic nature? Nathan, my petal, go and get your bag now.'

'We went to the beach,' Lily told me as Nathan slid off his stool and trailed off reluctantly down the hall. 'Me and Anaya made a big sandcastle.'

'Anaya,' I repeated. 'That's a pretty name.'

'It's Indian,' Dave told me. 'She's not Indian; her parents are Irish, actually, but they were aid workers for years in India and Pakistan.'

I nodded, a vision of a Sienna Miller-esque, boho-chic beauty with a lilting Irish accent arriving ready-made in my head.

'She's great with the kids.'

So was Sienna. She was Jude Law's nanny, wasn't she? 'That's good.'

'I hear you're getting pretty friendly with your new worker.'

No, I had that wrong; Jude *cheated* on Sienna *with* the nanny. 'Hmm?' I said.

'Harry,' Lily supplied.

'Lily, go and get your bag!' I snapped.

'But I want to hear what you're saying!'

'One,' I said menacingly. 'Two ...'

Lily fled.

'Shagging him?' Dave asked.

I smiled and shook my head.

'Why not?'

'Don't want to.'

'Might do you good,' he said provocatively.

I laughed in genuine amusement. 'Dave, give it up.'

* * *

Dropping Lily at school, Nathan and I sped home and thence to the ridge paddock, where Dad and Harry were drafting lambs off a mob of ewes up the portable race. John Mercer, wearing his orange bobble hat and a pair of overalls two sizes too big for him, was laboriously folding up the scrim that had been used as a makeshift barrier to funnel sheep into the docking yard.

'You can leave that, John,' Harry called, looking back over his shoulder. 'We'll need it for the next mob.'

John ignored him and kept folding. 'Good morning, young fella,' he said to Nathan. 'Helping out today, are you?'

'No,' said Nathan, not unkindly. 'I'm going to play. I'm only little.'

'So you are. My mistake.' He broke into a coughing fit, hunched over the pile of scrim.

'That doesn't sound very healthy,' I said.

John flapped a hand at me. 'Fine,' he gasped when he could speak again. 'Nothing to fuss about.'

It was a bright, cold, gusty day. The ranges to the south stood out sharp and clear, and John's too-big overalls snapped and billowed in the wind. I like docking – in these days when your silage is made by a contractor with a two-hundred-horsepower tractor and the shearers bring their own pressers and shed hands, it's almost the only all-pitch-in-and-work-together job left.

'Andrew's got some nice-sized lambs up there by the reserve,' Dad said to Harry as he adjusted the flame on the gas tail-docking iron. 'What are they, Suffolk cross?'

'No, one of those new composite breeds. Primera, I think.'

'Ugly, spotty things. Give me a Romney any time,' said John, staggering across the pen with a twenty-kilogram lamb – by far the biggest in the pen – in his arms.

'Who cares what they look like? They grow like weeds,' Harry said.

Ignoring him, John manhandled the lamb into the docking cradle, although not before it slammed its head back into his chin.

'Hang on, John,' Dad said. 'You vaccinate – the younger ones can pick up.'

'I can manage,' said John, stiffly and untruthfully, and broke into a coughing fit.

'I think you'd be better off at home in bed, John,' said Dad.

'No, no,' said John manfully, throwing back his shoulders and bearing down on the second-biggest lamb in the pen.

'You're a stubborn and difficult old man,' I told him, heading him off. 'Think how inconvenient it will be for the rest of us if you overdo it and pass out.'

John patted my shoulder. 'None of your lip, missy,' he said fondly.

Harry made throwing-up gestures behind his back.

We settled into a routine fairly quickly – Dad castrating and cutting tails, Harry and I picking up and earmarking, John vaccinating and getting in our way, and Nathan directing operations.

'Get *that* one, Mummy,' he ordered from across the lamb pen. 'No, the *other* one. *Beside* that one.'

'You catch him,' I said, 'and I'll pick him up next. You know, guys, I think the lambs look pretty good, considering how light the ewes were at scanning.'

'They do,' Dad agreed, releasing a small woolly victim onto the ground, where it bolted, yelling at the top of its voice, into the anxious knot of ewes waiting a few metres away.

'They always look good at docking,' said Harry. 'It'll be next month, when they're competing with the ewes for grass, that you'll notice them falling behind.'

'Thanks for that happy thought,' I said.

He smiled. 'Any time. You know me; every silver lining has its cloud.'

'We'll need to dock those lambs of mine at the cottage, too,' said John. 'They're a bonny pair, I must say.'

'That's good,' I said.

'Five feeds a day; that's the secret. And a little bit of crushed garlic in their bottles.'

'To keep the vampires away?' Harry said.

Dad and I laughed, but John did not.

* * *

I was helping Lily with her maths homework later that afternoon – an ongoing struggle in which I tried to make her work it out for herself and she tried to make me do it for her – when the phone rang.

'I'll get it!' she cried, leaping from her chair to pick it up. 'Hello, Lily Reynolds speaking.' There was a pause, and then she said, 'No, I'm afraid she's not available right now.'

I turned in my chair and skewered her with a disapproving glare. Sighing, she handed me the phone.

'Hello?' I said.

'Oh, er, hi, it's Andrew here. Faulkner. Sorry to disturb you. I was wondering if you've got a spare vaccinating gun I could use tomorrow. Mine's just bitten the dust.'

'Yes, no problem,' I said. 'I've got a whole boxful. Come down and grab a few, if you like.'

'Cheers. I'll be down shortly.' And he hung up.

I turned back towards the table, where Lily was now lying full-length, like the effigy on a medieval tomb. 'Lil, what did you mean by saying I wasn't available?'

'You were helping me,' she said.

'Next time, how about you ask me first?'

'Okay,' she said serenely, closing her eyes.

'It's going to be hard to do maths with your eyes shut,' I remarked.

She waved a languid hand. 'You can read the questions out to me.'

'Lily Amelia Reynolds,' I said in my by-God-my-girl-you've-pushed-me-far-enough voice. 'Get your bottom onto this chair im*med*iately!'

After which, pausing only to banish Nathan, who had decided to be a cruise missile launcher underneath the table, we finished the maths worksheet in record time and went out into the mellow evening sunshine.

We found Nathan in the orchard, lying on his back under a pink-tipped apple tree. His lamb Bob, perhaps the most placid and long-suffering ovine of all time, was sitting beside him with its legs neatly folded and its eyes half shut.

'We need to practise leading,' Lily announced.

'In the paddock, please, not in the garden,' I said.

They headed obediently for the gate, Tessa following as overseer, and I began unravelling clover out of a miniature hosta. Weeding clover is beautifully therapeutic – the stems pull off the soil as if they're fastened by rows of tiny domes – and I was reflecting that as a mindfulness exercise it beat adult colouring books hands down when I heard Andrew's ute come down the driveway and pull up in front of the carport. I stood up, dusted my earthy hands on the legs of my jeans, and went around the side of the house to see him standing on the lawn, admiring two fat wood pigeons who were sitting in a seedling kowhai tree, bending it nearly double.

'They've already stripped my plum tree,' I remarked, watching the larger pigeon stretch his neck to reach a shoot, lose his balance and flap clumsily back upright, breaking the spindly branch he was sitting on.

Andrew smiled. 'I'd rather have pigeons than plums,' he said.

'Me too. But still.'

'Your garden's lovely.'

'Thanks!' I said. 'Come and look at my pleiones – I'm very proud of them.' I led him around the corner to a little patch of lavender orchids – five centimetres high and with a single, neatly pleated leaf apiece – that were grouped fetchingly at the base of a flowering cherry. 'Don't they look classy?'

'Yes,' he said obediently. 'Very classy.'

I cast around for another remark. 'Oh, I never thanked you for getting Arnold Keller to take us on.'

He looked puzzled. 'All I did was give you his number.'

'Really? He said his diary was chock-a-block, but you'd asked him specially to fit us in.'

'I think that might just be the sort of thing advisers say, so they sound busy and important.'

'Very likely,' I said. 'Oh well, his advice seems to be pretty good, even if he's a bit of an egg.'

Andrew smiled, and the tired lines around his mouth vanished, making him look about ten years younger and more like Bruce Springsteen than ever. 'He'd be crushed to hear you say that. He thinks you're lovely, he told me.'

'*Me*? He can't even remember my name!'

'I don't think it's your name he's interested in,' he said.

There was a brief, mutually embarrassed silence.

'How's your docking going?' I asked hastily and at random. Andrew, being short on staff or unoccupied family members, hired a gang to help him dock.

'Pretty well. Should finish tomorrow.'

'Man, you're efficient,' I said.

'Hmm? Not really. Sorry, I was just remembering that my parents have threatened to come and stay this weekend.'

'Are they honestly that bad?' I asked.

'No, of course they're not. They're just hard work. You need to be feeling mentally strong.'

'Aren't you?'

'Not particularly.'

'It comes in waves, doesn't it?' I said. 'You feel like you're getting on top of it, and then all of a sudden you're not.'

'I shouldn't have told you,' he said abruptly.

I looked at him, startled.

'When I found them together. I don't know why I thought you needed to know.'

'I'm glad you told me,' I said.

'It would have blown over. And ignorance is bliss, right?'

'No,' I said, a hot, painful lump forming in the back of my throat. 'It was simpler before, maybe, but it sure wasn't bliss.'

He looked at me for a moment, and then put an arm around my shoulders in a brief, wholly unexpected hug.

'Don't be all nice and sympathetic,' I said shakily, absurdly touched. 'Or I'll cry, and nobody wants that.'

'Shit, no,' he said.

'How are *you* doing, anyway?'

'Fine.'

I looked at him sceptically.

He sighed. 'I'm more worried about losing my farm than losing my wife, to be honest.'

'You'll have to pay her out,' I said slowly, thinking about it for the first time. Which would mean that half of the debt-free bit of his farm would then belong to the bank. Which would increase his interest repayments. And if your interest repayments are larger than your income, that's a problem that no amount of fancy accounting can fix. 'Oh, Andrew.'

'It's not hopeless. She's said she'll leave her money in for two years, anyway.'

'Big of her,' I said.

He smiled faintly. 'It's better than I expected.'

'We might be selling up, too,' I said, surprising myself.

He looked at me quickly. 'I'm sorry.'

'The plan was always that my sister and I would inherit half the farm each, some day. And by the time that happened, Dave and I would have saved up enough to buy her out. But it doesn't work so well without him. We end up paying a manager, or if I stop work to farm full-time we lose my salary – and that's assuming I'd be any use whatsoever as a farmer ...' My throat lump began to swell again, and I swallowed desperately.

'You love this place a lot, don't you?' he said.

'Yes.' I looked across the garden, shadowy and mysterious in the fading light, to where Lily was piggybacking Nathan back up through the orchard. They were making very slow progress; they'd gone giggly, and they were collapsing every few steps and falling over in a tangle of arms and legs. In the paddock below them the pet lambs, released from leading class, raced across the hillside in a mad twilight game of tag. The air was soft and golden and full of the clamour of birds settling down for the night. 'Well, look at it. Who wouldn't?'

'Indeed,' he said.

'Anyway, that's enough whingeing at you, when you're going through exactly the same thing,' I said, pulling myself together.

'You're not whingeing. And I haven't lived here all my life.'

'But on the other hand you bought your farm yourself, rather than getting to live here because of Mummy and Daddy.'

'Good point,' he said, smiling. 'Pull yourself together, princess.'

I made a face at him. 'Careful, or I'll change my mind about that vaccinating gun.'

Chapter 19

The next morning John arrived in the pig paddock (named for the big black pig that, seventy years before, had met Great-Granddad unexpectedly in the fern and chased him up a tree) on foot, wheezing.

'John!' I said in alarm. 'What are you doing here?'

'Give you – a hand,' he rasped.

'You should be in bed!'

'Nonsense,' he said, clinging to a gate.

Dad, who was tying a length of netting to the fence to stop lambs getting through, looked up, frowned, and said, 'Jenny, ring the doctor and make him an appointment, will you?'

'Nons–' John started, and then fell into a coughing fit instead.

'Actually, ring your mother first and ask her to *take* him to the appointment.'

I nodded, already dialling.

Mum arrived at the woolshed fifteen minutes later, and Nathan and I bore a feebly protesting John up the hill to meet her.

'Your appointment's at ten,' she told him as I stopped the four-wheeler beside her car and turned it off.

'Waste of everybody's time,' John muttered, climbing laboriously off the back.

'Can I come with you, Nana?' asked Nathan.

'Of course, my love,' Mum said. 'You can help me stop Mr Mercer from running away.'

'His car seat's in the back of my car. It's not locked,' I told her.

'I'm not worth all this fuss,' said John. 'An old codger like me ...' Lifting a shaking hand, he wiped away a tear.

I had been reflecting with some annoyance that if the silly old fool wouldn't try to be such a bloody hero it would save everyone a lot of time and effort, but at this I leant forward and kissed his sandpapery cheek. 'No,' I said gently. 'I can't think why we bother.'

'God, he's a pain,' Harry remarked as I climbed back over the side of the docking pen.

'He just wants to be a part of things,' I said. As, let's face it, do we all.

'You do realise that the nicer you are to him, the tighter he'll cling?'

I sighed. 'Yes.'

'You are such a soft touch,' said the man who spent at least one evening a week regaling me with the ongoing saga of How Chris Is Breaking My Heart.

'Yes,' I said, a little sourly. 'I know.'

* * *

Mum, wonderful woman, kept Nathan for the day. The rest of us docked steadily, with one small break for a cup of tea and a cheese scone, until ten to three, when I left Dad and Harry pulling down the portable yards and flew down the hill to pick up Lily from school.

'So you weren't working today?' Amy Wallace said as I ran across the road to join the little group of parents at the school gate.

I looked down at my filthy shirt, spotted copiously with blood from the ear markers. 'It *felt* like work,' I said.

'I mean, you obviously weren't working in town at the council,' she said. She tittered. 'At least, I hope you weren't.'

'Oh, I often get home from council looking like this. I get really upset when people don't comply with the Building Code.'

'Jenny, you're *such* a dag,' she said. Then, looking at me sideways, 'Oh, that reminds me – the Pet Day Committee has asked Dave to be the steward for the lambs. Your Dave. I mean, *not* your Dave. Oh, *you* know what I mean.' She bit her lip. 'Is that okay?'

'Yes, of course,' I said.

'It won't be too hard for you?'

I wondered why it should be – and indeed why, if she was so concerned, she hadn't asked me *before* appointing him. But I shook my head and smiled.

'You're so strong, Jenny. I don't know *how* you do it.'

There would come a day, I thought, when I would smile sweetly at this woman and say, 'Shut up, you twat.' But perhaps not this day.

* * *

On the way home, Lily and I called in at Mum and Dad's to pick up Nathan. We found him lying on his back on the sofa, playing a game on Mum's cell phone. 'Hi, small person,' I said. 'Where's Grandma?'

'Outside,' said Nathan.

'Can I have a turn?' Lily asked, sitting down beside him.

Unusually, he smiled and handed her the phone. Even more unusually, she bent and hugged him. Feeling quite dazed by all this loving kindness, I let myself out the patio door and went to find my mother.

I found her pruning dead wood out of a Judas tree outside the bathroom window, armed with a pair of loppers and wearing an enormous, lopsided straw hat. 'Hello, love,' she said, pushing back her hair with a rubber-gloved hand.

'Hi. Thanks so much for having Nathan.'

'Oh, he's been very good.'

'And how was John?' I asked.

'Pleurisy and bronchitis,' Mum said. 'Dr Singh put him straight onto antibiotics.'

'Gosh,' I said, duly impressed. Dr Singh prescribed garlic, ginger, less white bread and more whole grains for almost everything. If she put you on antibiotics, by God you needed them.

'And I popped into the supermarket to stock him up on soup and some nice buns and things. Poor old thing.'

'Mum, you're a star.'

'Perhaps you could call in and see him. He seems very fond of you, Jenny.'

'I know,' I said, sighing. 'Yes, alright.'

Emerging from among the branches, she took off her hat and dropped it on a pile of prunings. 'Jenny, love ...'

'Mm?'

'Are you and Harry ...?'

I laughed. *Thank you, John.* 'No.'

'He's a nice, nice boy, but ...'

'He comes and has tea with us once a week when his brother's playing squash and tells me his troubles,' I said. 'The kids really like him. I think he sees me as an honorary aunt.'

Mum looked doubtful. 'It's a shorter step than you think from telling someone your troubles to falling for them,' she said.

'Mum, Harry's gay.'

'Gay?' she repeated blankly.

'Don't tell anyone, will you? He'd hate to have the whole district talking about it.'

'Oh,' said Mum. 'Of course I won't say a word.'

'Why the enthusiasm to keep me single, anyway?' I asked. 'It would actually be kind of nice to find someone, one day.'

'Well – now, don't eat me, Jenny; you know I only want you to be happy – I can't help wishing that maybe, someday, you and David ...'

'Mum,' I said gently, 'I think that ship has sailed.'

'He still loves you. He's told me so. Are you sure you wouldn't ...?'

'He's got a new girlfriend.'

'*What?*' she said. 'Who?'

'She's called Anaya. She's Irish. I haven't seen her, but he's introduced her to the kids.'

'But ...' said Mum, and stopped.

'And it turns out he didn't just have one piddly little affair. He cheated on me for years.'

Poor Mum looked as if I'd hit her over the head. 'But – but why didn't you –'

'Leave him earlier? I didn't *know*. A woman came up to me in the pub one night after work a few months ago and congratulated me for getting rid of him. She said she'd slept with him – she didn't know he was married – and that she wasn't the only one.' I looked at my hands. 'And Ange Miller said she'd heard rumours. I feel like such a fool, Mum. I had no idea.'

'Are you sure, love? This woman wasn't just making mischief?'

'No, he admitted it. But apparently it's my fault, for not being nice enough to him.'

'Oh, baby,' Mum whispered, putting her arms around me. And, thus encouraged, I succumbed to a combination of tiredness, loneliness and humiliation, laid my head on her shoulder and cried.

Chapter 20

On Tuesday, 18 October, the morning of the Pukewai School Pet Day, I was woken at dawn by Lily knocking on my bedroom window. 'Mum!' she called. 'Mum, wake up! Strawberry has poo on her legs!'

Getting up, I shuffled to the open window in time to see Lily's lamb Strawberry (formerly known as Milly, formerly known as Amelia), with the air of a connoisseur, select and bite off a creamy yellow freesia. 'Lily, please get her out of the garden,' I said.

'Can you come and help me clean her?'

Strawberry swallowed another freesia and looked speculatively at a pink dwarf alstroemeria.

'It's only quarter past six,' I protested. 'We don't have to be down at school until nine thirty.'

'*Please*, Mum!'

'Oh, alright. But take her *out of my garden*!'

Dave arrived, as per arrangement, at nine twenty. The picnic lunch was packed, Nathan was wearing both gumboots *and* his sunhat, and ten minutes' work with a damp flannel had restored Strawberry to a respectable, if not a pristine, state.

'Morning, all!' Dave said cheerfully, getting out of his ute. 'Ready to go?'

'We've got chippies!' Nathan shouted.

'Awesome. Where's Mum?'

'Here,' I said, straightening from the corner of the carport where I had been tying up Tessa. She gave me one long look of heartbreak and betrayal, turned her back on me and crawled into her basket.

It was a lovely day – still crisp, but promising to be hot later on. We arrived down at the school field to find it already ringed with vehicles. Two young men from the ANZ were setting up a barbecue over by the judging rings and several parents were wrestling with the school marquee, an enormous canvas structure with iron poles, circa 1950, that was guaranteed to crush the fingers of anyone foolish enough to try to tackle it.

Dave took the children off to register and, in a cowardly bid to avoid the Finger-crushing Marquee of Doom, I went to help Paul Denny carry a picnic table to the spot where old Mrs Ellison had sat in state, writing down each child's score, for about the last forty years.

Mrs Ellison was tiny – the type of little old lady who seems to be made of crepe paper stretched over chicken bones. She wore a very fetching straw hat with a pink ribbon and an enormous pair of fit-over sunglasses, and she smiled at us graciously as she took her seat. 'Paul, might I trouble you for a jug of water?' she asked. Then to me, as he went to get it, 'Now, dear, who are my judges today?'

I had no idea, not having been on the organising committee, but I looked around obediently for white coats. I saw one on a grey-haired woman over by the barbecue, and – oh, good *God*, that was Andrew Faulkner stalking across the field, wearing another. Perhaps, I thought without much hope, he was judging the calves.

'Could you ask them to step over and see me?' Mrs Ellison asked.

Andrew was the closest, talking to Lily's teacher in the middle of the field. 'Just remember to speak up,' she was telling him as I approached. 'They get so excited; they won't listen to your instructions unless you bellow ... Oh, hello, Jenny.'

'Hi, guys,' I said. 'Are you judging today, Andrew?'

He looked down glumly at his cheap nylon lab coat. It was about two sizes too small for him, and the sleeves stopped mid-forearm. 'So it would seem,' he said.

'Mrs Ellison would like to see you, please. The little lady over there in the big hat.'

'Alright.'

'She adds up the scores,' Sonia told him. 'Her eyesight's not what it was, so make sure you write nice and clearly, won't you?'

Andrew nodded stiffly and headed off across the grass.

'Man of few words, isn't he?' Sonia remarked.

'He is indeed,' I said. 'Is he judging the lambs or the calves?'

'Lambs. Ruth Kaye was going to do it, but her mother's just had a fall and broken her hip.' I must have looked as appalled as I felt, because she added reprovingly, 'I'm sure he'll do just fine, Jenny. We were lucky to get him.'

'What? No, it's – Sonia, they've asked Dave to be the lamb steward!'

Sonia looked blank for a moment, and then laughed. 'Won't *that* be fun?' she said.

'No!'

'They're both adults. I'm sure they'll manage.'

'I'm sure they will,' I said. Big, public, nostril-flaring showdowns, although common in soap operas, are rare in real life. But it would be uncomfortable, and there would be a quiet undercurrent of amusement among the spectators, and – and … Forgetting all about the other judge, I went to find Dave.

He was lifting Lily's lamb out of the pen. 'Right, hold tight to her, Lil,' he said. 'We don't want to be chasing her all over the paddock.'

'She's a *good* lamb, Daddy,' Lily protested. 'She loves me, don't you, Strawberry?'

Strawberry reached out and plucked a blade of grass, looking supremely uninterested in Lily or anyone else.

'Do you want your lamb, Nath?' Dave asked as Lily and Strawberry headed for a cluster of other little girls.

'No,' said Nathan, who, although quite fond of his lamb, had the attention span of a goldfish. 'There's Nana and Granddad!' And he darted away to meet them, leaving his hat at our feet.

'Hey, um, apparently Andrew Faulkner's judging the lambs,' I said to Dave, stooping to pick it up. 'Want me to be steward instead?'

'Why? Think he'll take a swing?' said Dave sardonically.

'No, it's just … awkward.'

'Nah. He can put up with it. Screw him.'

'No, that was his wife,' I said icily, before I thought.

'Why are you so concerned about Andrew fucking Faulkner?' Dave snapped.

'I'm not! But you're acting like *he's* shafted *you*!'

He turned on his heel and walked away.

* * *

The day, after this unpromising beginning, did improve somewhat. There was the list of registered lambs and calves in the program, always good for a laugh – this year's highlights were Maybelline, Rogue Warrior and Dennis. Dennis was a small, pot-bellied lamb with dags, accompanied by an equally small and pot-bellied child in a sagging disposable nappy, but the two of them obviously loved each other to distraction. And then Lily, due more to good luck than dedicated lamb training, came second in calling and first in leading, and my friend Ange arrived to man the bank-sponsored barbecue.

I was watching the preschoolers with lambs receive their little rosettes for participation – Nathan looked mildly pleased, but Dennis's handler in the low-slung nappy was radiant with delight – when Ange said beside me, 'I've been giving Dave the stink eye. It's good fun.'

I turned and hugged her – cautiously, because she was almost entirely circular. 'Thank you; you're a true friend. Surely it's above and beyond the call of duty for you to be cooking sausages when you're about to go into labour?'

'I'm not due for a whole week,' she said, absent-mindedly rubbing the small of her back. 'Besides, I'm the only one at the bank with a current sausage-sizzling certificate.'

'Well, we'll all sleep sounder knowing our sausages were cooked by someone with a valid certificate. Would you like a seat?'

Ange looked with distaste at the unoccupied camping chair nearby. 'No, I'd never get up again. Who's your man in the white coat who looks like Mr Darcy?'

'That,' I said, watching Dave and Andrew pin ribbons to collars, each of them pretending the other wasn't there, 'is Andrew Faulkner, whose wife and Dave …'

'Ah,' she said. 'Hi, Lorraine, how are you?' And as Mum joined us, the talk turned exclusively to babies.

Ange returned to the barbecue for the lunchtime rush, and I caught up with several neighbours, including, sadly, Amy Wallace. She told me in wearying detail about the family tree she was researching, asked me if the pretty girl – 'Early twenties at the *most*, Jenny' – she'd seen with Dave in the supermarket last week was his new 'lady friend' (she put in the inverted commas with her fingers) and threatened to introduce me to her brother, who was single and *just* my type.

It was after one by the time I escaped. I returned Lily's lamb, given to me to hold while she applied herself to sausages and poisonous-looking soft drink, to its makeshift pen and made my way rather wearily back towards the marquee, where people were beginning to gather for the final prize giving and inevitable speech from the chairman of the school board of trustees. Nathan, hatless yet again and badly in need of a hanky, was lying on his side at Dad's feet, sucking his thumb.

'Here you go, chicken,' I said, crouching down beside him and applying a tissue.

'Don't,' said Nathan crossly, turning his head away.

'Sorry. But you can't go around with snot all over your face.'

'Why not?'

'It's just not a good look.'

'Can we go home now?' he asked.

'Pretty soon.' Gathering him up I got to my feet, settling him on my hip. He rested his head against my shoulder and I rubbed my cheek on the top of his curly head.

'*Poor* little man,' said Amy, coming past with a chocolate cake wrapped in cling film. It was lavishly studded with Smarties, whose colour, in the heat, had leached into the surrounding icing in lurid streaks. She held it out to Andrew, frowning at his phone a few paces away, and said, 'The committee would like to thank you *so* much for all your help today. Especially' – she lowered her voice – 'under, um, *trying* conditions.'

Andrew looked up, still frowning, and then blinked and put his phone back in his pocket. 'Thanks,' he said, grasping the cake just after Amy let it go.

Amy gave a little cry of dismay as it fell face down onto the grass between them.

'Sorry,' he muttered, bending to pick it up and freezing suddenly with a little grunt of pain.

'It'll still taste just as good,' said Dad cheerfully.

'I thought you were holding it,' Amy wailed.

Andrew straightened slowly and stiffly, flattened cake in hand.

'Oh, have you hurt your back?' she cried.

'It's fine,' he said between his teeth.

'Well, a big, yummy piece of cake is sure to make it feel better.'

He gave her a faint, cold smile.

'I suppose you don't get a lot of cake these days,' she added sympathetically.

He didn't answer that, but just waited, with no expression on his face whatsoever, for her to leave.

Even Amy was quelled by this. 'Well, thanks again for helping us out at such short notice,' she said, retreating across the field.

'Ghastly woman,' said Dad as we watched her go.

'You ready to leave, Jen?' Dave called, coming around the corner of the marquee.

'We'd better stay for prize giving, hadn't we?' I said, surprised. During our years together I couldn't remember Dave ever wanting to leave *anything* early. 'I think Lily might get the cup for best junior lamb.'

'She can get it tomorrow. Nathan's shattered.' He reached out his hands, and Nathan leant obligingly out of my arms. 'Aren't you, little man?'

'Yes,' said Nathan sleepily, nestling into Dave's neck, and I felt a pang of most unreasonable jealousy. It would be awful if Dave didn't love the children and they didn't love him. Really, really awful. But ...

'Well, then, you take him and the lambs now, and Lily and I can hitch a ride with Mum and Dad,' I said. 'Is that okay, Dad?'

'Hmm? Yes, I – actually, no. Your mother's organised afternoon tea or something at Merv and Lou Carroll's after this. Sorry.'

'Can we go now?' Nathan said plaintively, taking his thumb out of his mouth to speak and then immediately plugging it back in again.

Personally I was all for this idea, but looking at the cluster of little girls sitting expectantly in front of the marquee, I said, 'Lily will be really disappointed.'

'She'll live,' said Dave shortly.

'Why not ask Andrew to take you home? It's on his way,' Dad said.

Andrew had retreated several metres and taken his phone out again. I hesitated for a moment – his back looked forbidding, somehow – and then saw the look on Dave's face. It would be silly not to ask Andrew to drop us off. He was passing our mailbox. And the chance to piss Dave off was in *no way* a deciding factor. It was merely a – a happy accident.

'Andrew?' I said. 'Would you mind giving Lily and me a lift home after prize giving?'

He gave me exactly the same look he'd given Amy Wallace. 'What? No, sorry, I'm leaving now,' he said. And, cake in one hand and phone in the other, he turned and strode off across the field.

I suppose it was poetic justice, of a sort. It's not very noble to take pleasure in annoying your ex-husband. But the amused satisfaction on Dave's face when I turned back towards him was almost unbearable.

Chapter 21

We weren't going to break even this year. I'd done a budget, after a lengthy struggle with my accounting software – a struggle made even less enjoyable by the sick, guilty feeling that I shouldn't have been struggling at all. Preparing a budget should have been a familiar, routine task, part of that strategic planning which is so fundamental to success in business but which I tended so often to put off until some nebulous future date.

Anyway, the budget was done, and no matter how optimistic I was about lamb prices, and how much I shaved off repairs and maintenance, we couldn't afford to put on fertiliser. Which would have been alright, perhaps, if it was a one-off – but we hadn't put on fertiliser last year either. And even I knew that saving money at the expense of growing grass really, *really* wasn't the road to profitability.

Dad and I had an appointment with the bank manager at one o'clock on Monday of the week after Pet Day. Not Ange, who had spent Friday producing baby number three. I was relieved, on the whole – it was always a pleasure to see her, but I preferred to ask someone other than a good friend for money.

Ange's stand-in was young and hearty, with very red cheeks. He shook hands so firmly that it hurt, and we sat down around the table in a glass-walled meeting room. He read my budget, drumming his fingertips on the pale wooden tabletop, looked up and said, 'Are you drawing any income from the farm, Jenny?'

'No,' I said. 'Well, that's not entirely true. I don't pay any rent, and the farm pays my power bill.'

'And you and Lorraine are drawing three thousand dollars a month, Brian?'

'We could get by with less,' Dad said.

He dismissed this with a shake of his head. 'So you'd like to extend your loan by one hundred and twenty thousand dollars.'

'Yes, please,' I said. 'Fifty thousand for fertiliser, and another fifty thousand for cattle. Friesian bulls, probably – they'll be the cheapest. It would just make the system a bit more flexible. With the dairy grazers you're locked in; you can't sell some in January if there's a drought. And then the other twenty thousand is just to give us a bit more of a buffer, so we're not right at the edge of the overdraft.'

He drummed his fingers a little more. It was quite hypnotic. 'I can't see why that would be a problem.'

'Thank you.'

He looked up and smiled. 'This is standard stuff. Your loan's well secured. But I see that you've budgeted to end this financial year thirty thousand further in debt than you were at the start.'

'We've done a lot of things wrong this year,' I said. 'We haven't got as many lambs, and we've had to send some calves home because we were short on feed, so income from grazing is down – but we plan to manage better next year. We've got a farm adviser helping us out.'

'You'll still be paying a manager to run the farm?'

'At this stage.'

'So the bulk of your income goes towards his salary.'

Neither Dad nor I replied.

'Have you considered how sustainable that is, long term?'

There was a pause, then Dad said slowly, 'In other words, have we considered how long we want to keep farming as a hobby rather than a source of income?'

The bank manager said nothing, the better to let Dad's words sink in. Irritation at this technique mingled in my breast with admiration of its effectiveness.

'We should be able to do a lot better than we're doing at the moment,' I said finally, when the silence became unbearable. 'We need to grow our lambs better, and we could look at intensive bull-beef ... Perhaps I should think about leaving my job and doing a lot more on the farm.'

'Do you really want to do that, Jenny?' Dad asked. 'Or do you feel you should?'

'Both ...' I said.

* * *

Mum was ironing when we got home. She routinely ironed every bit of clean washing as she folded it, down to knickers and fitted sheets. I could only assume it did for her what weeding clover did for me.

'Where's Nathan?' I asked, kicking off my shoes at the patio door and going inside. The kitchen smelt of clean, hot cotton and sweet peas from a jug on the counter.

'Asleep, bless him,' she said. 'How was your meeting?'

'Fine,' said Dad heavily, dropping the car keys into the wooden bowl beside the phone. 'They've extended the overdraft.'

Mum finished a pillowcase, laid it aside and reached for another one. 'Brian, what is it?' she asked.

'Oh, nothing we didn't already know,' Dad said. 'The farm pays a manager's salary and bugger-all else, and the bank manager just wondered how soon we were going to get sick of doing it for nothing.'

I leant against the edge of the dining room table. 'Do you want to sell up?' I asked.

Mum and Dad both looked at me. 'Jenny, love ...' said Mum.

'I do realise that something has to change. And if I lease the farm again – even if I can figure out how to actually run it at a profit, which is anything but certain – that won't give you guys enough money to travel, or Bex enough for her dream home.'

'We've never expected to sell the farm to fund our retirement,' Dad said. 'And we don't need to. We can afford the odd overseas trip, and we don't have any desire to retire to a mansion at the beach.'

Mum spread one of Dad's work shirts on the ironing board, a strange little smile on her face.

'Mum, what do *you* want?' I asked suddenly.

The iron stilled. 'I'd like a new house one day,' she said. 'Something smaller, that we could actually keep warm in winter. This house has never felt like mine.'

'It hasn't?' Dad said blankly.

'It's like a shrine to your mother, Brian. "Mum planted that rhodo; you can't cut it down."'

'*What* rhodo?'

'That hideous red thing outside our bedroom window.'

There was a slightly puzzled silence before Dad said, 'The one you cut down twenty years ago?'

'And you're still holding it against me!'

'I am not!'

'Anyway, that's beside the point,' Mum said, as indeed it was. 'What really matters is that you and Rebecca are happy.'

'Well, whatever decision you make only pleases one of us,' I said. 'So you might as well take our happiness out of the equation.'

'Do you *want* to run the farm, Jenny?' Dad asked.

All that responsibility. All those big, expensive decisions that make the difference between sinking and swimming, and that just aren't as obvious as you'd think. Fertiliser, crops, when and what to buy and sell. Having, finally, to pull myself together and learn how to work the bale feeder. Nutrient budgeting, Healthy Rivers, OSH and ACC and NAIT and many, many other depressing acronyms, each of them with their attendant costs and soul-eroding paperwork ...

'I don't know,' I said, looking down at my hands. 'It's a pretty intimidating thought. I suppose what I *really* want is to be married to a farmer, so he can have the responsibility while I get the lifestyle. But I've already had my chance at that and stuffed it up.'

'*You* didn't stuff it up,' said Mum, with a most refreshing change of perspective.

'You could do it,' Dad said. 'You're highly intelligent – much cleverer than your old man.'

'Rubbish,' I said, smiling at him.

'The question isn't whether you're competent. It's whether you want to do it. It's a full-time, physical job with pretty bloody mediocre returns. And it's lonely, working by yourself all day.'

I *didn't* really want to. I wished I did; I greatly admired those women who could fence and shear and back large trailers. I should have been one of them already; I shouldn't have just left the practical farming to Dave. Well, there was no point wasting time and energy in self-reproach. It wasn't too late to learn; I was reasonably smart and fairly fit, and I should at least try to step up, rather than just gazing misty-eyed over the ancestral acres and wishing things would magically sort themselves out. (Misty-eyed hope is, of course, a very tempting approach to problem solving – it's so much easier than action. The only real drawback is that it *doesn't work*.)

'Could you give me another year?' I asked. 'To – to have a decent crack at it, rather than just drifting along like we are now? I know Bex'll be disappointed ...'

'She'll live,' said Dad. 'There's no need to rush into any major decisions now. Arnold Keller's coming next week, isn't he? Perhaps he'll have some suggestions.'

'Rebecca's coming up next week as well,' Mum said. 'She's not been feeling very well, and Sean's going to Sydney.'

'She'll have some suggestions, too,' I said, sighing. 'Right, I'd better go and pick Lily up from school. Can I leave Nathan here for another quarter of an hour, Mum?'

'Yes, of course, love,' she said.

* * *

Rebecca and Caleb flew into Hamilton airport on Sunday afternoon, and that evening – a soft, fragrant evening with a most picturesque dusting of tiny apricot clouds in a pink and blue sky – she appeared suddenly around the corner of the house, wearing the very latest in fashion sportswear and looking glossy and urban.

Harry and I were sitting on the deck, drinking coffee, while the children played swingball on the lawn. Harry had been justifying to himself Chris the Ex's failure, as yet, to disentangle himself from the new boyfriend, while I tried to mingle sympathy with the warning, delicately conveyed, that people can usually manage these things if they really want to.

'Evening, all,' Bex said, making everybody jump. Tessa, who had been lying on her side beneath the table, nudging my bare foot whenever it ceased to scratch her tummy, sat up with a start and pattered self-importantly down the steps to greet her.

'Aunty Bex!' Lily squealed, joyfully tossing her swingball bat aside and hitting Nathan in the stomach.

This put an end to conversation for a little while, but eventually, when Nathan's wails had diminished and greetings and introductions had been completed, we all sat down.

'Where's Caleb?' Lily asked.

'He's at Nana's,' said Bex. 'He's looking forward to seeing you.'

'Can we go and see him now, Mum?'

'No, it's too late now, love. We'll see him tomorrow.'

'But *Mu-m* ...'

'He's in bed already,' Bex said.

I looked at my watch – it was half past seven. 'Crikey, you guys should be, too. Teeth, please.'

'But Aunty Bex is here!'

'I'll still be here tomorrow,' Bex said.

'But –'

'Zip it, sprat,' she said.

Lily looked at her for a moment, decided not to push it and changed tack. 'Can Harry read me a story?' she asked.

'Only if I get to pick it,' said Harry, who had not yet recovered from *The Tailor of Gloucester* the week before. (Tippets and pipkins and dressmaking mice were not, he said, features of any reasonable children's literature.)

'I want a story too!' Nathan cried.

'Well, go and brush your teeth,' said Harry. 'I'll be there in a minute.'

Both children vanished inside, and Bex yawned and stretched. 'You're a handy chap to have around,' she told Harry. 'You wouldn't consider moving to Wellington, would you?'

'Yes, actually,' he said with a sad little smile.

Rebecca, who never felt bad about ignoring conversational leads if they didn't interest her, ignored this one. 'Sean's in Sydney,' she said, hooking one knee over the arm of her chair and swinging a slim foot clad in a beautiful peach-coloured sneaker.

'Yeah, Mum said. For work?'

'Mm. Sorting out some project or other that's gone way over budget.'

'Wow. Go, Sean.'

She made a face. 'Any excuse to be away from home. I might as well be a single parent.'

'When's he back?' I asked.

'Thursday.'

Harry yawned and stood up.

'Thank you,' I told him. 'You're wonderful. You will be rewarded with cake.'

'That's alright, then,' he said, going inside.

While he was putting my offspring to bed, Bex told me about her job (exhausting) and her morning sickness (hideous). She did not, however, mention selling the farm, and I was grateful that Mum and Dad hadn't yet brought her up to date.

I got up to make hot drinks, and carried a loaded tray out onto the deck as Harry came back up the hall. 'Excellent,' he said, sinking into a chair and accepting a large slice of banana cake with chocolate icing.

'Bex?' I offered.

'No, thank you. I already look like a hippo.'

'You do not. And it's very tactless of you to say that you do, when you're two sizes smaller than me.'

'But you look great,' she said in surprise. 'You're so ... what's the word I want?'

'I shudder to think.'

'Statuesque,' she said.

'What, as in large and imposing?'

'As in elegant, you dribbler. Classically beautiful.'

'Yeah, she is reasonably easy on the eye,' Harry said, looking at me critically.

'Wow,' I said. 'Thanks, guys.'

'So, are you two an item?' Bex asked.

'No,' said Harry and I together.

'Why not?'

'I'm gay,' Harry said, and his voice was almost blasé. He really was coming along beautifully.

'Well, that's a shame,' said Rebecca. 'I'm sure it's time you got back on the horse, Jen.' She turned to Harry. 'What about your brother? Mum says he looks like Bruce Springsteen.'

'Bex, don't be an idiot,' I said, feeling my face get hot. So Mum thought so, too ...

'Well, well,' said Harry. 'She's blushing.'

'I am not!'

'Yes, you are,' Bex said. 'Well, well, indeed. Does *he* like *her*?'

'As much as he likes anyone, I suppose.' Harry said. 'He's a grumpy bastard. Yell at you as soon as look at you.' He took another bit of cake and inserted about half of it into his mouth.

'Probably just needs the love of a good woman,' Bex said briskly. 'Right. Jen, you need to have him around for dinner some night when you've got no kids. Cook something fabulous and talk about how big and cold and empty your bed feels these days.'

'Subtle,' I remarked.

'And wear lots and lots of lip gloss. And play with your hair. Like this.' She demonstrated.

'Yep, that's really alluring,' I said.

'Have you been doing your pelvic floor exercises?' she asked.

I threw a used teabag at her.

'Please,' said Harry. 'I have a delicate stomach.'

'Obviously,' Bex said, arching one delicate brow as she watched him swallow the last of his cake and reach for a packet of chocolate biscuits.

'If I wanted a relationship,' I said, 'which I don't, I wouldn't pick a grumpy prat with a thing for pot plants to have it with.' I was surprised by the stab of guilt that followed this statement – well, it served him right for being so mean at Pet Day. And he *was* grumpy. And he *did* like pot plants. And – and heaven forbid that Rebecca should think I liked him; she'd be quite capable of tracking him down and telling him so.

Chapter 22

On Tuesday morning after taking Lily to school, Nathan and I drove back up the hill to Mum and Dad's place for our bimonthly meeting with Arnold Keller. Harry's car was there already, but Arnold hadn't arrived yet.

'Aunty Jen!' Caleb shouted, meeting me at the door and thrusting a lump of greyish putty towards me.

'Wow!' I said. 'It's lovely.'

''Es,' said Caleb smugly, trotting off after his cousin, who was busily unpacking the toy box in the corner of the living room.

'We're baking,' Mum explained from the other side of the kitchen bench. 'I thought we'd have homemade bread for lunch.'

Bex came into the kitchen pink and fragrant from the shower, with a towel around her head. 'Good morning,' she said, selecting a mandarin from the fruit bowl. 'Mind if I sit in on your meeting?'

'Towel and all?' Dad asked.

'Why not?' she said, but she drifted out again, presumably to dry her hair.

It was a good half-hour later by the time Arnold had arrived and been introduced to Rebecca. Mum and I moved the two little boys outside to the sandpit with a piece of shortbread apiece, and we all sat down around the table.

'I've been thinking about this possibility you mentioned of selling the farm, Brian,' Arnold said, twirling a gold pen between his fingers.

This, as an opening statement designed to catch and hold his audience's attention, could scarcely have been bettered. Harry's eyes widened. Bex leant forward in her chair. I looked sharply at Dad.

'I just mentioned it to Arnold as one of the options that we *might* be looking at, sometime in the future,' he said uncomfortably.

'Yes, of course,' Arnold said. 'But I happened to be in touch with a friend of mine at the end of last week – Richard Green, from Greenfarm Investments. Do you know him?'

'Yes,' said Harry.

'The Greens are big wheels down in the Manawatu,' Arnold continued, as if he hadn't spoken. 'They own a number of farms, in partnership with various investors. They're keen to expand up this way – they're looking at buying Andrew and Toni Faulkner's place, actually.'

'Are they selling up?' I asked, surprised.

'Toni's certainly pushing him to,' Harry said.

'The joys of divorce, eh?' said Arnold jovially. 'Well, Richard mentioned it to me – he and Andrew and I were all at high school together, back in the mists of time – and it occurred to me that this might be just the opportunity you people are looking for.'

'What, they'd buy this farm, too?' Bex asked.

'They'd certainly consider it pretty seriously,' Arnold said, looking her up and down with unsubtle appreciation. 'The two farms fit together very nicely, and then Andrew's right here on the spot, keen to manage them both.'

He *was*? I felt a pang of betrayal that he hadn't told me, followed closely by one of humiliation. Why should he have told me, after all? And – and how had this farm sale idea gone so quickly from a vague future possibility to something real and imminent? 'Have you talked to him about it?' I asked.

'It's a pretty attractive option, from his point of view,' said Arnold. 'He could be an equity partner, you see, and maintain a share in the operation. Anyway, that's all by the way. It wouldn't affect you people – except that potentially it would raise your asking price a bit.'

'I – I don't think we're ready to take a step like that just yet,' said Mum. 'The farm's been in Brian's family for four generations – five, actually, if we count the children ...'

'Yes, but Mum, it'd be stupid to just dismiss the idea without considering it,' Bex said.

'It's never going to be an easy decision,' Arnold said. 'But I'd think seriously about it, if I were you. Greenfarm's a top-calibre organisation. They'd pay well, and they'd really look after the place. There's nothing worse than selling a farm that's been in your family for generations to someone who's going to rape and pillage it.'

'Hmm,' said Dad.

'Jenny, you could subdivide your house off,' Rebecca said kindly. 'Then you could stay here.'

'Hey, steady on,' Dad said, before I'd had time to do more than straighten indignantly in my chair. 'Let's not get ahead of ourselves. We haven't decided that selling the farm is the right option.'

'Dad, come on – it's the only option, and you know it,' she said.

Mum looked at me in wordless entreaty, her eyes begging me not to rise and smite my sister in front of strangers. So I didn't. But the temptation was great.

* * *

That meeting, I felt, pretty much spoilt Tuesday, and Wednesday started off no better. Lily decided for the first time that she didn't want to go to her father's that night, and clung to me, sobbing, when I dropped her off at school. At work our two-yearly government audit was looming, Microsoft Outlook crashed for an hour and a half and Greta went home sick. Then I discovered, when I rushed downtown to do the final inspection of the new wing at Grubb's Accountants, that whoever had installed the ventilation system had cut a nice roomy tunnel for it through three adjacent fire cells in the ceiling.

'But you've already signed it off!' said Michael Grubb, pacing the floor around my stepladder.

'I'm sorry, but the fire cells aren't airtight anymore.' I descended the ladder. 'If you had a fire up there it would race down the whole length of the ceiling. Go up and have a look.'

He did, and came down spluttering. 'This is unacceptable. I'm not paying for it to be fixed – they can bloody well come back and sort it out.'

I nodded. 'Absolutely. But I'm afraid that until they do, you can't use these rooms.'

He was exceedingly put out. Which was understandable, but I'd have preferred it if he hadn't blamed the whole thing on me.

As I came back into reception at council, Lyn said, 'Phillip McClintock would like you to give him a call.'

'Really?' I said. 'Man, it is *not* my day.'

'It's not Greta's, either. She looked terrible when she left. She *said* she had a migraine, but personally I think it's that boy she's been seeing.'

'I wouldn't be at all surprised. He's a horrible little bastard.'

'But what can you do?' Lyn said, shaking her head mournfully. 'You've got to let people work these things out for themselves.'

'I have tried to say something,' I admitted. 'But it only put her back up.'

'Nothing you can do,' said Lyn. 'Except help to pick up the pieces when it all turns to shit, as it inevitably will.'

'I know it's heartless and unsympathetic of me,' I said, 'but I can't help hoping it doesn't turn to shit until *after* the audit.'

'That is heartless,' she said. 'Off you go and call Phillip. I think he's got some queries about his bill. I told him you were the person he needed to talk to.'

'*I'm* heartless, you reckon?' I said, and headed for the stairs, pursued by her mocking laughter.

After talking to Mr McClintock I felt I needed caffeine, in lieu of stronger chemical support. I went along to the lunch room and made myself a strong coffee with two sugars, returning to find a text message from Harry on my phone.

Emergency! Forgot milk and toilet paper, can you grab me some to prevent Andrew losing plot?

Sweet as, I sent back.

Legend ☺

Duly, at five twenty-seven I drove past my own house, past Andrew Faulkner's woolshed and the downy new grass that had replaced his winter kale crop, and turned down his driveway. I parked in front of the nasty concrete patio and got out of the car, bearing two litres of milk and a pack of toilet paper rolls.

I crossed the patio and tried the big glass sliding door into the living room. It was unlocked, so I let myself in to drop the groceries on the kitchen bench. I was admiring the stair corner greenery, and was halfway across the brown shag-pile wasteland of the living room floor before I saw Andrew and his dog.

They were lying on the floor in a golden-brown square of sunlight, fast asleep. Meg's head was on his shoulder and his arm was around her woolly grey neck. I smiled – it was oddly touching to catch the Man of Granite in a vulnerable moment – and tiptoed past, hoping not to disturb them.

As I put the milk down softly on the bench Meg raised her head and growled. Andrew's hand moved to pat her vaguely, but she sat up, barking. He woke with a jerk.

Meg surged to her feet and took a stiff, outraged step towards me, poised to lunge. 'Shh,' I said, backing away. 'Hey, sit down, it's alright ...'

Apparently it wasn't. The barking rose in volume and frequency, and I retreated hurriedly behind the brown-tiled kitchen island.

Andrew scrambled upright, grabbed Meg's collar and dragged her across the living room to the door. He pushed her outside, shut the door and turned to face me, rubbing his face with his hands. His hair stood up on end and his face was creased with sleep.

'I'm so sorry,' I said. 'I, um – Harry asked me to get some things in town. Sorry to just let myself in; I didn't see you.'

He looked at the bags on the bench, frowning. 'Thanks, but we don't need anything.'

'Well, he ordered milk and toilet paper, so here they are.'

He gestured towards the sink, where a frozen three-litre bottle of milk was thawing. 'We've got plenty. Plenty of toilet paper too.'

'Fine,' I said shortly, picking everything up again. 'Sorry to disturb you. Would you mind holding onto your dog so I can get to the car?'

He rubbed his eyes again and opened the door. 'Go and sit down,' he told Meg.

She stood her ground, hackles raised and teeth bared. I hesitated in the doorway, and Andrew said impatiently, 'She won't hurt you.'

Ruffled by their blatant mutual desire to see the back of me, I said impulsively, 'Hey, you know what?'

'What?'

'It's none of my business who you sell your farm to –'

'Er, no,' he said, eyebrows lifting.

'But it wouldn't have hurt you to mention that you were planning a takeover.'

'What on earth are you talking about?'

'You know perfectly well what I'm talking about!'

'I assure you I don't,' he said coldly.

'Your little scheme with Richard Green, or whatever his name is.'

'What the hell has that got to do with you?' he snapped.

'It's my *home*!' I cried.

'Oh, fuck off, princess. Not everything in the world is about you.'

I stood and gaped at him, hurt and furious. '*God*, you're an arsehole! No wonder your wife left you.' And hot all over with anger and humiliation, I flew back across the patio to my car.

* * *

I could feel the tears building by the time I reached home, although most of them were evaporating before they reached the eyes, burned off in the heat of my rage. How *dare* he? What was *wrong* with him? Christ, poor Toni. I mean, I'd have preferred it if she hadn't picked my husband as the springboard from which to escape her shitty marriage, but you could sort of see her point. As I stormed up the back steps and into the kitchen I caught my hip, for perhaps the tenth time, on the box of chokos on the end of the bench beside the food processor. The lousy things were never going to rot and let me throw them away with a clear conscience – heaven only knew what they were made of, but surely it was nothing any right-minded person would actually ingest voluntarily ... I put down the unwanted milk and toilet paper, snatched up the choko box, bore it outside and hurled the lot of them into the compost heap.

Heading back towards the house with the box in my hands, I heard a vehicle on the road above pause and then turn down the driveway. My stomach gave an unpleasant little lurch.

But it was John Mercer's little white Toyota Corolla that appeared around the corner of the driveway. *You actually thought it might be Andrew, come to apologise. You poor, sad fool.* I drew a long breath and went to meet John.

'Good evening!' he called, opening his door. 'You're looking very lovely, Madam Jenny!' A leg, swathed from mid thigh to mid calf in an enormous white bandage, emerged from the car.

I looked down doubtfully at my charcoal coloured shirt-dress, which Dave had always said made me look like a prison guard. 'Thank you,' I said. 'What on earth happened to your leg, John?'

'Oh, it's fine. Just a tweak.'

'It doesn't look like a tweak. It looks like a chainsaw massacre.'

'Ah, well, I wrapped it up in cabbage leaves. Wonderful for swelling, but a bit bulky.'

'Cabbage leaves?' I repeated blankly.

'That's right. Can't beat 'em. Anyway –' He paused to heave himself to his feet, and I hurried forward to help him, dropping the box I was holding.

'Thank you, m' dear. Bit shaky on me pins at the moment. Light duties only. But I remembered I promised to fix up your compost bins, so I thought I'd pop round and measure them up. Nice easy job, even for a useless old fella with a gammy leg.'

He paused to allow me to express my gratitude and delight, but I merely looked at him in horror. He would be *destroyed* if he knew I'd thrown away his chokos. I was reminded of my social obligations by the look of hurt surprise that began to creep across his face, and I said quickly, 'Oh, John, that's so kind, but I'm sure you should have that leg up. It's not an urgent job at all.'

'No time like the present.' And he pulled a measuring tape from his trouser pocket with a conjuror's flourish.

I plucked it from his hand. 'You stay here, then, and I'll do it. The ground's a bit uneven …'

'Thank you kindly, but I never trust a woman's ability to measure things,' he said. He took hold of his tape measure, but I held on grimly. 'No offence, m' dear.'

I released the tape measure only because it was either that or actually wrestling him for it. 'I'm an excellent measurer, I'll have you know,' I said. 'It's part of my job.'

'Well, then, you'd better come along and make sure I'm doing it right, hadn't you?'

And just then, when all seemed lost, Andrew's ute came rattling down the driveway. He pulled up beside John's car and got out, and I beamed at him as if he was the answer to a prayer.

He looked extremely surprised by the warmth of his welcome, but he smiled back, in an uncertain sort of way.

'Have you two met?' I asked.

'No,' said Andrew.

'This is John Mercer, who lives in Grandma's little cottage by our woolshed,' I said. 'He worked on your place for years. John, this —'

'Managed,' John interrupted.

'Oh,' I said. 'Yes. Sorry, John. This is Andrew Faulkner. Um, excuse me a moment, guys; I just need to get the washing in.' A strange and unmannerly thing to do as guests arrive, but needs must. I sped around the corner of the house.

My two square post-and-rail compost bins stood at one end of the veggie garden. In the nearest, neon green and horribly visible, was a medium-sized choko pyramid. I snatched a sheet from the washing line, spread it on the lawn, vaulted the metre-high side of the bin with a grace born of desperation, and began flinging chokos out onto the sheet. Then I leapt out again and bundled them up. By the time the two men came around the side of the house the evidence was entirely hidden beneath a large heap of clean washing and I was taking the last bath towel off the line.

'There's a hell of a lot of clover on your airstrip,' John was saying. He had rolled himself a cigarette and was gesturing with it, unlit. 'You'll lose cattle with bloat; you mark my words.'

'I'm going to put ewes and lambs in there after shearing next week,' said Andrew.

'You're shearing ewes with lambs at foot?'

'Yes.'

John shook his head sadly as he applied his lighter to his cigarette. 'Oh, well, I suppose that's your business.'

Andrew smiled. 'Yes,' he said again, and bent to gather up my washing from the grass.

I took a hasty step to intercept him, realised I was too late and grimaced at him instead. He looked at me in some surprise, puzzled first by my increasingly odd behaviour and then by the strange and lumpy consistency of my washing pile.

'Thanks, Andrew,' I said. 'Come around and drop that in the lounge.'

We crossed the lawn together, leaving John getting out his tape measure, and as we went up the porch steps I hissed, 'They're chokos. In the sheet. John gave them to me, and I threw them in the compost, and now he's just turned up to measure it and I didn't want to hurt his feelings.'

'What's a choko?'

'A vegetable-y thing,' I said, opening the living room sliding door. Tessa, most indignant about having been accidentally shut in, shot out between my legs and glued her nose to Andrew's boots. 'Just drop the washing on the floor, thanks.'

'This isn't even *close* to straight,' John said as we rejoined him at the compost bins. 'That post needs to come a good inch this way.' He looked down, frowned and poked at something in the bottom of the bin with the end of his tape measure.

Suddenly cold with foreboding, I came up beside him. There in the corner, looking back up at me with – I swear – a smug expression on its puckered green face, lay a solitary choko.

'Surplus to requirements, eh?' said John.

I considered telling him it was rotten, decided he was quite capable of fishing it out to check and remained guiltily silent.

After a good long pause, so as to really let his reproof sink in, he straightened up again, tapped the ash from the end of his cigarette and retracted his tape measure. 'Well, it's getting to that time of day,' he said. 'I suppose I'd better shuffle off home again and find myself a crust.'

He was dying to be asked to stay for dinner, but I couldn't ask him when Andrew had obviously come to talk to me. Anyway, I wasn't feeling strong enough for two hours of ponderous anecdotes. So I said nothing and felt bad as we went slowly back towards the carport.

'Kiddies with their dad tonight?' John asked.

'Yes.'

He looked with sorrowful speculation from me to Andrew. 'I see. Well, you two have a nice evening. Can I trouble you to move your vehicle?'

There was ample room for him to get past Andrew's ute, but Andrew didn't bother to point it out. He got in, started his engine and backed around onto the lawn.

John limped across to his car and inserted himself with some difficulty behind the steering wheel.

'Goodnight, John,' I said.

'Goodnight.' And he drove sadly away.

'Tedious little man,' Andrew remarked, getting out of his ute again.

'He's lonely.'

'No wonder.' He took a deep breath. 'Jenny, I'm sorry,' he said. 'Harry just told me about this Greenfarm equity partnership fairy tale.'

'So you're not …?'

'First I'd heard of it. They're probably going to buy my place, but I haven't heard anything about them buying yours. And I certainly haven't heard that I'm going to be running the show.'

'I thought Toni was going to give you two years to try to sort something out.'

His mouth twisted. 'Changed her mind.'

'Can she?'

'Why not? It was only a verbal promise; it wasn't written down.'

'That's really rough,' I said.

'Yeah. Look, I should never have spoken to you like that. It's been a shit of a couple of weeks, but that's no excuse. I'm really sorry.'

'So am I,' I said. 'Saying it was no wonder your wife left you …' I held my hand out, and he took it. We shook.

'Do you want to come in and have a drink?' I asked.

'Um, sure,' he said. 'Sounds good.'

'Hot drink or a beer?' I asked, preceding him into the kitchen.

'Either or.'

'That's really not helpful.'

He smiled. 'Beer, then.'

I hunted through the fridge and emerged with a bottle of low-alcohol citrus-flavoured stuff in one hand and a can of Lion Brown in the other. 'Pickings are a bit slim. You might want to go for the cup of tea instead,' I said, holding them both out for inspection.

'No, this is fine,' he said, taking the Lion Brown.

There was an uncomfortable little pause. 'Come and sit out on the deck,' I said, leading the way across the living room. And at that moment yet another car came down the driveway. 'Oh, for goodness' sake.'

As I reached the kitchen door, Bex, her hair pulled back any old way and her face almost hidden behind enormous sunglasses, leapt out of Mum and Dad's car. 'What are you doing here?' I asked. She and Caleb should have flown out of Hamilton at lunchtime.

'Leaving the bastard,' she said, pushing Tessa, who was inspecting her shoes, aside with one foot and running up the steps.

'But –'

'I'm done. I'm not putting up with his bullshit anymore. I –' She brushed past me into the kitchen, saw Andrew and broke off abruptly. 'Fuck. Sorry.'

Andrew put his unopened beer down on the end of the bench. 'Look, I'll push off,' he told me.

'No!' said Bex. 'No, you stay. I'll go. No need to spoil your night too. As you were. Crack on.' She retreated towards the door, swiping a hand impatiently across her wet cheeks.

'Bex, hang on,' I said.

She shook her head, flashed me a bright, unconvincing smile and ran back down the steps.

I followed her. 'Bex, you twit, come *back*.'

'No, go and talk to him. Good on you.'

'No, we're not –' I began, and then realised he could probably hear and stopped abruptly.

'Why not?'

'Be *quiet*!' I hissed.

Andrew, at this point, appeared at the kitchen door and began to put on his boots.

'You're Andrew, right?' Bex demanded.

'Yes.'

'Stop it!' I snapped.

'And you find my idiot sister attractive?'

He didn't answer, but he looked at her as if she'd grown another head, which I appreciated.

'She really likes you,' Bex continued, undeterred. 'Fantasises about you all the time, thinks you look like Bruce Springsteen ...'

'Rebecca, piss *off*,' I said savagely.

'She's just got this abnormally enlarged sense of duty. Anything she wants, she automatically assumes she shouldn't have.' She shot Andrew a brittle smile. 'As opposed to me. *I* assume I'm entitled to everything I can think of.'

'And how's that working for you?' Andrew asked, pulling on his second boot.

Bex's mouth crumpled below the enormous sunglasses. 'Pretty shit, thanks for asking.'

'Mm.' He straightened up again and smiled at me. 'Night.'

'You don't have to run away; I'm going,' said Bex. 'Pull yourself together, Jenny, and stop being so fucking wet.' She ran across the gravel to Mum and Dad's car.

Perhaps I should have gone after her. She was only being revolting because she felt wretched. When Rebecca descended to the depths of self-loathing, she liked to encourage everyone around her to hate her as much as she hated herself.

But I didn't move. *Wet* rankled. I stood and watched her back the car around, and as it vanished around the bend in the driveway I said, 'Well, wasn't that fun?'

'Toni does that, too,' Andrew said. 'Says something just to get a reaction, and then gets carried away by the dramatic possibilities and forgets it's all made up.'

'It's bad enough in a sister; it must be a real joy to be married to.'

'It was.'

'And did you stop reacting, because you knew you'd just get sucked into a hysterical shouting match, only to be accused of being a hard, miserable bastard?'

He looked at me in surprise. 'Yes,' he said.

'You *do* do a good cold stare, when you want to.'

'I know.' He sighed. 'I'm sure I used to be nicer, once.'

'So did I,' I said. 'I think you get sort of ... tarnished, when you're unhappily married. You keep having the same arguments, and each time you get a little bit more bitter and sarcastic. Or maybe that's just me.'

'You're not tarnished,' he said quietly. 'You're lovely.'

My stomach turned over. 'Um,' I said, 'do – do you want to have another go at that drink?'

'Yeah,' he said.

Chapter 23

'Your lambs are looking nice. I was admiring them from the road the other day,' I said, picking a topic at random as we sat down at the outside table. Things had just changed, and although I thought I was pleased, it was hard to be sure beneath the panic.

'Yeah, they've done pretty well this year,' said Andrew.

'Particularly when contrasted with the little weedy ones across the boundary.'

'They're not that bad,' he said. 'And they'll be better again next year, now that you're sorting things out.'

'Assuming Mum and Dad haven't sold the farm to Richard Green.'

'Well, there is that.'

'So ... Arnold said you guys all went to school together?'

'Yes.'

'What's he like? Richard.'

Andrew made a face. 'Wouldn't trust him as far as I could kick him,' he said.

'Oh.'

'They've built themselves quite an empire. They buy farms with investors' money and put managers on them, and then they clip the ticket at every possible opportunity. They lease them bulls, and sell them their own special breed of rams, and do all the cartage, and one brother has a contracting business, so he does all the cropping …'

'Do they do a good job?'

He shrugged. 'Depends how you define a good job. I think the Greens do very nicely out of the whole set-up. I wouldn't be so confident about return on investment for the people actually paying for it.'

I nodded and took a sip of my beer. 'So you're not tempted by the thought of going into partnership with them?'

'Shit, no.'

'That'll disappoint them.'

'I'm sure they'll get over it.'

He was turning the little aluminium tab from his beer can over and over between his fingers. They were slim and brown and graceful, and I thought suddenly that he had beautiful hands. Or he would have had, if the nails hadn't been bitten to the quick.

'They look sore,' I said, and he frowned, puzzled. 'Your fingers, I mean.'

'Oh,' he said. 'Yeah, a bit. Terrible habit.'

Wishing I hadn't made such a personal remark, and uncomfortably aware that, even if he didn't actually believe that he had a starring role in my sexual fantasies, he must at least think I'd discussed him with my sister, I lost my head completely and said, 'It was Mum who said you look like Bruce Springsteen.'

He looked first taken aback, and then amused. 'Isn't he nearly seventy?'

'Like he used to look, obviously.'

'Right. Well, that's a relief.'

'Although he's aged very well, I must say.'

The little lurking smile at the corners of his mouth grew and spread.

'I think I should probably stop talking now,' I said.

The phone began to ring. 'Excuse me,' I said, getting up to answer it. 'Hello?'

'Do *you* know what's got into your sister?' Mum demanded.

'No idea.'

'She's shut herself in her room. I can't get a word out of her.'

'You should be thankful,' I said. 'I got quite a few words, and I didn't like any of them.'

'Jenny, she's very upset.'

I sighed. 'I know.'

'She says she's *left Sean*.' Mum's voice rose shrilly at the thought of not one but two single-parent daughters.

'I know.'

'*He's* not sleeping around, is he?'

'I don't know, Mum,' I said. 'I doubt it.'

'Why don't you come down and talk to her? She might listen to you.'

'Doubtful,' I said. 'Look, I can't just now. Why not let her sleep on it, and I'll come in on my way to work tomorrow and –'

'Is Andrew still there?'

Rebecca hadn't been *wholly* uncommunicative, then. I chalked up another sisterly grievance. 'Mm.'

'Oh,' she said. 'Right. Sorry, love. Be careful, won't you?' And she hung up.

I put the phone down, feeling like a cat stroked the wrong way. *Be careful? Of what?*

Andrew pushed back his chair as I came outside again. 'I think it's time I got out of your hair,' he said, standing up. 'Thanks for the drink.'

'You're welcome,' I said, accompanying him across the living room to the back door.

He opened it and bent to put his boots on. 'Have you got the kids this weekend?' he asked as he straightened up again. His eyes, I noticed suddenly, were exactly the same shade of blue as his shirt.

My stomach twisted painfully, partly in excitement and partly in sheer terror. I hadn't done this for so long – I'd forgotten the rules, if indeed I'd ever known them … 'No.'

'Would you like to come for a look around my place? There's a really nice waterfall in the bush – I don't know if you've seen it.'

'No,' I said. 'I mean no, I haven't seen it, but I'd like to. I remember Granddad talking about it. They used to go swimming there when he was a boy.'

'Maybe on Saturday afternoon, or something?'

'Sure,' I said. 'Just, um, give me a ring when it suits. And no worries if something else comes up …'

'Okay.'

I pulled myself together and smiled at him brightly. 'Excellent. Would you like a couple of chokos to take home?'

'No thank you,' he said, and taking a step forward he kissed me. It was a competent, decisive, serious sort of kiss. Of course it was, I thought numbly; Andrew did everything well. He was a good six inches taller than me, and his skin felt hot where it touched mine. I slid my arms up around his neck, and his tightened around my waist in response.

It was too much – too fast – too intense. I pulled back again, half afraid of how much I liked it, and he let me go immediately.

'Are – are you sure about the chokos?' I said shakily, taking refuge in weak humour. 'They're so versatile.'

'Are they?' He kissed me again, and it was even better the second time.

'And they keep for months …'

He held me at arm's length and looked at me with eyebrows raised.

'Is that a genuine cold stare?' I asked.

'Yes.'

'It's great. Some of your best work.'

He sighed, laughed and let me go. 'Goodnight, Jenny.'

'Goodnight.' And as he went down the steps I added softly, 'It was perfect. The kiss.'

'Yes,' he said, not turning around.

* * *

When he was gone, I took a deep breath and started unloading the dishwasher (the next day I found two glasses in the fridge and a little stack of bread and butter plates in a pot cupboard). What on earth were we getting ourselves into? Was it just fun – a nice boost to two battered egos – or might it turn serious? How could it, when he was on the verge of selling up and moving goodness knew where? What about Lily and Nathan? Should I have made it clear that they came first? But how do you do that? It's insulting, not to mention presumptuous … He smelt nice. Did he still love Toni? What on earth would Dave say, if he ever found out?

I slept patchily, waking at two a.m. for a good long worry and finally falling into a deep, rejuvenating slumber about ten minutes before my alarm went off. As you do. I felt about a hundred years old as I staggered up the hall to the bathroom, but makeup is wonderful stuff, and when I reached Mum and Dad's place at quarter to eight I looked human, if not fresh-faced and radiant. I let myself in to find Dad at the table, eating cornflakes and reading – for at least the fifteenth time – *All Quiet on the Western Front*.

'How are things?' I asked.

He looked up and made a face.

'Where's Caleb?'

'Your mother's taken him out to get the eggs.'

'Any sign of Bex this morning?'

'Not yet.'

'Hmm,' I said. 'Hey, Dad?'

'Yes?' His eyes were already back on his book.

'I was talking to Andrew Faulkner last night' – I was pleased with how offhand my voice was – 'and he hadn't heard of this plan Arnold told us about, where he'd run our farm and his together.'

Dad looked up again.

'In fact, he, um, he said that he wouldn't trust Richard Green as far as he could kick him. He might have to sell his farm to Greenfarm, but he wouldn't go into partnership with them. So – so I don't know whether they'd still be interested in our place.'

'Well,' said Dad, 'we don't know that we want to sell it to them, even if they want it.'

I smiled at him. 'We don't seem to know much, do we?'

'No, very little,' he said.

'What if they *do* make you an offer you can't refuse?'

He actually turned his book face down. 'Let's not get ahead of ourselves. We can worry about that if it happens.'

'Okay,' I said, kissing the top of his head. 'Well, wish me luck; I'm going in.'

He lifted his eyebrows. 'Luck.'

I went slowly up the hall and tapped on Rebecca's closed bedroom door. There was no answer, so I ignored the twenty-five-year-old sticker telling me to KEEP OUT and opened it. 'Hi.'

She was lying on her side with her eyes open and one hand beneath her cheek, looking fixedly at the wall. She was very pale, with hard little lines around her mouth.

'Oh, Bex,' I said, sitting down beside her on the edge of the bed. 'It'll be alright.'

'It won't,' she said flatly, not looking at me.

'What's happened?'

'I've left him.'

'Why?'

'Might as well. He's left me.'

'Honestly?'

Silence.

'Why?'

'Because he's an arsehole. He doesn't care about his family.'

'I'm pretty sure he does.'

'I'm not,' she said flatly.

I tried a different tack. 'Did you fly home?'

'No,' she said. 'No point.'

'Did he call you, or –'

'I don't want to talk about it,' she said.

The door creaked as Mum pushed it open and looked around it. 'Rebecca, love ...' she said.

'Leave me alone,' Bex said.

Mum sighed and withdrew.

'You too,' Bex told me.

'Nope.'

'Fine.' She closed her eyes.

I stroked her smooth black hair back from her forehead. Bex never was any good at silence. *One ... two ... thr–*

'He's not coming home,' she said.

'Ever?' I asked. 'For a week?'

'Forever, for all I care.'

'Becca ...'

'Go away, please,' she said.

I stood up. 'I'm here when you want me.'

'I know.'

Mum looked up anxiously as I came back into the kitchen. 'Well?' she asked.

'I don't know. She wouldn't talk to me either. She just said Sean's not coming home.'

'What, at all?'

'Goodness only knows,' I said, turning to pick up Caleb, who was trotting past with a whisk in one fat hand. 'Good morning, sausage.'

'Put me down,' he ordered, writhing. 'I *busy*.'

'Oh. Sorry.' I set him back on his feet and he vanished purposefully into the living room.

'Well, at least *he's* happy,' said Mum sadly. 'I was going to have lunch with Ngaire today.'

'Why can't you?' Dad asked.

'Well, Caleb ...'

'Has a perfectly good mother.'

'But –'

'This is ridiculous!' said Dad. 'As far as I can tell, she's leaving her husband because Jenny did and she doesn't want to be left out!'

'Anything you can do, I can do better?' I said. (I may not, after all, have entirely recovered from *wet*.)

'Exactly,' said Dad. 'And the more you hover around her wringing your hands and asking questions, the more you'll encourage her. Go away, Jenny. Go on.' He flapped his book at me.

I laughed, gave Mum a hug, and went to work.

* * *

So Rebecca had the dubious satisfaction of being taken at her word and left alone for the day, whereupon she discovered that, as annoying as anxious solicitude from your family might be, bland lack of interest is worse. She arrived at my place at half past four, looking for sympathy (although unwilling to admit it), pushing Caleb in his pram.

I was cutting Nathan's hair, and the buzz of the electric clippers covered the sound of their approach. Bex opened the kitchen door, and Lily, who was sitting cross-legged on the kitchen bench eating toast and offering hairdressing advice, jumped down and flew across the room to meet her. 'Mum has to cut off all Nathan's hair,' she announced. 'It's all knotted and the brush won't go through it.'

'That seems a bit drastic,' Bex said.

'It was the knot from hell,' I said. Five centimetres across and matted almost to the skin, like a dreadlock on steroids. I'd have liked to blame Dave, but a bird's nest like that doesn't grow in a day, and I couldn't actually remember when I'd last held my son down and brushed his hair. Poor parenting. I sighed and ran the clippers up the side of Nathan's head, felling a swathe of brown ringlets.

'Don't cut my ears off!' he shrieked, clamping them between his shoulders.

Caleb, clinging to his mother, burst into tears of fright.

'I'm not, you twit!' I said. 'Stop yelling and sit still; you're scaring Caleb.'

'It's probably the haircut that's distressing him,' Bex said. 'There, there, my love, Mummy will never let Aunty Jen do that to you.'

'It looks *good*!' Lily cried, rushing to my defence.

'I want to see it!' Nathan said.

'Hang on a second, there's a tufty bit on this side …' I turned off the clippers and stepped back to check my work.

The bird's nest was gone, along with all of Nathan's corkscrew curls. His hair was now one centimetre long all over, soft and fuzzy like teddy-bear fur, and the back of his neck looked very small and white and defenceless.

'He looks like the boy in the striped pyjamas,' said my sister, ever helpful and supportive.

'Can I go and look?' asked Nathan.

'Yes,' I said, and he slid off his stool and ran up the hall. 'Oh well, it'll grow.'

'I never noticed before that his ears are lopsided,' said Bex.

But Nathan returned beaming. 'It's cool!' he said.

'I know!' I said heartily, although I wasn't at all sure it was. 'Want me to put some gel in it so it sticks up like a hedgehog?'

'Yes!' He pounded away again.

'In the second drawer under the bathroom sink!' I called after him.

'Can we have some lollies?' Lily asked.

'Hmm?' I said, dismantling the clippers. 'No, not just now, love. Have an apple.'

'I don't like apples. Daddy always lets us have lollies.'

'He would,' said Bex, and I shook my head at her.

'You don't like my dad,' Lily said.

'No,' Bex agreed.

'Rebecca!' I said sharply.

'Is it because Mummy doesn't like him, and you're her sister?'

'Lily, of course I like Dad,' I said. 'Don't be silly.'

'I'm not! Daddy said it, not me!'

'Then *he* was being silly. Could you get me the vacuum cleaner, please?'

She went without arguing, which made a pleasant change, and Bex gave me a sardonic look. 'Don't,' I said, bending to gather up a handful of brown curls.

'Don't what?'

'Criticise Dave in front of the kids. It just makes things worse.'

'It makes *me* feel better,' she said.

'Oh, grow up!' I snapped.

I suspect my sister would have departed in high dudgeon, had she had anywhere better to go. Since she didn't, she turned cool and remote and withdrew to the couch with her phone.

I, on the other hand, turned noble and long-suffering. I tested Lily on her spelling words, made meatballs, emptied the lunchboxes and refilled them for the next day, bathed all three children and watered my Siberian irises, which, if irises could talk, would have expressed considerable surprise at this unprecedented concern for their welfare.

By the time we'd eaten and tucked our respective children into bed, enough time had passed for both of us to get over ourselves, and we wandered outside to sit on the porch steps. It was a lovely golden evening, the sunlight rich and buttery. It outlined every leaf on the poplars lining the track below the orchard and pooled between the shadows that were creeping across the garden. I turned my face up to it and closed my eyes, and said, 'Are you really going to leave Sean?'

'I don't know,' said Bex wearily.

I opened my eyes again and looked at her. 'What happened?'

She sighed. 'He sent me a text to say he wasn't coming home today; he was going sailing for the weekend with someone from the Sydney office. A *text*! Didn't even have the decency to ring. And then when I rang *him*, he wouldn't pick up. So I texted him back to ask when he *was* coming home, and he said he didn't know.' She picked a hawkweed flower from the grass at her feet and twirled it between her fingers. 'And that's it. I haven't heard anything else.'

I frowned. 'Did you guys have an argument before he left?'

'Not really.'

'Not really?'

'No more so than usual.'

'Maybe you *should* split up,' I said. 'You're not very happy together, are you?'

'Sometimes we are,' said Bex very softly.

'Oh,' I said. 'Good.'

'You don't need to sound quite so surprised.'

I said nothing, not knowing what to say, and tearing her flower deliberately in half she added, 'I think he's found someone else.'

'Why?'

'Well, not taking my calls is a hint!'

'Maybe,' I said slowly, 'he just decided that since he's going to get a hard time about being away anyway, he might as well do something to justify it for a change. He *has* to travel for work, but you always act as if he's swanning off for fun while you slave at home.'

'He is! His life's a bloody whirl of hotels and corporate lunches and drinks with clients on the company credit card.'

'Would you rather he hated his job?'

'Stop it,' she said. 'Stop being so *reasonable*. I *know* I'm a bitch. I hate myself.' She lay down flat on her back on the deck and looked morosely at the sky.

'Then there's your problem. Nobody can possibly be a nice person if they hate themselves.'

'You sound like a fucking self-help book,' she said, swatting irritably at Tessa, who was investigating her elbow with a wet black nose. 'Go away, you horrible little dog.'

'Stop it,' I said. 'Stop being such a brat.'

There was a breathless pause. Screaming tantrum or apology? Which was it to be? 'Can't help it,' Bex muttered at last, choosing neither option.

'You can,' I said firmly. 'Shitty things happen to everyone. What gives *you* the right to make everybody else's lives miserable when you're unhappy?'

She shrugged. 'Just a revolting human being, probably.'

'You're not, but you do a fairly good impression of it sometimes.'

There was another pause.

'Do you want my advice on your marriage?' I said. 'Seeing as I'm such an expert on the subject?'

Another shrug, which I decided to take as assent.

'When Sean comes home, just be pleased to see him. Say you're glad he's home. You could even go completely overboard and ask him if he had a nice time.'

'Why not cook him his favourite dinner and give him a blow job while I'm at it?'

I smiled at her. 'Well, why not?'

'Thank you, marriage expert.'

I sighed. 'It's always so much easier to see what other people are doing wrong.'

'Why *did* you marry Dave?' Bex asked curiously.

'Well, I was in love with him,' I said.

'Are you still?'

'No,' I said. 'God, no. I was such an idiot, Becca. I never bothered to get to know him when we started going out. I liked his looks, and I liked that he was a farmer, and I invented a personality to go with the rest of the package.' In my fevered twenty-four-year-old brain, sheep farmers were by definition quiet, capable, manly men with understated senses of humour and the ability to fix anything at all with duct tape, number eight wire or both. Like Dad. *Or Andrew*, I thought suddenly. *Or am I just doing it again?*

'So how long did it take you to figure out that he's a dick?' she asked.

'Hmm?' I gave myself a mental shake. 'Oh, I don't know. It was more of a gradual disillusionment than a lightning flash. And then – well, it was just easier to drift along, even if it wasn't the best marriage in the world.'

There was a long silence, while Bex spread her hands across her stomach and I stroked Tessa.

'So did whatshisname – Andrew – stay last night?' she asked.

'Only for a beer.'

'And?'

I lifted my eyebrows. 'And then he went home.'

'Jennifer!' she said sternly.

'He kissed me when he left,' I said to my feet. 'It was – it was nice.'

'Nice. Wow.'

I thought about kind, cynical, unhappy Andrew Faulkner – the way his eyes crinkled up at the corners when he smiled, and the slow, expert way he'd kissed me – and shivered. 'Very nice.'

'And yet he went home.'

'It *is* actually possible to find someone attractive and yet refrain from tearing all their clothes off and having wild sex with them on the spot,' I said.

Bex smiled. 'Not only possible but certain, if it's you we're talking about.'

I made a face at her. 'I have two children, and he's about to sell up and move, and he's only single in the first place because my brain-dead husband had an affair with his wife …'

'Moving?' she said. 'I thought he was going to stay here and start a district-wide takeover?'

'He says not. He says he wouldn't go into business with that Greenfarm lot; they're not to be trusted.'

'Bummer,' Bex said, stretching her arms languorously above her head. 'It seemed like such a good opportunity for you to have your cake and eat it.'

'What?'

'Well, if you shacked up with him you'd still be on the farm, even if it was sold.'

'You mean for me to have my cake and *you* to eat it,' I said dryly.

'Maybe. But I wouldn't worry,' she said. 'I'm sure the farm won't be sold if the favourite daughter says no.'

'I am not the favourite daughter, and you know it.'

'Well, your wishes certainly seem to carry a bit more weight than mine do,' she said.

'No, it's just that Dad would rather not sell the farm either.' I looked at her curiously. 'Bex, do you care about this place at all?'

'Of course I care about it. It's my home too. I'm just a bit more realistic than you are.'

We sat there in silence for a while, and then she reached out and took my hand. Her hand was slim and soft, with nicely manicured nails; mine was stubby and business-like, the fingers thickened from gardening. It looked much older than hers – a whole generation older, not just the two years that divided us. I wondered vaguely if there was a moral in that, and decided there probably wasn't.

'Please don't say anything to Mum about Andrew,' I said.

'Of course not!'

'Well, you told her he was here last night!'

'I was not myself last night, as you well know,' she said, squeezing my hand. Which was, for Bex, a pretty good apology.

* * *

The next day was Friday. Rebecca flew home in the morning, which was a positive step. And at work Greta looked reasonably cheerful, which was another. And Andrew wanted to see me on the weekend ... Things, I decided, sitting down at my desk and turning on my computer, were looking up. But before I could get too carried away by the general auspiciousness of the circumstances, my handbag chirruped. I hunted through it and extracted my cell phone. The message was from an unknown number.

Hi Jennie, Anaya here! I hope you don't mind my getting in touch (I got your number from Dave lol!). I realise this is a bit of an uncomfortable situation but I think it's best to be adult about the situation and accept that we're part of each others lives whether we like the idea or not lol!! 😉 😜

Definitely or not, I thought. *Lol.*

I'm so sorry for the short notice but my brothers home this weekend from south America and will be at my parents house at Coopers Beach. Its my only chance to see him and for him to meet David, but we both feel its unkind to drag Lily and Nathan (adore those kids!!) all that way for one night. Could we have them next weekend instead? I know that like me you only want whats best for them!!! Can't wait to meet you, Anaya ☺ ☺ ☺

Tight-lipped and white-knuckled, I put my phone down. It's bad enough being patronised, but being patronised by a birdbrain who sends novel-length, randomly punctuated text messages!

The phone extension on my desk rang before I'd formulated my reply. Then I had a site visit, and then a meeting. It was after twelve before I had the leisure to further consider the matter. What to write? How to convey scorn and contempt, and yet maintain the moral high ground? In the end I settled for, Okay. **Have a good weekend**, which failed on all counts, pressed send, and rang Dave.

'Jennifer,' he said, answering his phone.

'Don't you think Friday morning's a bit late to cancel having the kids?'

'Sorry. Unavoidable circumstances.'

'Like deciding to go to the beach with your girlfriend?'

He sighed.

'Lucky my weekend plans are so much less important than yours.'

'Yeah,' he said. 'Lucky.' And he hung up.

'You *fucking* bastard!' I said savagely, and Charlie the roading manager, passing the office doorway, stuck his head in and said, 'Bad day?'

I smiled at him shame-facedly. 'Just having a little private tantrum.'

'There's cake in the lunch room, if that would help,' he offered.

'Thanks.'

He carried on, and I looked at my watch. Lunchtime. I might catch Andrew at home. I might also catch Harry, of course. A risk that could be avoided by ringing Andrew's cell phone, if I only knew the number. But I didn't.

Sighing, I looked up A.C. and T.R. Faulkner, Pukewai Road, and dialled the number. The phone was answered with the inevitable, "Lo?'

'Which one is that?' I said, more crisply than I intended.

'Andrew. Hi, Jen.'

'Hi. I've just heard that Dave can't have the kids this weekend, so I won't be able to make it on Saturday. Well, not unless I bring them with me, and – and I don't know that …' I floundered to a standstill.

'Actually, I've, er, hurt my back,' he said. 'Maybe we should reschedule.'

'Okay,' I said unhappily. 'I hope it feels better soon.'

'It's no big deal. It'll be right in a day or two.'

'That's good. Oh well, catch you later.'

'Great,' he said awkwardly. 'Talk soon.'

'Bye.' I put down the phone and rested my forehead on my desk, which, although both foolish and theatrical, did actually make me feel a little bit better. Then I got up, temporarily ignoring the twenty-seven new emails that had arrived over the course of the morning, and went to get myself a piece of cake. I beat Todd Granger from roading to the last piece, so at least that was something.

Chapter 24

'I'm hungry,' said Lily, trailing up the hall on Sunday afternoon wearing my long floaty wraparound skirt, with an enormous plastic flower behind one ear.

'Sandwich?' I suggested, looking up from the washing pile. There's a mythical sort of quality to my washing pile – it reminds me of that poor Greek chap doomed to spend eternity pushing a boulder up a hill, only to watch it roll down again.

'Okay.' She opened the pantry. 'Where's the peanut butter?'

'On the shelf in front of you.'

'Yes, I *know*,' she said. 'But the jar is *empty*.'

'Then I suppose we're out. Have honey.'

'I don't like honey.'

'Since when?' I asked.

'Since *ages* ago. Anyway, there's none left.'

'Isn't there?' I said. 'Damn. Have a biscuit, then.'

'We've only got malt biscuits. They're gross. Can we go and see Nana? She has way nicer food than us.'

'Ouch,' I said, and she smiled. 'Not just now, love.'

'Why *not*?'

Because my parents had friends staying this weekend, a retired couple who had recently emigrated from Britain to be closer to their grandchildren. On the occasion of their previous visit they'd come to watch the pet lambs being fed. All had been going swimmingly – photos, cuddles, cries of, 'Oh, aren't they *sweet?*' – when Nathan came running down the orchard holding a small dead kitten by the tail.

'Look, Mum!' he'd cried. 'Harry got it with the grubber! Look, its eye's coming out!'

My subsequent efforts to explain the devastating effects of feral cats on the native bird population, and to reassure the lady that the poor little thing wouldn't have suffered, failed to make any impression whatsoever. She was escorted from the premises in tears, and a plan to introduce us to the rest of their family was repealed on the spot.

'Because ... we're going grocery shopping,' I said now. 'Where's your brother?'

Nathan was discovered in his bedroom, playing with his magic sand. On the carpet. 'Oh, *Nath*,' I said, stopping in the doorway.

'I put it on a mat,' he said, lifting big eyes to mine. 'But then it fell off.' He scrubbed at the edge of the pile with the corner of his cuddly blanket.

'Stop!' I cried.

'I'm cleaning it!'

'No you're not; you're making it worse.'

Having transferred the sand from the carpet to its box and the vacuum cleaner bag – about fifty percent each way – we drove into town. My cell phone beeped as we went down the hill, and Lily pounced on it. 'I'll read it!' she said. 'It's from Aunty Bex. "Smi – smiled! Cooked. Per-perf-or-m-ed –"?'

'Performed,' I said. 'It means "did".'

'"Fell–"' Lily continued slowly, '"–at–"'

Oh. Right. Good on her. 'Yep, that's okay, Lil, I know what she means,' I said quickly. 'Put the phone back in my bag; you'll get carsick.'

* * *

The supermarket was moderately crowded. We met Nathan's day care teacher in the vegetable aisle and the mayor beside the cereal. Local elections were getting close, so he smiled warmly and told the children they had a very clever and hard-working mummy.

'We know,' said Lily.

'Can we get ice cream?' Nathan asked.

Continuing on our way, we rounded the corner into the dairy aisle and found Andrew, wearing jeans and a free-with-drench rugby shirt, perusing tubs of yoghurt. 'Hi!' I said. 'How's your back?'

'Oh,' he said. 'Um, yeah, not too bad. Hi.' He seemed oddly taken aback at seeing us. And – and he could easily have dropped in over the weekend. I'd been telling myself for the last two days that it didn't matter, and I didn't mind ... *But I do mind*, I thought, relaxing my desperate grip on optimism with almost a sense of relief.

'Your dog bit Tessa,' Nathan informed him.

'I know,' he said. 'Sorry.'

'That's alright,' said Nathan graciously. 'Guess what?'

'What?'

'Tessa did a big spew by my bed this morning, and I standed in it.'

'Damn,' said Andrew. His eyes met mine, crinkling in amusement. 'I hate it when that happens.'

'Terrible start to the day,' I agreed, smiling.

And just then his wife came around the corner, saying, 'Babe, did you get hummus?'

Toni Faulkner was very thin and very fair, and she wore a pale grey jersey T-shirt dress and white canvas slip-on shoes which accentuated both thinness and pallor. I was struck, as I'd been struck before, by how tired she looked. How she'd ever managed to exert herself sufficiently to get off with my husband was a mystery.

Her eyes widened just the merest fraction as she saw me, and then slid away sideways.

'Hi,' I muttered, and bolted.

'Mum,' cried Lily, behind me. '*Mum!*'

I slowed and came to rest halfway down the next aisle. 'What?'

'What about the cheese?'

'What?' I said stupidly.

'You didn't get any cheese!'

'Oh,' I said. 'Um, we'll go back that way. Do you guys want some chips?'

'I want to choose them!' Nathan cried.

'You can both choose a packet.' And as they dashed off I took a long, shuddering breath. Where was I? Salsa, taco shells, two-minute noodles ... Did we want any of this stuff? No. Okay. Moving on.

'Jenny,' said Andrew, appearing beside me.

Frowning in concentration, I selected a jar of salsa. 'Hi.'

'It's not —' he started, and then stopped. 'Toni just turned up. We've got to go and see a lawyer tomorrow ...'

I tucked the salsa tenderly into my trolley between a leek and a box of eggs, straightened up and smiled at him brightly. 'Hope it goes well.'

'Jen ...'

'It's okay,' I said. 'I'll see you later.'

'Can we have these ones, Mum?' Lily called, running back down the aisle with a tube of Pringles in her hand.

'Yes. Sure.'

Suddenly Andrew put his hand over mine on the handle of the trolley. 'Please – please don't write me off just yet,' he said.

'Okay,' I whispered.

'Thank you.' He squeezed my hand, took his away and vanished swiftly back the way he'd come.

'Mum, what did he mean?' Lily asked.

'What? Oh, he – he was going to do something for me, but he hasn't got there yet,' I said.

'Oh,' she said. 'You look funny.'

I made a face at her. 'Not as funny as you. Nathan, my sweet, I said *one* packet of chips.'

* * *

As I put away the groceries I noted sadly that although I'd brought home salsa, which none of us liked, I'd forgotten both the peanut butter and the cheese. To make up for this, however, I had purchased two heads of broccoli, bringing the total in the fridge to four.

Chicken and broccoli stir fry? I mused, running the bath for the kids. *But it's so much better with peanut butter ... Broccoli and cheese sauce? Nope. What about that nice broccoli salad with bacon and toasted almonds ... and cheese. Oh, for fuck's sake.*

'Can we have some chippies?' Nathan asked.

'What, in the bath?'

'Yes!'

I kissed his shorn head. 'Why not?'

'You're the best mum *ever*,' he said, throwing his arms around my neck. 'Lily! Lily, Mum says we can eat chips in the bath!'

I was making chicken and broccoli stir fry (without peanut butter) to cancel out this debauchery when a vehicle came down the driveway. *Andrew*, I thought breathlessly, hastening to the door. *It won't be him. It won't be* ...

It wasn't.

'Bloody Toni's turned up,' Harry called, coming across the wet gravel. 'So I ran away.'

'When did she arrive?' I asked.

'This afternoon sometime, I suppose. I've been out topping thistles in the middle hay paddock.'

'On Sunday? That's above and beyond the call of duty.'

'I know,' he said. 'I'm amazing.'

'You are. Come on in.'

Pausing in the doorway to kick off his shoes, he shouted, 'Hi guys!' in the direction of the bathroom, whence came sounds of revelry and song.

'Hi, Harry!' the kids yelled back.

'I thought this was your ex's weekend to have them,' he remarked, closing the door behind him.

'It was, but he cancelled on Friday morning so he could go up north with his new girlfriend,' I said.

'What a guy.'

'Indeed. Would you like a drink?'

'Be rude not to,' he said.

I opened the fridge door and hunted for beer, which I had also forgotten to purchase. 'Export Citrus?'

'Anything else?'

'Milk?' I suggested.

'Export Citrus it is. Cheers.'

'So,' I said. 'How's Toni?'

'Buggered if I know. I left them to it.'

'To what?' I said tightly.

'What was that?'

'Nothing.'

'You okay, Jen?'

I smiled at him and nodded.

'I think they've got a meeting with a lawyer tomorrow. Andrew's being extra nice to her in the hope she'll give up on this instant sale idea of hers.'

'Is he?' I said stupidly, opening a drawer at random and hunting fruitlessly for a bottle opener among the tea towels.

Harry frowned at me for a second, and then light dawned and he said, 'Shit, sorry. You don't want to hear about her.'

'No, it's fine. Hey, Harry, how come you dislike her so much?'

'Because she sucks all the joy out of everyone and everything around her.'

I blinked. 'That's harsh.'

'You'd cook dinner, and she'd announce she was wheat- and dairy-free and she couldn't eat it. She didn't like any of Andrew's friends, but he wasn't allowed to see them without her. If they were out somewhere and he looked like he was having a good time, she'd suddenly get a terrible migraine and have to go home.'

'Wow. She sounds delightful.'

'She *is* bloody funny when she's in a good mood,' Harry conceded. 'She's an incredible mimic.'

At which point I discovered that, although I quite enjoyed hearing about Toni's failings, her merits were an entirely different kettle of fish. Better change the subject before I gave myself away. 'Are you staying for tea?' I asked. 'Although I warn you, it's nothing flash.'

'Yeah, why not?' he said. There was a shriek and a mighty splash from the bathroom. 'What on earth is happening down there?'

'I hate to think. I suppose I'd better go and investigate.'

'Sorry, Mummy,' said Lily in a very small voice as I appeared in the bathroom doorway.

'That's okay, chicken,' I said, surveying the lake at my feet. 'How about getting out now?'

The noise of the bath emptying covered all sounds of approaching vehicles, and when Dave said, 'Holy heck, Nath, what happened to your hair?' from just behind me I spun around so fast I almost gave myself whiplash.

'Mummy cutted it!' said Nathan, hurling himself at his father and nearly falling flat on his face as he collided with Tessa, who was rubbing herself ecstatically against Dave's shins.

'So I see. Hang on a tick, mate, you're sopping wet.' He held Nathan up with one hand and opened the cupboard under the sink where the towels lived with another.

A short, plump, sweetly pretty girl with smooth brown hair and lovely skin appeared in the doorway behind him. 'Oh,' she said sorrowfully. 'Oh, Nathan, sweetheart, your beautiful curls!'

'He had a really big knot,' Lily explained, trailing the end of her towel in the puddle on the floor.

Dave wrapped Nathan in a towel and pushed him towards the girl behind him. 'You sort him out, babe, while I organise Lily,' he said. 'Settle down, Tessa, would you?'

'Dave, I've got this,' I said, intensely irritated by this takeover, and then even more irritated with myself for sounding sour and ungracious.

Dave ignored me, relieved Lily of her towel, dropped it on the floor and began briskly to dry her hair with a fresh one. 'Had a nice weekend, baby?'

'Yes,' Lily said, slightly muffled by the towel. 'But it was a bit boring.'

'Well, we'll just have to see if we can fix that next weekend, won't we? Maybe we could go to the movies. Or the beach.'

Lily fought her way free of the towel. 'Can we go fishing?' she asked eagerly.

'Well, maybe. Anaya hasn't surf-casted before; we'll have to show her what to do.'

'Will you teach me, Lily?' Anaya asked, smiling. A fake, sickly sort of smile, I thought, although honesty forces me to admit that she was probably just trying to be nice.

'Yes,' Lily said.

Anaya turned her smile in my direction. 'Hello,' she said. 'You must be Jenny. It's lovely to finally meet you.'

'Hi,' I said, trying hard to look nicer than I felt. 'Did you have a good weekend?'

'Lovely, thank you. Although we missed these little people.'

I smiled mechanically and bent to gather an armful of sopping towels and drop them into the bath.

'Anaya, can you come and see my room?' Lily asked.

'And mine!' Nathan put in.

'I'd love to see *both* of them,' Anaya said, following the children along the hall into Lily's bedroom.

I picked up a wet towel and began to wring it out.

'How often is *he* here?' Dave murmured, pushing Tessa out of the way and spreading Lily's towel across the puddle on the floor.

'None of your business,' I murmured back, losing the unequal struggle with my better self.

'If he's hanging around my children, it's my business.'

I straightened with a jerk and turned to face him. 'Do you honestly think I'd let someone who might hurt the kids anywhere *near* them?'

'I'm just –'

'Just trying to throw your weight around. Yes, I noticed.'

'I'm just worried about you,' he corrected evenly.

This was the Last Straw. In capitals, no less. 'Go away,' I whispered savagely. 'Take your dippy little girlfriend and *go away*.'

'Don't take this out on Anaya,' he hissed.

'Then don't bring her around here and rub her in my face!'

Dave smiled at me kindly. 'Jenny, you're going to have to accept that she's a part of my life, now.'

I stood up. 'Get out,' I said softly, my voice shaking. 'I do *not* want to shout at you in front of the kids, and if you say another *word* I fucking will, so help me God.'

Dave retreated before me into the hall. 'Babe,' he called, eyeing me warily, 'we'd better go.'

Anaya appeared in Nathan's bedroom doorway. 'Okay,' she said. 'Thank you so much for showing me your beautiful rooms.'

We all proceeded up the hallway to the kitchen, where Harry was cutting an onion into thick slices, which the children would undoubtedly refuse to eat.

'Mm,' Anaya said, smiling at Nathan. 'It looks like you're going to have a yummy tea.'

Dave gathered up both children and hugged them. 'Bye, kidlets. See you on Wednesday,' he said.

'Bye, Daddy,' said Lily sadly, and I fought down another spike of rage. *Damn* Dave. Maybe he hadn't called in to flaunt his new girlfriend in my face – maybe he'd genuinely only wanted to see his children – but the effect was the same. It just reminded the kids yet again of the difference between life now and life the way it used to be, in the days when home was home and they weren't handed constantly from one parent to the other like human bargaining chips.

Harry looked up from his onions, winked at me and looked down again, and that small gesture of support and solidarity enabled me to smile at Anaya and say, 'Lovely to meet you. Thanks for calling in.'

She smiled back, obviously pleased that I was being reasonable. It seemed a shame that her pleasure was only going to last for about a minute and a half, until Dave delivered his verdict on my manners and morals in the car.

* * *

'Mummy?' said Nathan at bedtime, as I tucked the duvet in around his shoulders. He liked to sleep firmly wrapped.

'Mm?'

'Would a T-rex beat a lion?'

'I expect so,' I said. 'It'd be lots bigger. But I think a lion might run faster, so it could probably get away.'

'What about a shark? A big one?'

'Well, hard to know. Maybe the shark. I don't know if T-rexes were very good at swimming. In fact, I bet they weren't. Imagine trying to paddle with teeny little arms.' I did a tyrannosaur dog-paddling impression using only my index fingers, and he giggled.

'What about a ...'

'Sh,' I said, bending to kiss him. 'Sleep time.'

'No, but what about a boy with a gun? If he shot it right in the head.'

I stood up. 'You know, Nath, if you *did* happen to find a T-rex still alive, it'd be a bit of a shame to shoot it, don't you think?'

'But if it was going to eat you and Lily.'

'In that case,' I said, 'I'd let you away with it. Night, love.'

'Mummy?'

'That's enough. Go to sleep.'

'But – but – but can we have pizza tomorrow, and can I sprinkle the cheese with my fairy fingers?'

I smiled. Ruthless dinosaur assassin one second, dainty cheese sprinkler the next. 'Absolutely,' I said. 'Goodnight.'

* * *

'Is it reasonable that I'm mad at Dave for showing up unannounced with the new model in tow?' I asked Harry, going back up the hall into the living room and beginning to scrape the Lego littering the carpet into a pile with the side of my foot. 'Or am I just being a bitch, and I need to get over myself?'

'No, fair enough, I guess,' said Harry, which wasn't quite as reassuring as I'd have liked. 'Hey, I took your advice.'

'Did you? Very risky.'

'You were right. If Chris wants to be with me, he can bloody well tell Ryan, and break it off with him. I told him he's treating both of us like shit.'

'Good on you,' I said.

'So I gave him an ultimatum. If I haven't heard from him by tomorrow night, I'll assume it's all off and – and –'

'Go online and meet someone fabulous?'

'Hell, no,' said Harry. 'Probably just pine away and die. But at least I'll do it with dignity.' He smiled at me, then leant forward and extracted a large piece of the coffee cake I'd made that morning from its tin.

* * *

Andrew came over at half past eight the next evening, on foot. The air was fresh and spicy-smelling after a shower of rain, the kids were asleep and I was wandering restlessly around the garden in the dusk, hoping he would come, telling myself he wouldn't and failing entirely to do anything productive in the meantime. I heard his boots crunch across the gravel in front of the house and emerged from behind the lemon tree.

'Hi,' I said.

He jumped and spun around. 'Christ. Hi.'

'Sorry to give you a fright.'

'It's fine,' he said, and there was an awkward silence.

'Come – come and look at something,' I said at last.

We went around the corner of the house and along the wide, wet grass path between orchard and flower garden to where a snowball bush covered in creamy globes of blossom, overhung the edge of the lawn. The flowers glowed in the dusk and a wood pigeon, settled for the night in a cherry tree above our heads, shifted uncomfortably and then left his perch to swoop down across the orchard with a noise like tearing silk. 'Isn't it pretty?'

I said, reaching up to touch a soft ball of flowers and dislodging a shower of raindrops.

'Yes,' said Andrew. 'Beautiful. Jenny, I'm really sorry about yesterday afternoon.'

'Did you really hurt your back?' I asked, before I'd realised I was going to.

'What?'

'When I rang you on Friday you said you'd hurt your back.'

'Oh,' he said. 'Yes. Bending over to spit out my toothpaste. Not the most manly injury.'

I smiled, albeit a little weakly.

'I prolapsed a disc a few years ago. It's pretty good these days, but every now and then I tweak it and it goes into spasm.' He looked at me, frowning. 'Did you think it was an excuse to get out of seeing you on Saturday?'

'I wasn't sure,' I said.

He sighed. 'For what it's worth, which probably isn't much, I was really looking forward to Saturday. And I was expecting to meet Toni at the lawyer's office this morning.'

I looked at him for a moment, and said, 'Alright. Fair enough.'

He looked so surprised that I smiled. 'Did you manage to change her mind?'

'Pardon?' he said.

'About selling the farm straight away.'

'No.'

'I'm so sorry.'

'Oh well,' he said. 'Such is life.'

'When will it be sold?'

'March, I think.'

'Any idea what you'll do then? I'm sorry, I'm interrogating you ...'

'That's alright. I'll look for a manager's job, I guess.' He pulled a leaf off the snowball bush, and a whole drift of tiny white florets spiralled towards the ground. 'It'll have to be farming; I don't know how to do anything else.'

'I think you could do anything you wanted to,' I said.

'I don't want to do anything else.'

He'd worked so hard, and it didn't matter. He was losing everything anyway. Wanting somehow to comfort him, I took his face between my hands and pulled his head down so I could kiss him. It was quite a long time before we broke apart, and we stood and blinked at one another foolishly.

'Sorry,' I said at last.

'Don't mention it,' he said, and I noted with a certain amount of satisfaction that his voice shook.

'That probably wasn't the smartest idea.'

'Wasn't it? I liked it.'

'So did I. But – but we're both in the middle of nasty divorces, and I've got two small children ...'

'Mm,' he said. 'On the other hand, we could probably both do with something nice happening, for a change.'

'Just look at it as light relief?'

He smiled at me wryly. 'Why not?'

Why not indeed? Perhaps because when sensible people decide they'd like a little light relief, they go for binge-watching the *Outlander* series, not sleeping with the next-door neighbour. 'I might get all attached, and cling sobbing around your neck,' I said.

'So might I. Or you might decide I'm a complete tosser.'

'Or vice versa.'

'I doubt it, but I suppose it's possible ...' He turned serious. 'Jenny, if you don't want to take this any further, just say so.'

I felt a swift jolt of panic. It's one thing to point out what could go wrong, and quite another to actually sway the person you're pointing it out to. 'Andrew Faulkner, are you reverse-psychologising me?' I asked.

He smiled. 'Maybe. Is it working?'

'Yes, damn you,' I said, and his smile widened.

'Then I'll stop while I'm ahead.'

We walked silently back towards the house. 'Shall we have another go at looking at that waterfall?' he asked, pausing beside the carport.

'Okay. Yes.'

'It's Wednesday nights that you don't have the kids, isn't it?'

I nodded.

'So I'll pick you up at six on Wednesday?'

'Sounds good,' I said.

'Cool. Goodnight, Jen.'

'Goodnight.'

He strode off up the driveway. I stood quite still for a long time after his footsteps had faded into silence, hugging myself against the cold while the shadows thickened and the stars came out. Life was wonderful, magical, thrilling ... *Any minute*, I thought, *you're going to start singing about raindrops on kittens.* I smiled, and stretched, and went inside.

Chapter 25

When Nathan and I got home from taking Lily to school the next morning, we found John's little white car parked on the lawn. The boot was open, revealing a pile of planks, and as we pulled into the carport John himself came around the corner holding a draining spade. His leg was still heavily bandaged, and his customary wilted cigarette hung from his bottom lip.

'Morning,' he said, nodding to us as we got out of the car.

'Hi, John. What are you doing?'

'That compost bin isn't going to build itself, now, is it?'

'But your leg,' I said.

John smiled at me kindly. 'If I waited until I had no aches and pains before I did any work, m' dear, I'd never do anything at all.'

'And all this wood! You shouldn't have paid for —'

'I didn't,' he said cheerfully. 'Put it on your account. You can just tell your accountant it's fencing materials, and you won't pay any tax. Now, I'll struggle along here for a bit, and then we'll have a cup of tea and a chat, eh?'

'I'm afraid I'm a bit tied up this morning,' I said, somewhat taken aback by this freedom with my credit. 'I've got a lady coming over with some building plans for me to look at.'

'Adding another couple of rooms, are you? Must be nice to be a land baron.'

'Her house, not mine,' I said. 'Come on, Nathan, love.'

'I'm going to help Mr Mercer,' Nathan said.

'Well, thank you very much, young man,' said John, with such touching delight that my conscience pricked me uncomfortably. 'You can carry my spirit level, if you'll be so kind.'

'Would you like to have tea with us tonight, John?' I said impulsively, before remembering that it was Tuesday, and that my recurrent Tuesday dinner guest would be underwhelmed by this happy notion.

But John shook his head. 'Not tonight,' he said. 'I'm having a bite in at the club with friends. How about tomorrow?'

'No, I'm busy tomorrow.' Waterfall viewing, which indicated either a praiseworthy determination to seize the day or a reckless disregard for the consequences of my actions. If only one could tell the difference in advance.

'And me and Lily won't be here tomorrow, anyway,' Nathan said.

'Thursday?' I suggested, and John bowed his head in gracious assent.

* * *

My visitor was Claire Potter, a friend of Mum's, and she stayed for two hours. My mother had a somewhat unfortunate habit of assuring her wide circle of friends and acquaintances that in her free time Jenny liked nothing better than looking at the floor plans of their houses, perusing their LIM reports and fast-tracking their building consents. She asked me various questions – several times each, because she wouldn't stop talking to listen to the answers — drank two cups of coffee and told me all about her daughter-in-law's multiple failings as a wife and mother. At quarter past eleven I waved her off, sent up a short prayer of thanks that nothing had come of my going to the school ball with Lance Potter at the age of sixteen, and went outside to find my builders. They were sawing a plank — at least John was sawing while Nathan, with an expression of fierce concentration, held the free end steady.

'Hi, guys!' I said. 'Gosh, it's coming along in leaps and bounds!'

John straightened, saw in hand. 'Yes, we're doing nicely.'

'I digged in a post,' Nathan said proudly.

'Good on you,' I said. 'Thanks so much for letting him help, John.'

'A pleasure,' said John. 'We're having a good time, aren't we, young fella? Thirsty work, though.'

'I'm hungry,' Nathan said. 'Can we have popcorn?'

'Popcorn?' John repeated. 'What do you want with that nasty stuff? Sticks in your false teeth something awful.'

'Harry can catch popcorns with his mouth,' said Nathan. 'Like this. *Umph.*' He demonstrated. 'We're going to practise tonight when he comes for tea.'

'Coming for tea, is he?'

'He always comes on Tuesdays.'

'Does he now?' John said, looking at me with mournful disapproval.

Wrong brother, John, I thought, with a little shiver of nervous excitement.

* * *

I was in the council toilets the next afternoon, washing my hands and wondering, as usual, if the person responsible for painting the walls a shade of bluish mauve that made everyone look undead had actually liked the colour or whether it had been an act of covert rebellion, when the door burst open behind me and Greta shot in as if she'd been fired from a gun. Her eyes met mine in the mirror for one startled instant, and then she dashed into a cubicle and shut the door.

'Are you okay?' I asked. It was a stupid question – she obviously wasn't.

'Fine,' she said, in a sort of strangled gulp.

'Would you like a cup of tea? I was just going to make one.'

'No. But thank you. It's just that Marcus had to cancel dinner tonight. It's not his fault, something's come up, but my friend'll give me a hard time about it.'

'Mm,' I said sympathetically.

'Ignore me. I'm making a big deal out of nothing. He's – he's just been a bit stressed.'

'Greta, you don't have to stay with him if he's making you miserable,' I said, rushing in where angels may well have feared to tread. 'I know it never seems that simple when you're in the middle of these things, but –'

'Thank you so much for your advice,' said Greta, in a voice like a brick wall with broken glass on top.

I sighed and returned to my desk to ring Roy Whittaker and inform him that filling a five-centimetre gap between roof and chimney with Polyfilla did *not* meet the required standard.

* * *

Andrew arrived at my place on the dot of six to pick me up.

It'll be fine, I told myself as I went out to meet him. *It'll all be fine* ...

'Hi,' he said, getting out of his ute.

'Hi.'

'Good day?'

'Not bad,' I said. 'You?'

'Yeah, fine. Ready to go?'

'Yes. Sneakers or work boots?'

'Maybe work boots,' he said. 'Might be a bit muddy in places.'

I tied up an indignant Tessa, and we drove up the road and turned through a gateway just past Andrew's woolshed. A track led sharply downhill past his implement shed, where Harry was just shutting up his dog. He looked up as the ute approached, and his eyebrows lifted. I felt myself blushing, which of course made me blush even more. I do wish embarrassment didn't work on a positive feedback loop.

Andrew pulled up beside his brother but left the ute running.

'Where are you two off to?' Harry asked.

'Going to see the waterfall,' Andrew said.

'I've always wanted to see it,' I put in, 'but I've never got there. Granddad used to talk about it.'

'Right,' said Harry. He looked me up and down, and I had the sudden, uncomfortable conviction that he'd noticed I was wearing eyeliner and was leaping to conclusions. 'Have fun.'

Andrew started to let the clutch out, and Meg howled piteously from the next kennel along.

'We'd better bring her, hadn't we?' I said. 'That's unbearable.'

He sighed, stopped, got out of the ute and went to open the door of Meg's kennel. He picked her up and carried her over, setting her down on the back. She stalked forward, glared at me through the back window of the cab, and growled.

'What's her problem?' Harry said.

'Is she not like this with you?' I asked.

'No.'

'I thought she hated everyone.'

The growling deepened, and Andrew said sharply, 'Sit down, you old tart.'

She did, with an audible *humph* of disgust.

'No, just you,' Harry said. 'Obviously views you as competition.'

I looked at him with what was intended to be withering scorn, and he laughed.

Harry's dog was lying down, chin on paws, after his day's work, but the half-grown pup in the next kennel along was bouncing up and down and whimpering. Andrew looked at him, sighed again and let him out, and the little dog jumped at him ecstatically in a blur of flailing paws and wet pink tongue. 'Al*right*, Jake, you twit!' he said, batting him away.

'And there you have it,' Harry remarked. 'The final death blow to romance.'

'Oh, shut up,' said Andrew.

Harry grinned. 'He's such a grumpy bastard, Jen. Are you sure you've thought this through?'

'We're just going to see a waterfall,' I said. 'Why don't you come?'

It occurred to me just after making this suggestion that it would be spectacularly awkward if he did, but luckily he shook his head. 'Wouldn't dream of intruding.'

Slightly ruffled, we continued down the fenced laneway that ran past Andrew's house, up again and then down over the brow of a long hill that fell to the river flats below. The flats were in shadow and the bush-clad gully below us looked dark and mysterious, but the evening light warmed the hillside across the river to greenish gold.

'What a wonderful view,' I said. 'Where's your boundary, Andrew?'

He stopped the ute and turned the engine off. 'The far side of that block of bush,' he said, pointing. 'Then down to the river, and it does a funny little dog-leg across the flats – those white-faced steers are mine, but the poplars behind them are on Mick Cooper's place – and up again on the far side of that half-round hay barn.'

'It's lovely.'

He smiled. 'It's not bad, is it? Right, this is where we get out and walk.'

Accompanied by a wildly excited pup and watched balefully by Meg, we climbed the fence and walked downhill to meet a narrow grassy track, cut across the face of the hillside long ago. The bank to our left was thick with ladder fern, the new fronds unrolling in shades of pink and gold, and on the right the hillside fell from sheep track to sheep track in a series of furry green terraces. 'Track's a bit boggy here, I'm afraid,' said Andrew, jumping a patch of buttercups and turning to offer me a hand.

I didn't take it, being distracted by a tiny black-and-white bird that darted across the track in front of us, perched for a moment on a twig and then flitted on to vanish over the brow of the hill. I gasped. 'Did you see that?'

'What?'

'That was a *tomtit*! It must have been! Nothing else looks like that!'

'Yep,' he said. 'I see them around here from time to time.'

'That's *wonderful*,' I said, fending off Jake the pup, who was licking my right kneecap with inexplicable enthusiasm. 'I remember Granddad saying he'd seen tomtits around home when he was a boy, but never since the war.'

Andrew picked up his dog by the collar and dropped him down the hill, where he turned several somersaults with unabated good humour, regained his feet and bounded back towards us. 'You've probably still got a few lurking around,' he said. 'Royce hadn't seen them either, but I put bait stations through the bush when we came here, and the numbers are building up.'

'We need to do more predator control, too. I should have got on to it years ago. Man, I'm slack.'

'Yes,' he said. 'Appallingly slack. You've only got a farm and a job and two children and about three acres of garden. I don't know what you've been doing with your time.'

'I'm not nearly as impressive as you imply,' I said, shaking my head. 'Although it's nice of you to imply it.'

He smiled at me but didn't answer.

The waterfall, reached after another five minutes' walk and then a short slither down a steep slope through the bush, was a gem. It poured smoothly over the edge of a granite-lipped basin into a deep, round, black pool, where it seethed and churned energetically before collecting itself to hurry on downstream between slick black boulders. It was cool and dim beneath the trees, a tui somewhere nearby sang a counterpoint to the relentless, unhurried roar of water and the air smelt damp and spicy.

Jake the pup, who had been bouncing through a patch of begonia fern twice as tall as he was, lay down across my feet and panted happily. 'He's very sweet,' I said, tickling him under the chin with the toe of my left boot.

'I wonder how sweet you'd have thought he was this morning when he chased twenty sheep into the swamp below the woolshed.'

'Less sweet, I expect,' I said.

'It did occur to me after I'd been screaming at him for a while that it was lucky you were at work, or you might have heard me and decided I had some serious anger management issues.'

'Nah,' I said, smiling at him. 'You, angry? Inconceivable.'

'Sarcasm, my mother used to say, is the lowest form of wit,' he remarked.

'Next you'll be telling me you're grumpy.'

'Only under extreme provocation.'

'What about at Pet Day, when I asked you for a lift home and you acted like I was trying to sell you a vacuum cleaner?'

'I did not!'

'Yeah, you did, but I forgive you.'

'You're very kind,' he said. 'I'm sorry. Toni had just rung up and thrown this farm sale thing at me.'

'Ah.'

'And then when I got home Harry gave me a lecture about how I couldn't possibly understand what it feels like to be betrayed by the person you love.'

I grimaced. 'He is a bit oblivious at times. Did you crush him like a bug?'

'You mean the way I crushed you the other day?'

'Mm.'

He scratched his ear sheepishly. 'I may have.'

Jake the pup, evidently feeling refreshed and ready for action, stood up, shook himself and lunged upwards, swiping my chin with half a metre or so of wet tongue.

'Get down, you maniac,' said Andrew, swatting him away.

'At least this one likes me,' I remarked.

'He's really thick,' he said, and then thought about that statement and laughed.

I punched him in the arm, just gently, and he caught my fist and held it. There was a short, breathless silence. Then I smiled, and he smiled back at me, and we walked into one another's arms as easily and naturally as if we'd been doing it for years.

It was Jake, forcing his head between our bodies and panting happily, who eventually separated us. 'You smell nice,' I said shakily.

'Do I? Home Brand shower gel.' He touched my cheek very softly with the back of a finger. 'Are you hungry?'

'I, um – y-yes,' I said, shaken completely off what remained of my balance by the gesture.

'Me too.' He took my left hand and held it firmly, and, with Jake bounding around us in circles, we started back up the hill.

* * *

We drove back to the implement shed, where Andrew fed the dogs and shut them away for the night. 'Would you like to come in and have some dinner?' he asked.

I looked towards the house, and Harry's car parked outside. I was very fond of Harry, but … 'Let's get something at my place.'

'Sounds good,' he said, and we continued up the track, leaving Meg barking resentfully behind us.

'Right,' I said when we'd reached my house and had followed Tessa up the back steps and into the kitchen. 'What do you feel like eating? I can do steak, bacon and eggs, pasta-type stuff, risotto ...' I turned to look at him, and my throat closed up. He was watching me with that mixture of admiration and nervousness and sheer blazing excitement that you can't mistake for anything other than sexual attraction. Without really deciding to, I took a step towards him.

He took two steps, and kissed me.

'Come on,' I said a few minutes later, pulling back and taking his hand.

'Jen ...' he said, resisting.

I looked at him, not taken aback, exactly, but surprised.

'I don't have any condoms. Have you?'

'Oh,' I said. 'No, but I've got an IUD.'

'A what?'

'Intra-uterine device.'

He looked entirely blank.

'Little wire thingummy. Sits in your cervix, stops you getting pregnant.'

'Who knew?' he said.

'Sorry, it's not the most alluring concept ...'

He smiled slowly, and my stomach quivered. 'Want to bet?'

We went down the hall to my bedroom at the end. Tessa came too, but Andrew bent down, scooped her up and dropped her in the hallway, closing the door behind her. As he turned back towards me I said breathlessly, 'It's okay to do this, isn't it? We're not hurting anyone.'

He shook his head and held his hands out. I put mine into them, and he pulled me up against him.

'How's your back?' I asked.

'Fine, thank you,' he said, a touch repressively. 'How's your chlamydia?'

I laughed. 'Good. I mean gone. Successfully treated.'

'Marvellous,' he said, starting to undo my shirt. 'God, Jenny, you're beautiful.'

Chapter 26

Some time later, having very kindly supplied me with the nicest sexual experience of my life, he sighed and rolled away from me.

'Come back,' I whispered.

'I would, but I lack the strength.' He groped for my hand and squeezed it feebly.

'Like a salmon.'

'Pardon?'

'They mate and then die of exhaustion. Lily did a school project on them last term.'

He turned his head and smiled at me. 'I don't think it's quite that desperate. How are you?'

'Excellent,' I said, smiling back.

'No regrets?'

I shook my head. 'You?'

'Hell, no.'

I squeezed his hand. 'Do you still love Toni?'

'What sort of a question is that?'

'I know. It's a terrible thing to ask. But it's such a good opportunity, while you lack the strength to get up and run away.'

There was a pause, long enough for me to wonder if he was going to reply at all, before he said, 'I suppose I do, in a way. God knows the last few years weren't much fun, but – you don't just walk away from someone without a backward glance after twenty years.'

'Twenty years,' I said slowly. 'How old are you?'

'Er ... forty-one. Why?'

'Just – twenty years is a long time.' Half his life, in fact. *All* his adult life.

'Yeah, I suppose it is. She was my first serious girlfriend.'

'Where did you meet?'

'Napier Young Farmers.' He rubbed the side of his thumb across my knuckles. 'Do we really need to talk about Toni just now?'

'No, I suppose not.'

'What about you? How did you end up with ... him?' The pause where he considered saying Dave's name and decided not to was barely noticeable.

'Um ... We met in a bar in London. We were both travelling. I was twenty-four.' A young accountant with damp hands had bought me a drink, then excused himself to go to the bathroom. I was sipping my half-pint of lager and wondering if politeness demanded I stay and make conversation until I'd finished it when a voice behind me – a New Zealand-accented voice that made my throat tighten with homesickness – said, 'Don't do it.'

I'd turned to see a tanned, wiry young man with most beguiling dimples. 'Don't do what?'

The dimples flashed. 'Him ...'

'Do you still love him?' Andrew asked.

'No,' I said, looking up at the ugly little smear Nathan and a handful of homemade PVA glue and cornflour slime had made on the ceiling. I hadn't loved Dave for a long time. It had all been pretty bloody mediocre, to be honest. And I hadn't tried to fix it;

I'd just shuffled drearily along. What a – a *victim*. 'I stayed because it was easier. And for the kids ... I should have done something about it.'

Andrew rubbed his thumb across the backs of my knuckles. 'You did,' he said. 'You are.'

I turned my head and saw him watching me. He was beautiful, although he was too thin; perfectly put together, like a minimalist sculpture.

'So I am,' I said, smiling at him. 'Are you hungry?'

'Starving.'

'Right.' I sat up, and he reached across and pulled me down again.

'That,' I said, 'is not going to fix your hunger.'

He ran his hands down my sides. 'I don't care,' he said.

* * *

We did get up, in due course, and climbed rather self-consciously back into our clothes. I turned the kitchen lights on as I passed them, and the twilight outside deepened instantly to night. Tessa, curled up in her basket beside the table, got up, shuffled around a hundred and eighty degrees, and lay down again with her back ostentatiously towards us. You could almost hear her judgmental sniff.

'Bacon and eggs?' I offered.

'Sounds good.'

'Do you have a burning desire for salad to go with it?'

'No, thanks,' he said. 'I'd kill for a cup of coffee, though.'

We made dinner together, blushing like teenagers when our eyes met, and sat down at the dining room table to eat it.

Discovering at that point that fried eggs don't go well with stomach butterflies, I abandoned food and watched Andrew's hands instead. I liked Andrew's hands a lot.

'– sell?' he asked.

I ran a hasty mental replay of the previous few seconds and failed to resurrect the rest of the sentence. 'Sorry,' I said, reddening. 'What was that?'

'Harry tells me that your sister's very keen to sell your place.'

'Oh. Yes. There's a bit of a ceasefire just at the moment, while we wait to hear how much your friend Richard Green will offer. If anything.'

He nodded, busy arranging his coffee cup, the butter dish and a jar of plum jam in a precise equilateral triangle.

'And if he does make a decent offer, Bex's argument is that if the place has to be sold eventually it might as well be sooner rather than later.'

'And the sooner she gets her chunk the better,' he said.

I sighed. 'Well, yes. But it's not just that. Mum and Dad are in their sixties, and if they wait another ten years before they have a bit of cash to play with, that's a big chunk of their retirement gone. And that's assuming that neither of them develops some major health problem in the meantime.'

'Do they want to sell?'

'Yes and no,' I said. 'Dad doesn't really, but if it's going to happen anyway, he'd prefer not to watch his eldest daughter wasting her youth' – I wrinkled my nose to show I wasn't actually getting carried away on a tide of melodrama – 'on a lost cause.'

'Does it have to be split fifty-fifty? It can't be held in trust for the next generation?'

I shook my head. 'Not if there isn't going to be some hideous family schism, it can't. Bex already likes to think I'm the favourite daughter – she'd never get over it if I inherited the family farm.'

'Mm,' he said, grimacing.

There was a short silence. 'Hey, Andrew?' I asked, breaking it. 'Do you shear your lambs at weaning?'

He looked slightly startled, but he said, 'No.'

'Because they get pneumonia?'

'Yeah, they can do. It's a bit rough on them, doing two stressful things at the same time.'

'Right,' I said. That was what the Beef and Lamb website, which was providing all my current bedtime reading, said. We'd always shorn lambs at weaning; I'd thought it was just what you did. 'And Harry said that you don't get the stock agent to pick your fat lambs; you just go by weight.'

'You can do it either way,' he said.

'You don't find that you end up sending big skinny ones and getting penalised?'

He shook his head. 'Don't seem to.'

'What weight do you go down to?'

'Before weaning or after?'

'Does it make a difference?' I asked.

'Absolutely. The rumen's bigger when they're eating all grass, so the kill-out percentage falls.'

Who knew? 'What weight before weaning, then?'

'Depends on the season,' he said, smiling.

I beat my forehead against the table – just softly, for effect.

'Look, it *does*!' he said. 'If it looks like drying out, and grass is short, and the lamb schedule's falling like a stone, then you get rid of as many as you can. But if the grass is up to your knees and the prices are holding, you'd probably grow them as big as you could.'

I sat up again. 'Okay,' I said. 'Granted. But what would you do *this* year, if you were us?'

He readjusted his cup a fraction of a degree. 'Well, in your situation, where you don't have much spare feed ...'

'Tactfully put,' I remarked.

He smiled fleetingly. 'I'd probably wean early – first week in December. Send everything that's killable to the works – over thirty-four kilos, say – and sell everything between twenty-eight and thirty-four kilograms store. Then give all the little ones a drench and a B12 injection, and spread them out in your best grass.'

I got up and fetched a pad and pen from beside the phone. 'Thirty-four plus to the works,' I muttered, writing it down. 'Twenty-eight to thirty-four kilograms store ... thank you so much.'

'I feel I should be charging for this,' he said.

I smiled at him. 'You should. I'm taking shocking advantage of you.'

'You are. It's appalling.'

'D'you think you'll be able to forgive me?'

He reached across the table and touched the tip of my index finger with his. 'Oh, I expect so,' he said.

* * *

We left the dirty dishes in the sink and went back to bed, and then, although he'd meant to get up again and go home, we both fell rapidly asleep. Hours later, rolling over and meeting a warm bare leg, I woke up again with a start.

'Wha's wrong?' Andrew muttered.

I squinted at the digital alarm clock on the dresser across the room. Eleven fifty-seven. 'It's nearly midnight!'

He stirred and stretched. 'Are you going to turn into a pumpkin?'

I giggled. 'No, but Harry will be appalled.'

'Well, we can't have that,' he said, sighing and pushing himself slowly up to sit.

'Don't go. Unless you want to.'

'Are you sure?'

'Yes,' I said, although I wasn't, quite. Not about him staying, but about Harry knowing he had.

He lay back down and pulled me up against him, and I decided I didn't care if Harry, or indeed anyone else, knew.

* * *

I floated into work the next morning in a state of such unshakeable goodwill and happiness that not even a staff workshop focused on revising the council's mission statement and realigning ourselves with ratepayer core values could spoil my mood. Which was amazing, because normally wasting two or three hours at such a workshop and then having to take work home in order to actually meet the needs of a few ratepayers pisses me off like nothing else on earth.

John was hard at work on the compost bin when the kids and I got home. Nathan rushed to help, bless him, allowing me to escape without offence, and Lily followed me inside.

'Anaya says sugar is poisonous,' she told me. 'We weren't allowed ice cream for pudding. We had a frozen banana chopped up in the food processor.'

'Dad too?' I asked. Surely not; Dave routinely took sugar *and* sweetened condensed milk in his coffee.

'Yes.'

'Wow,' I said, reflecting that it really must be love. And such was my current mood that I reflected it with almost no sarcasm at all.

'It wasn't very nice. *Is* sugar poisonous, Mummy?'

'No. You just don't want to overdo it.'

'But Anaya *said*.'

'Well, she's kind of right,' I said. 'If you had Coke on your Weet-Bix instead of milk, and a packet of lollies every day, you'd start to feel pretty lousy. And your teeth would probably turn black and fall out, which isn't really the best look.'

Lily giggled.

'But a little bit of sugar here and there isn't going to do you any harm. And life's pretty depressing if it's all whole grains and frozen bananas.'

'Can I have a biscuit?' she asked.

'Yes, alright. But then have a drink of water.'

'I know, I know,' she said. She selected the biggest piece of ginger crunch from the tin and climbed up onto the kitchen bench beside me. 'Mummy?'

I opened the fridge to put away the milk I'd bought on the way home. 'Yessy?'

'Anaya says if she and Dad have a baby I can help look after it.'

My sweet and happy outlook faltered. What the *hell*? They'd only been a couple for about half an hour! Closing the fridge door I turned to look at Lily, who was sitting with her shoulders up beside her ears and her arms tight around her knees.

'Dad will always love you, Lil,' I said gently. 'No matter how many new babies he might have.'

'I know.'

'And babies are pretty cute.'

She shrugged, and I put my arms around her and hugged her. 'Never mind, my darling,' I said into her hair.

'Mummy?'

'Mm?'

'Will you ever have another baby?'

'I don't know,' I said slowly. 'Probably not.'

'Good,' said Lily, freeing herself and jumping down off the bench. 'Can I watch TV?'

* * *

John knocked off work promptly at five and came in, full of coy humour and long-winded anecdote. I asked him to test Lily on her spelling words, which occupied him beautifully for quarter of an hour, then poured him a beer ('Trying to get me drunk, eh? You're a wicked woman!') and turned my back on him to make cheese sauce.

Nathan galloped up the hall, waving a plastic cutlass from the two-dollar shop. 'Mum! I need a pirate belt!'

'Use my black scarf,' I said, grating cheese. 'But first you can set the table, please, love.'

'But *Mu-um* ...'

'It won't take you long.'

'Why doesn't Lily have to help?'

'Because *I* just emptied the dishwasher,' said Lily smugly. 'So *there*.'

'*Mu-uuum!*'

'Nathan!' I said. 'Don't make that noise in my ear! It's revolting.'

'You need to be careful, making a face like that,' John warned. 'The wind might change.'

Nathan ignored that, which was understandable, and stalked back down the hall again.

'You have to set the table!' Lily cried.

'I'm getting a pirate belt!'

'Mum, he has to set the table!'

'Yes, thank you, Lily,' I said. 'He will. Go and have a shower.'

'But *Mu-um*!'

'I can hear grizzling!' John said, shaking his head. And just then a vehicle came down the driveway, providing a most welcome distraction.

Lily flew to the kitchen door and opened it. 'It's Harry!' she cried, running down the steps.

'Is it now?' said John meaningfully.

'— and Shineya's getting a *pony* for Christmas!' Lily was saying as she accompanied Harry across the carport. 'I wish I could have a pony, but Mum says I'm too little.'

'Rubbish,' Harry said, stepping out of his jandals and coming in. 'You just need a little pony.'

I glared at him, and he laughed.

'Anyway, Lil, I thought you wanted a dolphin.'

'You can't ride a *dolphin*!'

'Of course you can. You sit on its back and hold onto the dorsal fin. It could live in the main dam.'

'*Really?*'

'Absolutely. I had a pet crocodile when I was your age. That wasn't quite so good, though; it had to be muzzled before I could ride it. And it used to eat the odd sheep, which annoyed my father.'

'Mum, is he telling the truth?' Lily asked.

'No,' said John. 'He's –'

'Hello, trouble!' Harry said.

Nathan dashed into the kitchen, bearing my black scarf. 'Harry, can you tie this around me to make a pirate belt?'

'What's the magic word?' John croaked, but nobody paid any attention.

'Harry, did you *really* have a pet crocodile?' Lily asked.

'Yes,' he said, winding the scarf around Nathan's middle.

'I don't believe you.'

'I'm crushed. How's that, Nath?'

'Good,' Nathan said, arranging his plastic cutlass. 'Will you play pirates with me?'

'Not now, mate. It looks like your tea's nearly ready.'

'You could stay for tea, and then we could play.'

'That would be lovely,' said Harry, purely to annoy John. He caught my warning eye and grinned. 'But not tonight. Your mum looks really tired. Didn't you sleep well last night, Jenny?'

The look I gave him this time was positively murderous.

'Alright, I'm done,' he said, holding up his hands in mock surrender. 'For now. Did you pick up that pump from Wrightson's?'

'Oh no!' I said, horrified. 'I forgot all about it!'

'Can't imagine why. Never mind; I'll go in and get it tomorrow. Be good to your mother, kids. See you, John.'

And off he went, leaving me to spend the next hour and a half listening to John explain that when you have kiddies they just have to come first, and I could call him an old fusspot if I liked, but nothing would ever convince him that the best thing for children wasn't a stable home with Mum and Dad.

Chapter 27

Anaya came to the door when I dropped the children at Dave's house the next evening. She greeted them effusively and me coldly, which was only to be expected, and ushered them inside with a pretty little display of maternal protectiveness. This irritated me, but only for about twenty seconds. I was going to see Andrew tonight, and there was very little room in my head for anything else.

Back at home I started dinner, and then wasted a fair amount of time looking through my wardrobe in case any of my clothes had magically become fabulous since last I'd looked at them, before selecting, inevitably, jeans and my black chiffon top. I put a couple of candles on the table, decided they looked cheesy and suggestive, took them away again and went out into the garden.

It was a beautiful evening. A tui was hunting insects up the trunk of a seedling peach tree – they're usually nectar feeders so it must have been feeding chicks – and the first flower on my Ville de Lyon clematis was open, deep magenta at the edges of the petals and clear lilac in the middle. It looked rich and luxurious against the hot pink rose it was using as a scaffold, just as planned (a rare event in my garden, where most of the really good effects are accidental), and I felt a thrill of artistic pride.

From Andrew's woolshed on the skyline a metallic crash rose above the faint, persistent clamour of ewes and lambs, followed by muffled but fervent sounds of wrath. Would he like a hand, I wondered, or prefer to be left alone to get on with it? Well, I could go and see, anyway. I went back to the house for my boots, tied Tessa up and set off up the driveway.

* * *

I found him in the covered yards behind his woolshed, panel-beating a small aluminium gate with a half-round post. The noise of six hundred ewes and nine hundred lambs yelling to one another from opposite ends of the yards rose into the still evening air like an audible mushroom cloud.

'Hi,' I said, climbing the rails beside him.

He looked up and smiled with gratifying pleasure. There were deep, tired lines at the corners of his eyes and his dark hair was stiff with dust and sweat. 'Hi,' he said, straightening up carefully, as if his back hurt.

'Hi,' I whispered, shaken by a wave of tenderness and pity that I'm sure he didn't want. But he looked so exhausted and thin and generally uncared for …

It dawned on me at this point that what he was mostly looking was amused. 'Yep, hi,' he said.

I felt my face get warm. 'Sorry.'

He propped his post against the railing, leant over and kissed me. He tasted of dust and lanolin. I slid my arms up around his neck and kissed him back with considerable enthusiasm.

'You don't think this'd be nicer if I washed first?' he said, pulling his mouth away from mine.

'Probably, but it's pretty nice now.'

He smiled and kissed me again.

'Can I give you a hand?' I asked when we broke apart.

'No, I'm nearly done,' he said. 'I've just got to rehang this gate and chase the lambs away.' He glanced at his watch. 'Sorry, I'm a bit later than I'd hoped.'

'And I'm making you later.'

'That doesn't matter. Always good to see you.'

I grinned, and he raised a questioning eyebrow. 'I was just imagining what you'd say if I came over to the shed mid-run tomorrow and draped myself over the wool press.' I reclined seductively against a pole and looked at him through my eyelashes to demonstrate.

'Better not,' he said. 'I might lose all control and ravish you on the wool table.'

I considered that idea for a moment, and smiled. And, as if someone had flicked a switch, the atmosphere changed from enjoyably flirtatious to electric with lust.

Andrew took half a step towards me. Then he looked down at himself, grimaced and stopped. 'You go on,' he said. 'I'll be there in half an hour.'

* * *

I paused on my way down the driveway to rescue a small, spindly camellia from underneath a large and thuggish blackvine. It was quite a job, blackvine being only marginally weaker than high-tensile wire. I was crossing the gravel in front of the carport when the phone started to ring. I ignored it, knowing I couldn't get there in time, but it rang again as I untied Tessa.

'Hello?' I said, picking it up just before the answer phone cut in.

'*Why* don't you carry your cell phone?' Bex asked plaintively.

'It's charging.'

'Where have you been?'

'Andrew's woolshed.'

Tessa looked pointedly at her empty bowl, and I got her biscuits (specially formulated for joint, gastrointestinal and dental health in elderly small-breed dogs, and costing slightly more per serving than fillet steak) out of the cupboard. 'He's penning up for shearing.'

'Oh, how romantic.'

She had no idea. 'Speaking of which,' I said, 'shouldn't you be bonding with your husband?'

'My husband's bonding with the TV.'

'You could always stand in front,' I suggested, opening the oven door to investigate a tray of lemon and rosemary chicken drumsticks. 'Slowly taking your clothes off.'

'He'd probably just throw scorched almonds at me to get me to move,' said Bex.

'Well, there you go. It's a win-win situation.'

She gave a little snort of laughter. 'Hey, not a bad offer from that Greenfarm lot, is it?'

'What?' I said blankly.

'Haven't Mum and Dad told you?'

'No.'

'Oh. Shit. Sorry.'

I was still standing like a statue in front of the open oven door. I bent, took out the tray of drumsticks and began to turn them. 'How much?' I asked, feeling mildly surprised that my voice sounded so normal.

'Four point seven million.'

Six hundred thousand dollars above government valuation. That was a *dream* offer, surely, not a good one. I felt slightly sick.

'Look, why *don't* you look at subdividing off your place?' she said.

'Mm,' I said, putting the chicken back in the oven and shutting the door with something approaching a slam.

'Jen, there's no point in sticking out your bottom lip. It just makes it harder for Mum and Dad. That's probably why they haven't said anything to you yet.'

I took a deep breath. 'I'm *not* sticking out my bottom lip, it's just ... Look, I have to go. I'm trying to make dinner.'

'Bruce coming over?'

'Yes.'

'Is he indeed? Shagged him yet?'

'Yes,' I said, only too happy to change the subject.

'You're *kidding*!' she squealed.

'I'm not.'

'*When?*'

'Wednesday.' I got out a bag of potatoes. 'Tell Mum and die.'

'Who made the first move?' she asked.

'Mutual decision, I think.'

'Well, well. There's hope for you yet. Tell me *everything*.'

'No,' I said. 'Go away and concentrate on your own sex life, rather than living vicariously through mine.'

'But mine's boring!'

I held the phone between ear and shoulder and crouched down to rummage through the pot cupboard. 'Well – go and read *Fifty Shades of Grey*, then, if you feel you need more spice in your life.'

'Is *that* the sort of sex you're having?'

'No!' After a moment's reflection I added, 'Thank goodness.'

'Bog standard missionary, then?'

'Good*night*, Rebecca,' I said.

'Never mind,' she said consolingly. 'He might improve with practice.'

A blatant attempt to goad me to further detail. 'He's not bad now,' I said.

'Even though he has a thing for pot plants?'

'Actually, I've decided I quite like men with a thing for pot plants. Look, I really do have to go.'

'Alright, alright. Off you go. Lucky cow.'

'Everything okay at your end?' I asked.

'Yes, of course it is,' she said. 'Love you.'

I stiffened, potato pot in hand. 'What's wrong?' Or was she just feeling guilty about the farm?

'Nothing, you idiot! Well, nothing apart from the depressing contrast between your Friday night and mine.'

'It is tough,' I said sympathetically. 'You'll be dodging scorched almonds; I'll be having sex ... Awesome sex, I might add.'

'Shut up,' she said, laughing as she put the phone down.

I followed suit, and turned to see Andrew standing in the kitchen doorway, holding a small potted orchid.

'Oh, shit,' I said feebly.

He leant against the doorframe and laughed for what I felt was an unnecessarily long time. His hair was still damp from the shower, and the collar of his blue paisley shirt was turned under.

'I wish you wouldn't keep sneaking up on me!' I said, pettish with embarrassment.

'I wasn't!'

'Well, I didn't hear your ute.'

'I left it at home to keep Meg happy,' he said.

I smiled unwillingly. 'How dare you have a reasonable excuse?'

'Here,' he said, holding out the little orchid. 'Peace offering. It's one of those pansy orchids you liked.'

'*Miltoniopsis*, as I recall.'

'Very good.'

'Thank you very much,' I said, taking it. 'How do I not kill it?'

'Put it somewhere out of direct sunlight, water it about once a week but don't leave it standing in a puddle. That's it.'

I put it down on the bench and kissed him. 'Thank you.'

'Who were you talking to just now?' he asked, putting his arms around my waist.

'Dave,' I said, succumbing to a sudden and irresistible temptation.

His transition from amusement to appalled disbelief was rapid and somewhat alarming.

'I'm kidding!' I said. 'I'm kidding! My sister.'

'You are a truly horrible woman.'

'I know.' I hugged him. 'I don't actually make a habit of discussing my sex life with other people. Just in case you were wondering.'

'I suppose it's alright, as long as you're complimentary.' He kissed me in a serious sort of way, sliding his hands up under my shirt and unhooking my bra.

'That's very nice,' I said breathlessly. 'But perhaps I should concentrate on dinner, for a bit.'

'Now *that's* crushing,' he remarked, taking his hands away.

I caught them in mine. 'No, no, I really *am* being swept away on a hot tide of passion. Honest.'

He laughed. 'Obviously.'

'Fine,' I said, with a long-suffering sigh, turning off the oven. 'But don't blame *me* when you're eating raw potatoes with your chicken.'

'I won't,' he said, taking my hand and pulling me towards my bedroom.

* * *

We dined at half past nine on chicken and bread and butter.

'Crikey,' I said, watching him salt his chicken sandwich with a startlingly heavy hand.

'Cramp prevention,' he explained. 'I've been dagging all day.'

'I've got a couple of electrolyte sachets somewhere,' I said. 'Those squeezy gel ones that people take on long-distance runs. Would you like one?'

'No, the salt should do the trick.' The corner of his mouth twitched. 'Depending on just how much more awesome sex you had in mind.'

'You're never going to let me forget that, are you?'

'Shit, no,' he said.

I sighed, and we ate in silence for a little while. Should I tell him about Greenfarm's offer? I wondered. No. Not now. Sufficient unto the day is the evil thereof, after all. 'What's Harry up to?' I asked instead.

'Harry, as we speak, is having dinner in town with his ex.'

'What, really?' I said, sitting up straight in surprise. 'Town as in Tipoi?'

'That's the one.'

'Wow. That's brilliant!' The ultimatum had evidently borne fruit after all.

'He was just heading out when I got home.'

'Fingers crossed that it all goes well.'

'I'm sure you'll hear all about it either way,' he said dryly.

'Will you?'

'I fear so.'

'Admit it; you'll miss him if he moves back to Wellington.'

He looked sceptical. 'Mm ... Think of what he'll be like if he doesn't.'

I thought of it and winced. Andrew laughed.

'I'm thinking of *him*,' I said haughtily.

'Right.'

I smiled. 'Well, mostly.'

* * *

''S too hot,' I muttered a couple of hours later, wriggling out from underneath Andrew's arm. 'Sorry.'

'Shh,' he said, clamping me back against him.

'No, I –'

'Be *quiet*.'

I froze in shock, but half a second later my dawning fear that perhaps I'd made a terrible mistake and fallen for a control freak was erased by a rustling sound from outside, and then a muffled, 'Shit.' Andrew shot upright as though he'd been electrocuted.

'*Dave?*' I said, sitting up too. 'What the *hell* are you doing here?'

The rustling grew louder. 'C'n I've the key for the diesel?' Dave whispered hoarsely through the open window.

'What?' I said, getting out of bed and groping in the wardrobe for my dressing-gown. 'Look, go around to the back doo–'

But alas, no. Dave, by this time, had reached calmly through the window, unlocked the French doors, let himself in and turned on the light. 'Well, bugger me,' he said.

'Get *out*!' I said, screwing up my eyes against the glare as I wrestled with my dressing-gown, the armholes of which seemed inexplicably to have vanished.

'Well, well,' Dave said, shaking his head. 'I thought you were doing the other brother.' His face was flushed and his eyes glazed – it dawned on me that he was very drunk. Unusually so; I hadn't seen him like this for years. 'Unless you're doing them both, 'course.'

'Did you *drive* here in that state?' I demanded, finally getting my arms into my sleeves and pulling the dressing-gown tightly around myself. Andrew was sitting up in bed, clutching the duvet around his waist and looking both furious and embarrassed.

'Nag, nag,' Dave said, swaying. 'You're such a drag … Hey, that rhymes! Nag, nag, Jen's a drag …' He looked at Andrew. 'Decent tits, though, eh? Has she done that thing where –'

At which point Andrew earned my undying gratitude by leaping up, grabbing him by the neck of his T-shirt and shoving him back, hard, against the wall.

'Whoa!' Dave wheezed, raising his hands. 'Settle down, buddy! You'll wake the kids.'

Andrew released him, slowly and deliberately, and turned to pull on his jeans.

'*You've* got the kids!' I snapped.

All this commotion had, by now, woken Tessa, who came barrelling down the hallway to hurl herself ecstatically at Dave's knees. 'Hey, Tess!' he said, crouching down to pull her ears. She promptly rolled onto her back, and he rubbed her tummy.

'Where – are – my – children?' I said through clenched teeth.

'At home with Anaya,' he said, looking up. 'Where else would they be?'

'Why aren't *you*? It's after one in the morning!'

Dave stood up, steadying himself against a handy wall. 'Oh, for –' He caught Andrew's eye and subsided. 'To be perf'ly honest, forgot I don't live here anymore.' He smiled his charming little-boy smile. 'Might've had one or two too many.'

Andrew looked at me. 'I suppose we'll have to take him home,' he said, picking up his shirt.

'Nah, mate,' Dave said. 'Just need a bit of diesel. Bloody ute stopped down by the quarry.'

'Go and wait in the kitchen,' I ordered, pulling a sweatshirt out of the wardrobe.

'It's not like I haven't already –' Andrew took a single step towards him, and he dried up mid-sentence. 'Jeez,' he muttered, backing out of the room, and we heard him weaving up the hall, hitting the wall at intervals. Tessa the peabrain followed him, tail wagging.

'Let's just kill him and bury him in a shallow grave,' I said, pulling up my jeans.

Andrew gave a snort of laughter as he buttoned his shirt. 'Tempting,' he said. 'Have you got something to put diesel in?'

'Um, the lawnmower petrol container will do. I think it's nearly empty.'

There was a crash from the direction of the kitchen, which turned out to be the sound of my new orchid hitting the floor. Andrew smiled at me suddenly. 'What are the chances of him throwing up in your car?' he said, following Dave up the hall.

* * *

Dave *didn't* throw up in the car, but that was almost the only good thing about the next hour. I emptied the lawnmower petrol into the car's tank, spilling quite a bit in the process, and we drove to the woolshed for diesel. Then, having forcibly discouraged Dave from taking the wheel, we resumed our journey down the hill and found Dave's ute in the mouth of an old quarry below Mum and Dad's house, half on and half off the road.

Dave got out of the car and opened the door of his ute, and I plucked his keys out of the ignition and pocketed them. 'Hey!' he said.

'Where's the button you push to open the petrol cap?' I asked.

''S not petrol, 's diesel.'

'Where's the button to open the *diesel* cap, then?'

'Here.' He leant past me into the ute, steadying himself by means of a hand on my bottom.

'Dave,' I said coldly.

'Bit squidgy,' he said, giving my right buttock a squeeze.

I rammed my elbow into his stomach.

'*Fuck*,' he gasped, staggering backwards. 'Bitch.'

Andrew put down the diesel container. 'Sit down and shut up,' he said. He spoke quietly, but something about his tone suggested that he'd be only too happy to enforce the order.

'I need a piss,' said Dave sulkily, retreating to the far side of the ute.

'You take the car; we'll follow you,' Andrew said to me as he screwed the cap back onto the diesel tank.

'No! I'll take him,' I said. Heaven alone knew what Dave would say during the drive.

'Like hell you will,' said Andrew.

'But –'

'Please, Jen.' He held out his hand for the keys, and I sighed and handed them over.

* * *

It was a half-hour drive to Dave's house. I spent it dwelling on his many failings as a human being – I had quite an exhaustive list by the time I pulled up at his mailbox.

'Cheers,' Dave said, getting out of the ute behind me and making his way unsteadily around the front to the driver's side.

'Nope,' said Andrew, shutting the door in his face.

Dave gave an offended huff.

'It'll be fine here till morning,' I said. 'Please don't wake the kids on your way in.'

'Al*right*,' he said, starting up the dark driveway. He fell over something and swore as he went up the porch steps, and a light came on inside.

'Idiot,' I said bitterly.

'Want me to drive?' Andrew asked.

'No, I'm fine, unless you'd rather.'

'You go ahead.'

We got into the car, and I started the engine. 'How was the trip here?' I asked, backing around.

'Oh, fine.' He yawned and ran a hand through his hair.

'Did he say anything particularly awful?'

'I guess that depends on your definition of particularly awful.'

That, I assumed, meant yes. I sighed.

'He's hurting, poor chap,' Andrew said. 'Apparently it's not very nice finding your wife in bed with someone else.'

'Wow,' I said. 'Who would've thought?'

'Although he does realise that you're only sleeping with me – oh, and Harry, he tells me – to get back at him.'

Which was so – so *Dave*-ish a piece of self-deception that I laughed.

* * *

'Three forty-one,' I said as we got back into bed. 'When d'you have to get up?'

'Half past five,' said Andrew, reaching up to turn the light off.

'Well, that sucks.' I wriggled closer and kissed his shoulder.

He ran a hand down my spine to my bottom, and I went rigid with embarrassment. 'No, definitely not squidgy,' he said thoughtfully. 'Soft, smooth, pliable ...'

'What, like bread dough?'

'Yeah,' he said, wrapping his arms around me. 'But much sexier.'

Chapter 28

Andrew got up and left at five thirty, and after twenty minutes of lying in bed worrying about what Dave might say to the kids, I gave up on sleep and got up too. By eight I'd reconciled two months' worth of accounts, drunk about a litre of coffee and vacuumed the spider webs off the corners of the ceilings. Feeling virtuous, if over-caffeinated, I went to see Mum and Dad.

It was a hot, grey morning, not sunny but surprisingly bright, without a breath of wind. Tessa and I walked down the road, curving between smooth green hills towards the river flats below. A skylark trilled exultantly somewhere high above us, and lambs called to mothers who, at this time of year, only bothered to respond to cries of full-blown panic.

I found my parents sitting down to their first post-breakfast cup of tea (they routinely had nineses as well as elevenses). 'Good morning, love,' Mum said as I opened the patio door. 'Cup of tea?'

'No, I've already had far too much coffee this morning.' I crossed the room and sat down at the table. 'Bex told me about the offer from Greenfarm.'

'And how, pray, did she know?' Dad asked, looking hard at Mum.

'I just happened to be talking to her on the phone last night,' she said, bristling. 'I *asked* her to let us tell Jenny. I do wish she wouldn't take these things on herself.'

'Does it matter?' I said. 'Or was it supposed to be a secret?'

'Of course not,' said Dad, and silence fell, while both my parents fiddled with their teacups.

'It's a good offer,' I said at last.

'Yes,' said Dad heavily.

'They haven't even seen the place, have they?'

'Well, Arnold has, of course.'

I took a deep breath. 'I've been thinking. If you just sold the river flats as a dairy support block, and I left my job and leased the rest ...'

'Oh, Jenny,' Mum said heavily.

'I think I could make it work. We can do a lot better with our sheep – I've been reading up on pasture management and condition scoring and all sorts of stuff. And I was wondering the other day about making the worker's cottage into a farmstay. I could make it really nice – paint it, and do up the garden, and have really lovely breakfasts ...'

'Jenny, no,' said Mum.

'Mum –'

'Love, *stop*. How are you going to do this, realistically? You might be able to manage the farm or a homestay, but not both; there simply aren't enough hours in the day. And you've got the children ... You'll have a nervous breakdown, and you'll make less money than you do working in town.'

'Why not let me try? I know Greenfarm have made this amazing offer, but surely they're not the only potential buyers. Surely they or someone else would still be interested in a couple of years. It'd be obvious by then whether or not I could pull it off.'

'And in the meantime, you'll be exhausted and miserable. Your skin will turn to leather, you'll look fifty by the time you're forty —'

'I always wear sunscreen,' I said, between tears and laughter. 'Even in winter.'

Mum dismissed the sunscreen with a distracted flap of the hand. 'And how are you ever going to meet someone nice if you never have time to get off the farm?'

'But — but I *have* met someone nice! Don't pretend Bex hasn't told you.'

'Andrew Faulkner? He won't be staying around here, if he isn't going to go into partnership with the Greens. And no relationship survives if you don't have time to *see* each other. *No*, Jenny. I will *not* sit by and watch you ruin your life.'

'Hey,' said Dad, who had been listening, startled, to this outburst. 'Lorraine, love, hang on. I don't think the outlook's quite as bleak as all that. But, Jenny ...'

'Yes?' I prompted, after a decent pause.

'Running the farm by yourself is a big job. You'd be completely tied to it — I know you know all this, but have you *really* thought about what your life will look like? Dragging the kids down the farm, rain or shine ... Although of course they could come here after school, and I can help with the farm work.'

He *would* help. They both would, if I insisted on doing this. But — the realisation swam sharply into focus — how *selfish* of me. *They didn't want to.* And fair enough. Mum and Dad had done their time on the farm, and they'd raised their children — they shouldn't have to raise mine while I set off on this quest to prove to myself that I could be a real live McLeod's Daughter.

'No,' I said, wiping my eyes with the back of my hand. 'No, you're right. I'm being unrealistic.'

Dad looked at me worriedly.

'If – if I'm honest, I don't *really* want you to say, "Of course, what a wonderful idea, let's do it." But if I offer and you say no, it lets me off the hook. I don't have to be the one who makes the decision to sell, and I don't have to try to farm it and maybe fail. I'm sorry. I'll grow up now.'

Both my parents sagged a little with relief.

'Don't think I haven't realised that if I'd been a better farmer, we might have actually handed quite a profitable outfit over to you and Dave when you took over,' Dad said quietly.

'No!' I cried. 'Dad, *no*! Dave and I had ten years to make it awesome.'

'So you did,' he said, smiling at me. 'How about we all make a concerted effort to stop flaying ourselves with guilt?'

* * *

I was grubbing up buttercups in the shrubbery at the bottom of my driveway that afternoon when my cell phone rang. After a short search, I found it wedged between two azalea branches, safely out of the way of flying dirt. 'Hello?' I said.

'Hey, Jen. How's your day going?' Harry said.

'So-so. How's Chris?'

'Can you come for dinner tonight and meet him?'

'Um, Andrew was going to come down here …'

'So I hear. But he says he'll come if you will,' Harry said.

'Okay, then, I'd love to come,' I said, my voice a little too hearty in order to disguise the fact that, actually, I'd rather have had Andrew to myself. How depressing to discover that I was the sort of girl who loses interest in her friends the second she gets a man. 'I'm dying to meet Chris. Shall I bring along the very delicious piece of pork belly I'm cooking?'

'I'm making Thai beef salad.'

'It wouldn't really go, would it?'

'Not really,' said Harry. 'But who cares? Never look a gift pork belly in the mouth, I say.'

* * *

And so at seven that evening, having put on a dress and wrestled my hair into a French roll that would, I hoped, elevate my look to one of timeless elegance, I drove up the road to the Faulkners'. I parked behind a gleaming silver Mercedes belonging, presumably, to the legendary Chris. No dogs growled as I approached the house, which made a pleasant change, and Andrew met me at the living room door. His shirt this evening was olive green, which gave him a most enticing military air. We stood smiling at one another for a while, until Harry cleared his throat pointedly and we both jumped. 'How did the shearing go?' I asked hastily.

'Good,' Andrew said, standing aside to let me in. 'All done.'

I crossed the living room and put my pork belly down on the kitchen bench, where Harry was doing something fiddly with an avocado. I kissed his cheek. 'Hi.'

'Good evening,' he said. 'So kind of you to join us.'

'Isn't it?' I said.

There was another, older man reading a newspaper on the sofa, his right ankle balanced on his left knee. He had fair hair, receding at the temples, a Roman nose and sharply defined cheekbones. The thickening around his middle was minimised by excellent tailoring, and he radiated self-assurance and command. I wasn't sure what I'd expected the love of Harry's life to look like, but this man wasn't it.

'Chris, this is Jenny,' Harry said to him nervously. 'My boss.'

Chris raised his eyes wearily from his paper, gave me an infinitesimal nod and dropped them again. At which I decided, partly because nobody enjoys being treated as an annoying interruption and partly because of that timid, anxious edge to Harry's voice, to go right ahead and dislike him.

'Hi, Chris,' I said. 'Nice to meet you.'

'You too,' he murmured, turning a page.

'Right,' said Harry with rather forced cheer. 'Dinner's ready.'

* * *

Harry's salad tasted very nice, but he'd overcooked the steak, and it had the consistency of rubber. 'Bugger. Sorry,' he said, watching the determined chewing around the table.

'Nothing wrong with it,' Andrew said.

'There are all sorts of things wrong with it.'

'Maybe you shouldn't call our attention to them,' said Chris, and Harry flushed.

'Any interesting projects on the go, Chris?' Andrew asked.

'Of course. I don't take on uninteresting projects.'

Dick, I thought.

'Lucky you,' said Andrew.

Chris raised his eyebrows. 'It's not luck,' he said. 'I know what I want, and I go out and get it.'

I upgraded him mentally from dick to wanker.

'I've got no patience with people who complain about their lives,' he continued. 'It's nobody else's job to sort your life out — you've got to get off your bum and do it yourself. If you're not happy with your lot, it's your own bloody fault.'

'Rubbish!' I said hotly. 'People can be miserable for all sorts of reasons that are completely out of their control! Other people die, or leave, or ...' Catching Harry's beseeching eye across the table, I broke off.

Chris's eyebrows rose again. 'No point in whingeing about it, though, is there?'

'True,' I said, forcing my lips into a conciliatory smile. 'But it's not necessarily your own fault if you're unhappy.'

'I never said it was.'

'Yeah, you did, actually,' said Andrew, pushing his chair back. 'Beer, anyone?'

There was an uncomfortable silence, which Harry broke by saying, 'Give us your professional opinion of this house, Chris.'

Chris picked up his wineglass and swirled it thoughtfully before taking a sip. Putting it down again, he shrugged and said, 'Decent bones. Of course, that stuff's all wrong.' He nodded towards the greenery clothing the stair corner.

'Why?' I asked.

He sighed. 'Because the design of this house calls for strong functionality and stark contrasts.'

'Ah,' said Andrew, turning back from the fridge with a beer in his hand and the corners of his mouth firmly tucked in.

'But hell, what would I know?'

What on *earth*, I wondered, had Harry ever seen in this horrible man? But perhaps, to someone diffident and nervous and unsure of himself, Chris's exceedingly high opinion of his own worth was somehow attractive …?

'Would that be alright, Jen?' Harry was saying.

'Pardon?' I said. 'Sorry, what was that?'

'I was just wondering if I could bring Chris down to your place tomorrow, and show him your garden.'

'Yes, of course.'

Chris looked unexcited at the prospect.

'Chris does quite a lot of landscaping himself,' Harry continued doggedly.

'It's an important part of the job,' said Chris. 'You need a connection between a building's architecture and the cultural vernacular of the site. Otherwise there's no sense of cohesiveness. No harmony.'

'I hope you kept the cultural vernacular of your site in mind when you laid out your garden,' Andrew told me, abandoning all attempts to keep a straight face.

'I certainly would have, if only I knew what it meant,' I said.

Chris merely looked bored, but Harry reddened and bit his lip, and I wished I'd kept my mouth shut.

So, I think, did Andrew. 'You went to the Indian place in town last night, didn't you?' he asked his brother. 'How was it? I haven't been for ages.'

'Pretty good,' Harry said.

'Very mediocre, I thought,' said Chris.

'You didn't order the fish curry, did you?' I asked, making an effort to redeem myself. 'The menu describes it as "straight from the beaches of Goa" and the one time I ordered it I got the feeling that the fish actually *had* washed up on a beach in Goa, and then someone had sent it over here on a very slow container ship.'

Andrew and Harry both laughed, more as encouragement than because I'd managed to be funny, but Chris said, 'God, no. Never eat seafood anywhere you can't see the sea.'

'They make a mean onion bhaji, though,' Andrew said.

'They do,' I said. 'And they're lovely people.'

'Being a lovely person doesn't actually rule out the possibility that you're a poor cook,' Chris informed me.

Just then my cell phone rang from the other side of the living room, where I'd left it with my shoes at the door. I shouldn't really have answered it, mid dinner party – I shouldn't have let it ring, come to think of it – but it provided a timely distraction from telling the man what I thought of him. 'Sorry – excuse me ...' I said, getting up.

The caller, I saw as I picked it up, was Dave. 'What?' I said coldly, turning away from the table.

There was a pause, and then a breathless wail of 'M-mu-mummeee ...'

'Lily! Hey, love, what's up?'

'M-mummy,' Lily gasped. 'M-mummeee ...'

'You're alright, sweet pea. Deep breaths.'

'I – I – I –'

'Do you want to give the phone to Dad so he can tell me?'

'*No!*'

'Okay,' I said.

There was a heroic gulp. 'I – I miss you, Mummy.'

'I miss you too. Did you go surf-casting today?'

'No,' she said. 'Daddy was sick.'

'Mm.' I bet he was.

'We're going t-tomorrow.'

'Well, that'll be fun,' I said brightly.

'Will you s-sing me a s-song?'

'Oh, Lil …'

She sobbed louder.

'Of course I will.' But not within earshot of anyone else. I answered Andrew's questioning look with a smile, let myself out onto the patio and closed the door behind me.

'T-Taylor Swift.'

'No worries, love.' There was a low, rumbling growl off to my left, and Meg appeared around the corner of the house, hackles up and gums bared. 'Oh, go away, you horrible animal!'

She advanced, and I beat a hasty retreat to the car, where I sat singing the bits of 'Shake It Off' that I could remember while she circled menacingly. After a little while Andrew came out, called her to heel and banished her, crushed and resentful, to the dog kennels at the shed.

Lily's sobs had subsided by the time the song was finished, proving that love is deaf as well as blind.

'Feeling a bit better, my darling?' I asked.

'Sort of,' she whispered.

'Anything bothering you in particular, or did you just suddenly feel you couldn't live another second without hearing me sing Taylor Swift songs out of tune?'

'I just miss you.'

'Well, I miss you too. I think you should go to sleep now; everything will be better in the morning.'

'What if I want you in the night?'

'Ring me up.'

'But what if you're asleep?'

'That is a concern, it's true,' I said. 'But I quite like you, so I'll probably get over it. Okay?'

'Okay,' she whispered.

'Is Dad handy?'

'He's in the lounge. Do you want to talk to him?'

I'd intended to, but it occurred to me that nothing I could say to Dave, or he to me, would be in any way productive. 'No, that's okay,' I said. 'Goodnight, love.'

'Goodnight, Mummy.'

Putting the phone back in my pocket, I got out of the car. The evening sun was reflecting back off the long windows, and it wasn't until I opened the door that I saw both Faulkners on their feet, Harry very red in the face and Andrew at his iciest and most expressionless. Chris, looking highly offended, was leaning back in his chair. Things had evidently deteriorated while I was away.

For a long moment nobody moved. Then Andrew looked at me and asked, 'Everything alright?'

'Fine,' I said. 'Just a small bedtime crisis.'

'Good. You ready to go?' Without waiting for an answer he crossed the living room, slid the door open and waited for me to precede him through it.

Crikey. I looked worriedly at Harry.

'Go,' he said, trying to smile. 'Honestly.'

'Thanks so much for dinner,' I said, as if we were ending a pleasant evening rather than leaving in a snit. There's no social situation so awkward it can't be papered over with polite nothings, after all. I bent down to pick up my shoes, and as I straightened up something – perhaps the extra blood flow to my head, or perhaps I was just more like my sister than I realised – inspired me to add,

'Harry, don't let him put you down, will you? He's not nearly as awesome as he thinks he is.'

Andrew and I drove away in silence. With considerable restraint, I waited until we'd reached the end of his driveway before I asked, 'What happened?'

'I thought it was time to leave,' he said.

'Well, yes, I gathered that.'

Silence fell again, and we were at my mailbox when he added, 'I got sick of it, and asked Harry how long he was going to put up with being patronised by that pompous fuckwit.'

'Did you actually say "pompous fuckwit"?'

'Yes.'

'Coldly and calmly?'

'I don't know,' he said irritably.

'Silly question. Of course you did,' I said, driving into the carport, and he smiled ruefully.

We got out of the car and I untied Tessa, who was whining and shivering at the end of her chain. Making a lightning transformation from piteous sufferer to bustling official she ran up the back steps and waited, panting, on the doorstep. The sun had reached the strip of clear sky between cloud and horizon, and was bathing the lawn and garden in mellow, pinkish light.

'I'm sorry for being such a grumpy bastard,' Andrew said suddenly.

I stopped on the bottom step and looked back at him. 'I wouldn't worry. Hanging out with that low-life would make anyone grumpy.' Even someone who hadn't spent much of the previous night driving Dave around the countryside and then all day shearing. 'Anyway, it's very sexy.'

He raised his eyebrows. 'It is?'

'Absolutely. Textbook romantic hero stuff. Think of Mr Darcy. Or Mr Rochester. Tall, dark, handsome, bad-tempered ...'

'Fictional ...' He came up the steps and put his arms around me.

'A minor detail,' I said, hugging him in return. 'You don't think Harry'll actually get back together with that twerp, do you?'

'Don't know. Hope not,' he said.

'I don't understand why he was so unpleasant.'

'Presumably because he's an unpleasant person.'

'Yeah, but after coming all this way to see Harry you'd think he'd at least make a *bit* of an effort to be charming.' Tessa barked impatiently, and I pulled away to open the door for her.

'Maybe he thinks Harry's such a pushover he'll put up with anything,' he said, following me into the kitchen.

I switched on the lights. 'I really hope he's wrong.'

'So do I,' Andrew said. He sighed, then smiled at me. 'Nothing we can do about it tonight, anyway.'

'True,' I said, sliding my arms up around his neck.

Chapter 29

I woke up on Sunday morning feeling warm and lazy and perfectly contented. Little flakes of sunlight, filtered through the leaves of the gingko tree on the eastern edge of the lawn, were dancing across the ceiling – if you could see baby's laughter, I thought dreamily, that's what it would look like. Andrew was asleep on his stomach with his head turned towards me, his long arms and legs sprawled like a starfish. He was smiling a little in his sleep, and I lay and watched him with a sort of aching tenderness until he reached out, not opening his eyes, and pulled me up against him.

'Morning,' he said sleepily against my hair.

'Hi,' I whispered, kissing his arm.

'What time's it?'

I consulted my watch. 'Five to six.'

'Good. 'S early. You feel nice.' And tightening his arm around my chest like a vice he went promptly back to sleep.

* * *

'Have you got much work to do today?' I asked an hour later, as we went up the hall to the kitchen.

'Just a couple of gates to open. You?'

My to-do list included mowing the lawn, doing the work I'd brought home for the weekend, trampling down the long grass from around the little trees we'd planted along the creek the year before last, packing up the spare pump to be sent away for servicing, collecting a vast pile of used silage bale wrap from the middle hay barn for recycling … 'Free as a bird,' I said, and we smiled at one another. 'What do you feel like eating?'

'What've you got?'

'I can do toast, Weet-Bix, cornflakes, bacon, eggs, pancakes, French toast …' I opened the fridge. 'Leftover chicken, chocolate custard …'

'Toast, please.'

'What would you like on it?'

'Have you got Vegemite?'

'No, just Marmite.'

'Foul black slurry,' he said. 'Honey?'

'Yep. It's in the pantry behind you.' I took the custard and a bottle of milk out of the fridge and put them down on the bench. 'Real coffee or instant?'

'Real, please, if you've got it.'

I hunted in the freezer compartment of the fridge and failed to find filter coffee. Hoping there might be some in the chest freezer in the carport, I went out to look and heard, with sadness but no real surprise, a car come slowly up the road and turn down my driveway. It was, of course, John.

He pulled up on the gravel and opened his door. A leg appeared, accessorised with cabbage leaves held in place by cloth bandages. It was like some awful parody of a supermodel emerging from a limo. 'Up bright and early, eh?' he said, levering himself to his feet. 'That's the ticket.'

'It's not really a good time …' I said weakly, as Tessa hurried up to inspect his gumboots.

'Don't mind me,' he said. 'You just carry on. I've got a few things to do later on, so I thought I'd pop up now and put in an hour or two.'

I smiled even more weakly and went back inside, forgetting the coffee.

Andrew looked at me questioningly as I shut the door, and I mouthed, 'John.'

'It's five past seven.'

'Yep.'

'For Christ's sake.'

'I know. It's not cool. I should say something.'

'I'll say it, if you like,' he said grimly.

'At least he's outside,' I said.

The kitchen door opened. 'Coo-ee?'

'*What?*' Andrew snapped.

There was a sharp wheeze of indrawn breath, and John's head appeared. He appeared to be torn between pious disapproval and satisfaction at the confirmation of his darkest suspicions, with satisfaction leading by a nose.

'What do you need, John?' I asked.

'Oh, er, string,' he said.

'There's a roll of baling twine in the garden shed.'

'That should, ah …'

'I *think* it's somewhere on the left as you go in,' I said brightly.

'Right you are,' John said, and reluctantly withdrew, closing the door softly behind him.

Peace reigned for five seconds or so, and was then broken by the sound of another vehicle.

'You've got to be kidding,' Andrew said.

'I wonder if it's Harry,' I said, going to the door again.

John had only got as far as the bottom step, so he was perfectly placed to receive the new arrival. It was indeed Harry, driving, for some reason, Andrew's ute. He pulled up and leapt out, jerking the handbrake on. 'Where's Andrew?' he asked.

John fairly quivered with delighted anticipation.

'Here,' Andrew said, coming to the door behind me. 'What is it?'

'I've killed Meg. God, Andrew, I'm so sorry. She was under the wheel, and I didn't see her ...'

I stepped aside and Andrew went past me down the steps.

'She's on the back,' said Harry miserably.

Andrew crossed the gravel towards his ute, and the rest of us fell in behind him, like acolytes behind a priest.

Meg lay on her side on the deck of the ute, her eyes glassy and staring. There was a small, bright pool of blood on the boards beneath her nose. Andrew put his hand on her head.

'I let the dogs out for a run, and then I thought I'd just drive to the top of the hill and check the river flats for a deer ...' Harry said. 'I'm so sorry.'

'You should always do a head count before you drive off,' John told him. 'You need to make it a habit, so you don't even have to think about it. Imagine if it had been a child.'

Harry looked at him, then at his watch, and frowned. '*Why* are you here?' he asked.

'I'm doing a little job for Jenny,' said John stiffly.

'At ten past seven on Sunday morning?'

'Harry, don't,' I said. 'But it *is* a bit early, John.'

John drew himself up to his full five foot five. 'So sorry to intrude,' he said, stricken yet dignified. 'I'll get out of your way, then.'

'John ...' I started apologetically, and a satisfied little smile flickered at the corners of his mouth. Remorse turned rapidly to annoyance. 'Thanks,' I said. 'Another time would be great.'

He limped sadly to his car, and my bad temper drained away, as bad temper so often does just when you could do with its bolstering effects. He was a tedious old thing, but he meant well. More or less.

'I'll leave you to it,' Harry said unhappily, distracting me from my guilt. 'Shall I take her home, or leave the ute here?'

'Leave her,' Andrew said.

'Do you want me to dig a hole? If you just tell me where, I can –'

'No, that's alright,' said Andrew. 'Look, don't worry about it. Just one of those things.'

'She wouldn't have suffered. It was so quick.'

'That's good,' he said, running a velvet ear through his fingers.

Harry and I looked at each other and quietly withdrew several paces.

'Has Chris gone?' I asked.

'Yes.'

'For good?'

'Yes.'

I gave him a thumbs-up.

'I'm such an idiot.'

'No you're not,' I said. 'Hence no Chris.'

'Careful, Jen,' said Andrew, turning towards us. 'Very dangerous to run down someone's ex. Next thing you know they're back together and they both hate you.'

I smiled at him. 'Does calling someone a pompous fuckwit count as running them down?'

'He is a pompous fuckwit,' Harry said heavily.

'How did this escape your notice until now?' asked Andrew.

'Stupid, I suppose.' He sighed. 'No, he can be very charming when he wants to. But he was pissed off last night because he wanted me to go to Spain with him, and I said I couldn't. I can't just bugger off for a month and leave you in the lurch at this time of year.'

'Well, you could, but I'm very grateful that you're not,' I said.

'I think I was supposed to feel honoured that he'd decided to pay attention to me again. Fuck, he thinks he's so much better than everyone else.'

'We all think that,' Andrew said, smiling faintly. 'It's just that most of us realise we're biased.'

'After you left he had a go at me about how dare I let you insult him like that, so I said that if he was going to be a prick I didn't see why you couldn't be one, too.'

'Um, thank you,' Andrew said.

'And then I told him to fuck off. So he did.' His lip quivered.

'Good on you,' I said, hugging him.

Tessa, recognising signs of distress, trotted over and sat on his right boot, gazing meltingly up at him.

'No boyfriend, no home, no job …' he said.

'It's like a country and western song,' Andrew remarked.

'You're such an arsehole,' Harry said, smiling unwillingly.

'That's true. But you did just kill my dog.'

'I *said* I was sorry.'

'Oh, well, that's alright then.'

'What exactly do you see in him, Jen?'

My eyes met Andrew's. What *did* I see? Kindness, humour, sarcasm, sharp intelligence, a complete intolerance of affectation and pretentiousness, carefully hidden vulnerability ... My heart gave a funny little skip, but I said lightly, 'Buggered if I know, to be honest.'

'Thank you,' Andrew said. 'Right. Enough chitchat. Graves to dig, gates to open ...'

We all, Tessa included, got into Andrew's ute and drove up the road to his house, where he pulled up beside his ugly concrete patio. 'Won't be a minute,' he told me, getting out and going inside. Tessa scrambled up out of the footwell, using my bare legs for purchase, and sat on the driver's seat, panting with self-satisfaction.

Harry opened the passenger-side door. 'Right, then,' he said, giving me a brave, sad little smile. 'I'll go and fix a fence, then.'

He had not the faintest intention of fixing a fence, but much can be forgiven those whose idols have just tumbled from their pedestals, and I responded dutifully to my cue. 'You will not. Why not hang out with us?'

He smiled suddenly as he got out of the ute. 'Thanks, but I'd rather chew off my own leg.'

'You're welcome,' I called after him.

* * *

Andrew returned wearing shorts and a cotton work shirt, carrying a fleece-lined oilskin vest. He drove along the track we'd taken on Wednesday and over the brow of the long hill that fell to the river flats, where he stopped above half-a-dozen round, lichen-covered boulders that rose like a miniature archipelago from a sea of grass.

He took a spade from the assorted fencing gear on the back of the ute, and after several attempts found a space between the rocks where the soil was deep enough to dig a hole. I got a shovel and helped him, and Tessa stretched out luxuriously across the seat of the ute and went to sleep. He lined the hole with his vest, furry side uppermost, and laid his dog gently on top.

'I'm so sorry,' I said.

'Thanks.'

'Beautiful spot.'

'Yes,' he said. 'It'd be a nice place for a house.' He sighed, picked up the shovel and began to fill in the hole, while I wondered with a hot, irrational stab of jealousy whether he and Toni had once planned to build one here.

'As long as you got the cultural vernacular right, of course,' he added.

'Well, yes. Obviously.'

He finished filling in the grave and stood looking down at it for a moment. His eyes were wet when he looked up, but all he said was, 'Can you last another twenty minutes without coffee?'

I thought I could, just, so we continued down to the river flats to open a gate for a mob of fat, glossy, white-faced steers. A little stand of totara trees, every branch trailing scarves and wisps of lichen, cast long shadows across the dewy grass. They were surrounded by a brand-new eight-wire fence that continued uphill, crested the next hill and vanished out of sight. 'Nice fence,' I said.

Andrew looked at it for a moment, and then said, 'I was working it out a couple of weeks ago. I've done seven point nine kilometres of fencing and put in twenty-eight new troughs in the last three years.'

'All by yourself?'

'Yep.'

And now he had to sell up. All that work for a future that wasn't going to happen. I moved my hand along the top of the gate to touch his. 'No wonder you have a bad back.'

'It's not that bad,' he said. 'I'm not quite as decrepit as you seem to think.'

'I don't think you're decrepit!'

He lifted his eyebrows in a sceptical sort of way.

'I asked you *once* if your back was alright, because I was about to have sex with you and I knew you'd just hurt it spitting out your toothpaste. That doesn't *really* qualify as going on and on about it, does it?'

'Hmph,' he said, but he looked sheepish.

'Does it?'

'No,' he said. 'You're right. I'm wrong. I apologise unreservedly. Would you like me to grovel?'

'No,' I said. I looked at him sideways and added, 'You might hurt your back.'

'Wench,' he said, and kissed me. 'It's lucky the sex is so awesome.'

Chapter 30

We went back to my place for breakfast rather than having it with Harry, which was perhaps a little callous. But we were amply punished, because when we rattled back down the driveway we found Dad's ute and Arnold Keller's shiny, sign-written SUV parked behind my car.

I looked at my watch. It was quarter to nine.

Dad, Arnold and a slim, dapper-looking fellow in the agricultural professional's uniform of moleskin trousers, collared shirt and glossy chestnut-coloured boots with pointy toes came around the corner of the house. 'Is that Richard Green?' I asked.

'Sure is,' said Andrew.

'Bloody hell. He doesn't waste any time.' He looked at me enquiringly, and I added, 'He did put in an offer. Just a day or two ago. Mum and Dad are going to accept it.'

'Morning, love!' said Dad with somewhat forced cheer as we got out of the ute. 'We've just been for a little look around the farm. This is Richard Green.'

'Hi,' I said, going slowly across the gravel towards them. 'Nice to meet you.'

Richard Green shook my hand in a brisk, professional fashion. 'Hello.'

Arnold dragged his fascinated gaze off me and said, 'G'day, Andrew! This is good timing – we were hoping to catch up with you while we were here.'

Andrew gave him a very small nod. 'Richard,' he said shortly.

'Andrew,' said Richard Green. 'Just tried to ring you. I'm keen to have a look around, if that suits.'

There was a long – awkwardly long – pause before Andrew said, 'Alright.'

I caught my father's eye and blushed, which was ridiculous. There was no need to feel, or to act, like a rebellious teenager caught smuggling her boyfriend into her bedroom in the dead of night. I straightened my shoulders self-consciously, found Arnold Keller eyeing me again with a knowing smirk, followed his gaze and discovered that my shirt was on inside out. I went hot all over.

'So this house is – what? Four bedrooms?' Richard asked Dad.

'Three,' I said. It was, after all, my house.

'Nice view, though,' Arnold put in.

'This house probably wouldn't be part of the sale,' I said.

'Yes, alright,' Richard said, as if I was being unnecessarily rude. He turned to Andrew. 'The house on your place is a decent size, isn't it?'

'I suppose so.'

'May as well head up there now, eh?'

Andrew frowned, sighed and said, 'May as well.'

'Great,' said Richard. 'We'll follow you.' He nodded briskly at Dad. 'Thanks very much for that, Brian. We'll be in touch shortly, no doubt.'

Andrew smiled at me fleetingly and got back into his ute. Arnold and Richard climbed into the SUV, and they all drove away. 'Coffee, Dad?' I asked.

'No,' he said. 'No, thanks.'

'What a *prat*.'

Dad smiled. 'Which one?'

'Richard Green!' I said indignantly. Andrew wasn't a prat; he was just a little curt …

'Ah. Right. Yes. Complete tosser, as far as I could tell.'

'What did he say about the farm?'

'Very little. He took quite a few pictures to take back and show the board.'

'He must be pretty keen, to rush up and inspect it on a Sunday morning.'

'Just the way it worked out, I think,' Dad said. 'He was up this way for a meeting, and he's flying to Christchurch early this afternoon. You were out bright and early – I tried to give you a ring before we came up.'

'We were out burying Andrew's dog,' I said.

'Right,' said Dad, looking a little bemused. As well he might.

'Harry turned up here first thing, all upset because he'd just run her over …' I trailed off in embarrassment as I realised I'd just made it perfectly clear that Andrew had spent the night with me.

'Very good,' Dad said. 'So, er … all going well, is it?'

'I – I think so …' Oh, for goodness' sake, I thought impatiently. I was an adult. I knew my father loved me and wanted to see me in a stable, happy relationship, but do you think we could talk about this stuff? 'It's – it's such a shame that he has to sell up. It's a beautiful farm, and he's done so much to it.'

'Where's he going to go?' Dad asked.

I shook my head. 'No idea.'

'Perhaps he'll consider staying on as a manager after all, since you're here.'

'I think that would be a disaster,' I said. 'Going from owning a place to taking orders from someone you don't like …'

'Yes, he didn't put too much effort into trying to hide his opinion of the man, did he?'

'No,' I said, smiling. 'No, I don't think Andrew would ever make a politician.'

* * *

I'd seen Dad off and was just pouring milk over my Weet-Bix when the phone rang. 'Hello?' I said, turning in my chair to pick up the phone.

'Hi, Mummy,' said Lily in a very small voice.

This did not bode well. 'Hi, love.'

'Mummy?'

'Yes?'

'Can we come home?'

'Now?' I asked, surprised.

'Y-yes …' And she started to cry.

'Hey, don't cry, love! Of course you can, if you want to. Can I talk to Dad?'

'He – he said it would be better if I asked you, 'cause then you wouldn't get so mad …'

'I'm not mad,' I said. This was a blatant lie – I was furious. Had Dave chosen to, he could have charmed his small daughter back to smiles in two minutes flat. Ergo, he wanted the kids out of the way. And there was nothing I could do about it, or they'd think that *neither* parent wanted them around. 'But I'd better talk to him and find out what the plan is.'

'Okay.' And then, her voice fainter, 'Daddy! Mummy wants to talk to you and find out what the plan is.'

I heard Dave say something indistinguishable, and then Lily was back. 'He's going to bring us. We're going to leave in half an hour.'

'Very good,' I said. That snivelling coward. Making a seven-year-old do his dirty work. 'See you soon.'

They were home in forty-five minutes, which meant they'd left in fifteen. I heard Dave's ute come down the driveway and went out to meet them. Nathan waved excitedly from his car seat as they pulled up, and I smiled and waved back.

Lily clambered out and ran to cling to me, face buried in my shirt. I picked her up and hugged her, allowing myself to glare at Dave over the top of her head.

'Hi, Mummy!' Nathan shouted.

Dave got out of the ute, keeping his back to me, and began to unbuckle him.

'Hi, love!' I said.

'Mum! Mum! Lily was sad this morning and Anaya made us a yucky breakfast and we didn't eat it and she cried and – and –'

'Stop wriggling, wriggle-bum,' said Dave, tickling him so he shrieked with laughter.

'Stop it, Daddy! So then we had McDonald's for breakfast! But we couldn't have chicken nuggets 'cause it was too early.'

'What did you have?' I said, letting Lily slide to the ground. 'Grab your bag, love.'

'I had a egg muff – Mc – thing … It was yuck so Dad let me have a hot chocolate instead. And it had marshmallows in! But we didn't get a toy.'

'Oh well, at least you got marshmallows. What did you have, Lil?'

'Pancakes,' she whispered. 'But I didn't eat them.'

Dave, holding a backpack in either hand, turned, tripped over Tessa and swore. Tessa yelped and shot inside.

'You stood on Tessa's foot, Dad!' Nathan cried. '*And* you said a bad word! You should say sorry!'

'Sorry,' Dave said, dropping the backpacks on the back step. 'Okay, kiddos, I think that's the lot. I'll see you soon, okay?'

'Bye, Dad,' said Nathan, throwing his arms around Dave's legs.

'Bye, trouble. Love you.' He stroked Nathan's shorn head and held a hand out to Lily, who clutched it tightly. 'Love you, precious.' And failing to meet my eyes at all, he detached himself from his clinging offspring and left.

'Can we play a game where you're a mummy unicorn and I'm your baby?' Lily whispered as Dave's ute disappeared up the driveway. She was paper white, with dark smudges beneath her eyes.

'Sure,' I said, picking up her backpack. 'What's your name?'

'Star. And I can fly, and I can go invisible.'

'*I'm* Dash from *The Incredibles*,' Nathan shouted. '*I* can run as fast as the wind.' He sped off around the corner of the house.

'Okay, Star,' I said, ushering my baby unicorn into the kitchen. 'What do unicorns like to have for breakfast?'

'I'm not hungry.'

'I think you should eat something anyway. Invisibility takes a lot of energy.'

Lily smiled wanly. 'I don't know what to eat.'

'Toast? Cereal? Banana?'

'Okay.'

'Which one?'

She shrugged limply. 'Banana.'

Nathan appeared at the living room door and hammered loudly on the glass.

'Hey!' I said, hastening to open it. 'Don't do that, you horror; you'll break it.' I scooped him up as he stepped in and carried him to the sink to wash the grass off his bare feet.

He bore this patiently, daintily extended first one foot and then the other for me to dry on the tea towel, and jumped down onto the floor. 'Can I have a banana too?'

'Sure,' I said, balling up the tea towel and throwing it through the laundry door.

He dragged a chair across the kitchen floor and climbed up on it to inspect the fruit bowl. 'Anaya cries all the time,' he said cheerfully.

'That's no good,' I said.

'Only because we wouldn't eat that porridge,' said Lily, leaning against the pantry door.

'No, she cried yesterday too, when Dad was sleeping.' A vehicle came down the driveway, and he jumped down from the chair, banana in hand. 'Someone's here!'

The someone was, of course, Andrew. Feeling that life was unnecessarily complicated all of a sudden, I followed Nathan outside to meet him.

He got out of his ute and looked from me to Nathan in surprise.

'Dave just dropped them off,' I said.

'Ah.'

'Where's your dog that bited Tessa?' Nathan asked suddenly.

'She died,' Andrew said.

'What of?'

'She got run over.'

'Oh,' said Nathan.

'Hey, I'm really sorry about this,' I said. 'I was ... steamrolled.' A small hand clutched the back of my shirt – Lily, who had crept across the carport and was now peering balefully at the visitor from beneath my left elbow.

'Mr Faulkner,' said Nathan, 'what did she look like? Your dog.'

Andrew looked puzzled. 'Well, grey and brown ...'

'*No!* When she was run-ded over! Did she go pop and all her guts came out?'

'Nathan!' I said.

'No, she just looked normal,' Andrew said.

Nathan's face fell. 'Only dead,' he pointed out.

'That's right.'

'Were you sad?'

'Yes.'

'Did you cry?'

'A little bit.'

'That's okay,' Nathan said kindly. 'It's okay for boys to cry. *I'm* going to cry when my mum dies, even though I'll prob'ly be growed up.'

'That's very kind of you,' I said. 'Could you go and unpack your bag, please?'

'Lily has to too!'

'Yes, she does. Off you go, guys.'

'I don't feel very –' Lily whispered, and threw up copiously on my feet.

* * *

I must say, I've had better days. Further conversation being impossible, Andrew went away. Poor Lily vomited with clockwork regularity all day, and by evening, although the worst seemed to have passed, she was as pale and limp as a piece of damp paper.

I felt pretty limp myself. Nathan, bored and irritated by the amount of attention his sister was getting, was being a fire siren in the sufferer's bedroom doorway, while Tessa scratched industriously at the carpet between his feet.

'Outside,' I ordered.

Neither obeyed. In fact, neither gave any indication of having heard me.

'*Out!*'

'Mum, what are we doing for my birfday?' Nathan asked, ceasing to be a siren and leaning against the doorjamb.

'The usual, I guess. Cake, party ...' Comprising Nana and Granddad, any other relatives who happened to be in the vicinity, Ange Miller and her kids, and a selection of unhealthy processed snack foods. Ange and I had sworn a solemn oath at the third birthday party of a mutual acquaintance's daughter (an occasion that had featured goodie bags, a croquembouche tower and a petting zoo) never to start down the slippery slope of competitive partying.

'Can we have marshmallows?' said Lily weakly, which I thought was an excellent sign.

'I want sausage rolls!' cried Nathan. 'And it's *my* birfday!'

'But –'

'We can have both!' I said. 'Nathan, run up and check the mailbox, please.' It would be empty, this being Sunday, but there would be peace for five blessed minutes.

* * *

At eight o'clock, when both children were finally asleep, I took the portable phone outside and sat down on the top porch step to ring Andrew.

''Lo,' said a Faulkner, picking up.

'Harry?' I guessed.

'Nope. Hi, Jen.'

'Oh, sorry. Hi.'

'How are the kids?'

'Lily hasn't been sick for three hours, now. How was your day?'

'I missed you.'

'Good,' I said.

'I've never known a woman who made me feel like you do ...'

Hmm. 'Hi, Harry.'

'What – what d'you –?' he said with unconvincing indignation.

'Nice try.'

Harry sighed and gave up. 'I suppose you want Andrew?'

'Yes, please,' I said.

'Are you sure? You're an attractive woman; I'm sure you could do better.'

'Give me the phone, you clown,' came Andrew's voice from somewhere in the distance.

'Listen to that. Not even a please. *And* he's broken.'

'Has he hurt his back?' I asked.

'Yep. Flat on the floor and groaning. Here he is.'

There was a clatter and a grunt, and then Andrew said, 'Hey, Jen.'

'Hey.'

'Ask him how he did it,' Harry called.

'Would you go away?' said Andrew, with no real hope.

'It wasn't spitting out toothpaste again?' I asked.

'No. I picked up a cycad in a pot.'

'A really *small* pot,' came Harry's voice.

I laughed – I couldn't help it. 'Today's been a bit average all round, hasn't it?'

'It sure has.'

'My only hope is that Lily managed to give Dave her tummy bug before he returned them.'

'Fingers crossed,' he said. 'How is she?'

'Flat as a pancake. But I think the worst has passed.'

'That's good.'

A thin wail sounded on the warm evening air, coming from the direction of Lily's open bedroom window. 'I may have spoken too soon,' I said. 'I'd better go.'

'Good luck. Night, Jen.'

'Love you,' Harry called in a quavering falsetto.

'Tell him he's fired,' I said. 'Goodnight, love.'

I was halfway to Lily's room before I realised what I'd said.

Chapter 31

None of us were throwing up the next day, luckily, but I kept Lily home from school in case. Whereupon she ate two scrambled eggs for breakfast and climbed with Nathan to the top of a peach tree.

They stayed there while I did the housework. Then I went out with an animal biscuit in either hand to retrieve them. 'Hey, chickens.'

'We're fantails, not chickens,' Lily informed me.

'Right. Even better. Animal biscuit?'

The fantails descended rapidly.

'Shall we go for a little walk down to Mr Mercer's place?' I asked.

'No, thank you,' said Nathan through a mouthful of biscuit.

'Could we go and see Nana instead?' said Lily.

I was just about to break it to them that it had, in fact, been a rhetorical question, when we heard a four-wheeler climbing the hill below the garden.

'Harry!' Nathan cried, dashing around the side of the house.

Lily and I followed more slowly, and reached the top of the orchard as Nathan climbed the fence at the bottom. Harry was turning off the four-wheeler.

'Good morning!' I called.

'Hi, guys,' Harry said. 'Still chundering, Lily?'

'What's that?' she asked.

'Throwing up.'

'No. But I'm still not a hundred percent. There was *blood* in one of my spews.'

'Wow.'

'About quarter of a mil,' I said, not wishing to figure in this story as the parent who didn't think gastric haemorrhage was cause for medical intervention. 'How are you doing, Harry?'

'Mental state? Work performance?'

'Mental state.'

'Melancholy,' he said.

I smiled at him. 'Yeah.'

'Do you want to come to my birfday?' Nathan asked him, climbing up onto the mudguard beside him.

'Sure, mate,' Harry said. 'When is this auspicious occasion?'

'The sevenf of December. I'm going to be *five*.'

'But he's not going to school until next year,' said Lily. '*I* started going to school on my birthday.'

'Your birthday wasn't two weeks before the Christmas holidays,' I said.

'Who else is coming to your party?' Harry asked hastily, observing the signs of imminent warfare.

'Nana and Granddad,' said Nathan, ticking them off on his fingers. 'Mummy, Lily, Aunty Bex and baby Caleb –'

'Probably not this year, love,' I said. 'They've only just been here for a visit.'

'Oh,' said Nathan sadly. Then he brightened. 'But they'll still send me a present.' He turned back to Harry. 'And Dad, and Anaya' – this was news to me – 'and Perry and Scarlett and baby Michael and their mum and dad, and you, and Nana and Granddad, and …'

'Sounds epic,' said Harry, shooting me an amused sideways glance.

'Doesn't it just,' I said. 'Oh, I've just remembered – the silage contractor rang last night to ask how much we had shut up and when we wanted to cut it.'

'Er, none,' Harry said.

'Really?' I said. 'But …' But we'd talked about this. We *always* cut silage at the end of November.

'I did shut up the cabbage tree paddock a couple of weeks ago, but, um – then I opened the gates again.'

'Why?'

'Well …' He looked down and fiddled with the petrol cap. 'Andrew said we didn't have a surplus, and shutting up silage while we underfed the ewes and lambs was a brain-dead thing to do.'

'Well, true,' I said. 'Cool.' But inadequacy rolled over me like a wave. How the hell had I ever thought I might be able to turn the farm around? I didn't even know what I didn't know.

'Please don't tell him I told you. He said it wasn't appropriate for him to be putting his oar in.'

'I'd much rather he said something than just watched us stuff things up,' I said.

'Yeah, that's what I told him. But he seemed to think you'd feel bad.'

'Never,' I said, smiling. It wasn't much of a smile, but he didn't notice.

* * *

Harry continued on his way to shift the heifers, and the kids, Tessa, three out of five pet lambs and I walked through the paddocks to John's cottage below the woolshed. It was warm and sunny, and a turkey with thirteen chicks hurried across the track in front of us to vanish, peeping hysterically, into the long grass beside the pond. The ewes and lambs we passed looked *fine*, I told myself firmly. Although – although those lambs of Andrew's I'd seen on Friday night were as big as their mothers ...

'Don't worry, Mummy,' Lily said, slipping her hand into mine.

I smiled at her. 'No, I'm just – how did you know?'

'You bite your lip when you're worrying about things.'

'Huh,' I said, impressed. 'Very observant. Well, I'll stop.'

'I'll tell you a joke to cheer you up, shall I?'

'Yes, please.'

'Okay. Um ... I know. You'll really like this one. Are you ready, Mum?'

'Yep. Hit me.'

'Hit you?' she asked.

'Figure of speech, love. I'm ready. Go.'

'Okay.' She cleared her throat. 'What's, um, what's yellow with sharks in it?'

'I have no idea,' I said.

'Yes you do! It's your joke, that one you like!'

'Oh. What's yellow and very dangerous?'

'Yes!' said Lily. 'That one. Do you feel better now, Mum?'

I smiled at her. 'Yep. Heaps better. Thanks, Lil.'

'You're welcome,' she said.

* * *

We found John in his veggie garden, digging laboriously. Torn between gratification at the visit and the desire to ensure that I was properly humbled, he greeted us with cool politeness and an air of sorrow, nobly borne.

This was fairly painful, but on my admiration of his seedling leeks and the children's admiration of his collection of concrete animals, lined up like an honour guard along the path, he veered back towards his normal state of patronising goodwill. Also painful, but less so.

'Just look at my early spuds,' he said, as Nathan and Lily began a variation of hopscotch along the crazy paving.

'They look wonderful,' I said.

'And what d'you think of me tomatoes?'

'They look won– great.'

'Bit ahead of yours,' he said smugly, getting out his tobacco and beginning to roll himself a cigarette.

'Miles ahead,' I agreed. 'You put me to shame, John.'

'Ah, well. Mind been on other things, eh?' And he gave me a wry look that said all too clearly that although he was – understandably – concerned by my wanton behaviour, he was far too tactful and considerate to say so.

'John …' I said.

'Spit it out, m' dear.'

'This isn't common knowledge yet, but Mum and Dad are thinking of selling the farm.'

His partly rolled cigarette fell into his tobacco pouch. 'They're *what?*'

'Dad doesn't want to be hands-on anymore, and – and I'm not a farmer.'

'You are not,' he said with grim and unflattering emphasis. 'Right. So that's that, is it? Thanks for getting the place into shape; now clear out.'

'No!' I said. 'There are four houses on this farm, and surely whoever buys it won't be using more than two of them. They'll probably be quite happy for you to stay on.'

'*Probably*,' said John sullenly.

'I know. I'm sorry, John. It's horrible having it all up in the air.'

'After everything I've done. After all the work and the money I've put into this place.'

Here I considered pointing out that nobody had asked him to do it, that he hadn't paid a cent of rent in six months and that his nice new wood burner and wetback system had come gratis. But of course I didn't.

'I've turned this place from a bloody hovel into a nice, snug little house ... Even if they don't kick me out, the rent will be through the bloody roof. *Look* at it.' He swept his arm in the direction of a gleaming lilac wall. 'New paint, nice garden, all shipshape ... And I've paid for the lot. Well, there's no fool like an old fool, is there?'

'I'm sorry, John,' I said again.

But he was not to be placated, so after a few minutes we went quietly away.

* * *

When I booted up my computer on Wednesday morning, I found forty-four new emails to go with the tottering stack of files on my desk. That was about normal, the building control department at

Tipoi District Council being chronically understaffed, but usually I cleared at least some of the backlog at home. Not for the last fortnight, though. New relationships, not to mention farm sales and sisters in crisis, are not conducive to quiet evenings with one's laptop.

'Oh, God,' I said aloud, and Greta looked across at me enquiringly. 'And this bloody government audit's in less than two weeks.'

'Tell me about it,' she said heavily.

At ten fourteen I got a text message from Anaya.

Hey chicky! When do you have lunch? Just wondering if we can catch up and have a chat about things ☺

What things, pray? Her new boyfriend's selfishness, lack of responsibility and general unfitness to be a parent? I turned the phone face down and carried on with the report I was writing. But two minutes later I sighed and turned it back up again.

Good idea. But not today, sorry, work is insane.

The reply came back straight away. I could meet you later on, if that suits. ☺ What time do you finish work?

Midnight, at this rate, I thought glumly.

The phone beeped again.

Sorry to be so pushy lol! But I feel its really important for us to talk for the kids sake ☺

Oh, for Christ's sake. 4 this afternoon? I wrote.

4 isn't so great for me ☹ 4.30?

Fine, I wrote grimly.

Yay! ☺ ☺ Where would you like to meet up?

I didn't know. Neither did I care. Hotel? It was conveniently near; just across the road.

There was a two-minute pause before she replied. Would you

mind if we went somewhere else? Not quite the ambience I had in mind. 😱 😓

I threw the phone into my top drawer and slammed it shut. Whereupon it immediately rang. 'Just *go away*!' I said aloud, opening the drawer again. Could she not wait even a minute for a reply? Bloody younger generation and their instant gratification issues ...

Andrew Faulkner, read the phone's screen. I snatched it up and swiped feverishly. 'Hi!'

'Hi,' he said. 'Sorry to call you at work.'

'It's fine,' I said warmly. 'Nicest thing that's happened all morning.'

'Thank you. I was just wondering if you could come for tea tonight.'

'I'd love to, but work's a bit crazy today – would seven thirty be too late?'

'Seven thirty's fine. Whenever you can come is fine.'

'Cool. See you later.'

'Have a good day,' he said.

'You too.' I hung up and wasted another three seconds of valuable work time smiling dreamily at nothing, before Anaya's next message arrived.

Sorry to be such a pain. 😓 Of course we can meet at the hotel, I just need to get over myself!!! Bad experience there. Anyway, water under the bridge 😬 See you then!

Not because I'm nice, but because I didn't feel strong enough to watch her bravely facing her demons during our meeting, I replied, Somewhere else is fine, you decide and I'll meet you there.

Aw, thanks chicky, you rock!! 😬 😓 How about at the war memorial?

Fine.

* * *

By four twenty my head ached and my eyes felt gritty. It was a relief to abandon my computer and walk down the main street to the war memorial at the south end of town. Anaya wasn't there when I crossed the square of worn grass in front of the cenotaph. I stretched my shoulders absent-mindedly and looked down the plaque listing Tipoi's fallen soldiers for *Smith, W.P. Cpl.* Corporal W.P. Smith had been my grandfather's favourite brother Billy, who played the piano like a dream and smoothed his hair down with mutton fat when his parents wouldn't buy him Brylcreem (thus attracting a horde of blowflies and much amusement at the Pukewai District Christmas Picnic of '38), and who lied about his age when he ran away from home to enlist. He was eighteen when he died in Egypt.

My musings on the senseless waste of war were interrupted by Anaya, approaching from across the main street. She was wearing a very pretty pink blouse and a somewhat less successful pair of skinny jeans. 'Hi, Jenny!' she called. 'How's it going?'

'Good, thanks,' I said. 'I like your top.'

'Oh, thank you!' She sat down on a bench and patted the seat beside her invitingly. The chill hauteur with which she had greeted me on Friday might never have been.

I sat beside her and tweaked the hem of my skirt straight. It was made of khaki-coloured canvas, with big square pockets on the front and a tie belt, almost but not quite too informal to wear to work, and I loved it dearly.

'I'm glad you agreed to meet me,' she said.

'No problem.'

'I'll just, um, jump right in, then, shall I?'

'Jump away,' I said.

'Okay.' She took a deep breath. 'I just thought – well, I thought that if we could meet up face to face we might be able to put aside our differences. Because when it comes down to it, the differences aren't that big. We *all* want what's best for Nathan and Lily, right? And we – David and I – know you'd never let your personal feelings get in the way of that.'

'Er, no,' I said, slightly bemused.

'And I hear you've got a new man in your life?'

'Er, yes ...'

'That's just *so* great. I really hope you can start to move on now, and find some healing. I've been crossing my fingers that you'd meet someone. It must be so hard watching your ex find love when you're alone.'

'No, it's ...' I began dazedly, and then gave myself a mental shake. 'Anaya, I'm sure Dave told you that I was a bit unhappy about him dropping off the kids on Sunday morning.'

She nodded and smiled encouragingly. I had a strong suspicion that this was a technique culled from an internet article titled 'How to Manage Your Partner's Hostile Ex-Wife'.

'Look, you guys can't just suddenly decide that the kids are cramping your style and pack them off back to me,' I said. 'It's – well, it's inconsiderate. And I don't want them to feel that their dad would rather not have them around.'

'We *love* having them around!' she said.

'And yet a weekend with them was too long.'

'They're *gorgeous* kids. Although – and don't take this the wrong way – Lily can sometimes have a *teensy* bit of an attitude ...'

I was startled by the intensity of my wrath. How *dare* this immature, patronising little *moron* criticise my child? How *dare* she?

'I just think it's really important not to burden children with our own emotional baggage,' she was saying kindly. 'Of course I understand, Jenny, how David's and my happiness might feel like a slap in the face to you, but the thing is that the kids are really going to pick up on that.'

'You and Dave can be as happy as you like,' I snapped. 'I'm delighted for you both. What *doesn't* delight me is you sending the kids home because you're sick of them!'

'We weren't sick of them! If you must know, I was ovulating on Sunday!'

'What?' I said blankly.

She folded her hands protectively across her stomach and said nothing.

'Anaya, how old are you?'

'Twenty-five. It's not *me* that's the issue. David's *thirty-seven*.'

Gosh. So he was, poor old thing. I choked back a burst of wild laughter and said, 'But – but men are perfectly capable of –'

'I don't want my baby's father to be an old man by the time he or she's a teenager!'

'Okay, but don't you think maybe you should hold off for another year, say, and get to know each other a bit better?'

'No,' she said. 'It's been eight months. Although, to be honest, I knew in eight minutes.'

Eight months? That was … March? April? And Dave was begging me to take him back in June … Oh, hell. 'Babies are awfully time-consuming,' I said gently. 'It's quite nice to have some time alone together before they come along.'

'*I* think the best times *start* when you have children,' she said.

Right.

'I do know that David has made some bad decisions in the past. He's told me all about it. We don't keep secrets from one another. But people make mistakes when they feel like they're trapped in a toxic relationship.'

'I see,' I said, standing up.

'You need to let him go, Jenny. He's with me, now.'

True, I thought suddenly, my anger evaporating in a wave of amusement. So he was. And it served him right.

Chapter 32

On that note, Anaya and I went our separate ways, me to return to my computer and she to spend the evening with my children. Heaven help them. I answered emails until seven and got home at half past to dash through the shower, drag a brush through my hair and speed out again, Tessa panting triumphantly beside me.

'Sorry,' I said as she preceded me through Andrew's living-room door and began a tour of inspection. 'She guilted me. She's been tied up all day.'

'She's fine,' he said, smiling as he came across the living room. He had a tea towel over his shoulder. 'Hi.'

'Hi.' I pulled his head down and kissed him fervently.

'Must you?' said Harry, appearing through the doorway behind the staircase. I withdrew in some haste.

'It's my house,' Andrew said.

'Still.' Harry opened the fridge, and Tessa sped towards him. She sat down at his feet and looked up piteously. 'Good evening, young Tessa.'

'Did those calves arrive?' I asked, trying to recover a little poise.

'Yep.' He selected a jar. 'They got off the truck, ran straight through two fences and ended up in the bull paddock. Oh, and they broke a tape gate.' Opening the jar, he fished something out and dropped it into Tessa's waiting mouth. She spat it out and pawed feverishly at her tongue.

'What on *earth* was that?' I asked.

'Pickled onion.' He shut the fridge again, jar in hand.

Tessa sneezed violently three times in a row and then cautiously picked up the onion again, in case she'd made too hasty a decision. 'Coming?' Harry asked her, and she followed him back down the hall, stumpy little tail going like a propeller.

Andrew opened a cupboard in the kitchen and took out two plates.

'Isn't Harry eating with us?' I asked.

'No,' he said. 'He's eaten.'

'Was he hungry, or is he avoiding us?'

'Both,' Harry called.

* * *

We had an excellent meal of beef rendang and Asian-ish coleslaw, stuffed into pita breads. Harry returned, Tessa at his heels, as we were finishing it. 'Terribly sorry to intrude,' he said, filling the kettle and switching it on.

'Oh, come off it,' Andrew said.

Harry smiled. 'Richard Green called earlier. Apparently he can't open the file you sent him, and you need to ring him back urgently.' He opened the pantry and extracted a packet of biscuits.

Andrew grimaced but said nothing.

'You ring him; I'll do the dishes,' I said, standing up.

'No, he can wait. Do him good.' At which moment his cell phone, sitting on the kitchen windowsill, rang.

'Apparently he can't,' Harry said, looking at the screen.

Andrew got up, picked up his phone and turned it off.

'Doesn't it just send a shiver down your spine when he goes all stern and manly, Jen?' Harry asked.

It did. 'Absolutely,' I said, carrying the dirty plates to the sink. 'But why have you turned camp all of a sudden?'

He shrugged. 'Just trying it out.'

He made his cup of tea and took it away, and Andrew and I silently cleared the table. There are plenty of varieties of silence – tense, awkward, comfortable, indifferent … This one practically quivered with anticipation and delight.

Andrew rinsed the dishcloth, wrung it out and folded it neatly over a tap. Then he looked at me and smiled. 'Shall we?' he said very quietly.

I smiled back, and then hesitated. 'Just a second,' I whispered.

Harry was stretched out on his bed with Tessa on his stomach, iPad in one hand and cup in the other. He raised his eyebrows at me enquiringly as I appeared in the doorway.

'Night,' I said. 'We're going to head off. Come on, Tess.'

Tessa yawned cavernously and snuggled down. Harry lay there and smirked.

'I'm sorry,' I said awkwardly, feeling my face burn.

The smirk vanished, and he sighed. 'Oh, don't be silly,' he said. 'I'm glad you're happy. Although' – the smirk made a brief reappearance – 'I'm still concerned about your taste in men.'

'It's better than yours,' I pointed out.

'It could hardly be worse. Leave Tessa; I'll drop her back in the morning.'

'Thank you,' I said.

* * *

'What are you smiling about?' Andrew asked some time later, disturbing a pleasantly sleepy silence. We were lying in my bed as the sky outside deepened from violet to indigo and a bright sliver of moon rose above the trees.

'I was wondering what you'd do if I asked how your back was.'

'It's fine, thank you.'

'Good,' I said. 'Hey, I won't keep asking – but you will tell me if it's sore and you don't want me jumping on you, won't you?'

'Probably not,' he said. 'I'd hate to discourage you.'

'Well, then, you'll have only yourself to blame. Oh, I never asked how your drive with Richard Green went.'

'Unenjoyable, on the whole.'

I found his hand and squeezed it. 'It's all just *crap*, when you've worked so hard.'

'But not, apparently, on the right things,' he said.

'Such as your marriage?'

'That's the one.'

'And how hard was *she* working on your marriage?' I said crisply. Of course I was jumping to conclusions in assuming that their break-up was mostly Toni's fault – not *entirely* her fault; I wasn't quite that naive – but the woman really did look like bloody hard work.

Andrew gave a noncommittal sort of grunt.

'Did she leave you, or did you tell her to get out?' I asked.

'She left.'

'And it *was* her who cheated. So I don't know that you have to feel completely racked with guilt.'

'Ah, but I drove her to it.'

'Funny; that's what Dave said.'

'Hey, speaking of guilt,' he said after a short silence, 'it's not your fault *your* farm's being sold, either.'

'Hmm,' I said. 'I could have tried harder, let's face it.'

'How?'

'I don't even *know*. I've just had this vague idea that we needed to do better, without any clear idea of how we might get there. Poor at best.'

'Stop it,' he said, putting a hand on my leg and giving it a little shake. 'Jen, I don't understand why you seem to think you should be some sort of farm systems expert, when you've never done it before.'

But I *should* have done it before. I should have made more of an effort to be involved with the decision-making stuff rather than leaving it all to Dave, whose practices, according to my bedtime reading, could have used an update. Although – let's be honest – it would have gone down like a cup of cold sick. Any input from me had been met by my husband with: 'Look, why don't *you* just do it, seeing as you know everything?'

I sighed.

'You've been in charge since – when did that little shit Marcus go?'

'June.'

'By which time the ewes were skinny and you had no grass. And yet you seem to think you should have been able to turn it all around in five months.'

I rolled over and hugged him tightly. 'You're a very comforting person, did you know that?'

Chapter 33

December arrived, adding, as always, a flood of sheep work to the standard annual pre-Christmas panic. I spent several days in the yards, drenching and dipping lambs with Dad while Harry mustered. Nathan fell off the wool press and knocked out two front teeth, which considerably increased one morning's excitement. The submersible pump for the shower dip broke and needed a replacement part sent from Australia, apparently via canoe. And then there was the costume for Lily's end-of-year school play (she was featuring this year as Chicken Little's mother), Nathan's fifth birthday, the government audit at work ...

I barely saw Andrew, who did all his sheep work by himself and was putting in fourteen-hour days. And worst of all, Mum and Dad accepted Richard Green's offer to buy the farm. No eleventh-hour reprieve. No fairy tale ending. Shit really does happen.

* * *

On a bright, hot Tuesday morning, Harry, Nathan and I were in the yards at the woolshed, mouthing ewes. Harry and I filled the drenching race and worked our way up side by side, checking every mouth for loose, missing or otherwise dodgy teeth, while

Nathan clung to the rails beside us, marking the culls with pink chalk.

'That one?' Nathan asked eagerly as I let go of a ewe's head.

'No, she's fine.'

'You haven't let me stripe one for *ages*!'

'This one,' Harry said. 'Two teeth missing. Just like you. Better put a mark on your head, too.'

'*I'm* not going to the works,' said Nathan haughtily, leaning over the rails and making bold swipes with his chalk.

'My mate Geoff rang last night,' Harry said, moving up the race and reaching for the next ewe's head. 'He's just got the contract to cull goats and deer on Mount Taranaki, and he was wondering if I'd be keen. The job starts on the first of March.'

'Hey, that sounds cool!'

'Yeah, it'd be good fun.'

'Go for your life,' I said, smiling at him.

'Thank you.'

'No, thank *you*. You've been a life saver, these last six months.'

'I know,' he said. 'I'm awesome.'

'I'm awesome too,' Nathan said, busily chalking the top rail of the race. 'I'm being really, really useful.'

'So you are,' I said.

'Can I get paid for helping?'

'That sounds fair enough,' Harry said. 'He *is* being really useful, after all.'

'How much dollars will I get?'

'Hmm,' I said. 'Let's say … fifty cents an hour, if you work really hard.'

'Is that lots?'

'Heaps,' Harry told him, and Nathan beamed.

'Mum, don't tell Lily! I want to!'

'Okay.'

'Blatant exploitation,' Harry remarked.

'I know,' I said. 'The place is practically a sweatshop.'

'What should I buy with all my dollars?' Nathan asked, frowning.

'Maybe we can go to the two-dollar shop the next time we're in town, and you can have a look around.'

'I'm going to buy something for you, Mummy,' he said, leaning perilously over the rails to kiss me.

'Thanks, sausage!'

'I'm going to miss you, Nath,' Harry told him.

Nathan nodded; well, of course.

'But you'll be back to visit, won't you?' I said, wrestling with an uncooperative ewe.

'Yeah, of course. And Andrew reckons he can give me bits and pieces of work back here, if I want it.'

I frowned. 'What?'

'Hasn't he told you?'

'Told me what?'

'That he's decided to manage the two farms after all.'

I stood up straight. Manage … 'But he hates Richard Green!'

Harry looked at me quizzically. 'Maybe he's got a really good reason for staying,' he said.

* * *

I rang Andrew's cell phone as soon as I got home. The call went straight to message. I'd have called him again as soon as the kids were in bed, but John, characteristically, chose that moment to descend.

It was, however, an unusually short visit. I'd just seen him off and turned to pick up Lily's schoolbag, abandoned at the bottom of the back steps, when I heard his car stall. It started again, reversed rapidly and then stalled a second time with an ominous crunch of breaking branches.

I dashed up the driveway to find his little car listing heavily, half on and half off the track, with both left-hand wheels over the bank. The downhill slide had been arrested by a large and rather special hydrangea, and Andrew was getting out of his ute twenty metres further up.

John was struggling fruitlessly with his door. 'Driving like a maniac,' he spluttered as I opened it. 'Paying no attention to where he's going – entirely too fast …'

'Don't get out,' Andrew told him. 'If you stay there and steer we'll push you back onto the track.'

John sat back, glaring.

Andrew and I pushed through the remains of my poor hydrangea to the back of the car and braced ourselves to push. 'Start her up,' Andrew called. 'Ready, Jen?'

The engine coughed and started. I considered and then dismissed the idea of asking if this would be good for his back, and said instead, 'On three?'

'One – two – *three* … John! Take your foot off the damn brake!'

We managed, after a brief but strenuous effort, to push the little car back up onto the track. Andrew got into his ute and reversed up the driveway while I went to John's window. 'There's not a scratch on the car,' I said. 'No harm done.' Except to my hydrangea.

'No thanks to him,' he said.

I drew breath to retaliate, and then thought better of it. John was in his car, headed not towards but away from my house – heaven forbid I should detain him, even in pursuit of justice. 'Goodnight!' I said brightly, beating a retreat.

'What was his problem?' Andrew said as he got out of his ute down at the house. 'If looks could kill ...'

'Well, the whole thing was your fault,' I explained kindly.

'How the hell is it *my* fault if he decides to back over a bank?'

'It was actually my fault,' I said, putting my arms around him. 'I just crushed all his hopes.'

He rested his chin on top of my head. 'You finally told him you wouldn't marry him?'

'No, I told him we wouldn't sell him the cottage for ten thousand dollars. Even though that's far more than it's worth, apparently.'

'How unreasonable of you,' he said.

'I know. He took it badly when I said that ten thousand dollars wouldn't even cover the cost of subdivision.' I leant against him, and felt his chest rise and fall gently as he breathed. He smelt of soap and clean cotton. 'Thanks for coming over.'

'Pleasure,' he said. 'Sorry I missed your call. My phone was flat. What's up?'

'Are you really planning to stay and work for Richard Green?'

There was a short pause, and then he sighed. 'Harry.'

'He assumed I knew! Why didn't you tell me?'

'I was going to,' he said, a trifle defensively.

'You *hate* Richard Green!'

'Well, hate's a strong word ...' he said, and I could hear that he was smiling.

I pulled away and looked at him. 'Are you doing this for me?'

'I'm doing it for me,' he said slowly.

'Because who wouldn't jump at the opportunity to go into business with the Greens?'

'I'm *not* going into business with them! I'm going to manage the two farms on a short-term contract. No investment, no strings attached.'

'But – but you'll have to do things their way, and you don't like their way.'

'Well, then, it'll be a valuable exercise in learning to compromise,' he said.

'It'll drive you nuts!' I said.

'And if nothing else, it'll give me a bit of time to look around and see what my options are.'

'That's all very well, but you could just as easily get a job you *enjoy* while you look at your options.'

'Well – there are other benefits to being here.'

'Ah, yes,' I said. 'The awesome sex.'

He gave me a long, thoughtful look. 'I don't actually do *all* my thinking with my dick, Jen.'

'I – I know,' I faltered. 'I'm sorry; that was a stupid thing to say.'

He looked down at his hands. 'I think you're lovely,' he said quietly.

My eyes filled with sudden tears. 'I think you are, too. It's just – it's too *soon* to start making big compromises. We don't really know each other; the whole physical attraction thing overrides everything else, so you can't tell … I mean – well, look at me. I *married* Dave! And then there are the kids …'

'What about them?'

'I haven't even told them about you, yet!'

'No,' he said, and his voice was dry as dust.

'Do – do you want me to?'

'Of course I do! But you haven't even considered it, have you?'

'*Yes!*' I said. 'I just thought we should wait till we were really sure …'

'I see. Well, let me know when that is.'

My stomach lurched. This was all going horribly, horribly wrong. I took a deep breath. 'Andrew …' And then the back door opened, and Lily quavered, 'Mummy.'

I closed my eyes. 'What, love?'

'I was crying and crying for you, and you didn't come.'

'Well, don't worry, I'm right here.'

Andrew opened the door of his ute. 'See you later,' he said.

'Please wait,' I said. 'Please.'

He stopped.

'Lil, go and jump into bed, and I'll be there in a second.'

'But –'

'*Lily.*'

The kitchen door closed.

'Look, I'd better go,' Andrew said. 'I've got a mob of steers to shift before it gets dark. I'll see you tomorrow night.' He kissed my cheek quickly, got into his ute and drove away.

Chapter 34

At four thirty-five the next afternoon, I was crossing the council car park on my way back from a site visit, wondering whether *I love you* would be better said with steak or Swedish meatballs, when someone behind me said, 'Jenny.'

I stopped and turned. 'Travis! Hi!'

'You're looking well,' he said.

'How are you? I haven't seen you for ages.'

'No.' He bit his lip. 'I hear you've, um, been busy.'

'Well, you know what December's like,' I said, feeling vaguely uncomfortable. What had I promised to do for Travis and then forgotten about? 'Why is it that we all descend into some sort of wild pre-Christmas panic?'

He ignored this lead. 'Congratulations are in order, I hear.'

'Congratulations?' Oh, shit. He'd heard about Andrew. Dave must have told him.

'Dave said he'd ... interrupted you.'

I wondered fleetingly just what Dave, that grass seed in the sock of my happiness, had said, and decided it would be much, much better not to know.

Travis gave me a pitiful, knife-twisting little smile. 'Anyway, I really hope it all works out for you.'

'Travis,' I said, and stopped. What was there to say, after all? *You know how I said I didn't want a relationship? Well — this is funny; you'll enjoy this — it turns out I just didn't want one with* you.

'It's fine, Jenny. Any chance you might have a second to print off the floor plans for the shop?'

'Sure,' I said, rather too heartily. 'I can email them through first thing tomorrow morning.'

'Actually, you couldn't do it now, could you? I'm sorry to be a pain in the neck, but I've got a draughtsman coming to have a look this evening ...' *And it's the least you can do, after trampling my heart into the dirt.*

I glanced at my watch. I had to — *had to* — get to Wrightson's before five. But there'd be time, just. 'Yes, of course.'

As we continued across the car park my cell phone rang, and I groped for it in my handbag as I walked. *Andrew Faulkner*, the screen said. Not now, alas. I silenced it and dropped it sadly back into my bag.

'What *is* your ringtone?' Travis asked. 'I know I should know it.'

'The theme song from *Get Smart*.'

As we went through the automatic sliding doors into reception I saw Greta and Marcus standing at the foot of the stairs. He shot me a filthy look, and I flinched internally. What *was* Greta doing with this revolting excuse for a human being?

'Fuck,' said Marcus as we approached. 'Just when you think your day can't get any worse.'

This open declaration of hostility was most unexpected. 'Lovely to see you too, Marcus,' I said, raising my eyebrows.

'Oh, piss off, bitch.'

'Hey —' said Travis.

'He thinks it's your fault he lost his job,' Greta said, her voice shaking and her face white and set. 'But it's not; it's just that he's a lazy, incompetent arsehole.'

My fault? I thought. *Huh?*

'Shut the fuck up,' Marcus spat at her.

And Travis, even more unexpectedly, lunged forward and hit him in the mouth.

Marcus reeled back, tripped on the bottom stair and flailed his arms wildly to regain his balance. I froze, Greta screamed, and there was a general flutter of alarm among the onlookers – Lyn behind the reception desk, the mayor's PA and a small pod of middle managers who had just emerged from a meeting room.

Marcus brought a hand slowly to his mouth, took it away again and looked at the smear of blood on his fingers.

'Get out,' said Travis.

Marcus took a step towards him. He was taller than Travis, and quite a lot heavier.

'I'm calling security,' Lyn called from across the room.

Travis brought his fists up, ready. There was a breathless pause, and then Marcus fell back again. 'You're not fucking worth it,' he muttered, and sidled past us towards the doors.

Shocked silence reigned for perhaps two seconds after the doors had slid shut behind him. Then everyone appeared to breathe out simultaneously. The mayor's PA said, '*Well!*' Greta burst into tears. Lyn hurried across the foyer towards her. Travis flexed his fingers, wincing.

'Wow,' I said, drawing a long, shaky breath. 'Go, Travis.'

He gave a deprecating, just-doing-my-duty sort of shrug.

'Thank you,' Greta whispered.

'My pleasure,' he said.

'Your hand …'

Travis threw out his chest and said nobly, 'It's nothing.'

Lyn caught my eye, and her lips twitched.

I looked at the clock. Four forty-six … 'Travis, I'm so sorry, but I've got to get to Wrightson's before they shut.'

'Go ahead,' he said. 'It's fine.'

'I'll come straight back. Unless maybe Greta could find them for you?'

'No!' he said, evidently quite shocked at my insensitivity. 'God, no! Not after what she's just been through.'

Greta smiled bravely. 'I'll survive. What do you need?'

'Oh, just a copy of some plans,' said Travis. 'But it really doesn't matter.'

'That won't take long,' she said, wiping her eyes. 'It's the least I can do.'

'No. No, honestly …'

Lyn and I looked at one another again, and quietly withdrew.

* * *

I made it to Wrightson's as they closed the door, and bought a new shearing comb, two cutters and a packet of discs for the grinder from a young man who obviously felt that closing-time customers were envoys of Satan. Safely in the car again, I got out my phone to ring Andrew back.

He'd left me a voice message. 'Hi, Jen. I'm sorry, I won't make it tonight. Toni's father's just had a massive stroke. I'm heading to Feilding now. Um … take care.'

I dithered briefly about whether to call him – he'd be driving – and then did anyway, to find that his phone was either turned off or out of range. 'Leave a message and I'll ring you back,' said his voicemail, with Andrew-ish brevity.

'Sorry I missed you,' I said. 'I hope everything's okay – well, obviously it isn't okay at all, but … Anyway, I – I miss you. And I'm sorry I was such a dick last night. Talk soon.' I hung up and wearily rested my head against the seat back, causing a passing Wrightson's employee to pause at my open window and ask if I was alright.

'Fine,' I said, crimson to the ears. 'Just having a moment.'

'I know the feeling well,' she said, smiling. 'Sorry to disturb. Carry on.'

After which I went home, ate a family-sized bag of corn chips and eight stale gingernuts, and watched a documentary about the impact of global warming on the Great Barrier Reef. Why, after all, be unhealthy, unproductive or depressed, when you can so easily achieve all three?

And, just to set the final seal of gloom on my evening, Andrew didn't ring me back.

* * *

I was at my desk the next morning when Greta arrived. 'Morning,' she said, dropping her gym bag on the floor.

'Good morning,' I said. 'How are you feeling?'

She drew a deep breath and let it out again. 'I feel free,' she said.

Well, that was encouraging. 'Great!'

'It's like – I've been walking on eggshells for months, trying to keep Marcus happy, and it's such a relief not to have to anymore.'

'Good on you,' I said warmly. Of course, the end of the relationship might not be *quite* this cut and dried – Marcus was just the sort to post naked photos of his ex-girlfriend on the internet – but no point in meeting trouble halfway. 'By the way, why does he think it's my fault he lost his job? I don't even know what his job *was*.'

'Installing HRVs,' Greta said. 'You know, those heating duct systems.'

'Oh!' I said. 'Was he the person who cut whacking great holes through all the fire cells at Grubb's?'

'Is that what happened? I just heard you got him fired because you're a bitch.'

I smiled beatifically. Revenge is nice, but *unwitting* revenge ... Just fabulous.

'I didn't believe it,' she added. 'I'm sure they were looking for a reason to sack him anyway.'

'I'm sure they were. Hey, thanks for getting Travis those plans last night.'

'Oh, no problem. He took me out for a drink – he said we needed to debrief. He's sweet, isn't he?'

Should I say something about Travis's fondness for damsels in distress? About how his kindness always came with a generous dollop of obligation; the implication that you'd taken advantage of him, but he knew – well, he hoped – that you hadn't *really* meant to? And you mustn't worry about him; he'd *hate* for you to feel guilty. Yes, I decided, I should. Greta had been through enough without stumbling headlong into another emotional minefield. 'He is, but –' I started.

'It was really nice to talk it all out with someone,' she said. 'And then he told me about *his* ex-girlfriend.'

'Irena?' I'd liked Irena; she was Portuguese, and had come to work on a local dairy farm several years ago on some sort of agricultural scholarship. Travis had nursed her through the throes of homesickness until she let him down gently and moved to Southland.

'He didn't tell me her name. He's pretty cut up about it – he only just found out that she's been cheating on him.'

'Oh,' I said.

'He reckons the ironic thing is that he was actually trying to figure out how to tell her it was over.' She smiled. 'He was saying that he knows he should feel relieved because he's off the hook, but it's hard not to resent all that time he wasted worrying about hurting her.'

'Oh,' I said again, unable to stop myself from wondering if this woman did in fact exist, or if she was a fabrication loosely based on me.

'So I told him he needs to work on putting himself first, for a change. And apparently *I* need to work on not falling for total bastards.'

'Sounds like a plan,' I said. 'Hey, Greta, Travis can be a bit … intense, at times …'

'Yeah, he's quite into the whole knight-in-shining-armour thing, isn't he?'

'Exactly,' I said.

She smiled dazzlingly. 'I love guys like that, don't you? They never let you pay for anything … He's going to come and have a look at my hot-water cylinder this weekend.'

Right.

Chapter 35

I was leaving for the day – actually on my feet and gathering up the files that were this evening's designated homework – when the phone extension on my desk rang.

'Hello?'

'Jenny, m' dear.'

'Hi, John,' I said.

'Just wondering if you might be able to help me out ...'

'Yes?'

'Well, I've got to leave me little car in at the garage – they say it needs new filters, or pumps, or something – I don't want to *think* about what *that*'ll cost ...'

'Do you need a lift home?' I cut in.

'Well, m' dear, I don't want to put you out ...'

I looked at my watch. Two forty. I had to pick up Nathan from day care, and Lily panicked if I wasn't at the school by three ... 'That's fine, John. I'll be there in five minutes. But could you wait out by the road? I'm a bit pushed for time today.'

'No problem at all,' he said. 'Thank you, m' dear; I know you're a busy lady –' And I expect he kept talking, but I hung up.

* * *

Having extracted Nathan from a group of children who were building a magnificent block fortress, I pulled up on the street in front of Tipoi Motors. No John. I leapt out and hurried across the gravel to the workshop to make enquiries.

'Is John Mercer here?' I asked a mechanic, who looked up at me as I approached. 'Little guy – bandaged leg – white Toyota …'

'Don't think so,' he said, frowning.

I scanned the cars in the workshop, and the ones parked around the edges of the yard. None of them was a small white Toyota. 'He asked me to pick him up from the garage.'

'Could be Abercrombie's,' the mechanic suggested, wiping his hands on the sides of his overalls.

'Oh yes, of course.' The *other* garage; the one on the far side of town, on the heavy traffic bypass. 'Thanks.'

'Mummy, you forgot to buckle me in,' Nathan said as I leapt back into the driver's seat.

'Why didn't you say?'

'I *am* saying.'

I leapt out again.

* * *

John was waiting outside Abercrombie's Automotive, his bandaged leg shining like a beacon in the sun. 'What time d'you call this, eh?' he said playfully, opening the passenger door.

'We went to the wrong garage,' Nathan told him.

'Oh, I *see*. No, I don't use them. Never have, since they quoted me *five hundred dollars* to change the –'

'Hop in, John,' I interrupted. 'I'm late to pick up Lily.'

'Right you are, ma'am.' He lowered himself into the car at glacial speed and began to fumble with the seatbelt.

As we sped out of town John said, 'I've got a proposition for you, m' dear. I've been looking at some numbers, and I think I might be able to manage more money for you. If I do without me little luxuries, and if your parents could possibly see their way clear to letting me pay over a couple of years, I think I can stretch to fifteen thousand.'

'John, I really don't think it's going to be a starter,' I said. 'For one thing, the minimum section size on Pukewai Road is two and a half hectares, and –'

'Oh, I don't need all that!'

'It's still the legal minimum, because of the way the land's zoned. And I can't imagine the buyers being very pleased to find we've cut off all the holding paddocks around the woolshed and sold them separately.'

There was a thoughtful silence. 'Tell you what,' John said at last. 'We can set up a long-term lease back to that Greenfarm crowd. Forty years, and they can have it for a dollar – that type of thing. That should satisfy the legal eagles.'

'Maybe,' I said doubtfully. 'But it's still not all that simple. Your water comes off the line to the woolshed, and your existing driveway probably doesn't comply.'

'Comply with what, for goodness' sake? Damn bureaucratic nonsense.'

'Well, maybe, but all these boxes need to be ticked.'

'Hmph,' he said.

'Can we have the radio?' Nathan asked suddenly from the back.

'Sure, love.' I turned it on.

'Sounds like someone being done to death,' John said. 'No, I'm sorry. Can't be doing with that,' he said. He leant forward and pushed a random button, changing the radio from FM to AM. The hiss of static filled the car.

I turned off the radio more forcefully than was strictly necessary.

'Mum!' said Nathan crossly. 'That was my favourite song!'

'Never mind,' I said. 'We're nearly at school.'

'Bit late, are you?' John said as I pulled up outside the school gates.

The buses had gone and the only remaining cars belonged to the teachers and Amy Wallace, who was leaning against the bonnet of her SUV, phone in her hand and Lily at her side. Arwen sat stolidly in the back seat.

'Amy, you're a lifesaver,' I said, opening my door. 'Thanks so much for waiting.'

'Oh, no problem! I knew you wouldn't be far away. We've been having a lovely catch-up, haven't we, Lily?'

Lily, who by this time was clinging to me like a demented limpet, didn't reply.

'Are you home for Christmas?' Amy asked.

'Yes,' I said. 'Well, *I* am ... How about you?'

'Yes, everyone's coming to us this year.' She grimaced and added in a stage whisper, 'Dave having the kids?'

I nodded, and she sighed sympathetically. 'It really sinks in at Christmas, doesn't it? Feel free to come to us, if you're at a loose end.'

'Oh,' I said, touched. 'Thanks so much, Amy, but Mum and Dad will be around.'

'And your new fella, no doubt,' croaked John.

'Jenny, you shady lady!' Amy cried. She looked meaningfully at the children and added, 'I'll have to give you a ring very soon and hear *all* about him.' She bent to look into the car. 'I'm sorry; I'm being so rude ... Oh! Hello! It's – Joe, isn't it? No, *John*. Sorry! How *are* you? Are you living around here now, or just visiting?'

John, normally so chatty, hunched his shoulders and muttered something inaudible.

'John sold a house to my parents last year, Jenny,' Amy said. 'Over at Whangamata. Gorgeous sea views. That leg doesn't look very good, John! Nothing too serious, I hope?' She paused for him to reply, but she paused in vain. 'Well, I'd better get on,' she said after a few seconds. 'I've got to get into town and pick up some things for Aaron.'

* * *

House at Whangamata, huh? I thought as we drove away. With sea views. Popular spot, Whangamata. Very pricey ... No, I told myself sternly. Don't jump to conclusions. He's not *necessarily* a property tycoon trying his luck with those gullible Smiths. I'd like it if he was, of course – it would absolve me from guilt at not having him over for dinner as often as he'd have liked to come – but it would be wrong to make assumptions. And having reached this virtuous conclusion I glanced at John, sagging resentfully in the seat beside me, and made them anyway.

We dropped off the property tycoon, bidding him a cheery farewell and receiving merely a grunt in return, and went home.

'Mum?' said Lily, stopping halfway up the back steps. Tessa collided with the backs of her legs and sneezed indignantly.

'Yes?'

'Have you got a boyfriend?'

Bloody John, I thought bitterly. 'Yes.'

'Dad said your boyfriend's Mr Faulkner.'

Sorry, John. Bloody Dave. 'Yes,' I said again. There. It was out. How would they take it ...?

'It took you quite a long time to get a boyfriend, didn't it?'

I blinked. 'What?'

'When Shineya's mum breaks up with *her* boyfriend she always gets a new one really quickly.'

In the case of Shineya's mum, I'd heard, the new boyfriend usually started before the old one ended, so to speak. 'Does she?' I said. 'Open the door, love.'

'I guess it's because she's so pretty,' Lily said, opening the door and following Tessa into the kitchen.

'M-maybe,' I said weakly. Shineya's mum was a florid, dumpy woman who appeared to apply her makeup with a palette knife.

'You're pretty too, Mum,' Lily said kindly.

I dropped my handbag on the end of the bench. 'Thank you, my darling.'

'Will you still love us if you have a boyfriend?' Nathan asked suddenly.

'What? Of *course*!'

'Dad doesn't.'

I stared at him, momentarily dumb with horror. 'Nathan, love, he *does*. He loves you guys to bits.'

'Of course Dad loves us, Nathan,' Lily said. 'He just gets sick of us after a little while.'

'Lil, that's not –' I started.

'Dad's nice,' she said hastily. 'He's just not so ... You're the one who always thinks about us.'

'We both think about you all the time,' I said, picking Nathan up and hugging him hard. And to think I'd actually fantasised about the children seeing through their father. 'It's a parent thing. Happens automatically. And we both love you more than anything, even when you're disgusting. Got that, munchkin?'

He nodded slowly against my shoulder.

'Will Mr Faulkner live at our house now?' Lily asked.

'No, but he might come and hang out with us from time to time. Hey, shall we have some afternoon tea?'

* * *

We had quite an exhaustive discussion on boyfriends. Why not Harry, if I had to have one? Did I *kiss* Mr Faulkner? Did I like it? Would Mr Faulkner be giving Nathan a birthday present, even though he hadn't been invited to the party? No? Oh. What about Christmas? He'd give them presents then, wouldn't he?

We dined on pancakes with ice cream, just because we could. It had been a pretty heavy afternoon, after all. The shearing contractor rang as we finished, and both children seized the opportunity to vanish outside, safe from dishes and other potential forms of child abuse, while I was otherwise occupied.

'Yes,' I said. 'Monday, weather permitting. Great. Thanks, Shane.' I put the phone down and picked up Nathan's plate, which he'd abandoned on the seat of his chair in his haste to escape. *Dad gets sick of us after a little while.* When I was five my father was my hero. I swallowed the lump in my throat.

My cell phone beeped from its spot on the bookcase, and I crossed the room to check it.

Toni's father died this morning. Funeral on Tuesday, I'd better stay until then. X

I bit my lip. Ring back, or text? No, I wanted to hear his voice. I rang.

'Hey,' he said, answering.

'Hey. I'm so sorry.'

'Yeah, bit of a shock.'

'I won't hold you up. I just wanted to say I miss you, and I'm thinking of you, and all that useless stuff.'

'Thank you.'

'Can I do anything? Move sheep? Water plants?'

'No, I think Harry's got it all under control,' he said. 'But thanks.' There was a clatter in the background, and a cry of, 'Andy!'

'I'd better let you go,' I said.

'No, it's –'

'Babe, come and tell this idiot he doesn't know what he's talking about!' someone else called. Toni. 'He's *ruining* this steak.' More clattering, and then a burst of laughter. '*Babe!*'

'Hang on a tick,' Andrew called back. He must have shut a door, because the background noise suddenly cut off. 'The place is a madhouse. Cousins and aunts and family friends have been arriving since lunchtime, and they're having a big barbecue …'

'That's nice,' I said idiotically.

'Well, yeah, it –'

'Andy, what are you doing lurking in here?' someone cried. 'Oh, sorry! Didn't realise you were on the phone …'

'*Babe!*'

I felt a most unworthy spasm of hatred for poor bereaved Toni. 'You'd better go,' I said. I'd wanted to apologise again for Tuesday night, but it patently wasn't the time.

'Yeah ... Goodnight, Jen.'

'Goodnight.'

* * *

When the phone rang at nine I was indulging in what I'd thought might be a nice therapeutic cry. But no. I wasn't feeling cleansed, or relieved, or any of the things people apparently feel after Letting It All Out – all I'd achieved was a headache. I let the answer phone pick up, and the phone rang again immediately.

Bex, I thought drearily, not moving from the old velvet wing chair.

The answer phone picked up again, and there was silence for about thirty seconds. Then my cell phone beeped. I blew my nose and got up to look at the message.

Busy shagging Bruce?

I smiled despite myself, replied, **Piss off**, and blew my nose again.

The phone rang.

'*What?*' I snapped, answering it.

'Don't give me that. You wouldn't have texted if you didn't want me to call you,' said my sister calmly. 'What's wrong? Trouble in paradise?'

'He's in Feilding,' I said. 'Toni's father just died, and he's down there being a wonderful son-in-law.'

'What a guy.'

Indeed. Go, Andy. I was jealous, of course – jealous of the history he had with these people, all of whom knew him better than I did. I didn't know his friends or favourite foods or whether he thought *Mrs Brown's Boys* was side-splitting or inane. Could he whistle with his fingers? Had he played rugby at school? What books did he like? Had he and Toni not wanted children, or not been able to have them? Hilarious Toni, with her wicked sense of humour ... 'She still calls him babe,' I said miserably.

'Bitch,' Bex said.

'*Yes*.'

'Never mind. He's with you now.'

'Maybe,' I said, with an unhappy little gulp of laughter.

'You don't *really* think he's boning his ex, do you?'

'No ... Becca, I'm such an idiot.'

'I know, hon. But why in particular?'

'He – he's staying on to manage his farm after it's sold. And this one. And he pretty much told me he was doing it for me, and I ...'

'Let me guess. You said, "Oh no, Bruce, you mustn't! I can't let you! We barely *know* each other!"'

I winced.

'Didn't you?'

'Yep,' I said.

'Jenny, Jenny, Jenny.'

I started to cry again.

'Hey,' she said, sounding alarmed. 'Hey, come on, I'm kidding! It'll be *fine*. If that's all it takes to put him off you, he's not worth it.'

'It's just – we didn't sort it out before he went, and the longer you leave things unsorted the worse they get. And – and it's so lovely that he should take the job so he can stay with me, but he'll *hate* it! And he doesn't have kids – he doesn't realise how a-annoying they are ...'

'You're scared he'll end up resenting you.'

'Yes.'

'Well ... only one way to find out,' she said. 'If it all goes horribly wrong, it was probably always going to. And if the job's unbearable, he can leave.'

'I guess,' I said dully.

'Any other little problems you've blown way out of perspective and need me to sort out?'

'Sure,' I said. 'Dave's getting sick of having to look after his children every other weekend, and the farm's being sold.'

'Mum said you were alright about the farm now,' she said, sounding aggrieved.

'No. I'm *gutted* about the farm.'

She sighed. 'Jenny, surely we've been over all this. It's just one of those things. Shit happens. I'm sorry, but you're just going to have to grow up and get over it.'

'It is *not* just one of those things! The farm's being sold purely so *you* can fund your upwardly mobile lifestyle. You're the most selfish person I've ever known.'

At which, unsurprisingly, she hung up on me.

Oh, *shit*, I thought. Now I'd gone and done it.

Chapter 36

The next few days passed in a dreary, plodding fashion. Dave had the kids for the weekend, and I missed them horribly. Andrew and I spoke on the phone once or twice – stilted, unsatisfactory conversations – and sent each other text messages like **Goodnight x** and **Miss you**, which, although better than nothing, wasn't much better. It poured with rain, and we had not a snowflake's chance in hell of getting the ewes dry for shearing.

On Tuesday evening – the evening of Toni's father's funeral – I emptied Lily's schoolbag and found last Friday's school newsletter. I smoothed it out and read it, thus learning that there was a full dress rehearsal for *Chicken Little* on Friday, followed by a barbecue. And that there were hotdogs for lunch tomorrow – please get your order slip back no later than Monday.

'Lil, I'm afraid we've missed the deadline for you to have a hotdog,' I said. 'Maybe you could have a spaghetti and cheese toastie in your lunch instead.'

'No, I'm having a hotdog and a lemonade iceblock,' she said, pausing halfway through a forward roll and peering at me through her legs.

'Oh, did Dad fill the form in?'

'No, I did it. Mrs van der Wetering said I can just bring my money tomorrow.'

'It helps to actually tell me about these things, Lil! How much money?'

'Um ... it was on the piece of paper.'

'But you've handed it in.'

'Well, *I* don't know.' She rolled across the kitchen floor, narrowly missing Tessa's water bowl.

'Actually, it doesn't matter *what* it costs, because I don't have any change.' I'd emptied my wallet of what little it contained on Friday, when the girl guides had washed my car windscreen in the supermarket car park.

Lily sprang up, this time kicking the water bowl across the floor, and hunted frantically through my handbag. Finding that I was speaking the truth, she burst into tears. 'Mrs van der Wetering will growl at me!'

'No, she won't,' I said. 'I'll write you a note, and you can pay the next day.'

'No! No, I can't! Mrs van der Wetering said we're not allowed to do that anymore, because people never ever pay her back!' She cast herself on the floor and abandoned herself to grief.

I looked at her for a moment and decided *not* to take this opportunity to deliver a valuable life lesson on consequences. 'Why don't we see if Nana and Granddad have got any money?'

With Lily still sobbing weakly, we got into the car and drove down the road to Mum and Dad's. It was starting to rain again, and big, sparse drops splattered against the windscreen. 'I want to ask Nana!' Nathan said.

'It's *my* hotdog!' said Lily.

Both of them flung open their doors as the car came to a halt, and dashed headlong towards the house. Cries of '*Li-leee!*' and 'No, *I* want ...' faded as they ran.

I closed the car doors and ran after them, head down against the thickening rain. I scurried across the patio, shuffled my bare feet hastily on the mat to get the leaves off and opened the door.

'Mum, Mr Faulkner's here!' Nathan said.

I looked up, shaking my wet hair back off my face. And he was. He was getting up from the table, tall and thin and strangely unfamiliar in dark tailored trousers and a pale blue dress shirt. He looked wonderful.

We stared at each other – the sort of searing, devour-one-another-with-your-eyes stare that, I fear, makes onlookers wonder uneasily if you're about to do something indecent on the spot. He was here. He was mine, and I was his, and –

We were dragged from this rapt mutual contemplation by Nathan's voice. 'Nana,' he said, 'did you know Mr Faulkner is Mummy's boyfriend?'

'Is – is that right, love?' said Mum weakly.

One corner of Andrew's mouth lifted, and my stomach quivered.

'Yes. But she still will love me and Lily the best. Mr Faulkner's dog bit Tessa once, but then it died. It got run-ded over.'

'Nathan!' Lily hissed. 'You're embarrassing yourself!'

'No I'm not,' said Nathan, with perfect truth. 'Mr Faulkner, will you get us a Christmas present?'

'I hadn't actually thought about it,' said Andrew.

'I *wish* I had a 'mote control helicopter. I thought I was going to get one for my birthday, but I didn't. I was so sad.'

'Hey, zip it, small fry,' I said, scooping him up. 'Andrew, what are you doing here?'

Andrew hesitated and looked at my parents.

'We – we asked him to pop in,' Mum said.

How very mysterious. What on earth might my parents want to discuss with Andrew that I wasn't to know about? Well, presumably he'd tell me later, if they wouldn't. 'We're here to scrounge,' I said. 'Lily needs change to buy a hotdog at school tomorrow, and I have no cash at all.'

'*And* an iceblock,' Lily said. 'Can I look in your purse, Nana?'

'Yes, of course, love,' said Mum. 'It's just in –'

'I know!' Lily said, and ran out of the kitchen. Nathan squirmed to get down and ran after her.

'So,' said Dad. 'I suppose you'd better sit down, Jenny, now you're here.'

Mum looked like she'd just eaten a mouthful of shield beetles.

'Don't worry about it,' I said, half laughing. 'You guys carry on; we'll just clean you out of small change and be on our way.'

'No,' said Mum slowly, and sighed. 'Sit down, love. Would you like a cup of tea?'

'No, thank you.' But I was curious now, so I sat down in the chair beside Andrew's.

'Nana, you've got lots of dollars!' said Nathan, following Lily back into the room. 'Can I have some?'

'You can both have five dollars,' Mum said.

'Mum, no,' I protested – unheeded, of course, by either her or my rapacious offspring.

'You have the silver ones, and I'll have the gold ones,' Lily told Nathan.

'Lily,' I said sternly.

'He can't tell, Mum; he won't mind.'

'Small people!' Dad said. 'You can go and play on my computer, if you like.'

'Take Nana's credit card and buy things online,' I called after them as they vanished.

'Good idea,' said Dad. 'Right. We asked Andrew to come and see us to ask how he might feel about leasing the farm.'

I stared at him. *'This* farm?'

'Yes. With a view to eventually buying half of it, all things being equal.'

I sat still and gazed at him in shock.

'And of course half of it will be Jenny's one day,' Mum said to Andrew.

'But you've agreed to sell it to Greenfarm!' I said.

'We haven't signed anything,' Dad said. He wrinkled his nose. 'And, personally, I'm not going to lie awake at night worrying about disappointing Richard Green.'

But – but – *what*? How was this mad scheme going to work? Well, I thought dazedly, a bit like it would have worked if Dave and I had bought Bex out, according to the old succession plan. But would Andrew want to do it? And surely it *couldn't* work, or we'd have thought of it sooner. Wouldn't we?

'That's a very generous offer,' said Andrew slowly. 'But I don't think I could afford it. Toni's parents helped us out a lot when we bought next door, and of course that all has to be paid back when it sells. And – and this farm's bigger ...'

Dad frowned. 'Look, I can't see why that would necessarily be a problem,' he said. 'You wouldn't have to buy the lot in one fell swoop. You could do it gradually – I'm sure we could work something out. And we thought it would be sensible for you to lease the place for a while anyway – three years, say – to give everyone a bit of breathing space.'

'Bex wouldn't like that,' I said. She wanted her share – or some of it, at least – now, not in goodness only knew how many years.

'This was her idea, Jenny,' Mum said quietly.

Again I stared in shock.

'She knows how much the farm means to you – well, to all of us – and she's willing to put her and Sean's plans on hold if that's what the rest of us want.'

'But surely –'

'She says,' Dad told me, 'that it's her turn to be the awesome daughter for a change, whether you like it or not.' He smiled. 'Look, we know it's far too soon for you two to start considering whether you'd like to go into partnership one day. There would be all sorts of things to work out. But it might be worth considering.'

I looked at Andrew. He was looking at his hands, wearing his very blankest and most unreadable expression.

'What do you think, both of you?' Mum asked.

Andrew continued to look at his hands. Well, fair enough, after my stupid little diatribe last week.

'I think –' I said, and stopped. It was the perfect solution. Everything I wanted, handed to me on a plate. It was terrifying. *Be careful what you wish for. You don't get nothing for nothing. If it seems too good to be true, it probably is ...*

And then – well, it was all a bit humiliating, wasn't it? Jenny can't sort out her own life; Mummy and Daddy have to bribe her boyfriend to look after her. *Stop that,* I told myself savagely. *Stop thinking about yourself for half a minute.* Mum and Dad didn't really want to sell up. Rebecca wanted – at the moment, at least – to be noble. Andrew wanted to stay here with me, and to keep his farm. Well, we couldn't do anything about his farm, but maybe the farm next door was a reasonable alternative.

I took a deep breath. 'It would be wonderful,' I said.

Andrew looked at me and smiled slowly. 'Even with a grumpy prat who likes pot plants?'

I stiffened. 'Did Harry tell you that?' The *rat*! How *could* he?

'No, your sister did. She called me on ... Saturday, I think it was.'

'Oh dear Lord,' I said.

His smile widened. 'Apparently she quite likes you, even though you're a total pain in the bum. And since for some strange reason you seem to think the only thing that will make you happy is a grumpy prat who likes pot plants ...'

'It is,' I said.

'Good to hear. Anyway, since that's what you want, and you can't be trusted not to stuff it up if left to your own devices, she thought she'd better step in.'

Epilogue

It was hot already, at quarter past seven in the morning.

'Mum! Where's my book bag?' Nathan shouted from the far end of the house.

'In the middle of the living room,' I called back.

'What?'

'It's here!'

'*What?*'

'*It's here!*'

He pounded up the hallway into the kitchen. 'I need my book bag!' Nathan had been going to school for three weeks now, and his self-importance was immense.

I pointed silently.

He turned to look, and dashed across the room to get it. 'We need to do my reading!'

'We did it last night, remember?'

'But Andrew was at squash. He didn't hear me.' He trotted across the living room and shoved the bag at Andrew, who was leaning against the table, frowning at his phone.

'Hmm?' Andrew said absently, taking it. 'They've changed their minds about that rain this afternoon, damn it …' He put his phone down. 'Right, which one are we reading?'

'*The Lion and the Mouse*,' Nathan said. 'Mum, I need two Marmite sandwiches for my lunch today.'

'Okay,' I said. 'What would you like, Lil? Ham?'

'Two ham, please,' said Lily, looking up from her rice bubbles. 'And two Marmite and cheese.'

'Can you eat all that?'

'It's a Dad day. Some is for afternoon tea.'

'I'm pretty sure Dad and Anaya will feed you,' I said, repressing a smile.

'Dad might take us to McDonald's,' Nathan suggested, settling himself at the table and opening his junior reader.

'*No*, Nathan, he won't,' said Lily crossly. 'Because last time *you* told *her* we'd been, and now we're not allowed to go anymore.'

'Anaya cried,' said Nathan, sighing. 'And then Daddy was mad at me.'

'And then *Nathan* cried,' Lily added. 'And then Anaya shouted at Dad for making Nathan cry, and *then* she went to bed with the iPad and we couldn't play on it.'

'Goodness,' said Andrew mildly, coming up to the bench beside me. I passed him the coffee plunger, and he kissed my ear.

'Andrew! We need to do my reading!' said Nathan.

'I'm getting there,' Andrew said. 'I can't possibly read without coffee.'

'Coffee's bad for you,' Lily informed us. 'Anaya says that if you drink coffee when you've got a baby inside you, the baby will get poisoned. It can't choose what to eat; it has to have what you're eating.'

'Well, Lil,' Andrew said, taking the milk out of the fridge, 'seeing as there's absolutely no chance I'll ever have a baby inside me, I think I'll go ahead and risk it.'

'Because men can't have babies,' Nathan said.

'Exactly.'

'Ladies can.'

'So I hear.'

'Mum, you should have a baby,' said Lily.

I jumped, and my knife dug a hole in the piece of bread I was buttering.

'I could read it stories,' said Nathan, with the air of royalty conferring a boon.

'Well, there's an offer you can't refuse,' Andrew said, putting the milk down on the bench.

'Will you, Mum?' Lily asked.

'I …' Andrew didn't even officially live here, although in practice he only went home to water his plants. I looked at him, but he was pouring coffee with serene absorption. 'Maybe. Someday.'

'What's the date?' Nathan asked, turning laboriously to the back of his homework book.

'Someday soon, d'you reckon?' asked Andrew.

'Yeah, I reckon,' I said softly, and he covered my hand with his.

'What's the *date*?' Nathan demanded, as if nothing of any particular significance had just happened.

'What?' I said, glancing at the calendar. 'The twenty-third of February.'

The twenty-third of February. One year exactly since our lives were turned upside down. Should I say something? Should I draw Andrew's attention to this momentous anniversary; this transformative journey from mediocre to wonderful? *Nah*, I thought, squeezing his hand.